With a "sidekick" named Shakespeare, Inspector
Alleyn singles out a killer from a glittering array
of suspects . . .

LORD CHARLES LAMPREY—a high-gloss
nobleman with no money

COLIN AND STEPHEN—his twin sons, both of
whom claim to have ushered the victim to
the scene of the crime

**VIOLET, MARCHIONESS OF WUTHER-
WOOD**—his sister-in-law and a black-
magic woman

ROBERTA GREY—pretty young houseguest in
love with a Lamprey—if not the truth . . .

Death of a Peer

"A STORY THAT STRENGTHENS NGAIO MARSH'S CLAIM TO A
PLACE AMONG THE CLEVEREST AND MOST ENTERTAINING OF
OUR MYSTERY-MONGERS."
—*The New York Times*

NGAIO MARSH
Death of a Peer

JOVE BOOKS, NEW YORK

DEATH OF A PEER

A Jove Book / published by arrangement with
Little, Brown and Company, Inc.

PRINTING HISTORY
Little, Brown and Company edition published 1940
Jove edition / January 1980

ISBN: 0-515-08691-6

Jove Books are published by The Berkley Publishing Group,
200 Madison Avenue, New York, New York 10016.
The name "JOVE" and the "J" logo
are trademarks belonging to Jove Publications, Inc.

PRINTED IN THE UNITED STATES OF AMERICA

10 9 8

For Sir Hugh and Lady Acland with my love. For the one since he has helped me so often with my stories and for the other since she likes stories about London.

Contents

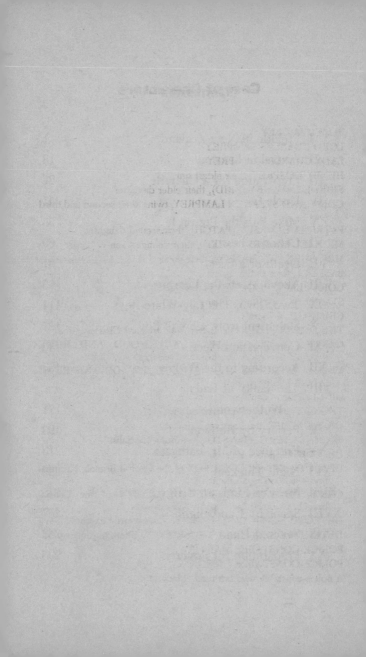

Cast of Characters

ROBERTA GREY

LORD CHARLES LAMPREY

LADY CHARLES LAMPREY

HENRY LAMPREY, their eldest son

FRIEDE LAMPREY (FRID), their elder daughter

COLIN AND STEPHEN LAMPREY, twins, their second and third sons

PATRICIA LAMPREY (PATCH), their second daughter

MICHAEL LAMPREY (MIKE), their youngest son

MRS. BURNABY (NANNY), their nurse

BASKETT, their butler

CORA BLACKBURN, their parlour-maid

STAMFORD, a commissionaire

GRIMBALL, a "bum"

THE LADY KATHERINE LOBE, aunt to Lord Charles

GABRIEL, MARQUIS OF WUTHERWOOD AND RUNE (UNCLE G.), elder brother to Lord Charles

VIOLET, MARCHIONESS OF WUTHERWOOD AND RUNE (AUNT V.), his wife

GIGGLE, their chauffeur

TINKERTON, Lady Wutherwood's maid

DR. KANTRIPP, the Lampreys' doctor

SIR MATTHEW CAIRNSTOCK, a brain specialist

DR. CURTIS, police surgeon

DETECTIVE-INSPECTOR FOX of the Central Branch, Criminal Investigation Department

CHIEF DETECTIVE-INSPECTOR ALLEYN of the Central Branch, Criminal Investigation Department

DETECTIVE-SERGEANT BAILEY, a finger-print expert

DETECTIVE-SERGEANT THOMPSON, a photographic expert

POLICE-CONSTABLE MARTIN

POLICE-CONSTABLE GIBSON

A police-constable who has read "Macbeth"

DETECTIVE-SERGEANT CAMPBELL, on duty at 24 Brummell Street

NIGEL BATHGATE, Watson to Mr. Alleyn

MRS. MOFFATT, housekeeper at 24 Brummell Street

MOFFATT, her husband

MR. RATTISBON, solicitor

Death of a Peer

CHAPTER I

Prelude in New Zealand

Roberta Grey first met the Lampreys in New Zealand. She was at school with Frid Lamprey. All the other Lampreys went to school in England: Henry, the twins and Michael to Eton; Patch to an expensive girls' school near Tonbridge. In the New Zealand days, Patch and Mike were too little for school. They had Nanny and, later on, a governess. But when the time came for Frid to be bundled off to England there was a major financial crisis and she became a boarder at Te Moana Collegiate School for Girls. Long after they had returned to England the family still said that Frid spoke with a New Zealand accent, which was nonsense.

In after years Roberta was to find a pleasant irony in the thought that she owed her friendship with the family to one of those financial crises. It must have been a really bad one because it was at about that time that Lady Charles Lamprey suddenly got rid of all her English servants and bought the washing machine that afterwards, on the afternoon it broke loose from its mooring, so nearly-killed Nanny and Patch. Not long after Frid went to board at Te Moana an old aunt of Lord Charles's died, and the Lampreys were rich again, and all the servants came back, so that on Roberta's first visit Deepacres seemed very grand indeed. In New Zealand the Lampreys were a remarkable family. Titles are rare in New Zealand and the younger sons of marquises are practically nonexistent.

In two years' time Roberta was to remember with nostalgic vividness that first visit. It took place during the half-term week-end, when the boarders at Te Moana were allowed to go home. Two days beforehand, Frid asked Roberta if she would spend the half-term at Deepacres. There were long-distance telephone calls between Deepacres and Roberta's parents.

Frid said: "Do come, Robin darling, such fun," in a vague, kind voice.

She had no idea, of course, that for Roberta the invitation broke like a fabulous rocket, that Roberta's mother, when Lady Charles Lamprey telephoned, was thrown into a frenzy of sewing that lasted until two o'clock in the morning, that Roberta's father bicycled four miles before eight o'clock in order to leave at Te Moana a strange parcel, a letter of instruction on behaviour, and five shillings to give the housemaid. Frid always sympathized when Roberta said her people were poor, as though they were all in the same boat, but the poverty of the Lampreys, as Roberta was to discover, was a queer and baffling condition understood by nobody, not even their creditors, and certainly not by poor Lord Charles with his eye-glass, his smile and his vagueness.

It was almost dark when the car arrived at Te Moana. Roberta was made shy by the discovery of Lady Charles in the front seat beside the chauffeur, and of Henry, dark and exquisite, in the back one. But the family charm was equal to more than the awkwardness of a child of fourteen. Roberta yielded to it in three minutes and it held her captive ever afterwards.

The thirty-mile drive up to the mountains was like a dream. Afterwards, Roberta remembered that they all sang an old song about building a stairway to Paradise, and that she felt as though she floated up the stairway as she sang. The surface of the road changed from tar to shingle; stones banged against the underneath of the car; the foothills came closer and salutary drifts of mountain air were blown in at the window. It was quite dark when they began to climb the winding outer drive of Deepacres. Roberta smelt native bush, cold mountain water and wet loam. The car stopped, and Henry, groaning, got out and opened the gate. That was to be Roberta's clearest picture of Henry—struggling with the gate, screwing up his face in the glare of the headlights. The drive up to Deepacres seemed very long indeed. When at last they came out on a wide gravelled platform before the house, something of Roberta's shyness returned.

Long after the Lampreys had gone to England Roberta would sometimes dream that she returned to Deepacres. It was always at night. In her dream the door stood open, the light streamed down the steps. Baskett was in the entrance with a young footman whose name Roberta, in her dreams, had forgotten. The smell of blue-gum fires, of the oil that Lady Charles burnt in the drawing-room, and of cabbage-tree bloom would come out through the open door to greet her. There, in the drawing-room, as on that first night, she would see the family. Patch and Mike had been allowed to stay up; the twins, Stephen and Colin, that week arrived from England, were collapsed in arm-chairs. Henry lay on the hearthrug with his shining head propped against his mother's knee. Lord Charles would be gently amused at something he had been reading in a month-old *Spectator*. Always he put it down out of politeness to Roberta. The beginning of the dream never varied, or the feeling of enchantment.

The Lampreys appeared, on that first night, to scintillate with polish, and the most entrancing worldly-wisdom. Their family jokes seemed then the very quintessence of wit. When she grew up Roberta had still to remind herself that the Lampreys were funny but, with the exception of Henry, not witty. Perhaps they were too kind to be wits. Their jokes depended too much on the inconsequent family manner to survive quotation. But on that first night Roberta was rapturously uncritical. In retrospect she saw them as a very young family. Henry, the eldest, was eighteen. The twins, removed from Eton during the last crisis, were sixteen; Frid was fourteen, Patricia ten, and little Michael was four. Lady Charles—Roberta never could remember when she first began to call her Charlot—was thirty-seven, and it was her birthday. Her husband had given her the wonderful dressing-case that appeared later, in the first financial crisis after

Roberta met them. There were many parcels, arrived that day from England, and Lady Charles opened them in a vague pleased manner, saying of each one that it was "great fun," or "charming," and exclaiming from time to time: "How kind of Aunt M.!" "How kind of George!" "How kind of the Gabriels!" The Gabriels had sent her a bracelet and she looked up from the cards and said: "Charlie, it's from both of them. They must have patched it up."

"The bracelet, darling?" asked Henry.

"No, the quarrel. Charlie, I suppose that, after all, Violet can't be going to divorce him."

"They'll have six odious sons, Imogen," said Lord Charles, "and I shall never, never have any money. How she can put up with Gabriel! Of course she's mad."

"I understand Gabriel had her locked up in a nursing-home last year, but evidently she's loose again."

"Gabriel's our uncle," explained Henry, smiling at Roberta. "He's a revolting man."

"I don't think he's so bad," murmured Lady Charles, trying on the bracelet.

"Mummy, he's the *End*," said Frid, and the twins groaned in unison from the sofa. "The *End*," they said, and Colin added: "Last, loathsomest, lousiest, execrable apart."

"Doesn't scan," said Frid.

"Mummy," asked Patch who was under the piano with Mike, "who's lousy? Is it Uncle Gabriel?"

"Not really, darling," said Lady Charles, who had opened another parcel. "Oh, Charlie, *look!* It's from Auntie Kit. She's knitted it herself, of course. What can it be?"

"Dear Aunt Kit!" said Henry. And to Roberta: "She wears buttoned-up boots and talks in a whisper."

"She's Mummy's second cousin and Daddy's aunt. Mummy and Daddy are relations in a weird sort of way," said Frid.

"Which may explain many things," added Henry, looking hard at Frid.

"Once," said Colin, "Aunt Kit got locked up in a railway lavatory for sixteen hours because nobody could hear her whispering: 'Let me out, if you please, let me out!'"

"And of course she was too polite to hammer or kick," added Stephen.

Patch burst out laughing and Mike, too little to know why,

broke into a charming baby's laugh to keep her company.

"It's a hat," said Lady Charles and put it on the top of her head.

"It's a tea-cosy," said Frid. "How common of Auntie Kit."

Nanny came in. She was the quintessence of all nannies, opinionated, faithful, illogical, exasperating and admirable. She stood just inside the door and said:

"Good evening, m'lady. Patricia, Michael. Come along."

"Oh *Nanny*," said Patch and Mike. "It's not time. Oh *Nanny!*"

Lady Charles said: "Look what Lady Katherine has sent me, Nanny. It's a hat."

"It's a hot-water-bottle cover, m'lady," said Nanny. "Patricia and Michael, say good night and come along."

ii

It was the first of many visits. Roberta spent the winter holidays at Deepacres and when the long summer holidays came she was there again. The affections of an only child of fourteen are as concentrated as they are vehement. All her life Roberta was to put her emotional eggs in one basket. At fourteen, with appalling simplicity, she gave her heart to the Lampreys. It was, however, not merely an attachment of adolescence. She never grew out of it, and though, when they met again after a long interval, she could look at them with detachment, she was unable to feel detached. She wanted no other friends. Their grandeur, and in their queer way the Lampreys were very grand for New Zealand, had little to do with their attraction for Roberta. If the crash that was so often averted had ever fallen upon them they would have carried their glamour into some tumbledown house in England or New Zealand, and Roberta would still have adored them.

By the end of two years she knew them very well indeed. Lady Charles, always vague about ages, used to talk to Roberta with extraordinary frankness about family affairs. At first Roberta was both flattered and bewildered by these confidences. She would listen aghast to stories of imminent disaster, of the immediate necessity for a thousand pounds, of the impossibility of the Lampreys keeping their heads above

5

water, and she would agree that Lady Charles must economize by no longer taking *Punch* and *The Tatler*, and that they could all do without table napkins. It seemed a splendid strategic move for the Lampreys to buy a second and cheaper car in order to make less use of the Rolls Royce. When, on the day the new car arrived, they all went for a picnic in both cars, Roberta and Lady Charles exchanged satisfied glances.

"Stealth is my plan," cried Lady Charles as she and Roberta talked together by the picnic fire. "I shall wean poor Charlie gradually from the large car. You see it quite amuses him, already, to drive that common little horror."

Unfortunately, it also amused Henry and the twins to drive the large car.

"They must have *some* fun," said Lady Charles, and to make up she bought no new clothes for herself. She was always eager to deny herself, and so gaily and lightly that only Henry and Roberta noticed what she was up to. Dent, her maid, who was friendly with a pawnbroker, made expeditions to the nearest town with pieces of Lady Charles's jewellry, and as she had a great deal of jewellery this was an admirable source of income.

"Robin," said Henry to Roberta, "What has become of Mummy's emerald star?"

Roberta looked extremely uncomfortable.

"Has she popped it?" asked Henry, then added: "You needn't tell me. I know she has."

For twenty minutes Henry was thoughtful and he was particularly attentive to his mother that evening. He told his father that she was overtired and suggested that she should be given champagne with her dinner. After making this suggestion Henry caught Roberta's eye and suddenly he grinned. Roberta liked Henry best of all the Lampreys. He had the gift of detachment. They all knew that they were funny, they even knew that they were peculiar and rather gloried in it, but only Henry had the faculty of seeing the family in perspective, only Henry could look a little ruefully at their habits, only Henry would recognize the futility of their economic gestures. He, too, fell into the habit of confiding in Roberta. He would discuss his friends with her and occasionally his love affairs. By the time Henry was twenty he had had three vague love affairs. He also liked to discuss the family with Roberta. On the very afternoon when the great blow fell, Henry and Roberta had walked up through the bush above Deepacres and had come out on the lower slope of Little Mount Silver. The real name for Deepacres was Mount Silver Station but Lord Charles on a vaguely nostalgic impulse had rechristened it after the Lampreys's estate in Kent. From where they lay in the warm tussock, Henry and Roberta looked across forty miles of plains. Behind them rose the mountains, Little Mount Silver, Big Mount Silver, the Giant Thumb Range, and, behind that, the back-country, reaching in cold sharpness away to the west coast. All through the summer the mountain air came down to meet the warmth of the plains and Roberta, scenting it, knew contentment. This was her country.

"Nice, isn't it?" she said, tugging at a clump of tussock.

"Very pleasant," said Henry.

"But not as good as England?"

"Well, I suppose England's my country," said Henry.

"If I was there expect I'd feel the same about New Zealand."

"I expect so. But you're only once removed from England, and we're not New Zealand at all. Strangers in a strange land and making pretty considerable fools of ourselves. There's a financial crisis brewing, Roberta."

"Again!" cried Roberta in alarm.

"Again, and it seems to be a snorter."

Henry rolled over on his back and stared at the sky.

"We're hopeless," he said to Roberta. "We live by windfalls and they won't go on for ever. What will happen to us, Roberta?"

"Charlot," said Roberta, "thinks you might have a poultry farm."

"She and Daddy both think so," said Henry. "What will happen? We'll order masses of hens,—and I can't tell you how much I dislike the sensation of feathers,—we'll build expensive modern chicken-houses, we'll buy poultrified garments for ourselves, and for six months we'll all be eaten up with the zeal of the chicken-house and then we'll employ someone to do the work and we won't have paid for the outlay."

"Well," said Roberta unhappily, "why don't you say so?"

"Because I'm like all the rest of my family," said Henry.

7

"What do you think of us, Robin? You're such a composed little person with your smooth head and your watchfulness."

"That sounds smug and beastly."

"It isn't meant to. You've got a sort of Jane Eyreishness about you. You'll grow up into a Jane Eyre, I daresay, if you grow at all. Don't you sometimes think we're pretty hopeless?"

"I like you."

"I know. But you must criticize a little. What's to be done? What, for instance, ought I to do?"

"I suppose," said Roberta, "you ought to get a job."

"What sort of job? What can I do in New Zealand or anywhere else for a matter of that?"

"Ought you to have a profession?"

"What sort of profession?"

"Well," said Roberta helplessly, "What would you like?"

"I'm sick at the sight of blood so I couldn't be a doctor. I lose my temper when I argue, so I couldn't be a lawyer, and I hate the poor, so I couldn't be a parson."

"Wasn't there some idea of your managing Deepacres?"

"A sheep farmer?"

"Well—a run-holder. Deepacres in a biggish run, isn't it?"

"Too big for the Lampreys. Poor Daddy! When we first got here he became so excessively New Zealand. I believe he used sheep-dip on his hair and shall I ever forget him with the dogs! He bought four—I think they cost twenty pounds each. He used to sit on his horse and whistle so unsuccessfully that even the horse couldn't have heard him and the dogs all lay down and went to sleep and the sheep stood in serried ranks and gazed at him in mild surprise. Then he tried swearing and screaming but he lost his voice in less than no time. We should never have come out here."

"I can't understand why you did."

"In a vague sort of way I fancy we were shooting the moon. I was at Eton and really didn't know anything about it, until they whizzed me away to the ship."

"I suppose you'll all go back to England," said Roberta unhappily.

"When Uncle Gabriel dies. Unless, of course, Aunt G. has any young."

"But isn't she past it?"

"You'd think so, but it would be just like the Gabriels. I

wish I could work that Chinese Mandarin trick and say in my head, 'Uncle G. has left us!' and be sure that he would instantly fall down dead."

"Henry!"

"Well, my dear, if you *knew* him. He's the most revolting old gentleman. How Daddy ever came to have such a brother! He's mean and hideous and spiteful and ought to have been dead ages ago. There were two uncles between him and Daddy but they were both killed in the Great War. I understand that they were rather nice, and at any rate they had no sons, which is the great thing in their favour."

"Henry, I get so muddled. What is your Uncle Gabriel's name?"

"Gabriel."

"No, I mean his title and everything."

"Oh. Well, he's the Marquis of Wutherwood and Rune. While my grandfather was alive Uncle G. was Lord Rune, the Earl of Rune. That's the eldest son's title you see. Daddy is just a younger son."

"And when your Uncle G. dies your father will be Lord Wutherwood and you'll be Lord Rune?"

"Yes, I shall, if the old pig ever does die."

"Well, then there'd be a job for you. You could go into the House of Lords."

"No; I couldn't. Poor Daddy would do that. He could bring in a bill about sheep-dip if peers are allowed to bring in bills. I rather think they only squash them, but I'm not sure."

"You wouldn't care about being a politician, I suppose?"

"No," said Henry sadly, "I'm afraid I wouldn't." He looked thoughtfully at Roberta and shook his head. "The only thing I seem to have any inclination for is writing nonsense-rhymes and playing cricket and I'm terribly bad at both. I adore dressing up of course, but only in funny noses and false beards, and we all like doing that, even Daddy, so I don't imagine it indicates the stage as a career. I suppose I shall have to try and win the heart of an ugly heiress. I can't hope to fascinate a pretty one."

"Oh," cried Roberta in a fury, "don't pretend to be so *feeble!*"

"I'm not pretending, alas."

"And don't be so affected. 'Alas'!"

"But it's true, Robin. We are feeble. We're museum pieces.

9

Carry-overs from another age. Two generations ago we didn't bother about what we would do when we grew up. We went into regiments, or politics, and lived on large estates. The younger sons had younger son's compartments and either fitted them nicely or else went raffishly to the dogs and were hauled back by the head of the family. Everything was all ready for us from the moment we were born."

Henry paused, wagged his head sadly and continued:

"Now look at us! My papa is really an amiable dilettante. So, I suppose, would I be if I could go back into setting, but you can't do that without money. Our trouble is that we go on behaving in the grand leisured manner without the necessary backing. It's very dishonest of us, but we're conditioned to it. We're the victims of inherited behaviourism."

"I don't know what that means."

"Nor do I, but *didn't* it sound grand?"

"Do you?" asked Henry anxiously. "Anyway, Robin, we shan't last long at this rate. A dreadful time is coming when we shall be obliged to do something to justify our existence. Make money or speeches or something. When the last of the money goes we'll be for it. The ones with brains and energy may survive but they'll be starting from a long way behind scratch. They say that if you want a job in the City it's wise to speak with an accent and pretend you've been to a board school. A hollow mockery, because you're found out the moment you have to do sums or write letters."

"But," said Robin, "your sort of education—"

"Suits me. It's an admirable preparation for almost everything except an honest job of work."

"I don't think that's true."

"Don't you? Perhaps you're right and it's just our family that's mad of itself without any excuse."

"You're a nice family. I love every one of you."

"Darling Robin." Henry reached out a hand and patted her. "Don't be too fond of us."

"My mother," said Robin, "says you've all got such a tremendous amount of charm."

"Does she?" To Robin's surprise Henry's face became faintly pink. "Well," he said, "perhaps if your mother is right *that* may tide us over until Uncle G. pops off. Something has got to do it. Are there bums in New Zealand?"

"What do you mean? Don't be common."

"My innocent old Robin Grey! A bum is a gentleman in a bowler hat who comes to stay until you pay your bills."

"Henry! How awful!"

"Frightful," agreed Henry who was watching a hawk.

"I mean how shaming."

"You soon get used to them. I remember one who made me a catapult when I was home for the holidays. That was the time Uncle G. paid up."

"But aren't you ever—ever—"

Roberta felt herself go scarlet and was silent.

"Ashamed of ourselves?"

"Well—"

"Listen," said Henry. "I can hear voices."

It was Frid and the twins. They were coming up the bush track and seemed to be in a state of excitement. In a moment they began shouting:

"Henry! Where are you-oou! Henry!"

"Hullo!" Henry shouted.

The manuka scrub on the edge of the bush was agitated and presently three Lampreys scrambled out into the open. The twins had been riding and still wore their beautiful English jodpurs. Frid, on the contrary, was dressed in a bathing suit.

"I say, what do you think?" they cried.

"What?"

"Such a thrill! Daddy's got a marvellous offer for Deepacres," panted Frid.

"We'll be able to pay our bills," added Colin. And they all shouted together: "And we're going back to England."

CHAPTER II

Arrival in London

Now that the last trunk was closed and had been dragged away by an impatient steward, the cabin seemed to have lost all its character. Surveying it by lamplight, for it was still long before dawn, Roberta felt that she had relinquished her ownership and was only there on sufferance. Odd scraps of paper lay about the floor; the wardrobe door stood open; across the dressing-table lay a trail of spilt powder. The unfamiliar black dress and overcoat in which she would go ashore hung on the peg inside the door and seemed to move stealthily, and of their own accord, from side to side. The ship still creaked with that pleasing air of absorption in its own progress. Outside in the dark the lonely sea still foamed past the porthole, and footsteps still thudded on the deck above Roberta's head. But all these dear and familiar sounds only added to her feeling of desolation. The voyage was over. Already the ship was astir with agitated passengers. Slowly the blackness outside turned to grey. For the last time she watched the solemn procession of the horizon, and the dawn-light on cold ruffles of foam.

She put on the black dress and, for the hundredth time, wondered if it was the right sort of garment in which to land. It had a white collar and there was a white cockade in her hat so perhaps she would not look too obviously in mourning.

"I've come thirteen thousand miles," thought Roberta. "Half-way round the world. Now I'm near the top of the world. These are northern seas and those fading stars are the stars of northern skies."

She leant out of the porthole and the sound of the sea surged up into her ears. A cold dawn-wind blew her hair back. She looked forward and saw a string of pale lights strung like a necklace across a wan greyness. Her heart thumped violently, for this was her first sight of England. For a long time she leant out of the porthole. Gulls now swooped and mewed round the ship. Afar off she heard the hollow sound of a siren. Filled with the strange inertia that is sometimes born of excitement Roberta could not make up her mind to go up on deck. At last a bugle sounded for the preposterously early breakfast. Roberta opened her bulging handbag and with a good deal of difficulty extracted the two New Zealand pound notes she meant to give her stewardess. It seemed a large tip but it would represent only thirty English shillings. The stewardess was waiting in the corridor. The steward was there too and the bath steward. Roberta was obliged to return to her cabin and grope again in her bag.

Breakfast was a strange hurried affair with everybody wearing unfamiliar clothes and exchanging addresses. Roberta felt there was no sense of conviction in the plans the passengers made to sustain the friendships they had formed, but she too gave addresses to one or two people and wrote theirs on the back of a menu card. She then joined in the passport queue and in her excitement kept taking her landing papers out of her bag and putting them back again. Through the portholes she saw funnels, sides of tall ships, and finally buildings that seemed quite close to hand. She had her passport stamped and went up to B deck where the familiar notices looked blankly at her. Already the hatches were open and the winches uncovered. She stood apart from the other passengers and like them gazed forward. The shore was now quite close and there were many other ships near at hand. Stewards, pallid in their undervests, leant out of portholes to stare at the big liner. Roberta heard a passenger say, "Good old Thames." She heard names that were strange yet familiar: Gravesend, Tilbury, Greenhithe.

"Nearly over, now, Miss Grey," said a voice at her elbow. An elderly man with whom she had been vaguely friendly leant on the rail beside her.

"Yes," said Roberta. "Almost over."

"This is your first sight of London?"

"Yes."

"That must be a strange sensation. I can't imagine it. I'm a Cockney, you see." He turned and looked down at her. Perhaps he thought she looked rather small and young for he said:

"Someone coming to meet you?"

"At the station, not at the boat. An aunt. I've never met her."

"I hope she's a nice aunt."

"I do too. She's my father's sister."

"You'll be able to break the ice by telling her that you recognized her at once from her likeness to your father—" He broke off abruptly. "I'm sorry," he said. "I've said something that's—I'm sorry."

"It's all right," said Roberta, and because he looked so genuinely sorry she added: "I haven't got quite used to talking ordinarily about them yet. My father and mother, I mean. I've got to get used to it, of course."

"Both?" said her companion compassionately.

"Yes. In a motor accident. I'm going to live with this aunt."

"Well," he said, "I can only repeat that I do hope she's a nice aunt."

Roberta smiled at him and wished, though he was kind, that he would go away. A steward came along the deck carrying letters.

"Here's the mail from the pilot boat," said her companion.

Roberta didn't know whether to expect a letter or not. The steward gave her two and a wireless message. She opened the wireless first and in another second her companion heard her give a little cry. He looked up from his own letter. Roberta's dark eyes shone and her whole face seemed to have come brilliantly to life.

"Good news?"

"*Oh yes! Yes.* It's from my greatest friends. I'm to stay with them first. They're coming to the ship. My aunt's ill or something and I'm to go to them."

"That's good news?"

"It's splendid news. I knew them in New Zealand, you see, but I haven't seen them for years."

Roberta no longer wished that he would go away. She was so excited that she felt she must speak of her good fortune.

"I wrote and told them I was coming but the letter went by air-mail on the day I sailed." She looked at her letters. "This one's from Charlot."

She opened it with shaking fingers. Lady Charles's writing was like herself, at once thin, elegant and generous.

"*Darling Robin,*" Roberta read, "*we are all so excited. As soon as your letter came I rang up your Kentish aunt and asked if we might have you first. She says we may for one night only which is measly but you must come back soon. She sounds quite nice. Henry and Frid will meet you at the wharf. We are so glad, darling. There's only a box for you to sleep in but you won't mind that. Best love from us all.*

Charlot"

The wireless said: "AUNT ILL SO WE ARE ALLOWED TO KEEP YOU FOR A MONTH. HURRAH DARLING SO GLAD AUNT NOT SERIOUSLY ILL SO EVERYTHING SPLENDID LOVE CHARLOT."

The second was from Roberta's aunt.

My dearest Roberta [it said], I am so grieved and vexed that I am unable to welcome you to Dear Old England but alas, my dear, I am prostrated with such *dreadful sciatica* that my doctor insists on a visit to a very special nursing home!! So expensive and worrying for poor me and I would *at whatever cost to myself* have defied him if it had not been for your friend Lady Charles Lamprey, who rang me up from London which was quite an excitement in *my humdrum life* to ask when you arrived and on hearing of my dilemma very kindly offered to take you for a *month or more*. At first I suggested *one night* but I know your dear father and mother thought very highly of Lady Charles Lamprey and now I feel I may with a clear conscience accept her offer. This letter will, I am assured, reach you while you are still on your ship. I am so *distressed* that this happened but all's well that ends well, and I'm afraid you will find life in a Kentish village *very quiet* after the gaiety and *grandeurs* of your London friends!!! Well, my dear, Welcome to England and believe me I shall look forward to our meeting as soon as ever I return!

With much love,
Your affectionate
AUNT HILDA

P.S. I have written a little note to Lady Charles Lamprey. By the way I hope that is the *correct* way to address her! Should it perhaps be Lady *Imogen* Lamprey? I seem to remember she was The Hon., or was it Lady, Imogen Ringle. I do hope I have not committed a *faux pas!* I think her husband is the Lord Charles Lamprey who was at Oxford with dear old Uncle George Alton who afterwards became rector of Lumpington-Parva but I don't suppose he would remember. AUNT H.

P.P.S. On second thoughts he would be *much too* young!! A. H.

Roberta grinned and then laughed outright. She looked up to find her fellow-passenger smiling at her.

"Everything as it should be?" he asked.

"Lovely," said Roberta.

II

As the distance lessened between wharf and ship the communal life that had bound the passengers together for five weeks dwindled and fell away. Already they appeared to be strangers to each other and their last conversations grew more and more desultory and unreal. To Roberta, the ship herself seemed to lose familiarity. Because she had so much enjoyed her first long voyage she was now aware of a brief

17

melancholy. But only a ditch of dirty water remained and on the wharf a crowd waited behind a barrier. Isolated individuals had begun to flutter handkerchiefs. Roberta's eyes searched diligently among the closely packed people and she had decided that neither Henry nor Frid was there when suddenly she saw them, standing apart from the others and waving with that vague sideways sweep of the Lampreys. Henry looked much as she remembered him but four years had made an enormous difference to Frid. Instead of a shapeless schoolgirl Roberta saw a post-debutante, a young woman of twenty who looked as if every inch of herself and her clothes had been subjected to a sort of intensive manicuring. How smart Frid was and how beautifully painted; and how different they both looked from anyone else on the wharf. Henry was bare-headed and Roberta, accustomed to the close-cropped New Zealand heads, thought his hair rather long. But he looked nice, smiling up at her. She could see that he and Frid were having a joke. Roberta looked away. Lines had been flung to men on the wharf. With an imperative rattle, gang-planks were thrown out and five men in bowler hats walked up the nearest one.

"We won't be allowed ashore just yet," said her friend. "There's always a delay. Good Lord, what on earth are those two people doing down there? They must be demented! Look!"

He pointed at Henry and Frid who thrust out their tongues, rolled their eyes, beat the air with their hands and stamped rhythmically.

"Extraordinary!" he ejaculated. "Who can they be?"

"They are my friends," said Roberta. "They're doing a *haka*."

"A what?"

"A Maori war-dance. It's to welcome me. They're completely mad."

"Oh," said her friend, "yes. Very funny."

Roberta got behind him and did a few *haka* movements. A lot of the passengers were watching Henry and Frid and most of the people on the wharf. When they had finished their *haka* they turned their backs to the ship and bent their heads.

"What are they doing now?" Roberta's friend asked.

"I don't know," she answered nervously.

The barrier was lifted and the crowd on the wharf moved

towards the gangways. For a moment or two Roberta lost sight of the Lampreys. The people round her began laughing and pointing, and presently she saw her friends coming on board. They now wore papier-mache noses and false beards and they gesticulated excitedly.

"They must be characters," said her acquaintance doubtfully.

The passengers all hurried towards the head of the gangplank and Roberta was submerged among people much taller than herself. Her heart thumped; she saw nothing but the backs of overcoats and heard only confused cries of greeting. Suddenly she found herself in somebody's arms. False beards and nose were pressed against her cheeks; she smelt Frid's scent and the stuff Henry put on his hair.

"Hullo, darling," cried the Lampreys.

"Did you like our *haka?*" asked Frid. "I wanted us to wear Maori mats and be painted brown but Henry wanted to be bearded so we compromised. It's such fun you've come."

"Tell me," said Henry solemnly, "What do you think of dear old England?"

"Did you have a nice voyage?" asked Frid anxiously.

"Were you sick?"

"Shall we go now?"

"Or do you want to kiss the Captain?"

"Come on," said Frid. "Let's go. Henry says we've got to bribe the customs so that they'll take you first."

"Do be quiet, Frid," said Henry, "it's all a secret and you don't call it a bribe. Have you got any money, Robin? I'm afraid we haven't."

"Yes, of course," said Roberta. "How much?"

"Ten bob. I'll do it. It doesn't matter so much if I'm arrested."

"You'd better take off your beard," said Frid.

The rest of the morning was a dream. There was a long wait in the customs shed where Roberta kept remeeting all the passengers to whom she had said good-bye. There was a trundling of luggage to a large car where a chauffeur waited. Roberta instantly felt apologetic about the size of her cabin trunk. She found it quite impossible to readjust herself to these rapidly changing events. She was only vaguely aware of a broad and slovenly street, of buildings that seemed incredibly drab, of ever-increasing traffic. When Henry and Frid told her that this was the East End and murmured about Limehouse and Poplar, Roberta was only vaguely disappointed that the places were so much less romantic than their associations, that the squalor held no suggestion of illicit glamour, that the Road—looked so precisely like its name. When they came into the City and Henry and Frid pointed uncertainly to the Mansion House or suggested she should look at the dome of St. Paul's, Roberta obediently stared out of the windows but nothing that she saw seemed real. It was as if she lay on an unfamiliar beach and breaker after breaker rolled over her head. The noise of London bemused her more than the noise of the sea. Her mind was limp; she heard herself talking and wondered at the coherence of the sentence.

"Here's Fleet Street," said Henry. "Do you remember 'Up the Hill of Ludgate, down the Hill of Fleet'?"

"Yes," murmured Roberta, "yes. Fleet Street."

"We've miles to go still," said Frid. "Robin, did you know I *am* going to be an actress?"

"She might have guessed," said Henry, "by the way you walk. Did you notice her walk, Robin? She sort of paws the ground. When she comes into the room she shuts the door behind her and leans against it."

Frid grinned. "I do it beautifully," she said. "It's second nature to me."

"She goes to a frightful place inhabited by young men in mufflers who run their hands through their hair and tell Frid she's marvellous."

"It's a dramatic school," Frid explained. "The young men are very intelligent. All of them say I'm going to be a good actress."

"We'll be passing the law courts in a minute," said Henry.

Scarlet omnibuses sailed past like ships. Inside them were pale people who looked at once alert, tired and preoccupied. In a traffic jam a dark blue car came so close alongside that the men in the back seat were only a few inches away from Roberta and the Lampreys.

"That's one of the new police cars, Frid," said Henry.

"How do you know?"

"Well, I know it is. I expect those enormous men are Big Fours."

"I wish they'd move on," said Frid. "I wouldn't be surprised if we fell into their hands one of these days."

"Why?" asked Roberta.

"Well, the twins were saying at breakfast yesterday that they thought the only thing to be done was for them to turn crooks and be another lot of Mayfair boys."

"It was rather a good idea, really," said Henry. "You see Colin said he'd steal incredibly rich dowager's jewels and Stephen would establish his alibi at the Ritz or somewhere. Nobody can tell them apart, you know."

"And then, you know," added Frid, "if one of them was arrested they'd each say it was the other and as one of them must be innocent they'd have to let both of them go."

"From which," said Henry, "you will have gathered we are in the midst of a financial crisis."

Roberta started at the sound of that familiar phrase.

"Oh, *no!*" she said.

"Oh, yes," said Henry, "and what's more it's a snorter. Everybody seems to be furious with us."

"Mummy's going to pop the pearls this afternoon," added Frid, "on her way to the manicurist."

"She's never done *that* before," said Henry. "This is the Strand, Robin. That church is either St. Clement Dane or St. Mary-le-Strand and the next one is whatever that one isn't. We'd better explain about the crisis, I suppose."

"I wish you would," said Roberta. In her bemused condition the Lampreys' affairs struck a friendly and recognizable note. She could think sharply about their debts but she could scarcely so much as gape at the London she had greatly longed to see. It was as if her powers of receptivity were half-anesthetized and would respond only to familiar impressions. She listened attentively to a long recital of how Lord Charles had invested a great deal of the money he still mysteriously possessed in something called San Domingoes and how it had almost immediately disappeared. She heard of a strange venture in which Lord Charles had planned to open a jewellery business in the City, run on some sort of commission basis, with Henry and the twins as salesmen. "And at least," said Frid, "there would have been Mummy's things that she got out of pawn when Cousin Ruth died. It would have been better to sell than to pop them, don't you think?" This project, it appeared, had depended on somebody called Sir David Stein who had recently committed suicide, leaving Lord Charles with an empty office and a ten years' lease on his hands.

"And so now," said Henry, "we appear to be sunk. That's

Charing Cross Station. We thought we would take you to a play to-night, Robin."

"And we can dance afterwards," said Frid. "Colin's in love with a girl in the play so I expect he'll want her to come whizzing on with us which is rather a bore. Have you asked Mary to come, Henry?"

"No," said Henry. "We've only got five seats and the twins both want to come and anyway I want to dance with Robin, and Colin's actress isn't coming."

"Well, Stephen could take Mary off your hands."

"He doesn't like her."

"Mary is Henry's girl," explained Frid. "Only vaguely, though."

"Well, she's quite nice really," said Henry.

"Charming, darling," said Frid handsomely.

Roberta suddenly felt rather desolate. She stared out of the window and only half-listened to Henry who seemed to think he ought to point out places of interest.

"This is Trafalgar Square," said Henry. "Isn't that thing in the middle too monstrous? Lions, you see, at each corner, but of course you've met them in photographs."

"That building over there is the Tate Gallery," said Frid

"She means the National Gallery, Robin. I suppose you will want to see one or two sights, won't you?"

"Well, I suppose I ought to."

"Patch and Mike are at home for the holidays," said Frid. "It will be good for them to take Robin to some sights."

"Perhaps I could look some out for myself," Roberta suggested with diffidence.

"You'll find it difficult to begin," Henry told her. "There's something so cold-blooded about girding up your loins and going out to find a sight. I'll come to one occasionally if you like. It may not be so bad once the plunge is taken. We are getting a very public-spirited family, Robin. The twins and I are territorials. I can't tell you how much we dislike it but we stiffened our upper lips and bit on the bullets and when the war comes we know what we have to do. In the meantime, of course, I've got to get a job, now we're sunk."

"We're not definitely sunk until Uncle G. has spoken," Frid pointed out.

"Uncle G.!" Robin exclaimed. "I'd almost forgotten about him. He's always sounded like a myth."

"It's to be hoped he doesn't behave like one," said Henry. "He's coming to see us to-morrow. Daddy has sent him an SOS. I can't tell you how awful he is."

"Aunt V. is worse," said Frid gloomily. "Let's face it, Aunt V. is worse. And they're both coming in order to go into a huddle with Daddy and Mummy about finance. We hope to sting Uncle G. for two thousand."

"It'll all come to Daddy when they're dead, you see, Robin. They've no young of their own."

"I thought," said Roberta, "that they were separated."

"Oh, they're always flying apart and coming together again," said Frid. "They're together at the moment. Aunt V. has taken up witchcraft."

"What!"

"Witchcraft," said Henry. "It's quite true. She's a witch. She belongs to a little black-magic club somewhere."

"I don't believe you!"

"You may as well, because it's true. She started by taking up with a clergyman in Devon who has discovered an evil place on Dartmoor. It seems that he told Aunt V. that he thought he might as well sprinkle some holy water on this evil place but when he went there the holy water was dashed out of his hands by an unseen power. He lent Aunt V. some books about black magic and instead of being horrified she took the wrong turning and thought it sounded fun. I understand she goes to the black mass and everything."

"How can you possibly know?"

"Her maid, Miss Tinkerton, told Nanny. Tinkerton says Aunt V. is far gone in black magic. They have meetings at Deepacres. The real Deepacres, you know, in Kent. Aunt V. is always buying books about witchcraft and she's got a lot of very queer friends. They've all got names like Olga and Sonia and Boris. Aunt V. is half-Roumanian, you know," said Frid.

"Half-Hungarian, you mean," corrected Henry.

"Well, all Central European anyway. Her name isn't Violet at all."

"What is it?" asked Roberta.

"Something Uncle G. could neither spell nor pronounce so he called her Violet. A thousand years ago he picked her up in Budapest at an embassy. She's a very sinister sort of woman and quite insane. Probably the witchcraft is a throwback to a gypsy ancestress of sorts. Of course Uncle G.'s simply furious

23

about it, not being a warlock."

"Naturally," said Frid. "I suppose he's afraid she might put a spell on him."

"I wouldn't put it past her," said Henry. "She's a really evil old thing. She gives me absolute horrors. She's like a white toad. I'll bet you anything you like that under her clothes she's all cold and damp."

"Shut up," said Frid. "All the same I wouldn't be surprised if you were right. Henry, do let's stop somewhere and have breakfast. I'm ravenous and I'm sure Robin must be."

"It'll have to be Angelo's," said Henry. "He'll let us chalk it up."

"I've got some money," said Roberta rather shyly.

"No, no!" cried Frid. "Angelo's *much* too dear to pay cash. We'll put it down to Henry's account and I've got enough for a tip, I think."

"It may not be open," said Henry. "What's the time? The day seems all peculiar with this early start. Look, Robin, we're coming into Piccadilly Circus."

Roberta stared past the chauffeur and, through the windscreen of the car, she had her first sight of Eros.

In the thoughts of those who have never visited them all great cities are represented by symbols: New York by a skyline, Paris by a river and an arch, Vienna by a river and a song, Berlin by a single street. But to British colonials the symbol of London is more homely than any of these. It is a small figure perched slantways above a roundabout, an elegant, Victorian god with a Grecian name—Eros of Piccadilly Circus. When they come to London, colonials orientate themselves by Piccadilly Circus. All their adventures start from there. It is under the bow of Eros that to many a colonial has come that first warmth of realization that says to him: "This is London." It is here at the place which he learns, with a rare touch of insolence, to call the hub of the universe that the colonial wakes from the trance of arrival finds his feet on London paving stones, and is suddenly happy.

So it was for Roberta. From the Lampreys' car she saw the roundabout of Piccadilly, the great sailing buses, the sea of faces, the traffic of the Circus, and she felt a kind of realization stir in her heart.

"It's not so very big," said Roberta.

"Quite small, really," said Henry.

"I don't mean it's not thrilling," said Roberta. "It is. I—I feel as if I'd like to be—sort of inside it."

"I know," agreed Henry. "Let's nip out, Frid, and walk round the corner to Angelo's."

He said to the chauffeur: "Pick us up in twenty minutes, will you, Mayling?"

"Here's a jam," said Frid. "Now's our chance. Come on."

Henry opened the door and took Roberta's hand. She scrambled out. The voyage, the ship, and the sea all slid away into remoteness. A new experience took Roberta and the sounds that are London engulfed her.

CHAPTER III

Preparation for a Charade

The Lampreys lived in two flats which occupied the entire top story of a building known as Pleasaunce Court Mansions. Pleasaunce Court is merely a short street connecting Cadogan Square with Lennox Gardens and the block of flats stands on the corner. To Roberta the outside seemed forbidding but the entrance hall had lately been redecorated and was more friendly. Pale green walls, a thick carpet, heavy armchairs and an enormous fire gave an impression of light and luxury. The firelight flickered on the chromium steel of a lift-cage in the centre of the hall and on a slotted framework that held the names of the flat owners. Roberta read the top one: No. 25 & 26. LORD AND LADY CHARLES LAMPREY. IN. Henry followed her gaze, crossed quickly to the board and moved a chromium-steel tab.

"LORD AND LADY CHARLES LAMPREY. OUT, I fancy," muttered Henry.

"Oh, are they!" cried Roberta. "Are they away?"

"No," said Henry. "Ssh!"

"Ssh!" said Frid.

They moved their heads slightly in the direction of the door. A small man wearing a bowler hat stood on the pavement outside and appeared to consult an envelope in his hands. He looked up at the front of the flats and then approached the steps.

"In to the lift!" Henry muttered and opened the doors. Roberta in a state of extreme bewilderment entered the lift. A porter, heavily smart in a dark green uniform and several medals, came out of an office.

"Hullo, Stamford," said Henry. "Good morning to you. Mayling's got some luggage out there in the car."

"I'll attend to it, sir," said the porter.

"Thank you so much," murmured the Lampreys politely, and Henry added, "His lordship is away this morning, Stamford."

"Indeed, sir?" said the porter. "Thank you, sir."

"Up we go," said Henry.

The porter shut them in, Henry pressed a button and with a metallic sigh the lift took them to the top of the building.

"Stamford doesn't work the lift," explained Henry. "He's only for show and to look after the service flats downstairs."

In three days, photographs of the Pleasaunce Court lift would appear in six illustrated papers and in the files of the criminal-investigation department. It would be lit by flash lamps, sealed, dusted with powder, measured and described. It would be discussed by several million people. It was about to become famous. To Roberta it seemed very smart and she did not notice that, like the entrance hall, it had been modernized. The old liftman's apparatus, a handle projecting from a cylindrical casing was still there but above it was a row of buttons with the Lampreys' floor, the fourth, at the top. They came out on a well-lit landing with two light green doors numbered 25 and 26. Henry pushed No. 25 open and Roberta crossed a threshold into the past. The sensation of Deepacres, of that still-recurrent dream, came upon her so poignantly that she caught her breath. Here was the very scent of Deepacres, of the scented oil Lady Charles burnt in the drawing-room, of Turkish cigarettes, of cut flowers and of moss. The sense of smell works both consciously and subconsciously. About many households is an individual pleasantness of which human noses are only half aware and which is so subtle that it cannot be traced to one source. The Lampreys' house-smell, while it might suggest burning cedarwood, scented oil and hothouse flowers, was made up of these things and of something more, something that to Roberta seemed the very scent of their characters. It carried her back through four years and while the pleasure of this experience was still new she saw, in the entrance hall, some of their old possessions: a table, a steel-engraving, a green Chinese elephant. It was with the strangest feeling of familiarity that she heard Lady Charles's voice crying:

"Is that old Robin Grey?"

Roberta ran through the doorway into her arms.

There they all were, in a long white drawing-room with crackling fires at each end and a great gaiety of flowers. Lady Charles, thinner than ever, was not properly up and had bundled herself into a red silk dressing-gown. She wore a net over her grey curls. Her husband stood beside her in his well-remembered morning attitude, a newspaper dangling from his hand, his glass in his eye, and his thin colourless hair brushed across his head. He beamed with pale, myopic eyes at Roberta and inclined his head forward with an obedient air, ready for her kiss. The twins, with shining blond heads and solemn smiles, also kissed her. Patch, an overgrown schoolgirl in a puppy-fat condition, nearly knocked her over, and Mike, eleven years old, looked relieved when Roberta merely shook his hand.

"Such fun, darling," said all the Lampreys in their soft voices. "Such fun to see you."

Presently they were all sitting before the fire, with Charlot in her chair and Henry in his old place on the hearthrug and the twins collapsed on the sofa. Patch hurled herself onto the arm of Robin's chair, and Frid stood in an elegant attitude before the fire, and Lord Charles wandered vaguely about the room.

"Dear me," said Henry, "I feel like Uriah Heep. It's as good as the chiming of old bells to see Robin Grey in the flesh."

The twins murmured agreeably and Colin said: "You haven't grown much."

"I know," said Roberta. "I'm a pygmy."

"A nice pygmy," said Charlot.

"Do you think she's pretty?" asked Frid. "I do."

"Not exactly pretty," said Stephen. "I'd call her attractive."

"Really!" Said Lord Charles mildly. "Does Robin, who I must say looks delightful, enjoy a public dissection of her charms?"

"Yes," said Roberta. "From the family, I do."

"Of course she does," shouted Patch, dealing Roberta a violent buffet across the shoulders.

"What do you think of *me?*" asked Frid, striking an attitude. "Aren't I quite, quite lovely?"

"Don't tell her she is," said Colin. "The girl's a nymphomaniac."

"Darling!" murmured Lady Charles.

"My dear Colin," said his father, "it really would be a good idea if you stick to the words you understand."

"Well," Frid reasoned, "you may thank your lucky stars I am so lovely. After all, looks go a long way on the stage. I may have to keep you all, and in the near future, too."

"Apropos," said Henry, "I fancy there's a bum downstairs, chaps."

"Oh *no!*" cried the Lampreys.

"The signs are ominous. I told Stamford you were out, Daddy."

"Then I suppose I'd better stay in," muttered Lord Charles. "Who can it be this time? Not Smith & Weekly's again, surely? I wrote them an admirable letter explaining that—"

"Circumstances over which we had no control," suggested Stephen.

"I put it better than that, Stephen."

"Mike," said Lady Charles, "be an angel and run out on the landing. If you see a little man—"

"In a bowler," said Henry and Frid.

"Yes, of course in a bowler. If you see him, don't say anything but just come and tell Mummy, darling, will you?"

"Righto," said Mike politely. "Is he a bum, Mummy?"

"We think so but it's nothing to worry about. Do hurry, Mikey darling."

Mike grinned disarmingly and began to hop out of the room on one leg.

"I can hop for miles," he said.

"Well, run quietly for a change."

Mike gave a Red-Indian call and began to crawl out. The twins rose in a menacing fashion. He uttered a shrill yelp and ran.

"Isn't he heaven?" Lady Charles asked Roberta.

"There's the lift!" Colin ejaculated.

"It'll only be Mike t-taking a run down and up," said Stephen. "I understand that Mike's playing with the lift is rather unpopular."

"I bet it's the bum," said Colin. "Has Baskett been warned? I mean he may just lavishly show him in."

"If Baskett doesn't know a bailiff's man," said Lord Charles warmly, "after having lived with us for fifteen years, he is a stupider fellow than I take him for."

"There's the bell!" cried Lady Charles.

"It's all right," said Henry. "It'll only be Robin's luggage."

"Thank heaven! Robin darling, you'd like to see your room, wouldn't you? Frid, darling, show Robin her room. It's too tiny and absurd, darling, but you won't mind, will you? Actually it was meant for a hall, but Mike and Patch turned it into a sort of railway-station so we're delighted to have it made sane again. I really must dress myself but I can't resist waiting to hear the worst about the bum."

"Here's Mike," said Frid.

Mike came back, still hopping on one leg, and singing:

> "Hallelujah, I'm a bum!
> Hallelujah, bum again!
> Hallelujah, give us a hand up to..."

"Shut up," said Stephen and Colin. "What do you mean? Is he there?"

"Nope," whispered Mike. "Only *her* luggage."

"Don't say 'her,'" said Stephen.

Mike began to hop up and down in front of the twins singing:

> "Two, two, the lily-white boys,
> clothed all in green, oh."

Colin took him by the shoulders and Stephen seized his heels. They swung him to and fro and flung him, screaming with pleasure on the sofa.

"Lily-white boys!" yelled Mike. "I bet she doesn't know which is which. Do you?" He looked engagingly at Roberta. "Do you—Robin?"

The twins turned to her, and raised their eyebrows.

"Do you?" they asked.

"I do when you speak," said Roberta.

"I hardly stammer at all, now," said Stephen.

"I know, but your voices are different, Stephen. And even if you didn't speak I'd only have to look behind your ears."

"Oh," said Mike, "It's not fair. She knows the secret. Stephen's old mole. Old mole-dy Stephen doesn't wash behind his ears, yah, yah, yah!"

"Let's go to your room," said Frid. "Mike's turning mad dog, and the scare seems to be over."

ii

Roberta liked her room which was in 26. As Lady Charles had told her it was really the entrance hall but heavy curtains had been hung across it making a passage, through which the others would have to go to reach the real passage and their bedrooms. Frid showed her the rest of 26 which was all bedrooms with Nanny Burnaby living in the ex-kitchen where she could make the cups of Ovaltine that she still forced the Lampreys to drink before they went to bed. Nanny was sitting by the electric stove which she had converted into a sort of bureau. Her hair had turned much greyer. Her face was netted over with lines as if, thought Roberta, each good or ill deed of the young Lampreys had left it sign on that one face alone. She had been playing patience and received Roberta exactly as if four days instead of four years had gone by since their last meeting.

"Nanny," said Frid, "things are gloomy. We're up the spout again and there's liable to be a bum at any moment."

"Some folk will do anything," said Nanny darkly.

"Well, I know, but I suppose they rather want their money."

"Well, his lordship had better pay them and be done with it."

"I'm afraid we haven't got any money at the moment, Nan."

"Nonsense," said Nanny.

She looked at Roberta and said, "You don't grow much, Miss Robin."

"No, Nanny. I rather think I've finished. I'm twenty now you know."

"Same age as Miss Frid and look how she's shot up. You need nourishing."

"Nan," said Frid. "Uncle Gabriel's coming tomorrow."

"H'm," said Nanny.

"We hope he'll pull us out of the soup."

"So he ought to with his own flesh and blood in need."

Henry looked in at the door. By the singular scowl Nanny gave him, Roberta saw that he was still the favourite.

"Hullo, Mrs. Burnaby," he said. "Have you heard the news? We're in the soup."

"It's not the first time, Mr. Henry, and it won't be the last. His lordship's brother will have to attend to it."

Henry looked fixedly at his old nurse. "If he doesn't," he said, "I think we'll really go bust."

Nanny's hands, big-jointed with rheumatism, made a quick involuntary movement.

"You'll be all right, Nan," added Henry. "We fixed you up with an annuity, didn't we?"

"I'm not thinking of that, Mr. Henry."

"No. No, I don't suppose you are. I was, though."

Nanny put on a pair of thick-lens spectacles and advanced upon Henry.

"You put your tongue out," she ordered.

"Why on earth?"

"Do as you're told, Mr. Henry."

Henry put out his tongue.

"I thought so. Come to me before you go to bed this evening. You're bilious."

"What utter rot."

"You've always shown your liver in your spirits."

"Nanny!"

"Talking a lot of rubbish about matters that are beyond your understanding. His other lordship will soon send certain people about their business."

"Meaning us?"

"Stuff and nonsense. You know what I mean. Miss Robin, you'd better take a glass of milk with your lunch. You're over-excited."

"Yes, Nanny," said Roberta.

Nanny returned to her game of patience.

"The audience is over," said Henry.

"I'd better unpack," said Roberta.

"Leave out your pressings," said Nanny. "I'll do 'em."

"Thank you, Nanny," said Roberta and went to her room. Now she was alone. The floor beneath her feet seemed unstable as though the sea, after five weeks' domination, were not easily to be forgotten. It was strange to feel this physical reminder of an experience already so remote. Roberta unpacked. The clothes that she had bought in New Zealand no longer pleased her but she was too much preoccupied by the affairs of the Lampreys to be much concerned with her own. During the last four years, Roberta had passed through adolescence to womanhood. The emotional phases proper to those years had been interrupted by tragedy. Two months ago, when the languors and propulsions of adolescence had not yet quite abated, Roberta's parents had been killed, and a kind of frost had closed about her emotions so that at first, though she felt the pain of her loss, it was with her reason rather than with her heart. Later, when the thaw came, she found that something unexpected had happened to her. Her affections, which had been easily and lightly bestowed, had crystallized, and she found herself indifferent to the greater number of her friends. With this discovery came another: that in four years her heart was still with an incredible family now half the world away. Her thoughts returned to Deepacres and she wanted the Lampreys. More than anyone else in the world she wanted them. They might be scatter-brained, unstable, reprehensible, but they suited Roberta and she supposed she suited them. When her father's sister wrote to suggest that Roberta should come to England and live with her, Roberta was glad to go because, by the same mail, came a letter from Lady Charles Lamprey that awoke all her old love for the family. When it became certain that she would see them again she grew apprehensive lest they should find her an awkward carry-over from their colonial days, but as soon as she saw Henry and Frid on the wharf she had felt safer, and now, as she put the last of her un-smart garments in a drawer that already contained several pieces of a toy railway, she was visited by the odd idea that it was she who had grown so much older and that the young Lampreys had merely grown taller.

"Otherwise," thought Roberta, "they haven't changed a bit."

The door opened and Lady Charles came in. She was now

34

dressed. Her grey hair shone in a mass of small curls, her thin face was delicately powdered, and she looked and smelt delightful.

"How's old Robin Grey?" she asked.

"Very happy."

Lady Charles turned on the electric heater, drew up a chair, sat in it, folded her short skirt back over her knees and lit a cigarette. Roberta recognized, with a warm sense of familiarity, the signs of an impending gossip.

"I hope you won't be too uncomfortable, darling," said Lady Charles.

"I'm in Heaven, Charlot darling."

"We do so wish we could have you for a long time. What are your plans?"

"Well," said Roberta, "my aunt has offered very nicely to have me as a sort of companion, but I think I want a job, a real job, I mean. So, if she agrees, I'm going to try for a secretaryship in a shop, or, failing that, an office. I've learnt shorthand and typing."

"We must see what we can do. But of course you *must* have *some* fun first."

"I'd love some fun but I've only got a tiny bit of money. About £200 a year. So I've got to start soon."

"I must say I do think money's *awful*," said Lady Charles. "Here are we, practically playing mouth-organs and selling matches, and all because poor darling Charlie doesn't happen to have a head for sums. I'm so dreadfully worried, Robin. It's so hard for the children."

"Hard for you, too."

"Well, if we go bankrupt it'll be rather uncomfortable. Charlie won't be allowed on a race-course for one thing. There's one comfort, he *has* paid his bookmaker. There's something so second-rate about not paying your bookmaker and the things they do to you are too shaming."

"What sort of things?"

"I think they call out your name at Sandown and beat with a hammer to draw everybody's attention. Or is that only if you are a Mason? At any rate we needn't dwell on it because it's almost the only thing that is *not* likely to happen to us."

"But, Charlot, you've got over other fences."

"Nothing like this. This isn't a fence; it's a mountain."

"How did it all happen?"

"My dear, how does one run into debt? It simply occurs, bit by bit. And you know, Robin, I have made such enormous efforts. The children have been wonderful about it. The twins and Henry have answered any number of advertisements and have never given up the idea that they must get a job. And they've been so good about their fun, enjoying quite *cheap* things like driving about England and staying at second-rate hotels and going to Ostend for a little cheap gamble instead of the Riviera where all their friends are. And Frid was so good-natured about her coming-out. No ball; only dinner and cocktail parties which we ran on *sixpence*. And now she's going to this drama school and working so hard with the most appalling people. Of course the whole thing is the business of Charlie and the jewels. Don't ask me to tell you the complete story, it's too grim and involved for words to convey. The gist of it is that poor Charlie was to have this office in the City with buyers in the East and at places like the Galle Face Hotel at Colombo. He was in partnership with a Sir David Stein who seemed a rather nice second-rate little man, we thought. Well, it appears that they had a great orgy of paper-signing and no sooner was that over than Sir David blew out his brains."

"Why?"

"It seems he was in deep water and one of his chief interests had crashed quite suddenly. It turned out that Charlie had to meet a frightful lot of bills because he was Sir David's partner. So many, that we hadn't any money left to pay our own bills which had been mounting up a bit anyhow. And there's no more coming in for six months. So there you are. Well, we must simply keep our heads and take the right line with Gabriel. Charlie wrote him a really charming telegram, just *right*, do you know? We took great trouble with it. Gabriel is at Deepacres and he hates coming up to London so we rather hoped he'd simply realize he couldn't let Charlie go bust and would send him a cheque. However he telegraphed back: 'ARRIVING FRIDAY. SIX O'CLOCK. WUTHERWOOD,' which has thrown us all into rather a fever."

"Do you think it'll be all right?" asked Roberta.

"Well, it's simply *so* crucial that we're not thinking at all. Never jump your fences till you meet them. But I'm terribly anxious that we should take the right *line* with Gabriel. It's a bore that Charlie loathes him so wholeheartedly."

"I don't think he ever loathed anybody," said Roberta.

36

"Well, as far as he can, he hates Gabriel. Gabriel has always been rather beastly to him and thinks he's extravagant. Gabriel himself is a miser."

"Oh dear!"

"I know. Still he's also a snob and I really don't believe he'll allow his brother to go bankrupt. He'd *crawl* with horror at the publicity. What we've got to do is decide on the line to take with Gabriel when he gets here. I thought the first thing was to consider his comfort. He likes a special kind of sherry, almost unprocurable, I understand, but Baskett is going to hunt for it. And he likes early Chinese pottery. Deepacres is full of leering goddesses and dragons. Well, by a great stroke of luck, one of the things poor Charlie bought with an eye to business is a small blue pot which was most frightfully expensive and which, in a mad moment, he paid for. I had the really brilliant idea of letting Mike give it to Gabriel. Mike has quite charming manners when he tries."

"But, Charlot, if this pot is so valuable, couldn't you sell it?"

"I suppose we could, but how? And anyway my cunning tells me that it's much better to invest it as a sweetner for Gabriel. We've got to be diplomatic. Suppose the pot is worth a hundred pounds? My dear, we want two thousand. Why not use the pot as a sprat to catch a mackerel?"

"Yes," said Roberta dubiously, "but may he not think it looks a bit lavish to be giving away valuable pots?"

"Oh, no," said Lady Charles with an air of dismissal, "he'll be delighted. And anyway if he flings it back in poor little Mike's face, we've still *got* the pot."

"True," said Roberta, but she felt that there was a flaw somewhere in Lady Charles's logic.

"We'll all be in the drawing-room when he comes," continued Lady Charles, "and I thought perhaps we might have some charades."

"What!"

"I know it sounds mad, Robin, but you see he *knows* we're rather mad and it's no good pretending we're not. And we're all good at charades, you can't deny it."

Roberta remembered the charades in New Zealand, particularly one that presented the Garden of Eden. Lord Charles, with his glass in his eye, and an umbrella over his head to suggest the heat of the day, had enacted Adam. Henry was the serpent and the twins angels. Frid had entered into the spirit of the part of Eve and had worn almost nothing but a brassiere and a brown-paper fig-leaf. Lady Charles had found one of the false beards that the Lampreys could always be depended upon to produce and had made a particularly irritable deity. Patch had been the apple tree.

"Does he like charades?" asked Roberta.

"I don't suppose he ever sees any, which is all to the good. We'll make him feel gay. That's poor old Gabriel's trouble. He's never gay enough."

There was a tap at the door and Henry looked in.

"I thought you might like a good laugh," said Henry. "The bum has come up the back stairs and caught poor old Daddy. He's sitting in the kitchen with Baskett and the maids."

"Oh *no!*" said his mother.

"His name is Mr. Gremball," said Henry.

iii

During lunch Lady Charles developed her theory of the way in which Lord Wutherwood—and Rune—was to be received and entertained. The family, with the exception of Henry, entered warmly into the discussion. Henry seemed to be more than usually vague and rather dispirited. Roberta, to her discomfiture, repeatedly caught his eye. Henry stared at her with an expression which she was unable to interpret until it occurred to her that he looked not at but through her. Roberta became less self-conscious and listened more attentively to the rest of the family. With every turn of their preposterous conversation her four years of separation from them seemed to diminish and Roberta felt herself slip, as of old, into an attitude of mind that half accepted the mad logic of their scheming. They discussed the suitability of a charade—Lady Charles and her children with passionate enthusiasm, Lord Charles with an air of critical detachment. Roberta wondered what Lord Charles really felt about the crisis and whether she merely imagined that he wore a faintly troubled air. His face was at no time an expressive one. It was a pale oval face. Shortsighted eyes that looked dimly friendly, a colourless moustache and an oddly youthful mouth added nothing to its distinction, and yet it had distinction of a gentle kind. His voice was pitched rather high and he had a trick of letting his sentences die away while he opened his eyes widely and stroked the top of his head. Roberta realized that though she liked him very much she had not the smallest inkling as to what sort of thoughts went on in his mind. He was an exceedingly remote individual.

"Well anyway," Frid was saying, "we can but try. Let's fill him up with sherry and do a charade. How about Lady Godiva? Henry the palfrey, Daddy the horrid husband, one of the twins Peeping Tom, and the rest of you the nice-minded populace."

"If you think I'm going to curvet round the drawing-room with you sitting on my back in the rude nude—" Henry began.

"Your hair's not long enough, Frid," said Patch.

"I didn't say *I*'d be Lady Godiva."

"Well, you can hardly expect Mummy to undress," said Colin, "and anyway you meant yourself."

"Don't be an ass, darling," said Lady Charles, "of course we can't do Lady Godiva. Uncle G. would be horrified."

"He might mistake it for a Witches' Sabbath," said Henry, "and think we were making fun of Aunt V."

"If Frid rode on you, I expect he would," said Patch.

"Why?" asked Mike. "What do witches ride on, Daddy?" Lord Charles gave his high-pitched laugh. Henry stared thoughtfully at Patch.

"If that wasn't rude," he said, "it would be almost funny."

"Well, why not do a Witches' Sabbath?" asked Stephen, "Uncle G. hates Aunt V. being a witch. I daresay it would be a great success. It would show we were on his side. We needn't make it too obvious, you know. It would be a word charade. Ipswich for instance."

"How would you do Ips?" asked Colin.

"Patch could waggle hers," said Henry.

"You are *beastly*, Henry," stormed Patch. "It's foul of you to say I'm fat. Mummy!"

"Never mind, darling, it's only puppy-fat. I think you're just right."

"We could do Dulwich," said Stephen. "The first syllable could be a week-end at Deepacres. Everybody yawning."

"That would be *really* rude," said his mother seriously.

"It wouldn't be far wrong," said Lord Charles.

"I know, Charlie, but it would never do. Don't let's get all

39

wild and silly about it. Let's just think sensibly of a good funny charade. Not too vulgar and not insulting."

There followed a long silence broken by Frid.

"I know," Frid cried, "we'll just be ourselves with bums in the house. It could be a breakfast scene with Baskett coming in to say: 'A person to see you, m'lord.' You wouldn't mind, would you, Baskett?"

With that smile demanded by the infinite courtesy of service, Baskett offered Frid cheese. Roberta wondered suddenly if Baskett thought the Lampreys as funny as she did. Frid hurried on with her plan.

"It really would be a good idea, Mummy. You see, Baskett could bring in the bum, and we could all plead with him and Daddy could say all the things he really wants Uncle G. to hear. Robin could do the bum, she'd look heaven in a bowler and a muffler. It would seem sort of gay and gallant at the same time."

"What would be the word?" asked Patch.

"Bumptious?"

"The second syllable's impossible," Colin objected.

"Bumboat?"

"Too obvious."

"Well, bumpkin. The second syllable could be about relations. We could actually have Uncle G. in it. Robin could be Uncle G. His coat and hat and umbrella will be in the hall ready to hand. We'd all plead with her and say: 'Your own kith and *kin*, Gabriel, dear fellow, your own kith and *kin*.'"

"Yes, that's all very well," said Stephen, "but you've forgotten the 'p.'"

"It could be silent as in—"

"That will do, Frid," said Lord Charles.

CHAPTER **IV**

Uncle G.

On the morning after her arrival Roberta woke to see a ray of thin London sunshine slanting across the counterpane. A maid in a print dress had drawn the curtains and put a tray on the bedside table. Dream and reality mixed themselves in Roberta's thoughts. As she grew wide awake she began to count over the wonderful events of the night that was past. In the hour before dawn she had been driven through London. She had seen jets from hose-pipes splayed fanwise over deserted streets, she had heard the jingle of milk-carts and seen the strange silhouette made by roofs and chimney pots against a thinning sky. She had heard Big Ben tell four of a spring morning and the clocks of Chelsea answer him. Before that she had danced in a room so full of shadows, abrupt lights, relentless music, and people, that the memory was as confused as a dream. She had danced with Colin and Stephen and Henry. Colin had played the fool, pretended he was a Russian, and spoken broken English. Stephen with his quick stutter had talked incessantly and complimented Roberta on her dancing. She had danced most often with Henry who was more silent than the twins. He said so little that Roberta in a sudden panic had wondered if he merely danced with her out of a sense of hospitality and regretted the absence of the person called Mary. In those strange surroundings Henry had become remote, a sophisticated grandee with a white waistcoat, and a gardenia in his coat. Yet, when she danced with him, behind all her bewilderment Roberta had been aware of a deep satisfaction. Now, lying still in her bed, she called back the events of the night so potently that though her eyes were still open she had no thought for the sunlight on her counterpane but anxiously examined the picture of herself and Henry. There they were, moving together among a shadowy company of dancers. He did not wait to see if Stephen or Colin would ask her to dance, but himself asked her quickly and danced on until long after the others had gone back to their table. There was a sort of protective decisiveness in his manner that pleased and embarrassed Roberta. Perhaps after all, he was only worried about the financial crisis. "Heaven knows," thought Roberta, "it's enough to worry anybody but a Lamprey into a thousand fits." She realized that the crisis lay like a nasty taste behind the savor of her own enjoyment. It was not discussed during that dazzling evening until they got home. Creeping into the flat in the half light, they found Nanny's thermos of Ovaltine and sat drinking it round the heater in Roberta's room. Henry laughed unexpectedly and said: "Well, chaps, we may not be here much longer." Frid, very elegant and pale, struck a tragic attitude and said: "The last night in the old home. Pause for sobs." There was a brief silence broken by Stephen.

"Uncle Gabriel," Stephen said, "has s-simply g-got to stump up."

"What if he won't?" Colin had asked.

"We'll bribe Aunt V. to bewitch him," said Frid. She pulled her cloak over her head, crouched down, crooked her fingers and croaked:

"Weary se'nnights nine times nine
Shall he dwindle, peak and pine."

The twins instantly turned themselves into witches and circled with Frid round the heater.

"Double, double toil and trouble;
Fire burn, and cauldron bubble."

"Shut up," said Henry. "I thought you said it was unlucky to quote 'Macbeth.'"

"If we gave Aunt V. the ingredients for a charm," said Colin, "I expect she'd be only too pleased to make Uncle G. dwindle, peak and pine."

"They're awkward things to beat up in a hurry," said Frid.

Stephen said: "I wonder what Aunt V.'s friends d-do about it. It must be rather dull to be witches if you can't cast murrains on cattle or give your husband warts."

"I wish," Roberta cried, "that you'd tell me the truth about your Aunt V. and not go rambling on about her being a witch."

"Poor Robin," Henry said. "It does sound very silly, but as an actual fact, if her maid is to be believed, Aunt V. has taken up some sort of black magic. I imagine it boils down to reading histories of witchcraft and turning tables. In my opinion Aunt V. is simply dotty."

"Well," Frid said, "let's go to bed, anyway." She kissed the air near Roberta's cheek and drifted to the door. "Come on, twins," she added.

The twins kissed Roberta and wandered after Frid.

Henry stood in the doorway.

"Sleep well," he said.

"Thank you, Henry," said Roberta. "It was a lovely party."

"For once," said Henry, "I thought so too. Good night, Robin!"

Roberta, as she watched the sun on her counterpane, reviewed this final scene several times and felt happy.

ii

The visit of Lord Wutherwood was prejudiced from the start by the arrival of Lady Katherine Lobe. Lady Katherine was a maiden aunt of Lord Charles. She was extremely poor and lived in a small house at Hammersmith. There she was surrounded by photographs of the Lamprey children to whom she was passionately devoted. Being poor herself, she spent the greater part of her life in working for the still-poorer members of her parish. She wore nondescript garments: hats that seemed to have no connection with her head, and grey fabric gloves. She was extremely deaf and spoke in a toneless whispering manner, with kind smiles, and with many anxious looks into the faces of the people she addressed. But for all her diffidence there was a core of determination in Lady Katherine. In her likes and dislikes she was immovable. Nothing would reconcile her to a person of whom she disapproved, and unfortunately she disapproved most strongly of her nephew Wutherwood, who, for his part, refused to meet her. At Christmas she invariably wrote him a letter on the subject of good-will towards men, pointing out his short-comings under this heading and enclosing a blank promise to pay yearly a large sum to one of her charities. Lord Wutherwood's only reply to these communications was an irritable tearing across of the enclosures. For his younger brother Lady Katherine had the warmest affection. Occasionally she would travel in a bus up to the West End in order to visit the Lampreys and beg, with a gentle persistence, for their old clothes or force them to buy tickets for charitable entertainments. They were always warned by letter of these visits, but on this occasion Lady Charles, agitated by the crisis, had forgotten to open the note, and the only warning she had was Baskett's announcement, at six o'clock in the evening, of Lady Katherine's arrival.

The Lampreys and Roberta had assembled in the drawing-room to await the arrival of Lord Wutherwood. They were unnaturally silent. Even Mike had caught the feeling of tension. He stood by the wireless and turned the control knob as rapidly as possible until told to stop, when he flung himself moodily full length on the hearthrug and kicked his feet together.

"There's the lift," cried Lady Charles suddenly. "Mike, stay where you are and jump up. Remember to shake hands with Uncle Gabriel. Sprinkle some 'sirs' through your conversation, for heaven's sake, and when I nod to you you are to give him the pot."

"Mike'll break it," said Patch.

"I won't," shouted Mike indignantly.

"And remember," continued his mother, "if I suggest a charade you're all to go out and come back quietly and do one. Then, when you've finished, go out again so that Daddy can talk to Uncle Gabriel. And remember—"

"Can't we listen?" asked Patch.

"We'll probably hear Uncle G. all over the flat," said Henry.

"And remember not to mention witchcraft. Uncle G. hates it."

"Ssh!"

"Can't we be talking?" Frid suggested. "You'd think there was a corpse in the flat."

"If you can think of anything to say, say it," said her father gloomily.

Frid began to speak in a high voice. "Aren't those flowers over there *too* marvellous?" she asked. Nobody answered her. In the distance a bell rang. Baskett was heard to walk across the hall.

"Lovely, darling," said Lady Charles violently. She appealed mutely to the children who stared in apprehension at the door and grimaced at each other. Lady Charles turned to Roberta.

"Robin, darling, do tell us about your voyage Home. Did you have fun?"

"Yes," said Roberta, whose heart was now thumping against her ribs. "Yes. We had a fancy-dress ball."

Lady Charles and Frid laughed musically. The door opened and Baskett came in.

"Lady Katherine Lobe, m'lady," said Baskett.

"Good God!" said Lord Charles.

Lady Katherine came in. She walked with short steps and peered amiably through the cigarette smoke.

"Imogen, darling," she whispered.

"Aunt Kit!"

The Lampreys kept their heads admirably. They told Lady Katherine how delighted they were to see her and seated her by the fire. They introduced Roberta to her, teased her gently about her lame ducks and, with panic-stricken glances at each other, asked her to remove her raincoat.

"So nice to see you all," whispered Lady Katherine. "Such luck for me to find the whole family. And there's Michael home for the holidays and grown enormously. Patricia too. And the twins. Don't speak, twins, and let me see if I can guess. This is Stephen, isn't it?"

"Yes, Aunt Kit," said Colin.

"There! I knew I was right. You got my note, Imogen darling?"

"Yes, Aunt Kit. We're so pleased," said Charlot.

"Yes I wondered if you had got it because you all looked quite surprised when I walked in. So I wondered."

"We thought you were Uncle Gabriel," shouted Mike.

"What, dear?"

"Uncle Gabriel."

Lady Katherine passed a grey-fabric finger across her lips. "Is Gabriel coming, Charles?"

"Yes, Aunt Kit," said Lord Charles. And as she merely gazed dimly at him he added loudly: "He's coming to see me on business."

"We're going to have some charades," bawled Mike.

"I'm very glad," said Lady Katherine emphatically. "I wish to see Gabriel. I have written to him several times but no response did I get. It's about our Fresh Air Fund. A day in the country for a hundred children and a fortnight in private homes for twenty sickly mites. I want Gabriel to take six."

"Six sickly mites?" asked Henry.

"What, dear?"

"Do you want Uncle Gabriel to take six sickly mites at Deepacres?"

"It's the least he can do. I'm afraid Gabriel is inclined to be too self-centred, Charles. He's a very wealthy man and he should think of other people more than he does. Your mama always said so. And I hear the most disquieting news of Violet. It appears that she has taken up spiritualism and sits in the dark with a set of very second-rate sort of people."

"Not spiritualism, darling," said Charlot. "Black magic."

"What, dear?"

"Magic."

"Oh. Oh, I see. That's entirely different. I suppose she does it to entertain their house-parties. But that doesn't alter the fact that both Violet and Gabriel are getting rather self-centred. It would be an excellent thing for both of them if they adopted two children."

"For mercy's sake, Aunt Kit," cried Charlot, "don't suggest that to Gabriel."

"Don't suggest anything," said Lord Charles. "I implore you, Aunt Kit, not to tackle Gabriel this afternoon. You see—" he peered anxiously at his watch and broke off. "Good God,

Immy," he whispered to his wife, "we must do something. She'll infuriate him. Take her to your room."

"Under what pretext?" muttered Charlot.

"Think of something."

"Aunt Kit, would you like to see my bedroom?"

"What, dear?"

"It's no good, Mummy," said Frid. "Better tell her we're bust."

"I think so," said Lord Charles. He bent his legs and brought his face close to his aunt's.

"Aunt Kit," he shouted, "I'm in difficulties."

"Are you, dear?"

"I've no money."

"What?"

"There's a bum in the house," yelled Patch.

"Be quiet, Patch," said Henry. His father continued. "I've asked Gabriel to lend me two thousand. If he doesn't I shall go bankrupt."

"Charlie!"

"It's true."

"I'll speak to Gabriel," said Lady Katherine quite loudly.

"No, no!" cried the Lampreys.

"Lord and Lady Wutherwood, m'lady," said Baskett in the doorway.

iii

Roberta knew that the Lampreys had not reckoned on Lady Wutherwood's arrival with her husband, and she had time to admire their almost instant recovery from this second and formidable shock. Charlot met her brother and sister-in-law half-way across the room. Her manner held a miraculous balance between the over-cordial and the too-casual. Her children and her husband supported her wonderfully. Lady Katherine for the moment was too rattled by the Lampreys' news of impending disaster to make any disturbance. She sat quietly in her chair.

Roberta found herself shaking hands with an extremely odd couple. The Marquis of Wutherwood and Rune was sixty years of age but these years sat heavily upon him and he looked like an old man. His narrow head, sunken between high shoulders, poked forward with an air that was at once mean and aggressive. His face was colourless. The bridge of his nose was so narrow that his eyes appeared to be impossibly close-set. His mouth drooped querulously and the length of his chin, though prodigious, was singularly unexpressive of anything but obstinacy. His upper teeth projected over his under lip and hinted at a high and a narrow palate. These teeth gave him an unpleasingly feminine appearance increased by his chilly old-maidish manner, which suggested that he lived in a state of perpetual offence. Roberta found herself wondering if he could possibly be as disagreeable as he looked.

His wife was about fifty years of age. She was dark, extremely sallow, and fat. There was a musty falseness about the dank hair which she wore over her ears in sibylline coils. She painted her face, but with such inattention to detail that Roberta was reminded of a cheap print in which the colours had slipped to one side, showing the original structure of the drawing underneath. She had curious eyes, very pale, with tiny pupils, and muddy whites. They were so abnormally sunken that they seemed to reflect no light and this gave them a veiled appearance which Roberta found disconcerting, and oddly repellent. Her face had once been round but like her make-up it had slipped and now hung in folds and pockets about her lips, which were dragged down at the corners. Roberta saw that Lady Wutherwood had a trick of parting and closing her lips. It was a very slight movement but she did it continually with a faint click of sound. And in the corners of her lips there was a kind of whiteness that moved when they moved. "Henry is right," thought Roberta. "She is disgusting."

Lord Wutherwood greeted the Lampreys without much show of cordiality. When he saw Lady Katherine Lobe his attitude stiffened still further. He turned to his brother and in a muffled voice said: "We're in a hurry, Charles."

"Oh," said Lord Charles. "Are you? Oh—well—"

"Are you?" Charlot repeated. "Not too much of a hurry, I hope, Gabriel. We never see anything of you."

"You never come to Deepacres when we ask you, Imogen."

"I *know*. We'd adore to come, especially the children, but you know it's so frightfully *expensive* to travel, even in

England. You see we can't all get into one car—"

"The fare, third-class return, is within the reach of most people."

"*Miles* beyond us, I'm afraid," said Charlot with a charming air of ruefulness. "We're cutting down *everything*. We never *budge* from where we are."

Lord Wutherwood turned to Henry.

"Enjoy your trip to the Cote d'Azur?" he asked. "Saw your photograph in one of these papers. In my day we didn't strip ourselves naked and wallow in front of press photographers but I suppose you like that sort of thing."

"Enormously, sir," said Henry coldly.

There was a slight pause. Roberta felt uncomfortably that Charlot's plan should be amended and that they should leave the field to Lord Charles. She wondered if she herself should slip out of the room. Her thoughts must have appeared in her face for Henry caught her eye, smiled, and shook his head. The Wutherwoods were now seated side-by-side on the sofa. Baskett came in with the sherry.

"Ah, sherry," said Lord Charles. Henry began to pour it out. Charlot made desperate efforts with her brother-in-law. Lady Katherine leant forward in her chair and addressed Lady Wutherwood.

"Well, Violet," she said, "I hear you have taken up conjuring."

"You couldn't be more mistaken," said Lady Wutherwood in a deep voice. She spoke with a very slight accent, slurring her words together. After each phrase she rearranged her mouth with those clicking movements and stealthily touched away the white discs at the corners, but in a little while they reformed.

"Aunty Kit," cried Frid, "will you have some sherry? Aunt Violet?"

"No thank you, my dear," said Lady Katherine.

"Yes," said Lady Wutherwood.

"You'd better not, V.," said Lord Wutherwood. "You know what'll happen."

Mike walked to the end of the sofa and stared fixedly at his aunt. Lord Charles turned to his brother with an air of cordiality. "It's a sherry that I think you rather like, Gabriel, don't you?" he said. "Corregio del Martez, '79."

"If you can afford a sherry like that—" began Lord

Wutherwood. Henry hurriedly placed a glass at his elbow.

"Aunt Violet," asked Mike suddenly, "can you do the rope trick? I bet you can't. I bet you can't do that and I bet you can't saw a lady in half."

"Don't be an idiot, Mike," said Patch.

"Mikey," said his mother, "run and find Baskett, darling, and ask him to take care of Uncle Gabriel's chauffeur. I suppose he's there, isn't he, Gabriel?"

"He'll do very well in the car. Your aunt's maid is there, too. Your aunt insists on cartin' her about with us. I strongly object, of course, but that makes no difference. She's a nasty type."

Lady Wutherwood laughed rather madly. Her husband turned on her. "You know what I mean, V.," he said. "Tinkerton's a bad lot. Put it bluntly, she's damn well debauched my chauffeur. It's been goin' on under your nose for years."

Charlot evidently decided that it would be better not to have heard this embarrassing parenthesis. "Of course they must come up," she said cheerfully. "Nanny will adore to see Tinkerton. Mikey, ask Baskett to bring Tinkerton and Giggle up to the Servants' sitting-room and give them a drink of tea or something. Ask politely, won't you?"

"O.K.," said Mike. He hopped on one foot and turned to look at Lady Wutherwood.

"Isn't it pretty funny?" he asked. "Your chauffeur's called Giggle and there's a man in the kitchen called Grumble. He's a—"

"Michael!" said Lord Charles. "Do as you're told at once."

Mike went out, followed unostentatiously by Stephen who shut the door behind him. Stephen returned in a few moments.

"I wish you'd tell me, Violet," said Lady Katherine, "what it is you have taken up. One hears such extraordinary reports."

"She's dabblin' in some damn-fool kind of occultism," said Lord Wutherwood, turning pale with annoyance.

Roberta noticed that when he stopped speaking his upper teeth closed firmly on his under lip, causing his whole mouth to settle down at the corners in an expression of maddening complacency.

"Gabriel," said his wife, "believes in what he sees. Nothing else. He thinks himself fortunate in that. He is not so fortunate as he supposes."

"What the devil d'you mean?" demanded Lord Wutherwood. "Don't look at me like that, V., I don't like it. These friends of yours are makin' a damned unpleasant woman of you. Of all the miserable footlin' crew! What d'you think you're doin' huntin' up a parcel of spooks? A lot of trickery. I've told you before, I've a damn good mind to speak to the police about the whole affair. If it wasn't for draggin' my name into it—"

"You had better be careful, Gabriel. It is not wise to sneer at the unseen."

"The unseen what?" asked Lady Katherine who had caught this last phrase.

"The unseen forces."

Lord Wutherwood made exasperated sounds and turned his back.

"What sort of forces?" persisted Lady Katherine against the combined mental opposition of the Lampreys.

"Do you seek," asked Lady Wutherwood with a formidable air of contempt, "to learn in a few words the wisdom of all the ages? A lifetime is too short to reach full understanding."

"Of what?"

"Esoteric Lore."

"What's that?"

Charlot suddenly made a bold dash into this strange conversation, and Roberta with something like terror saw that she had decided on the line she would take with her sister-in-law. Evidently it was to be a line of gentle banter. Charlot leant towards Lady Wutherwood and said gaily: "I'm as bewildered as Aunty Kit, Violet. Is esoteric lore the same as—what? Witchcraft? Don't turn into a witch, darling."

Lady Wutherwood stared at Charlot. "It's a great mistake," she said in her deep voice, "to laugh at necromancy, Imogen. There are more things in Heaven and earth—"

"I suppose there are, Violet, but I don't want to meet them."

"The church," said Lady Katherine in her loudest whisper, "takes a firm stand in such matters. I imagine you know, Violet, that you are in danger of—"

The Lampreys all began to talk at once. They talked persistently, not raising their voices but overpowering their guests with a sort of gentle barrage. They seemed by tacit

51

agreement to have split into two groups: Frid, Patch and their mother tackling Lord Wutherwood, while Henry and the twins concentrated on his wife. Lord Charles, nervously polishing his eye-glass, stood aside like a sort of inadequate referee. The scene now developed in accordance with the best traditions of polite drawing-room comedy. Roberta was irresistably reminded of the play she had seen the previous night and, once possessed of this idea, it seemed to her that the Lampreys and their relations had begun to pitch their voices like actors and actresses and to use gestures that were a little larger than life. The scene was building towards some neat and effective climax. There was perhaps a superfluity of character parts and with Lady Katherine Lobe smiling and nodding in her corner the eccentric dowager was not lacking. Partly to dispel this idea and in the hope that she might be of some service to the cause, Roberta moved to Lady Katherine who, true to family form, instantly began to confide in her, saying that she had heard most disquieting news of Violet and asking Roberta if she thought the Lampreys would rather she went away as poor Charles must be given a free hand with Gabriel. All this was fortunately uttered in such a muffled aside that Roberta could hear no more than half of it. Lady Katherine was too insistent, however, for Roberta to divide her own attention and she had no idea of what went forward between the Lampreys and the Wutherwoods until she heard Frid say: "No, Uncle Gabriel, I shall be bitterly humiliated if you don't ask us to do one for you." Roberta saw that Lord Wutherwood looked slightly less disagreeable. Frid was presenting herself as a lovely and attentive niece.

"I'm so glad you agree with me," whispered Lady Katherine. "There is no doubt at all, in my mind, of our duty to these poor things." Roberta did not know if she spoke of the Lampreys, of ailing children, or of Jewish refugees, in all of whom she seemed to be passionately interested. Frid had refilled her uncle's glass. Lady Wutherwood was droning interminably to Henry and the twins who appeared to be enraptured with the recital. Charlot suddenly broke up this comparatively peaceful picture by making the much-discussed announcement.

"Children," she said gaily. "Frid's been telling Uncle Gabriel about your charades. Do you think you could do a very quick rhyming charade now, for Aunt Violet and Aunt

Kit and Uncle Gabriel? Don't take ages deciding what to do; just do the first thing that comes into your heads. We'll give you a word. Out you go."

"Come on, Robin," said Henry.

Robin, full of misgivings, followed the Lampreys into the hall.

CHAPTER V

Mike Puts the Pot on It

"This is a mistake," said Henry gloomily as soon as he had shut the door. "Obviously Uncle G.'s in a foul temper and we won't improve it by cutting capers in front of him. I must say he's a loathsome old man."

"Well, let's compromise," said Frid. "We won't do one about bums. Let's do one about witchcraft. Uncle G. will like that because he'll think it's making nonsense of Aunt V. and Aunt V. will be interested if we do it well enough."

"She's quite m-mad, you know, poor thing," said Stephen. "D-don't you consider she's mad, Colin?"

"Stark ravers," said Colin. "Where's Mike?"

"Talking to Giggle about toy trains, I think. He's better out of this."

"Let's get going," said Patch. "Mummy said we were to hurry."

The door opened and Charlot looked out. "It's to rhyme with 'pale,'" she said loudly and then lowering her voice she hissed: "It's 'nail.' Don't do either of the other things. Too risky." The door shut and Charlot called from the other side: "Hurry up!"

Frid made a helpless gesture. "Well, there you are," she said. "No bums and no witches and the word is 'nail.' Evidently Mummy wants us to get it right at the first stab. What shall we do?"

"Bite our nails?" suggested Patch.

"Put a nail in Uncle G.'s coffin," said Henry viciously.

"Nailing our colours to the mast?"

"I know," said Frid. "We'll do Jael and Sisera."

"What did they d-do?" asked Stephen.

"Something with a nail. What was it, Robin?"

"Didn't Jael hammer a nail through Sisera's head?"

"That's right," said Colin. "Well, we can be clever and do wail and hail and Jael and nail all at once. A compound charade."

The Lampreys threw open the door of their enormous hall cupboard and began to dress themselves up.

"I'll be Jael," said Frid, "and Henry can be Sisera and the twins guards and Robin a faithful slave."

"What am I?" demanded Patch, putting on Lord Wutherwood's bowler.

"Another faithful slave. Wait a moment."

Frid ran down the passage towards the kitchen. Roberta could hear her shouting: "A skewer, Baskett, a skewer! We're doing a charade. Quick!"

"Did Jael make love to Sisera," asked Colin, "before he slew her?"

"Jael's the female," said Stephen.

"Oh. Give me that ghastly scarf, will you. Is it Uncle G.'s?"

"Yes. I want it for a loin cloth."

"I'm going to be a Circassian slave," said Patch.

"This is most frightfully bogus," said Henry, taking two yachting caps out of the wardrobe. "I can't tell you how much I object to cavorting in front of these repellent people. You could use yachting caps as breast-plates, Robin. There's some string."

"Thank you. Aren't you going to dress up, Henry?"

Henry hung a pair of field-glasses round his neck. "I shall play it modern," he muttered. "Colonel Sisera Blimp." He drew a pair of fur-lined motoring gloves over his hands.

Frid came back with a long silver-plated skewer.

"Be careful how you muck about my head with that thing," said Henry.

"I want a hammer."

"Use your boot. Let's get it over."

"In you go, Robin and Patch. Take that rug and hold it like a tent. You too, twins. Say how beautiful I am," ordered Frid, "and wonder if the day has been Sisera's."

Robin, Patch and the twins entered the drawing-room unnoticed. Their audience was sitting with its back to the door.

"We've begun," said Patch loudly. "I wonder how the battle went. Dost thou know if the day is Sisera's?"

"Nay," said Stephen.

"Dost thou?"

"Nay," said Colin.

"And thou?" continued Patch, irritably, to Robin.

"Nay, I wot not," said Robin and she added hurriedly: "How beautiful Jael is!"

"She is like the new-blown moon," agreed Patch.

"Lo," said Colin, "here she comes."

"How beautiful she is!" said Stephen.

Frid made an entrance. She had removed her stockings and shoes and had hitched her dress up with scarves. She carried the skewer in her sash and a shoe in her hand. She shut the door and leant against it in a dramatic manner.

"That's my scarf," said Lord Wutherwood. He turned his back on the charade and began talking in a low, querulous voice to his brother.

"I am aweary with watching," said Frid. "Praise to Allah the day is ours. Ho, slaves!"

Patch and Robin threw themselves on their faces. The twins saluted.

"Lie down, O Jael," said Colin abruptly.

Frid crawled into the tent. "I am aweary unto death," she repeated.

"Here comes S-S-Sis-Sis—" began Stephen.

"Hist!" shouted Patch, coming to his rescue. "I hear footprints. Stand to!"

"Stand!" said the twins.

The door opened and Henry came in. He wore a solar

topee and his gauntlet driving gloves. He had turned up his trousers to resemble shorts. He focussed his field-glasses on the audience and said: "An arid desert, by gad!"

" 'Tis Sisera," said Frid. "Lure him hither, slaves."

Roberta and Patch made winning gestures. Henry watched them through his field-glasses. When they drew nearer he seized Roberta by the arm. "A damn fine girl, by gad," he said.

"Come hither, O Sisera," invited Roberta uneasily. "Come to yonder tent."

Henry was led to the tent. Frid writhed on the carpet and extended her arms. "Do I behold the valiant Sisera?" she asked. "All hail O Captain."

Henry was dragged down to the floor. A rather confused scene took place in the course of which Frid gave him a few lines from Titania's speech to Bottom and he began to snore.

"Vengeance is mine," observed Frid. "Quick, the nail." She drew the skewer from her sash and hammered it into the carpet behind Henry's head. Henry yelled, gurgled, and lay still.

"Wail," muttered Frid. The twins, Patch and Roberta wailed loudly.

"That's all," said Frid. "Were we right? It was a compound charade."

Charlot and Lady Katherine clapped their hands. Lord Wutherwood glanced at them with annoyance and resumed his conversation. Lady Wutherwood stared out of the window with lack-lustre eyes.

"And now tidy up the mess," Charlot ordered. "I want to show Aunt Violet and Aunt Kit how we fitted into 26. Where's Mike?"

"We'll find him, Mummy," said Frid. "Come on, chaps. That's that."

ii

When they returned to the hall Roberta saw that the Lampreys were in a family rage. Henry and Frid were white and the twins and Patch scarlet with fury. Roberta wondered

58

if these reactions were the natural consequences of their complexions, if fair people were always more choleric than dark ones. Henry, she saw, was the angriest. He walked off down the passage calling "Michael!" in a voice that brought Mike running. "Your mama is asking for you," said Henry.

"I've lost the pot," said Mike. Henry turned on his heel and came back into the hall. He picked up rugs and hats and slung them indiscriminately into the cupboard.

"That was a howling success, wasn't it?" said Frid. "Did either of them so much as glance at us, do you happen to know?"

"They've got the manners of hogs," said Patch violently.

"Uncle Gabriel," muttered Stephen slowly, "is without doubt an old—"

"Shut up," said Colin.

"Well, isn't he?"

"I hope Mummy's pleased," said Henry. "She's seen us make as big fools of ourselves as can reasonably be expected in one afternoon."

"It's not Mummy's fault," murmured Colin uncomfortably.

Mike came in looking scared. "I can't find the pot I've got to give Uncle Gabriel," he said. His brothers and sisters paid no attention; Roberta hunted helplessly round the littered hall. Mike, looking anxious, wandered into the drawing-room.

"Shut that d-door," said Stephen.

Patch hurled Lord Wutherwood's bowler to the far end of the hall.

"Don't be a fool, Patch," said Henry. Colin picked the bowler up and pretended to be sick into it. The others watched him moodily.

"This has been great fun for Robin," said Henry. "We're sorry our relations are so bloody rude, Robin."

"What *does* it matter?" said Roberta.

Henry stared at her. "You're quite right," he said, "it doesn't matter. But if any of you think that noisome old treasure-trove in there is going to hand us two thousand pounds, you're due for a disappointment. Daddy could go bankrupt six times over before his charming brother would help him."

"You th-think we're for it then?" asked Stephen.

"I do."

"We'll wriggle out," said Frid. "We always have."

"Wolf, wolf," said Henry.

"Why? I don't see it."

"Let's get out of this," suggested Patch. "Mummy's going to take the aunts into 26, isn't she?"

"Let's go into the dining-room," said Frid.

Colin reminded them of Mike and the Chinese vase and wondered vaguely if they ought to look for it. Stephen said Lord Wutherwood could be depended upon to take the vase and go away without offering them any assistance. Frid and Henry said they thought the gesture with the vase should be attempted.

"Was it wrapped up?" asked Roberta suddenly.

"Yes. Mummy bought a smart box for it," said Patch.

"Then I know where it is. It's in her bedroom."

"There let it lie, say I," said Stephen.

"But if Charlot wants it?"

"Robin," said Frid, "be a darling and go into the drawing-room. Hiss to Mummy where the pot is and then if she wants it she can send Mike."

"All right," agreed Roberta, and returned nervously to the drawing-room. She managed to give Charlot the message.

"Where's Mike?" murmured Charlot.

"Didn't he come in here?"

"Yes, but he's wandered away."

"Shall I find him?"

"No, never mind."

As Roberta made for the door she heard Charlot say brightly: "Come along, Violet, come along, Aunt Kit, we'll leave the boys to talk business." Roberta hurried through into the dining-room where she found the Lampreys lying close together on the floor with their heads to the wall.

"Lock the door," they whispered.

Roberta locked the door. Henry moved slightly and invited her with a gesture to lie between Frid and himself.

"What's this in aid of?" asked Roberta.

"Ssh! Listen! Get closer."

Roberta now saw that this part of the wall consisted of a boarded-up door which evidently had at one time opened into the drawing-room. The Lampreys were listening at the crack. The voices of Lord Charles and his brother could be clearly heard above the comfortable sounds made by the drawing-room fire.

"I'd better not," breathed Roberta, diffidently.

"It's all right," said Frid in her ear. "Daddy wouldn't mind. Ssh!"

"... so you see," said Lord Charles's voice, "it's been a series of misfortunes rather than any one disaster. The jewellery and *objets-d'art* idea seemed a capital one. I really couldn't foresee that poor Stein would shoot himself, you know. Now could I?"

"You go and tie yourself up with some miserable adventurer—"

"No, no, he wasn't that, Gabriel, really."

"Why the devil didn't you make some enquiries?"

"Well I—I did make a good many. The truth is—"

"The truth is," said Lord Wutherwood's voice edgily, "you drifted into this business as you have drifted into every conceivable sort of blunder for the last twenty years."

There was silence for a moment, and then Lord Charles's voice: "Very well, Gabriel. I'll take that. It's quite useless in my predicament to offer excuses. I readily confess that the sort of explanation I have to make would seem quite ridiculous to you."

"And to anyone else. I may as well tell you at the outset that I can't do anything about it. I've helped you twice before and I might as well have thrown the money into the sea."

"We were extremely grateful—"

"Is it too much to suggest that you might have shown it by pullin' yourselves together? I told you then that you should recognize the fact that you were a man with a small income and a large family and should cut your coat accordingly. It's preposterous, the way you live. Butlers, maids, cars, bringin' gels out, doin' the season, trips here, gamblin' there. Good God, you ought to be livin' like a—like a clerk or something! Why haven't you got some post for yourself where you earned a wage? What are those three boys doin'?"

"They've tried extremely hard to get jobs."

"Nonsense. They could have gone into shops since they're not qualified for any professions. I said when they were at school that they ought to face the facts and work for professions!"

61

"We couldn't afford the University."

"You could afford half a dozen white elephants. You could afford to traipse around the world in luxury liners, you could afford to take that place in the Highlands, entertain, and God know what."

"My dear Gabriel! The amount of entertaining we do!"

"You dribble money away. Why don't those gels run the house? Plenty of gels one knows are doin' that sort of thing. Domestic."

"Frid's going on the stage."

"Yah!" said Lord Wutherwood. "Was that display she treated us to just now a sample? Showin' her legs and droppin' about in other people's scarves like a dyin' duck in a thunderstorm!"

Roberta felt Frid go rigid with hatred. Stephen and Colin thrust their fists into their mouths. Patch snorted and was savagely nudged by Henry.

". . . I may tell you, Charles, that I'm plaguely hard pressed myself. Deepacres nearly kills me keepin' it up. I'm taxed up to the gullet. Looks as if I'll have to put down the London house. You don't know the calls there are on me in—well, in my position. When I remember what it'll end in I sometimes wonder why the devil I take the trouble."

"What do you mean, Gabriel?"

"I've no boy of my own."

"No."

"And to be frank with you I don't imagine Deepacres is likely to survive the treatment of my heirs."

"You mean Henry."

"Oh you'll outlive me, no doubt," said Lord Wutherwood.

"Then you mean me?"

"Put it baldly, I mean the pair of you."

There was a long pause. Roberta heard the fire in the next room settle down in the grate. She heard the breathing of the young Lampreys and the flurried ticking of a carriage-clock on the dining-room mantelpiece. When Lord Charles at last broke the silence, Robert felt her companions stir a little as though something for which they had waited was about to appear. Lord Charles's voice had changed. It was at once gentler and more decisive.

"I think," he said, "that I can promise you neither Henry nor I will do much harm to Deepacres. We might possibly care to let other people share its amenities occasionally. That's all."

"What do you mean?"

"I was thinking of your regard for Deepacres and wondering if after all it amounts to very much. As you say, one day it will be Henry's. Yet you are content to let him go down with the rest of us."

"If he's got any guts he'll make his way."

"I hope he will. I almost believe I am glad to go bankrupt without your aid, Gabriel. I've had to ask you for money. No doubt you would say I've come begging for money. You choose to refuse me. But please don't plead poverty. You could perfectly well afford to help me but you are a miserly fellow and you choose not to do so. It is not a matter of principle with you—I could respect that—it is just plain reluctance to give away money. I hoped that your vanity and snobbishness, for you're a hell of a snob, would turn the balance. I was wrong. You will go away bathed in the vapour of conscious rectitude. I doubt if you have ever in your life been guilty of a foolish generous action. Everything you have said about us is true; we *have* dribbled money away. But we've given something with it. Imogen and the children have got gaiety and warmth of heart and charm; over-rated qualities perhaps, but they are generous qualities. Indeed there is nothing ungenerous about my undisciplined children. They give something to almost everybody they meet. Perhaps they cheat a little and trade a little on their charm but I don't think that matters nearly so much as being tight-lipped monsters of behaviourism. They are full of what I dare to call loving-kindness, Gabriel, and that's a commodity I don't expect you to understand or applaud."

"Oh Daddy!" whispered Frid.

"That's a damned impertinent stand to take," said Lord Wutherwood. "It's as much as to say that people with a conscience about money are bound to be bores."

"Nothing of the sort, I—"

"You're as good as puttin' a premium on dishonesty. It's the way people talk these days. 'Charm!' Plenty of scamps have got charm; wouldn't be scamps if they hadn't, I daresay. Where's this lovin'-kindness you talk about when it comes to lettin' down your creditors?"

"Touché, I'm afraid," muttered Henry.

"If I hadn't thought of that," said Lord Charles, "nothing would have induced me to ask for your help."

"You won't get it."

"Then, as I fancy the Americans say, it is just too bad about my creditors. I rather think the poor devils have banked on you, Gabriel."

"Insufferable impertinence!" shouted Lord Wutherwood, and Roberta heard the angry sibilants whistle through his teeth. "Sulking behind my name, by God! Using my name as a screen for your dishonesty."

"I didn't say so."

"You as good as said so," shouted Lord Wutherwood. "By God, this settles it."

The scene which had hitherto maintained the established atmosphere of drawing-room comedy now blossomed agreeably into a more robust type of drama. The brothers set about abusing each other in good round terms and with each intemperate sally their phrases became more deeply coloured with the tincture of Victorian rodomontade. Incredible references to wills, entails, and family escutcheons were freely exchanged. Lord Charles was the first to falter and his brother's peroration rang out clearly.

"I refuse to discuss the matter any further. You can drag yourself and your fool of a wife and your precious brood through the bankruptcy court. If Deepacres wasn't entailed I'd see that you never got a penny of Lamprey money. As it is—"

"As it is you will no doubt rewrite as much of your will as is not covered by the entail."

"I shall do so, certainly."

"You're a delightful fellow, Gabriel! I wish to God I'd left you alone."

"You appear even to make a failure of the noble art of sponging."

This, as Roberta and the Lampreys afterwards agreed, was the climax. Lord Charles and his brother in unison began to speak and in a moment to shout. It was impossible to understand anything but the fact that they had both lost their tempers. This lasted for perhaps fifteen seconds and stopped so abruptly that Roberta thought of a radio-knob turned off in the midst of a lively dialogue. So complete was the ensuing silence that she heard a far door open and footsteps cross the drawing-room carpet.

Mike's voice sounded clearly: "Uncle Gabriel, this is a little present from all of us with our love."

Roberta and the four Lampreys sat on the dining-room floor and gaped at each other. Next door all was silence. Lord Charles had merely said: "Michael, put that parcel down, will you, and come back later."

The brothers had moved away and their following remarks were inaudible. Then Lord Wutherwood had marched out of the room, not neglecting to slam the door. Lord Charles had said: "Run away, Mike, old man," and Mike had hopped audibly to the door. Everything was quiet. Lord Charles, only a few inches away, must be standing motionless. Roberta wondered if he still looked after his brother, if he was white like Frid and Henry, or scarlet like Patch and the twins. She wished with all her heart that he would make some movement and pictured him staring with an air of blank wretchedness at the door his brother had slammed. The silence was unendurable. It was broken at last by a step in the passage outside. The dining-room door-handle rattled and Henry walked across and turned the key. The door opened and Mike stood on the threshold. He looked doubtfully at his brothers and sisters. "I say, is anything up?" he asked.

"Not much," said Henry.

"Well, anyway, I bet something's up," Mike persisted. "I bet Uncle G.'s in a stink about something. He looks absolutely fed-up and he and Daddy have been yelling blue murder. I say, do you know Giggle's fixed up my Hornby train? He's absolutely wizard with trains. I bet he could—"

"Mike," said Henry. "Did Mummy tell you to give the pot to Uncle Gabriel?"

"What? Oh. Well, no. You see Giggle and I were trying my Hornby in the passage and it goes absolutely whizzer now because—"

"The pot," said Stephen.

"What? Well, I saw it through Mummy's door so I just—" A distant voice yelled "Violet!"

"Who's that?" asked Frid.

"It's Uncle G.," explained Mike. "He's in the lift. Giggle had his coat off because he says—"

"I'd better go to Mummy," said Frid. "She may be in difficulties with the aunts. Come on, Patch." They went out.

"What *is* the matter with Uncle G.?" asked Mike with casual insistence.

Stephen looked at him. "If you must know," he said violently, "Uncle Gabriel is—"

"Never mind that," said Colin. "Come on out of this, Step. We need air."

"I think we had better go and talk to Father," said Henry. "It's beastly to leave him alone in there. Come on you two."

The three boys went out together. Roberta was left in the dining-room with Mike.

"I suppose you're not interested in Hornby trains," said Mike with an unconvincing air of casualness.

"I'd like to see yours," said Roberta.

"We *could* play with it now, of course. It's in the passage in 26. That's if you'd like it."

"Aren't there rather a lot of people about?" hedged Roberta lamely. "I mean aunts and people."

"Well, of course I *could* bring it here. I'm allowed. Shall I, Robin? Shall I bring my Hornby in here?"

"Yes, do."

Mike ran to the door but there he hesitated. He looked rather a solemn, pale little boy. "I say," he said, "as a matter of fact I think Uncle Gabriel's pretty ghastly."

"Do you?" said Roberta helplessly.

A tall figure in chauffeur's uniform appeared in the passage behind Mike.

"Oh, hullo Giggle," cried Mike.

"Beg pardon, Miss," said Giggle. "Beg pardon, Master Michael, but I've got to go. There's that coupling—I've got it fixed. His lordship's in a hurry, so if you—"

"I'll come with you, Giggle," said Mike warmly.

They disappeared together. Roberta heard Mike's eager voice die away. "Violet!" yelled the distant voice again. She heard the groan of the lift. Roberta waited.

The tick of the carriage-clock came up again. In a distant part of the flat a door banged. The lift groaned once more. Outside, far beneath the windows and reaching away for miles and miles, surged the ocean of sound which is the voice of London. People were talking, now, in the room next door: A low murmur of voices.

Roberta felt lonely and irresolute and, for the moment, isolated from the calamity that had befallen her friends. She felt that wherever she went she would be hideously in their way. Perhaps if she played trains with Mike it would be a help.

Mike was taking a long time. Roberta took a cigarette from a box on the sideboard and hunted about the room for matches. At last she found some. She lit her cigarette and leant over the window sill. She became aware of a new sound. It came up through her conscious thoughts, gaining definition and edge. It was a thin blade of sound, sharp and insistent. It grew louder. It was inside the building, an intermittent, horridly shrill noise that came closer. A hand closed round Roberta's heart. Someone was screaming.

CHAPTER VI

Catastrophe

When Roberta realized that this intolerable sound was on the landing, close at hand, part of the flat itself, she was filled with a strange irresolution. Someone was screaming in the Lampreys' flat and there didn't seem to be anything for Roberta to do about it. She was unable to feel the correct impulses and run helpfully towards the source of these unpleasing noises. No doubt the Lampreys were doing that. Roberta, with a leaping heart, could only stand and wonder at her behaviour. While she still hung off on this queer point of social procedure, someone pounded down the passage. Without conscious volition Roberta followed. She was just in time to see Baskett's coat-tails whisk round the corner. As she passed the drawing-room Henry ran through the hall from the landing. The screaming stopped suddenly like a train whistle.

"Frightfulness!" said Henry as he passed Roberta. "Robin, for God's sake, get the kids out of it, will you? I'm for the telephone."

Abruptly filled with initiative, Roberta ran through the hall to the landing.

All the other Lampreys were on the landing with Baskett, Nanny and Lady Wutherwood. They were gathered round the lift. Patch and Mike were on the outskirts of this little crowd. Charlot held Lady Wutherwood by the arms. Roberta knew now that it was Lady Wutherwood who had screamed. Lord Charles and one of the twins seemed to be inside the lift. Frid, sheet-white, stood just behind them with the other twin. When Lord Charles and the boys turned, Roberta saw that their faces were as white as Frid's. They looked like people in a nightmare. From within the lift came a curious sound, as if somebody were gargling. It persisted. The Lampreys seemed to listen attentively to this noise. Nobody spoke for a moment and then Roberta heard Lord Charles whispering "No! No! *No!*"

"Hullo," said Mike, seeing her. "What's happening to Uncle Gabriel?"

Patch took his hand. "Come along, Mike," she said. "We'll go into the dining-room."

So Roberta did not have to give Henry's message.

"Come on, Mike," repeated Patch in a strange voice and dragged at Mike's hand.

They moved away. Roberta was about to follow them when the group at the lift broke up. Roberta saw inside the lift. Lord Wutherwood was sitting in there. A ray of light from the roof of the lift-well had caught the side of his head. For the fraction of a second she had an impression that in his left eye he wore a glass with a wide dark ribbon that clung to the contours of his face. Then she saw that the thing she had mistaken for a glass was well out in front of his eye. Lord Charles moved aside and the interior of the lift became lighter. Roberta's whole being was flooded with an intolerable nausea. She heard her own voice whisper, hurriedly, *"But it can't—it can't—it's disgusting."* She could not drag her gaze off the figure in the lift. She felt as though her entire body strained away from the frozen pivot of her sight. His mouth and his right eye were wide open and inside his mouth the sound of gargling grew louder, and still Roberta could not move.

"Better out of that, m'lady," said Nanny's trembling voice. "Folks will be ringing for the lift. If Mr. Baskett and one of the twins got the top of the ironing trestle—"

Charlot said: "Yes. Will you, Baskett? And you, Colin, help him."

The nearest twin went away with Baskett. Nanny followed them.

"Come away for a moment, Violet," said Charlot. "Violet, *come away*." Lady Wutherwood opened her mouth. "*No!*" said Charlot. She propelled Lady Wutherwood forward into the hall and saw Roberta.

"Robin, get some brandy. Top shelf in the pantry."

Robin had not been in the pantry. On the way she saw a maid's face looking palely out of a distant door. She found the pantry. Her brain worked frantically to push down, thrust out of mind, the picture of the figure in the lift. It must be repudiated, displaced, covered up. She must do things. How did one know which of these bottles was brandy? Cognac meant brandy. She took it with a glass to the drawing-room. Henry stood over the desk-telephone. "At once. Couldn't be more urgent. Yes, to the head. Through his eye. I said his eye." He put the receiver down. "Dr. Kantripp's coming, Mummy."

"Good," said Charlot. Roberta had given her a tumbler half full of brandy. The edge of the tumbler chattered like a castanet against Lady Wutherwood's teeth. Henry, with an expression of disgust, glanced at his aunt.

"Better have some yourself," he said to his mother. She shook her head. Henry added quickly: "And I rang up the police."

"Good."

Feet stumbled on the landing beyond the hall.

"They're moving him," said Charlot.

"I'd better go, then."

Henry went out.

"Can I do anything?" asked Roberta. She had spoken to nobody since Mike left her alone in the dining-room. Her voice sounded oddly in her ears.

"What?" Charlot saw her. "Oh, Robin, ask the maids to get plenty of boiling water. Doctors are so fond of boiling water, aren't they? And Robin, I don't know where the servants went, Tinkerton and Giggle, I mean. Could you find them and tell them there's been an accident. And the lift. Somebody may want the lift. The doctor will. Did we shut the door?"

"I'll see."

"Thank you so much."

Roberta hurried away and found time confusedly to marvel at Charlot's command of her nerves and of the situation. The Lampreys, she thought hurriedly, do rise to situations. She delivered the message to the maids. Now she must return to the landing. The lift was still open. Roberta stood stock-still with her hands on the doors, drilling her thoughts, telling them that he was gone, that she must look inside the lift. And, with a great effort, she lifted her head and looked. A little above the place where Lord Wutherwood had sat was a bright steel boss in the lift wall. In the centre of the boss was a small hollow which seemed to be stained. As she stared at it the stain grew longer. She heard a tap, a tiny dab of sound. She looked at the leather top of the seat. In the dent made by Lord Wutherwood she saw a little black pool where his blood had dropped from the stain on the wall. Back to the pantry, running as fast as she could go....A yellow duster.... Then the lift again.... It had looked so small a pool but it spread into her cloth and smeared over the leather...Now the wall. She heard a bell ringing. That would be someone who wanted the lift. Back on the landing, she slammed the doors and the lift at once sank beneath her fingers. Henry came out from 26 and looked at the cloth in her hands. He seemed like a figure in a dream and spoke like one.

"Clever Robin," said Henry. "But it won't do much good, you know. You can't wipe away murder."

Roberta had pushed that word out of her thoughts. She said: "It's not that—I mean I wasn't trying to do that. Only people will be using the lift. It looked so frightful."

Henry took the cloth from her.

"There's a fire in the dining-room," he said.

Roberta remembered her errands. "Have you seen Tinkerton and Giggle?"

"I don't think they're in the flat. Why?"

"They must be in the car. Charlot wants them told."

"I'll go," Henry offered.

"No, please. If you'll do—that."

"All right," said Henry and went away with the cloth.

Roberta was running downstairs...Four landings with blank walls and steel numbers...Long windows...Heavy carpet under her feet. The lift passed her, bearing an immobile man in an overcoat and a bowler hat, carrying a bag in his hand...Now the entrance hall with the porter who looked bewildered and perturbed and stared at Roberta. She remembered his name.

"Oh, Stamford, have you seen Lord Wutherwood's chauffeur?"

"Yes, Miss. He's in his lordship's car. My Gawd, Miss, what's gone wrong?"

"Someone has been taken ill."

"The screaming, Miss. It was something frightful."

"I know. A fit of hysterics. We're sorry about the lift. There's been an accident."

Better, she thought, to say something about it. The doctor might have said something. She walked quickly through the entrance into the street. The sun had set on London and there was an evening coolness in the air. The sensation of dream receded a little. There was the car, a large grand car with Giggle sitting at the wheel and a woman in a drab hat beside him. They did not notice Roberta and she had to tap on the window, making them jump. Giggle got out and came round to her, touching his cap.

"Giggle," Roberta began, wishing he had another name, "there's been an accident."

He looked at her, maddeningly stolid.

"An accident, Miss?"

"Yes, to Lord Wutherwood. He's hurt himself. Lady Charles thinks you had better come up."

"Yes, Miss. Will Miss Tinkerton be needed, Miss?"

Roberta didn't know. She said: "I think perhaps you should both come. Lady Wutherwood may want Tinkerton."

They followed her into the hall. The lift was down again. Stamford opened the doors. Conquering a sudden and violent reluctance, Roberta went in. She saw that the two servants were preparing to walk up. English servants, she thought, and said: "Will you both come up in the lift, please?"

They got in and Giggle pressed the button. Tinkerton was a small woman with black eyes and a guarded expression. They won't speak until I do, thought Roberta.

"The doctor has come," she said. "It's an upset, isn't it?"

They both said: "Yes, Miss," and Tinkerton added in a mumbling voice, "Is her ladyship much hurt, Miss?"

"It's not her ladyship," said Roberta, "it's his lordship." She remembered insanely that someone once said you had to use "Your Majesty" in every phrase of a letter written to the King. Your Majesty, your lordship, his lordship, her ladyship.

"His lordship, Miss?"

"Yes. He has hurt his head. I don't really know what happened."

"No, Miss."

The lift reached the top landing. Roberta felt as if she were followed by two embarrassingly large dogs. She asked them to wait and left them standing woodenly on the landing.

Now she was back in the flat and didn't know where to go. Perhaps Patch and Mike were still in the dining-room. She stood in the hall and listened. There was a murmur of voices in the drawing-room. Baskett came along the passage carrying a tray with a decanter and glasses. Extraordinary sight, thought Roberta. Can they possibly have settled down for another glass of sherry? Baskett dated from the New Zealand days; he was an old friend of Roberta's and she did not feel shy with him.

"Baskett, who's in the drawing-room?"

"The family, Miss, with the exception of his lordship. His lordship is with the doctor, Miss."

"And Lady Wutherwood?"

"I understand her ladyship is lying down, Miss."

Baskett lingered for a moment, looking down in a kindly and human manner at Roberta.

"The family will be glad to have you with them, Miss Robin," he said.

"Have you heard how—how he is?"

"He seemed to be unconscious, Miss, when we carried him into his lordship's dressing-room—but alive. I haven't heard any further report."

"No. Baskett."

"Yes, Miss?"

"What was the matter with—his eye?"

The network of threadlike veins across Baskett's cheekbones started out against his bleached skin. The glasses on the tray jingled.

"I shouldn't worry about it, Miss. You'll only upset yourself."

He opened the drawing-room door and stood aside for her to go in.

ii

The Lampreys were nice to Roberta. She kept saying to herself, they *are* nice to think about me. Henry gave her a glass of sherry and Charlot said what a help she had been. They

74

were all very quiet and seemed to listen attentively for something to happen. Charlot had just left Lady Wutherwood who was lying on her bed. She was no longer hysterical and had asked for Tinkerton. Roberta took Tinkerton to the door of the room and then rejoined the others. Nanny came in and in the usual way dragooned Mike off to bed. Charlot asked Patch to go with Nanny and Mike.

"But, Mummy—" Patch began—"it's hours before my bedtime. Can't I—"

"Please be with Mike, Patch."

"All right."

"What *is* the time?" asked Frid.

"Quarter to eight," said Nanny from the door. "Come along, Michael and Patricia."

"Can it be no more than an hour since they came!" said Charlot.

"Aunt Kit got here earlier," said Colin.

"*Aunt Kit!*" Charlot looked from one to another of her children. "For pity's sake, what has become of Aunt Kit?"

"Has anybody seen her?" asked Frid.

Nobody, it appeared, had seen Lady Katherine since the brothers were left alone in the dining-room and Charlot took the aunts to her bedroom.

"We stayed there for about ten minutes I suppose," said Charlot, "and then she said she wished to 'disappear.' She knows the flat quite well so I didn't lead the way or anything. Stephen—go and see if you can find her."

Stephen went away but returned to say that unless Aunt Kit was in with the doctor and Lord Charles she was not in the flat.

"Well," said Henry, "she told you, Mummy, that she wished to disappear and she has."

"But—"

"Darling," said Frid jerkily, "we can't be worried about Aunt Kit. Honestly."

"At least," said Stephen, "she had behaved with d-decent reticence. Did you ever hear anything more disgraceful than Aunt V.?"

"Poor thing," said Charlot.

"I simply can't feel sorry for her," said Henry.

"I can only feel sick," said Stephen. "I feel very sick indeed. Does anyone else?"

"Shut up," said Colin automatically.

"Here's Daddy," said Frid.

Lord Charles came in at the far door. He walked slowly across the room to his family. Charlot made a quick, contained movement with her hands. Her husband stood before her.

"Well, darling?" she asked.

"Immy," said Lord Charles, "he's not dead. He's alive still."

"Will he live?"

"It doesn't seem possible."

"Charlie—if he dies?"

"It seems that if Gabriel dies he will have been murdered."

There was a dead silence and then Henry said in a strange voice: "Isn't there a book called *It Can't Happen Here?*"

Stephen said: "Of c-course he's murdered. Of course he'll die. With that thing through his b-brain, why didn't he die at once?"

"Shut up," said Colin.

Lord Charles sat on the arm of his wife's chair and put his hand on her shoulder. It was the first time Roberta had ever seen him do this. "Where's Patch?" he asked.

"I sent her away with Mike and Nanny. She—didn't see, but I thought—"

"Yes. She and Mike will know of course but it might be as well, Imogen, if you told them. The rest of you had better hear the whole story now. Unless Robin—"

Roberta said, "If it's private of course—"

"Private! My dear child, it will be front-page news in every paper by to-morrow."

"So it will!" Frid ejaculated. "I say, we ought to tell Nigel Bathgate. It'd be a lovely scoop for him, wouldn't it?"

"I must say, Frid," said Henry, "I think that a particularly mad suggestion of yours."

"I don't see why. As Daddy says, it will be in all the papers anyway so why not give Nigel a break? I daresay he'd fight off all the other press-men for us. Shall I ring him up, Mummy?"

"Not now, Frid. And yet I don't know. Nigel might be a sort of protection, Charlie."

"I really do not consider," said Lord Charles with emphasis, "that one rings up young journalists, however charming, and tells them that one's relations have been murderously assaulted! You none of you seem to realize..."

He broke off and looked at Roberta who was still hovering

doubtfully. "Robin, my dear, we have no secrets from you. I'm only so sorry that you should have been plunged into this nightmare. Stay by all means, if you will."

"Don't go away, Robin," said Henry.

"No, don't go," said the others. So Roberta stayed.

Lord Charles beat gently on his wife's shoulder with his thin hand. Without looking up at him she leant towards him.

"I'm glad it's Dr. Kantripp," she said. "He knows us so well. It would have been much worse if he had been a stranger."

"It would have made no difference."

"None?" asked Charlot on an indrawn breath.

"Very little, at any rate."

"What will happen?" she asked.

"A man from the police-station is here. At the moment he is telephoning Scotland Yard. There's another man in there with Gabriel."

There was a short silence broken by Charlot.

"Well," she said, "none of us tried to kill him, of course, so I suppose we simply tell the truth."

Nobody answered her.

"Don't we?" Charlot persisted.

"We'll tell the truth," said Lord Charles, "certainly." He looked at his children. "I want you to listen carefully. Your uncle was alone in the lift for some time before he and Aunt Violet were taken down. It seems that he was sitting in the lift with his hat pulled forward and his head bent. Your aunt only discovered that he was hurt after the lift had gone some way down. You all must have heard the return. Now each of you may have to account for your movements after your—after he got into the lift. Try to remember exactly what you did and where you were. If . . ."

He broke off abruptly. The doctor had come into the room.

Dr. Kantripp was stocky and dark, with a pleasingly ugly face. He looked profoundly unhappy.

"They're coming," he said, "immediately."

"Good," said Lord Charles.

"Dr. Kantripp," said Charlot, "will he live?"

"He may—survive for a little, Lady Charles."

"Will he be able to speak?"

"I think it most unlikely."

"Pray God he does!"

77

He looked sharply at her and it would have been impossible to say whether he felt doubt or relief at her exclamation.

"We shall have a second opinion, of course," he said. "I've telephoned Sir Matthew Cairnstock. He's a brain man. I've sent for a nurse."

"Yes. Will you look at Violet—my sister-in-law? She's in my room."

"Yes, certainly."

"I'll come if you want me. She asked to be alone with the maid."

"I see." Dr. Kantripp hesitated and then said: "They'll want to talk to the servants, you know."

"Why the servants, particularly?" asked Lord Charles quickly.

"Well—the instrument. You see it looks as if it came from their part of the world. The kitchen."

Frid spoke abruptly on a hard, shrill note. "It was a skewer, wasn't it?"

"Yes."

"Then it wasn't in the kitchen. It was left on the hall table."

"Dinner is served, m'lady," said Baskett from the door.

iii

Roberta would never have believed that dinner with the Lampreys could be a complete nightmare. It seemed incredible that they should be there, sitting in silence round the long table, solemnly helping themselves to dishes that repelled them. Charlot left the room twice, the first time to take another look at Lady Wutherwood, the second time to see the nurse and to ask if there was anything she needed for her patient. The specialist arrived at the same time as the men from Scotland Yard. Lord Charles went out to meet them but returned in a few minutes to say Dr. Kantripp was still there and that he, with one of the police, had gone into the room where Lord Wutherwood lay. Only two of the police were in the flat now. They were plain-clothes men, Lord Charles said, and seemed to be very inoffensive fellows. The others had gone but he did not know for how long. Robert wondered if the Lampreys shared her feeling that the flat no longer belonged to them. When they had chopped their savouries into small pieces and pushed them about their plates for a minute or two, Charlot said suddenly: "This is too much. Let's go into the drawing-room."

Before they could move, however, Baskett came in and murmured something to Lord Charles.

"Yes, of course," said Lord Charles. "It had better be in here." He looked at his wife. "They want to see us all in turn. I suggest they use the dining-room and we go to the drawing-room. In the meantime they want me, Immy. There's a change in Gabriel's condition and the doctors think I should be there."

"Of course, Charlie. Shall I tell Violet?"

"Will you? Bring her to the room. You don't mind bringing her in?"

"Of course not," said Charlot, "if—if she'll come."

"Do you think—"

"I'll see. Come along, children."

Lord Charles moved quickly to the door and held it open. For as long as Roberta had known the Lampreys he had made the same movement each night after dinner, always reaching the door before his sons and holding it open with a little bow to his wife as she passed him. To-night they looked into each other's faces for a moment and then Roberta saw Lord Charles walk by on his way to his brother. That one glance gave her a vivid, indelible impression of him. The light from the hall shone on his head, making a halo of his thin hair and a bright-rimmed silhouette of his face. He wore that familiar air of punctiliousness. The placidity and the detachment to which she was accustomed still appeared in that mild profile, but she afterwards thought she had seen a glint of something else, a kind of sharpness so foreign to her idea of Lord Charles that she attributed the impression to a trick of lighting or of her overstimulated imagination. The hall door slammed. Roberta was left with the others to sit in silence and to wait.

CHAPTER VII

Death of a Peer

Inspector Fox sat in a corner of the dressing-room, his notebook on his knee, his pencil held in a large, clean hand. He was perfectly still and quite unobtrusive but his presence made itself felt. The two doctors and the nurse were much aware of him and from time to time glanced towards the corner of the room where he sat waiting. A bedside lamp cast a strong light on the patient and a reflected glow on the faces that bent over him. The only sound in the room, a disgusting sound, was made by the patient. On a table close to Fox was a bag. It contained, among a good deal of curious paraphernalia, a silver-plated skewer, carefully packed.

At thirty-five minutes past eight by Fox's watch there was a slight disturbance. The doctors moved; the nurse's uniform crackled. The taller of the doctors glanced over his shoulder into a corner of the room.

"It's coming, I think. Better send for Lord Charles." He pressed the hanging bell-push. The nurse went to the door and in a moment spoke in a low voice to someone outside. Fox left his chair and moved a little nearer the bed.

The patient's left eye was hidden by a dressing. The right eye was open and stared straight up at the ceiling. From somewhere inside him, mingled with the hollow sound of his breathing, came a curious noise. His complicated mechanism of speech was trying unsuccessfully to function. The bedclothes were distrubed and very slowly one of his hands crept out. The nurse made a movment which was checked by Fox.

"Excuse me," said Fox, "I'd be obliged if you'd let his lordship—"

"Yes, yes," said the tall doctor. "Let him be, nurse."

The hand crept on laboriously out of shadow into light. The finger tips, clinging to the surface of the neck, crawling with infinite pains, seemed to have a separate life of their own. The single eye no longer stared at the ceiling but turned anxiously in its deep socket as though questing for some attentive face.

"Is he trying to show us something, Sir Matthew?" asked Fox.

"No, no. Quite impossible. The movement has no meaning. He doesn't know—"

"I'd be obliged if you'd ask him, just the same."

The doctor gave the slightest possible shrug, leant forward, slid his hand under the sheet, and spoke distinctly.

"Do you want to tell us something?"

The eyelid flickered.

"Do you want to tell us how you were hurt?"

The door opened. Lord Charles Lamprey came into the half light. He stood motionless at the foot of the bed and watched his brother's hand move, lagging inch by inch, up the sharp angle of his jaw.

"There's no significance in this," said the doctor.

"I'd like to ask him, though," said Fox, "if it's all the same to you, Sir Matthew."

The doctor moved aside. Fox bent forward and stared at Lord Wutherwood.

A deep frown had drawn the eyebrows together. Some sort of sound came from the open mouth. "You want to show us something, my lord, don't you?" said Fox. The fingers crawled across the cheek and upwards. "Your eyes? You want to show us your eyes?" The one eye closed slowly, and opened again, and a voice oddly definite, almost articulate, made a short sound.

"Is he going?" asked Lord Charles clearly.

"I think so," said the doctor. "Is Lady Wutherwood—"

"She is very much distressed. She feels that she cannot face the ordeal."

"She realizes," said Dr. Kantripp, who had not spoken before, "that there is probably very little time?"

"Yes. My wife says she made it quite clear."

The doctors turned again to the bed and seemed by this movement to dismiss Lady Wutherwood. The patient's hand slipped away from his face. His gaze seemed to be fixed on the shadows at the foot of his bed.

"Perhaps," said Fox, "if he could see you, my lord, he might make a greater effort to speak."

"He can see me."

Fox reached out a massive arm and tilted the lamp. The figure at the foot of the bed was thrown into strong relief. Lord Charles blinked in the sudden glare but did not move.

"Will you speak to him, my lord?"

"Gabriel, do you know me?"

"Will you ask him who attacked him, my lord?"

"It is horrible—now—when he—"

"He might manage to answer you," said Fox.

"Gabriel, do you know who hurt you?"

The frown deepened and the one eye and mouth opened so widely that Lord Wutherwood's face looked like a mask in a nightmare. There was a sharp violence of sound and then silence. Fox turned away tactfully and the nurse's hands went out to the hem of the sheet.

ii

"I am very sorry, my lord," said Fox, "to have to trouble you at such a time."

"That can't be helped."

"That is so, my lord. Under the circumstances we've got to make one or two inquiries."

"One or two!" said Lord Charles unevenly. "Do sit down, won't you? I'm afraid I don't know your name."

"Fox, my lord. Inspector Fox."

"Oh, yes. Do sit down."

"Thank you, my lord."

Fox sat down and with an air of composure drew out his spectacle case. Lord Charles took a chair near the fire and held out his hands to the blaze. They were unsteady and with an impatient movement he drew them back and thrust them into his pockets. He turned to Fox and found the Inspector regarding him blandly through steel-rimmed glasses.

"Before I trouble you with any questions, my lord," said Fox, "I think it would be advisable for me to ring up my superior officer and report this occurrence. If I may use the telephone, my lord."

"There is one on that desk. But of course you'd rather be alone."

"No, thank you, my lord. This will be very convenient. If you will excuse me."

He moved to the desk, dialled a number, and almost immediately spoke in a very subdued voice into the receiver. "Fox, here, Mr. Alleyn's room." He waited, looking thoughtfully at the base of the telephone. "Mr. Alleyn? Fox, speaking from Flats 25-26 Pleasaunce Court Mansions, Cadogan Square. Residence of Lord Charles Lamprey. The case reported at seven-thirty-five is a fatality.... Circumstances point that way, sir.... Well, I was going to suggest it, sir, if it's convenient. Yes, sir." Here there was a longish pause during which Fox looked remarkably bland. "That's so, Mr. Alleyn," he said finally. "Thank you, sir."

He hung up the receiver and returned to his chair.

"Chief Detective-Inspector Alleyn, my lord," said Fox, "will take over the case. He will be here in half an hour. In the meantime he has instructed me to carry on. So if I may trouble you, my lord ..." He took out his note-book and adjusted his glasses. Lord Charles shivered, hunched up a shoulder, put his glass in his eye and waited.

"I have here," said Fox, "the statement taken by the officer who was called in from the local station. I'd just like to check that over, my lord, if I may."

"Yes. It's my own statement, I imagine, but check it by all means if you will."

"Yes. Thank you. Times. I understand Lord Wutherwood arrived here shortly after six and left at approximately seven-fifteen?"

"About then. I heard seven strike some little time before he left."

"Yes, my lord. Your butler gets a little closer than that. He noticed it was seven-fifteen before his lordship rang for his man."

"I see."

"His lordship was alone in the lift for some minutes before anyone went out to the landing," read Fox.

"Yes."

"Thank you, my lord. After he had been there for some minutes he was joined by her ladyship—Lady Wutherwood—that is—and by Lady Charles Lamprey and by Mr. Lamprey. Which Mr. Lamprey would that be, my lord?"

"Let me think. You must forgive me but my thoughts are intolerably confused."

Fox waited politely.

"My brother," said Lord Charles at last, "left me in the drawing-room. Soon after that the boys, I mean my three sons, joined me there. Then I think my wife opened the door and asked if one of the boys would take my brother and sister-in-law down in the lift. They never take themselves down. One of the boys went out. That will be the one you mean?"

"Yes. That is so, my lord."

"I don't know which it was."

"You don't remember?"

"Not that exactly. It was one of the twins. I didn't notice which. Shall I ask them?"

"Not just yet thank you, my lord. Do I understand you to say that the two young gentlemen are so much alike that you couldn't say which of them left the room?"

"Oh, I should have been able to tell you if I had looked at all closely but you see I didn't. I just saw one of the twins had gone. I—was thinking of something else."

"The other two remained in the drawing-room with you? Mr. Henry Lamprey and the other twin?"

"Yes."

"Yes, my lord. Thank you. Then you will have noticed the remaining twin if I may put it that way?"

"No. No, I didn't. He didn't speak. I didn't look at the boys. I was sitting by the fire. Henry, my eldest son, said something, but otherwise none of us spoke. They'll tell you themselves which it was."

"Yes, my lord, so they will. It would be correct to say that while the lift went down you remained in the drawing-room with Mr. Lamprey and his brother until when, my lord?"

"Until..." Lord Charles took out his glass and put it in his waistcoat pocket. It was an automatic gesture. Without the glass the myopic look in his weak eye was extremely noticeable. His lips trembled slightly. He paused and began afresh. "Until I heard there was—until I heard my sister-in-law scream."

"And did you realize, my lord—"

"I realized nothing," interrupted Lord Charles swiftly. "How could I? I know now, of course, that they had gone down in the lift and that she had made that—that terrible discovery, and that it was while the lift returned that she screamed. But at the time I was quite in the dark. I simply became aware of the sound."

"Thank you," said Fox again, and wrote in his notebook. He looked over the top of his spectacles at Lord Charles.

"And then, my lord? What would you say happened next?"

"What happened next was that I went out to the landing followed by the two boys. My wife and my girls—my daughters—came out of 26 at the same time. I think my youngest boy, Michael, appeared from somewhere but he wasn't there for long. The lift was returning and was almost up to our landing."

"Up to the landing," repeated Fox to his notes. "And who was in the lift, my lord?"

"Surely that's clear enough," said Lord Charles. "I thought you understood that my brother and his wife and my son were in the lift."

"Yes, my lord, that is how I understand the case at present. I'm afraid this will seem very annoying to you but you see we usually take statements separately for purposes of comparison."

"I'm sorry, Mr. Fox. Of course you do. I'm afraid I'm—"

"Very natural, my lord, that you should be, I'm sure. Then I take it that Lady Wutherwood must have begun to scream while the lift was near the bottom of the shaft?"

Lord Charles twisted his mouth wryly and said yes.

"And continued as it returned to your landing?"

"Yes."

"Yes. Would you mind telling me what happened when the lift stopped at the top landing?"

"We were bewildered. We couldn't think what had happened. We couldn't think what had happened. She—she—I should explain that she is rather highly-strung. A little hysterical, perhaps. The lift stopped and Henry opened the doors. She rushed out, almost fell out, into my wife's arms. My son, the twin—I—it's too stupid that I can't tell you which it was—came out without speaking, or if he did speak I didn't hear him. You see I was looking in the lift."

"That must have been a great shock to you, my lord," said Fox simply.

"Yes. A great shock."

"I saw my brother," said Lord Charles loudly and rapidly. "He was sitting at the end of the seat. The injury—it was there—I saw it—I—I didn't understand then, that they—my sister-in-law and my son—had gone down in the lift without at first realizing there was anything the matter."

"When *did* you realize this, my lord?"

"As soon as my wife had calmed her down a little she began to speak about it. She was very wild and incoherent, but I made out as much as that."

"You did not question your son, my lord? Whichever son it was," inquired Fox, as if the confusion of one's children's identities was the most natural thing in the world.

"No. There doesn't seem to have been any time to talk to anybody."

"And of course if you had questioned him you would have known which he was?"

"Yes," rejoined Lord Charles evenly, "of course."

"Did any of the others talk to him, my lord?"

"I really don't know. How could I? If I had heard that, I would—" He stopped short. "I really can't tell you more than that."

"I understand, my lord. I must thank you for your courtesy and apologize again for causing you so much pain. There are only one or two other points. Did you touch your brother?"

"No!" said Lord Charles violently. "No! No! They carried him out and took him to my room. That is all."

"And you did not see him again until you came into his room while I was there?"

"I took Dr. Kantripp to the room and waited with him. The children's old nurse was there. She helped the doctor until the trained nurse arrived."

"I take it that Dr. Kantripp—" Fox paused for a moment—"the doctor did everything that was necessary? I mean, my lord, that the injury was unattended until he came?"

Lord Charles made an effort to speak, failed to do so, and nodded his head. At last he managed to say: "We thought it better not to—not to try to—we didn't know whether it might prove fatal to—"

"To remove anything? Quite so."

"Is that all?"

"I shan't trouble you much further, my lord, but I should like to ask if you know whether his lordship had any enemies."

"Enemies! That's an extravagant sort of way to put it."

"It's the way we generally put it, my lord. I daresay it does sound rather exaggerated but you see the motive for this sort of crime is usually something a bit stronger than dislike."

To this bland rejoinder Lord Charles found nothing to say.

"Of course," Fox continued, "the term enemies is used rather broadly, my lord. I might put it another way and ask if you know of anyone who had good reason to wish for Lord Wutherwood's death."

Lord Charles answered this question instantly with a little spurt of words that sounded oddly mechanical.

"If you mean, do I know of anyone who would benefit by his death," he said, "I suppose you may say that his heirs will do so. I am his heir."

"Well, yes, my lord. I know Lord Wutherwood had no son."

"Do you, by God!" said Lord Charles. The exclamation was completely out of key with the level courtesy of his earlier rejoinders but Fox took it in his stride.

"I have heard that is the case," he said. "I understand that two of his lordship's servants were here. It's not very nice," continued Fox with an air of one who apologizes for a slight error in taste, "to have to think of people in this light, but—"

"Murder," said Lord Charles, "is not very nice either. You are quite right, Mr. Fox. My brother's chauffeur and my sister-in-law's maid were both there."

"Might I trouble you for their names, my lord?"

"Tinkerton and Giggle."

"Giggle, my lord?"

"Yes. That's the chauffeur."

"Quite an unusual name," said Fox, placidly busy with his

notes. "Have they been long with his lordship?"

"I believe that Tinkerton was with my sister-in-law before she married and that's twenty-five years ago. Giggle began at Deepacres as an odd boy and under-chauffeur. His father was coachman to my father."

"Family servants," murmured Fox, placing them. "And of course your own servants would be in the flat?"

"Yes. There's Baskett, the butler; and the cook and two maids. They may not all have been in. I'll find out."

He stretched his hand out to the bell.

"In a minute, thank you, my lord. These are all the servants you employ?"

"Yes."

"I thought you spoke of a nurse, my lord."

"Oh—you mean Nanny," said Lord Charles who now seemed to have himself very well in hand. "Yes, of course there's Nanny. We don't think of her as one of the servants."

"No, my lord?"

"No. She's the real head of affairs, you see."

"Oh, yes!" said Fox politely. "I would be much obliged if you would send for the butler now."

Baskett came in with his usual ineffable butler's walk, executed with the arms held straight down, the hands lightly closed and turned out with the palms downwards. It was the deliberate relaxed pose of a man whose deportment is an important factor in his profession. Baskett did it superbly.

"Oh, Baskett," said Lord Charles, "Inspector Fox would like to ask you about the people who were in the servants' quarters this evening. Were all the maids in?"

"Ethel was out, my lord. Mrs. James and Blackmore were in." He glanced at Fox. "That is the cook and the parlour-maid, sir," he explained.

"Any visitors in your quarters?" asked Fox.

"Yes, sir. Lord Wutherwood's chauffeur and Lady Wutherwood's maid. The chauffeur was in the staff sitting-room, sir, for some time, and then went into No. 26 to help Master Michael with his trains. Miss Tinkerton was with Mrs. Burnaby in her room."

"Mrs. Burnaby?"

"That's Nanny," explained Lord Charles.

"Thank you, my lord. And that is the entire household at the time of the occurrence?"

"I think so," said Lord Charles. "Was there anyone else in your part of the world, Baskett?"

Baskett looked anxiously at his employer and hesitated.

"You will of course tell us," said Lord Charles, "if you know of anyone else in the flat."

"Very good, my lord. There was another person, sir, in the kitchen."

Fox paused, pencil in hand. "Who was that?"

"Good God!" ejaculated Lord Charles. "I'd entirely forgotten him."

"Forgotten whom, my lord?"

"What's the miserable creature's name, Baskett?"

"Grumball, my lord."

Fox said sharply: "You mean Giggle. I've got him."

"No, sir. This person's name is Grumball."

Fox looked scandalized. "Who is he, then?" he asked. Baskett was silent.

"He's the man in possession," said Lord Charles.

"A bailiff, my lord?"

"A bum-baliff, Mr. Fox."

"Thank you, my lord," said Fox tranquilly. "I'll see the rest of the staff, now, if it's agreeable."

iii

"Would it be one of these society affairs, sir?" asked Detective-Sergeant Bailey, staring with lack-lustre eyes through the police-car window.

"What society affairs, Bailey?" murmured Chief Detective-Inspector Alleyn.

"Well, you know, sir. Cocktails, bottle parties, flats and so forth."

"One of the messy sort," said Detective-Sergeant Thompson, moving his photographic impedimenta a little farrther under the seat.

"That's right," agreed Bailey.

"I've no idea," said Alleyn, "in what sort of country we shall find ourselves."

"The flat belongs to deceased's brother, doesn't it, sir?"

"Yes. Lord Charles Lamprey."

The police-surgeon spoke for the first time. "I fancy I've heard something about Lamprey," he said. "Can't remember what it was."

"Wasn't he mixed up in that Stein suicide?" said Bailey.

Alleyn glanced at him. "He was, yes. Stein left him with the baby."

"The baby, sir?"

"Figuratively, Bailey. Lord Charles appeared to have developed an amazing flair for signing himself into every conceivable sort of responsibility. He turned out to be Stein's partner, you remember."

"Did he go bust?" asked the doctor.

"I don't think so, Curtis. Must have felt the draught a bit, one would imagine."

"Was the deceased a wealthy man, sir?" asked Bailey. "This Lord Wutherwood, I mean."

"Oh, pretty well, you know," said Alleyn vaguely. "There's a monstrous place in Kent, I think. Not that that tells one anything. May have been hanging on by the skin of his teeth."

"It sounds an unpleasant business," said Dr. Curtis. "Through the eye, didn't you say?"

"Yes. Beastly, isn't it? Fox was very guarded when he rang up. I recognized his suspect-listening manner."

"Large family of Lampreys?" asked Dr. Curtis.

"Masses of young, I fancy. Damn! We're in for a nasty run, no doubt. Why the devil do these people have to get themselves messed up in a case like this?"

"Another instance," said Dr. Curtis drily, "of the aristocracy mixing with the commonalty. They've tried trade and they've tried big business. Why not a spot of homicide? Sorry!" he added uncomfortably. "Silly statement. Very unprofessional. The peer was probably pinked by a—what? A servant? A lunatic? Somebody with an axe to grind? Here we are in Sloane Street. Cadogan Gardens, isn't it?"

"Pleasaunce Court. Do you know the doctor, Curtis? His name's Kantripp."

"I do, as it happens. He was in my first year at Thomas's. Nice fellow. Awkward business for him if, as one supposes, he's the family doctor."

"It may not be awkward. Let's hope it's a simple matter. Some nice homicidal maniac wandering about the top story of Pleasaunce Court Mansions and going all hay-wire at the sight of an elderly peer in a lift. Let's hope there are no axes to grind. Here's the turning. How anybody can get a kick out of homicide is to me one of the major puzzles of psychology."

"Was there never a time," asked Dr. Curtis, "when you read murder cases in your newspaper with avidity?"

"Oh, yes. Yes."

"And do they always bore you, nowadays?"

Alleyn grinned. "No," he said. "I'm not bored by my job. One gets desperately sick of routine at times but it would be an affectation to pretend one was bored. People interest me and homicide cases are so terrifically concerned with people. Each locked up inside his mental bomb-proof shelter and then, suddenly, the holocaust. Most murders are really very squalid affairs, of course, but there's always the element that press-men call the human angle. All the same, Curtis, it's a beastly sort of stimulus. One would have to be very case-hardened to feel nothing but technical insterest. O Lord, here we go! There's a gaggle of p.c.'s coming along in the car behind. Fox said we might need some spare parts."

The car pulled up. With that unmistakable air of being about their business, the four men got out and walked up the steps. A knives-to-grind returning from a profitable day in Chelsea paused at Pleasaunce Court corner and addressed himself to a newsboy.

"Wot's up in vere?" asked the knives-to-grind.

"Wot's up in where?"

"In vere. In vem Mensions."

The newsboy looked. "Coo! P'lice."

"P'lice!" said the knives-to-grind contemptuously. "I believe you! 'Ere! Know 'oo that is? That's 'Endsome Ell-een."

"Cripey, you're right, mate! Fency me missin' 'im! I've doubled me sales on 'Endsome Ell-een many an evenin'. Coo, there's 'is cemera-bloke. That's a cemera orl right in that box. And t'uvver bloke'll be 'is fingerprint expert."

"It's a cise for the Yawd," said the knives-to-grind.

"Ar. Murder," agreed the newsboy.

"Not necessairilly."

"Garn! Wot's the cemera for if it's not murder? Taking photers of the liftman? *Not necessairilly!* 'Ere wite on! I'll git orf a *Stendard* on the old bloke in the 'all."

The newsboy ran up the steps crying in a respectful manner, "*Stendard*, sir, *Stendard?*" The knives-to-grind thoughtfully salvaged a cigarette butt from the kerb and put it in his waistcoat pocket. A second car drew up and four constables got out and entered the flats.

The newsboy reappeared and with an unconvincing show of nonchalance returned to his post.

"Well," asked his friend, "'ow abaht it?"

"Been an eccident."

"What sorta eccident?"

"Old bloke 'ad is eye jabbed aht in the lift."

"Garn!"

"Yeah," said the newsboy, assuming a slightly hard-boiled transatlantic manner. "And it's just too bad abaht 'im. 'E's a gorner."

"Dead?"

"Stiff."

"Cor!"

"Eccident!" said the newsboy with ineffable scorn.

"Eccident! Oh yeah?"

"Wiv cops and cemeras floatin' in by dozins," agreed his friend. "Oh, yeah? Not 'alf. I *don't* fink."

And taking up the shafts of his grindstone he trundled down Pleasaunce Court, pausing at the corner to raise the mournful cry of his trade.

"Knives to grind? Knives to grind?"

His voice floated up in the evening air. Alleyn heard it as he rang the Lampreys' doorbell.

"Any old knives to grind?"

CHAPTER VIII

Alleyn Meets the Lampreys

Fox had lavished the most delicate attention on the skewer. It was tied down to a strip of cardboard and lay in a long box. Alleyn held the box under the lamp. The plated ring at the broad end of the skewer caught the light and glinted. The blade did not glint. It had had time to dry a little.

"Disgusting," said Alleyn. He laid down the box. "Yours, Bailey. The blade has obviously been lifted by the point."

"That's me," said Dr. Kantripp. "I thought it better to avoid the ring as much as possible, though of course in drawing it out—"

"Of course," said Dr. Curtis.

"Well, you'd better try the ring and top of the shaft, Bailey," said Alleyn.

"It's a whale of a great skewer," said Dr. Curtis.

"Yes. An old one. People use them nowadays for paper-knives."

"They got this one from the kitchen," said Fox.

"Did they? We'd better take a look at the body, if you please, Dr. Kantripp."

They moved to the bed. Fox tilted the lamp. Dr. Kantripp drew back the sheet.

"Nothing's been done," he said. "I thought, under the circumstances—"

"Yes, of course. His wife hasn't seen him like this?"

"No. She wouldn't come. Just as well perhaps."

"Yes," agreed Alleyn, staring at the gargoyle's head on the sheet. "Just as well."

"No. He's not very pretty," muttered Dr. Curtis absently. He bent down. Fox moved the lamp.

"It seemed a bit queer to me his lasting so long, Doctor," said Fox.

"The head's a queer thing," observed Dr. Curtis. "There have been cases of survival—What was the angle, Kantripp?"

"Slightly upward. But it may have shifted."

"Yes."

"You say, Fox," said Alleyn, "that he tried to speak?"

"Well, sir, not to say speak. He made noises."

"It wasn't likely, I thought, that he could say anything," said Dr. Kantripp, "but Mr. Fox thought there was just a chance. As Curtis says, queer things happen with injuries to the brain. There have been cases—"

"I know. What are those marks beside the eyes? Hypostases?"

The two doctors exchanged glances.

"I didn't think so," said Dr. Kantripp diffidently.

"Bruises, more likely," said Dr. Curtis. "You don't get hypostases there. Not with the way he's lying."

"They said, Fox, that he sat on the right-hand end of the seat?"

"Yes, sir."

"Have a look at the left temple, would you, Curtis?"

Dr. Curtis began to take away the dressing over the left eye.

"You're quite right, Alleyn," said Dr. Kantripp. "There's a cut on the temple under the bandage. I was going to show you. Yes, there it is."

With a swift and delicate gesture Alleyn placed his long left hand across the staring right eye and the left socket. The heel of his hand was against the right side of the face, thumb downwards.

"There's a sort of fancy steel fretwork affair in the wall of the lift," said Fox. "With knobs on. There's a bit of a smear on one of the knobs. It looks as if it had been wiped."

"Does it, indeed?" Alleyn murmured and swiftly drew away his hand. "We'll get him out of here," he added.

"I've left orders for the mortuary van."

"Yes. Thank you, Curtis. You'll do the post-mortem tomorrow?"

"Yes."

"I think before I see the family we'll take a look at the lift. You can get to work in here, Bailey. Try those bruises for prints. You'd better go all over the face. It's a faint hope but you'd better have a shot at it. Then the skewer. Then come along to the lift. And, Thompson, you get some shots of the head, will you?"

"Very good, Mr. Alleyn."

Alleyn did not move away from the bed. He stared at the face on the pillow and the single eye in the face seemed, in return, to glare sightlessly at him. Alleyn stooped and touched the jaw and neck.

"No rigor yet?"

"Just beginning. Why?"

"We may have to perform an unpleasant experiment. Is the nurse still here?"

"Yes," said Dr. Kantripp.

"When Bailey and Thompson have finished, get her to tidy him up. He's a nightmare as he is. Come on, Fox."

ii

Fox had caused the mechanism of the lift to be switched off, had sealed the doors and had posted a uniformed constable on the landing. The lift was dark inside and, waiting there at the Lampreys' landing, it wore an air of expectancy.

"Window at the top of the door," said Alleyn.

"That's right, sir."

"Didn't you say that he sat in here, yelling for his wife? With the doors shut?"

"So the butler said."

"He might have been whisked down below."

"Perhaps he kept his thumb on the stop button, Mr. Alleyn."

"Perhaps he did." Alleyn switched on the light. "Now, where was he?"

"From all accounts he was sitting in the right-hand corner with his head leaning against that steel grid affair and his bowler hat tilted over his face. Of course the lift's been used since then. The doctor, for one, came up in it. As soon as our chaps came in they attended to that. Still, it's a pity."

"It is." Alleyn peered at the steel fretwork of the wall. "There's the smear you talked about on that bulge or knob or what-you-will."

"Very fancy design, isn't it, sir?"

"Very, Br'er Fox. Grapes, you see, mixed up with decorative lumps. Modern applied art. How tall was he?"

"Six foot and a half-inch," said Fox immediately.

"Good. You're six foot, aren't you? Just sit at the other end, Foxkin. Yes. Yes, I fancy that if you sat there and I caught you a snorter on the right side of your head your left temple would miss that corresponding knob by half an inch or so. However, that's altogether too vague. It looks as if we'll have to get him in here to try. I see these knobs have got slight depressions in the surface. Look at our particular one. Somebody, as you capably observed, has wiped it. And the seat, as well. Not very proficiently. Bailey will have to deal with this. Hullo!"

Alleyn stooped and flashed his torch under the seat. "I suppose you've already spotted those, you old devil," he observed.

"Yes, sir. I thought I'd leave them for you."

"What delicacy! What tact!" Alleyn reached under the seat and drew out a pair of heavy driving gloves with long gauntlets. He and Fox squatted on the floor and examined them.

"Bloody," said Fox.

"Blood, or something that looks like it. Between the middle and the third fingers of the left hand, and on the inner surface of those fingers. And a little on the palm. Can you see any on the right-hand glove? Yes. Again, a little on the palm. Bless my soul, Fox, we must take care of these. Give them to Bailey, like a good chap, and then tell me the whole story as far as you've got."

Fox went into 26. The constable cleared his throat. Alleyn gazed at the lift well. The door into 25 opened and a good-looking, pale young man peered out onto the landing.

"Oh, hullo," he said politely. "I'm sorry to bother you. You're Mr. Alleyn, I expect."

"Yes," said Alleyn.

"Yes, I'm so sorry to make a nuisance of myself, but I thought I'd just ask if it was likely to be a very long time before you began to pitch into us. I'm Henry Lamprey."

"How do you do," said Alleyn politely. "We'll be as quick as we can. Not long now."

"Oh, good. It's just that my mother is rather exhausted, poor thing, and I think she ought to go to bed. That is, of course, if my Aunt Violet can be moved off the bed or even out of the room which I must say seems to be doubtful . . . What is the right technique, do you know, with widows of murdered men who are also one's near relations?"

"Is Lady Charles with Lady Wutherwood at the moment?" asked Alleyn. Henry came out on the landing and shut the door. He stood in the shadow of the lift.

"Yes," he said. "My mother is in there and so is Tinkerton who is my Aunt Violet's maid. It appears that my Aunt Violet is in a sort of coma or trance and really doesn't notice who goes or comes. But you won't want to be bothered with all that. I was only going to suggest that if you could see my mother first and then Aunt Violet it would give us a chance to bundle Mama off to bed."

"I'll see what can be done about it. I'm afraid in this sort of business—"

"Oh, I know," agreed Henry. "The rest of us are all quite prepared for the dawn to rise on our lies and evasions."

"I hope not," said Alleyn.

"Actually we are a truthful family, only the things that happen to us are so peculiar that nobody ever believes in them. Still, I expect you've got a sort of winnowing ear for people's testimonies and will know in a flash if we try any hanky-panky."

"I expect so," agreed Alleyn gravely. From the shadow of the lift Henry seemed to look solemnly at him.

"Yes," he said. "I'm afraid I expect so too. My father suggested that you ought to be offered a drink and some sandwiches but the rest of us knew you wouldn't break bread with suspected persons. Or is that only in books? Anyway, sir, if you would like us to send something out here or if you would like to join us for a drink, we do hope you will."

"That's very kind of you," said Alleyn, "but we don't on duty."

"Or if there's anything at all that we can do."

"I don't think there's anything at the moment. Oh, as you're here, I may as well ask you. Who is the owner of those gloves?"

"What gloves?" Henry's voice sounded blank.

"A pair of heavy driving gloves with stiff gauntlets."

"Lined with rather disgusting fur?"

"Fur-lined, yes."

"Sound like mine," said Henry. "Where are they?"

"I'll return them to you. My colleague took them into the flat."

"Where did you find them?"

"In the lift," said Alleyn.

"But I wasn't in the lift."

"No?"

"No. I expect..." Henry stopped short.

"Yes?"

"Nothing. I can't imagine how they got there. You needn't return them, sir. I don't really think I want them any more."

"I don't think you would," agreed Alleyn, "if you saw them."

Henry's face shone like ivory on that dimly lit landing. His eyes were like black coals under the cold whiteness of his forehead.

"What do you mean?" he asked.

"They are stained."

"Stained? With what?"

"It looks like blood."

Henry turned on his heel and went blindly into the flat.

Fox returned with Bailey.

"I want to go all over the inside of the lift, Bailey," said Alleyn. "Try the stops and the doorknobs—everything. Get Thompson to take a close-up shot of the seat and wall."

"Very good, sir."

"And, Fox, we'll go over your notes and then I think I'd better see the family."

iii

The twins stood side-by-side on the hearthrug. The lamp-light glinted on their blonde heads. They wore grey flannel suits and dark green pull-overs that their mother had knitted for them. Their hands were in their pockets; their heads were tilted slightly to one side. Their faces were screwed into an expression of apologetic attentiveness. From her stool by the fire Roberta watched them and felt a cold pang of alarm. For behind the twins Roberta saw not the coal fire of a London grate but the sweetly aromatic logs that burnt in the drawing-room at Deepacres in New Zealand. And with the sharpest emphasis of memory she heard each twin confess that he had taken out the forbidden big car, and had driven it through a water-race into a bank. She saw herself sitting mum, knowing all the time that it was Stephen who had taken the car while Colin was indoors. She heard herself asking Colin privately why he had made this Quixotic gesture and she again heard his answer. "It's a kind of arrangement we have!" "Always?" she had asked him, and Colin, rumpling up his fair hair, had answered, "Oh, no. Only when there's a really major row." "A twinny sort of arrangement." Roberta had said, and Colin had agreed. "Yes, that's the idea. As between twins." So insistent was this memory that the past was clearer for a moment than the present and she was unaware of the voices in the drawing-room. Her mind seemed to change gear and she found herself thinking of the Lampreys as strangers. "I don't know what they are like," thought Roberta in her cold panic. "I have no knowledge of their reality. I have fitted their words and actions into my own idea of them but my idea may be quite wrong." And she began to wonder confusedly if anybody had a complete secret reality or if each layer of thought merely represented the level of someone else's idea of the thinker. "This won't do," thought Roberta. "Stop!" Her mind changed gear again and Lord Charles's voice came back, familiar, gentle, a voice she knew and loved.

"Now listen to me," Lord Charles was saying. "There is going to be no more of this. One of you went down in the lift with Violet and with him. Which was it?"

"I d-did," said Stephen.

"Shut up," said Colin. "I did."

"Do you realize," said Henry, "that one of you is making things look just about as murky as may be for the other?"

"If you imagine," said Lord Charles, "that the police are to be checked by a childish trick of this sort, you are..." He paused and with a deflated air added hurriedly: "you simply couldn't be more mistaken."

"What about fingerprints?" said Frid.

"I didn't touch anything," said Colin.

"I kept my hands in my p-pocket," said Stephen.

"Whichever it was, must have worked the lift," Frid pointed out.

"The lift's been used twice since then," said Stephen.

"Twice, at least," said Colin. "There won't be any fingerprints worth talking about."

"At any moment now," Henry said, "Alleyn will come in and begin to ask questions. As soon as he sees what you are up to he'll talk to you separately. If you think you've one sickly misbegotten hope of taking him in, you're bigger bloody fools than anybody outside a bug-house."

"Mummy'll be back in a minute," said Frid. "Don't let's have this going on when she comes in."

Lord Charles said: "Stephen, did you commit this crime?"

"No, Father, I didn't."

"Colin?"

"No, Father, honestly."

"On your most solemn word of honour, both of you."

"No, Father," repeated the twins. And Stephen added: "We're not sorry he's dead, of course, but it's a filthy way to k-kill anybody."

"Lousy," agreed Colin cheerfully.

"I know very well that it seems grossly stupid and fantastic to ask you," said Lord Charles. "Of course you are quite incapable of it. What I—I implore you to believe is that it is the last word in dangerous lunacy for an innocent man to lie to the police."

"That's what I keep t-telling Colin," said Stephen.

"Then why don't you take your own advice?" asked Colin. "Don't be a fool. I went down in the lift, Father, and Stephen stayed in the drawing-room."

"Which is a complete and sweltering lie," added Stephen.

"So there you are," said Frid. "Come off it, twins. It's jolly clever, we all admit it's jolly clever, but this is a serious affair. You can't pit your puny wits against the master brain of Handsome Alleyn. You know, chaps, if it wasn't for the fact that Uncle G. was murdered, it'd be rather a big moment for me having Handsome Alleyn in the flat. I've nursed an illicit passion for that man ever since the Gospell murder. Is he really the answer to the maiden's prayer, Henry?"

"Do stop being crisp and modish, Frid," begged Henry irritably. "You know that, like all the rest of us, you're nearly dead with terror."

"No, I'm not, honestly. I may wake up in the night bathed in a cold sweat but at the moment I'm sort of stimulated. Only I wish one of the twins would stop being mad."

"I wish to God you'd all stop being mad," said Lord Charles with sudden violence. "I feel as if I were looking at you and listening to you for the first time. Someone in this flat killed my brother."

There was an awkward silence broken by Frid.

"But, Daddy," said Frid, "you didn't like Uncle G. Now did you?"

"Be quiet, Frid," ordered Henry. "You don't think any of the family did it, do you, Father?"

"*Good God, of course I don't!*"

"Well, who does everybody think did it?" asked Frid brightly.

"Tinkerton," said Colin.

"Or Giggle," said Stephen.

"You only say Tinkerton or Giggle because you don't know them as well as Baskett and the maids," Henry pointed out.

"And Nanny," added Frid.

"If I'd been Uncle G.'s or Aunt V.'s servant," said Colin, "I'd have murdered both of them long ago. I must say I'm rather glad it's going to be Alleyn. If we've got to be grilled it may as well be by a gent. But then I'm a snob, of course."

"I th-think it'll be rather uncomfortable," said Stephen. "I'd rather it was the old-fashioned sort that says: ' 'Ere, 'ere, 'ere, wot's all this?' "

"Which shows how ignorant you are," said Frid. "No detective speaks like that. But I *do* think, Daddy, that Henry ought to ring up Nigel Bathgate. You know how he raves about Mr. Alleyn. He's his Watson and glories in it."

"Why should I ring him up?" Henry demanded. "Ring him up yourself."

"Well, I will presently. I think it's only kind."

"What's Alleyn like?" asked Colin.

"Oh, very nice," said Henry. "Sort of old-world without any Blimpishness. Rather frighteningly polite and quiet."

"Hell!" said Stephen.

The drawing-room door opened and Patch came in wearing pyjamas and a dressing-gown. Her hair had been lugged off her forehead by Nanny with such ferocious emphasis that her eyebrows were slightly raised. Two hard plaits hung between her shoulders. Her round face shone and she smelt of bath-powder. To Roberta she was a mere enlargement of herself at twelve and still very much of the nursery.

"Mike's asleep," said Patch, "and I've never been wider awake in my life. Please, Daddy, don't send me back. My teeth keep chattering."

"Oh, Patch, darling!" said Lord Charles helplessly. "I'm so sorry. Come up to the fire."

"You can't face the police like that, Patch," said Frid, "You're too fat for *neglige* appearances."

"I don't care. I'm going to sit by darling Roberta and get warm. Daddy, are the police here now?"

"Yes."

"Where's Mummy?"

"With Aunt Violet."

"Was Uncle G. murdered? Nanny's being so maddening. She won't talk about it."

"Yes, he was," said Frid impatiently. "It's no good trying to fob Patch off with a vague story, Daddy. Uncle G.'s been dotted one, Patch, and he's dead."

"Who dotted him one?" asked Patch, rubbing her hands slowly over her knees.

"It must have been someone—" Lord Charles waved his hand "—some lunatic who wandered up here. A wandering lunatic. Obviously. Don't think about it, Patch. The police will find out about it."

"Golly, how thrilling," said Patch. She had squatted down by Roberta who could feel her quivering like a puppy. "Daddy," she said, "I've thought of something."

"What is it?" asked her father wearily.

"You'll be able to get rid of the bum."

"Be quiet, Patch," said Henry. "You're not to talk about the bum."

"Why not?"

"Because I tell you."

Patch looked impertinently at Henry. "O.K., Rune," she said.

"What!" cried Roberta.

"It's quite right," said Patch. "Henry's to be called the Earl of Rune now. Isn't he, Daddy?"

"Good God!" said Henry slowly. "So I am."

"Yes," said Patch with a certain complacency, "you are. And I, for instance, am now the Lady Patricia Lamprey. Aren't I, Daddy?"

"Shut up, Patch," said Colin.

"Yes, yes," said Lord Charles hurriedly. "Never mind about it now, Patch."

"And Daddy," Patch persisted stubbornly, "you're now—"

The drawing-room door opened. Alleyn stood on the threshold with Fox behind him.

"May I come in, Lord Wutherwood?" asked Alleyn.

iv

Afterwards, when Roberta had time to review the events of that incredible day, she remembered that until Alleyn appeared an image of a fictitious detective had hung about at the back of all her thoughts; an image of a man coldly attentive, with coarse hands and a large, soapy-shining face. Alleyn was so little like this image that for a moment she thought he must be some visitor, fantastically *de trop*, who had dropped in to see the Lampreys. The sight of Fox disabused her of this idea. There was no mistake about Fox.

The new Lord Wutherwood put his glass in his waistcoat pocket and, with his usual air of punctilious courtesy, hurried forward. He shook hands, bending his elbow sharply and holding his hand out at a right angle to his fore-arm—a modish, diplomatic handshake.

"Do come in," he said. "We have left you very much to yourselves out there but I hoped if there was anything we could do you would let us know."

"There was nothing, thank you so much," said Alleyn, "until now. I felt I should go over the information Fox had already got before I bothered all of you. But now—"

"Yes, yes, of course. My wife and my small son are not here at the moment but this is the rest of the family . . . My eldest son you have already met. My daughter . . ."

The introductions were solemnly performed. Alleyn bowed to each of the Lampreys. Roberta on her footstool was so much in shadow that Lord Charles forgot her, but Alleyn's dark eyes turned gravely to the small figure.

"I beg your pardon, Robin, my dear," said Lord Charles. "Miss Grey is a New Zealand friend of ours, Mr. Alleyn."

"How do you do," said Roberta.

"New Zealand?" said Alleyn.

"Yes. I only got here yesterday," said Roberta and wondered why he looked so gently at her before he turned to Lord Charles.

"This is a dreadful thing, Alleyn," Lord Charles was saying. "We are quite bewildered and—and of course rather shaken. I hope you will forgive us if we are not very intelligent about remembering everything."

"We know that it must have been a very grave shock," agreed Alleyn. "I shall try to be as quick as possible but I am afraid that at the best it will be a long and unavoidably distessing business."

"What happens?" asked Henry.

"First of all I want to get a coherent account of the events that preceded the moment when Lord and Lady Wutherwood entered the lift. I think I should tell you that Fox has seen the commissionaire downstairs. He was on duty in the hall all the afternoon and although he does not work the lift he can account for everybody who used it after Lord and Lady Wutherwood arrived. He also states very positively that no strangers used it earlier in the afternoon. There is of course the outside stairway, the iron fire-escape. To get into this flat by its aid you must pass through the kitchen. Your cook is prepared to make a definite statement that during the afternoon nobody came in by that entrance. Of course the commissionaire and the cook may be mistaken but, on the face of it, it appears that no strangers have been up here since lunch."

"I see."

"We shall, of course, make much more exhaustive inquiries on this point. But you will see that under the circumstances—"

"It m-must have been been someone in the flat," said Stephen loudly.

"Yes," said Alleyn, "it looks like that. I only stress this point to make it clear to you that we must have a very accurate picture of everybody's movements."

The Lampreys all murmured "Yes." Alleyn placed his hands palm down on the arms of his chair and looked round the circle of faces. Patch, huddled in her woollen dressing-gown, still sat by Roberta. The twins, long-legged and blond, were collapsed as usual on the sofa; Henry sat in a deep chair, his hands driven into his trousers pockets, his shoulders hunched, his head dipped a little to one side. Henry, thought Roberta, looks like a watchful bird. Lord Charles sat elegantly on a thin chair and swung his glass like a pendulum above his crossed knees. Frid still leant against the mantelpiece in an attitude that was faintly histrionic.

"Before all this business starts," Alleyn began, "there is just one thing I would like to say. It is not very much use my pretending to avoid the implications in this case. It is scarcely possible that it can be a case of suicide or of accident. The word that must be in all your minds is one that, unfortunately, calls up all sorts of extravagant images. Detective fiction has made so much of homicide investigations that I'm afraid to most people they suggest official misunderstandings, dozens of innocent persons in jeopardy, red herrings by the barrowload, and surprise arrests. Actually, of course, the investigation in a case of homicide is a dull enough business and it is extremely seldom that any innocent person is in the smallest degree likely to suffer anything but the inconvenience of routine."

He was sitting with his back to the hall door. His face was strongly lit and the attention of the Lampreys was fixed upon it. Roberta, watching them, wondered if his assurances brought them any sense of relief. The quiet voice went on, clearly and without emphasis.

"... so, if I may, I would just like to ask you all to remember that, apart from the distress and sorrow that are the consequences of this crime, innocent people have nothing to fear beyond an exacting and wearisome series of questions.

Presently I shall ask to see each of you separately. At the moment I think we shall get along a little quicker if we discuss things together. If Lady Wutherwood and—" Alleyn hesitated, confronted by the embarrassment of twin titles.

"And Lady Wutherwood. Trap for young players," said Frid in a sprightly manner.

"Frid!" said her father.

"Well, it is, Daddy. Aunt V. is the dowager now, isn't she? Violet, Lady Wutherwood. Or is she? Mr. Alleyn wants both the Ladies Wutherwood, I expect."

"Please," said Alleyn.

"I'll go and ask. I don't somehow think you'll have much luck, Mr. Alleyn. My mother will come, of course. I'd better get Nanny while I'm at it. What about Aunt Kit, Daddy?"

Fox, who had seated himself discreetly in the background, glanced up in surprise and Alleyn said: "Is there someone else?"

"I can't *imagine,*" said Lord Charles with an air of vexation, "why nobody can remember Aunt Kit."

"Well, she just popped off," said Frid. "We do remember her from time to time. Mummy said, about an hour ago, 'For pity's sake, what's become of Aunt Kit?' Shall I ring her up?"

"It's my aunt, Alleyn," explained Lord Charles apologetically. "Lady Katherine Lobe. She was here this afternoon but I'm afraid this terrible business put her out of our minds. She was with my wife just before it happened. I suppose she must have slipped away without realizing—I quite forgot to say anything about her. I'm so sorry. Shall we ring her up?"

"I think it might be as well," said Alleyn. "Her name is Lady Katherine Lobe did you say?"

"Yes. Why?"

"The commissionaire saw her leave a few minutes before the accident was discovered."

"Well," said Lord Charles, "I call it very odd to go off like that without a word. I hope to heaven that nothing was the matter with her. We'd better ring her up. Frid, darling, will you?"

"Am I to tell her to come trundling in from Hammersmith?"

"I'll send the car," said Lord Charles. "Tell her I'll send the car, Frid, and then you'd better ring up Mayling. Mayling's my chauffeur, Alleyn. He wasn't here this afternoon so I imagine—"

"That will do admirably."

Frid knelt on a chair beside the desk and dialled a number.

"Aunt Kit," said Henry, "is almost quite deaf and not very bright. Shall I go and fetch my mother?"

"If you please."

"And Aunt V.," Frid reminded Henry. She began talking into the telephone.

"Tell her about it gently, Frid," said Lord Charles.

"She'll go into a flat spin anyway," said Patch gloomily.

Henry went out into the hall. Colin said to nobody in particular: "Isn't it rather a shame to summon Aunt Kit? I know maiden aunts are fashionable as murderesses but Mr. Alleyn told us not to go by the detective novels. And honestly—Aunt Kit!"

"Even as a witness," said Stephen, "she'll be quite hopeless. She n-never knows what's going on under her own n-nose even."

"Shut up," hissed Frid. "I can't hear. What did you say? What? But—oh well, thank you so much. Would you just say Miss Lamprey rang up. She knows our number. No, I'm afraid we don't but I expect it's quite all right really. Don't worry, Gibson. Good night."

Frid replaced the receiver and gazed blankly at her father.

"It's a bit funny," she said. "Aunt Kit said she'd be in to dinner and there's someone coming to see her by appointment and, well, she'd not telephoned or anything but she's simply not turned up."

CHAPTER IX

"Two, Two, The Lily-White Boys"

Alleyn had been confronted with the Lampreys for only some twenty minutes but already he had begun to feel a little as though they were handfuls of wet sand which, as fast as he grasped them, were dragged through his fingers by the action of some mysterious undertow. He sent Fox off to find out, if possible, from the commissionaire when Lady Katherine Lobe had left the flat and what direction she had taken. Privately he instructed Fox to set the machinery of the department at work. Hospitals would be rung up, street accidents reported. And in the end, thought Alleyn, Lady Katherine would arrive home at half past eleven after an impulsive visit to the cinema. In the meantime he concentrated on the Lampreys still in hand.

Henry came back, bringing his mother and his old nurse. Again there were vague, polite introductions for which Lady Charles did not wait. She advanced with a swift graciousness which Alleyn at once recognized as the fruit of an excellent social technique. They shook hands. Alleyn saw the small

New Zealander give her hostess a startled glance and he wondered if Lady Charles Lamprey was usually so pale. But she greeted him with a perfection of manner that sketched with subtlety relief at his arrival, deference to his ability, and a delicate suggestion that they spoke the same language.

"Please forgive me," she said, "for keeping you waiting. My sister-in-law—" she made a rueful grimace "—too terribly upset. Henry says you want to see her."

"I'm so sorry," said Alleyn. "I'm afraid I do."

"At the moment she simply *can't* come. I mean I can't *move* her. Her maid may manage her better. She's going to try."

"She must come, Immy," said Lord Charles.

"Charlie darling, if you *saw* her. I mean *honestly*."

"We'll carry on as we are for the present," said Alleyn quickly. "Has Dr. Kantripp seen Lady Wutherwood?"

"Yes. He's given her something and the nurse is going to stay here to-night. Dr. Kantripp guessed that you would ask to speak to her and said he would look in again later and see if she was up to it. Of course she'd had the most appalling and overwhelming shock."

"Of course."

"She's not English," said Lord Charles uncomfortably. Frid and Henry exchanged glances and grinned.

"Well," said Alleyn hurriedly. "To begin with—"

"Do sit down, everybody," said Charlot. "Nanny came too in case she was wanted."

They sat down.

As he waited for a moment, collecting his thoughts and the attention of his audience, Alleyn received a sudden and extremely vivid impression of a united family.

Whatever their qualities of elusiveness, vagueness or apparent flippancy might be, he felt sure these qualities would never be used by the Lampreys against each other. They would always present a united if slightly ridiculous front. Until Lady Charles came in he had thought the children markedly resembled their father. He now saw that they bore in their faces and mannerisms confusing and subtle traces of both their parents. It was odd to see the complete separateness of Roberta Grey. Alleyn's attention had been arrested by Roberta, by her small, compact figure, her pale face with its pointed chin and dark eyes set so very wide apart, by a certain air of grave watchfulness, by the Quakerish tidiness of her black dress and white collar. She had only arrived yesterday from New Zealand and yet she looked as though she had often sat on that Moroccan stool with her back set against the wall and her hands folded in her lap. And during the few seconds in which these impressions passed through his mind, Alleyn wondered if the Lampreys would close their ranks, and if in that case Roberta Grey would fall in with them. He had taken notes of Fox's inquiries. He now opened his book and laid it on the arm of his chair. He began to speak.

"As far as we have gone," he said, "This is what seems to have happened. Lord Charles Lamprey and Lord Wutherwood were together in this room up to about ten minutes past seven. Lord Wutherwood decided to leave and went out of the room. He first rang the bell in the hall. Your butler, Baskett, answered it. Lord Wutherwood ordered his car. Baskett helped Lord Wutherwood into his coat and so on. I understand you didn't go out with your brother, sir?"

"No," said Lord Charles. "No. We said good-bye in here."

"Yes. Baskett then opened the hall door. Lord Wutherwood went out to the lift. Baskett says that he was told not to wait and so returned to the servants' sitting-room. These notes, you will see, account for the movements, or some of the movements, of five persons during the few minutes after Lord Wutherwood left this room. Now, as Baskett left the hall and returned to the servants' sitting-room, he heard Lord Wutherwood call loudly for Lady Wutherwood. I should like to know next, if you please, how many of you also heard this call. Lady Charles—please forgive me if I still call you Lady Charles—"

"It will be much less muddling if you do, Mr. Alleyn."

"It will, won't it? Did you hear this call?"

"Oh, yes. Gabriel, my brother-in-law, always shouted like that for people."

"Where were you, please?"

"In my bedroom."

Alleyn glanced at his note-book.

"I've made a very rough sketch plan of both flats," he said. "Your room is the second from the lift end of No. 26?"

"Yes."

"Were you alone?"

"When he shouted? No. My sister-in-law and—Good heavens, Charlie, for pity's sake—"

113

"Yes, Immy, I know. Aunt Kit hasn't got home yet."

"Not got *home?* But honestly, darling, it's too queer of Aunt Kit. We don't even know when she left. Why did she vanish like that, do you suppose?"

"I expect she just slipped away," said Henry.

"She probably thought she'd said good-bye," said Frid. "You know how absent-minded she is."

"I expect she *did* say good-bye, Mummy," said Patch, "and you didn't hear her. She talks in a whisper, Mr. Alleyn."

"What nonsense!" exclaimed Lady Charles. "Of course I would know she was saying good-bye. For one thing she'd kiss me."

"You might have thought she was just being effusive." said Frid.

"She's always kissing people," agreed Patch.

"Well, she didn't suddenly kiss me in the bedroom out of a clear sky," said Lady Charles positively. "Don't be absurd, Patch."

"Lady Katherine was in your bedroom with Lady Wutherwood then," Alleyn interposed adroitly, "when you heard the first call?"

"Yes, she was, and perfectly normal. She didn't hear Gabriel, of course, because she's deaf, but Violet did. Violet is my sister-in-law. Lady Wutherwood, you know."

"Yes. What did they do?"

"Violet said she'd better not keep Gabriel waiting. She said she would like to go into the bathroom, so I told her about the one at the end of the passage."

Lady Charles, who was sitting next to Alleyn, leant over and looked at his note-book. "Is that your plan?" she said. "Let me see."

"Immy, my dear!" protested her husband.

"Well, Charlie, I'm not going to read any of Mr. Alleyn's notes and he'd snatch it away from me if there was anything secret in the drawing. There, it's as clear as daylight. That's the bathroom, Mr. Alleyn. I told her where it was and off she went. And then Aunt Kit began to whisper—you know how that generation does—only even more so because, as Patch says, she whispers anyway. So she went off to the other place which I see you've also got marked very neatly, and now I think of it that's the last I saw her."

"It's as clear as glass," Frid interrupted. "She probably

whispered: 'I'll *have* to go. Bless you, my dear,' and you thought she said: 'Lavatory. I'll just disappear.'"

"Anyone would think it was I who was deaf instead of Aunt Kit! She didn't say anything of the sort. She went down the passage in that direction."

"Well, perhaps she's locked in," suggested Frid. "It happened to her once before, Mr. Alleyn, in a railway station, and nobody heard her whispering."

"Good heavens, I wonder—"

"No, m'lady," said Nanny firmly and unexpectedly.

"Oh. Are you certain, Nanny?"

With a scarlet face and a formidable frown Nanny said that she was certain.

"Then, *that's* no good," said Lady Charles. "And then, Mr. Alleyn, I waited for Violet. She was rather a long time and I remember that my brother-in-law shouted again for her. The two girls, Frid and Patch, came in, and then at last *she* came back and she reminded me that she and Gabriel didn't like working the lift themselves, so I came along here leaving her on the landing, and asked one of the boys to take them down."

It seemed to Alleyn that as Lady Charles reached this point a curious stillness fell upon the room. He looked up quickly. The Lampreys had returned to their former postures. Lord Charles again swung his eyeglass, Henry's hands were again driven into his trousers pockets, and again the twins stared at the fire while Patch, her chin on her knees, squatted on the floor by Roberta Grey. And Miss Grey still sat erect on her stool. Alleyn was reminded of the childish game of Steps in which, whenever the "he" has his back turned, the players creep nearer, only to freeze into immobility whenever he turns round and faces them. Alleyn felt sure that some signal had passed between the Lampreys, a signal that, by the fraction of a second, he himself had missed. At this hated and familiar sign of guardedness his own attention sharpened.

"Ah, yes," he said. "We may as well clear up this point as we come to it." He looked at the twins. "Mr. Fox tells me that Lord Charles didn't notice which of you went down in the lift. Which was it?"

"I did," said the twins.

So complete a silence fell upon the room that Alleyn heard a voice in the street below call for a taxi. The fire settled down in the grate with a little sigh and, as clearly as if, instead of sitting stone-still in their chairs, the Lampreys had made a swift concerted movement, Alleyn heard them close their ranks.

ii

"Hullo," he said amiably, "a difference of opinion! Or did you both go down in the lift?"

"I went down, sir," said the twins. Lord Charles, very white in the face, put his eyeglass away.

"My dear Alleyn," he said, "I must warn you that these two idiots have got some ridiculous idea of stonewalling us over this point. I have told them that it is extremely foolish and very wrong. I hope you will convince them of this."

"I hope so, too," said Alleyn. Out of the tail of his eye he saw Lady Charles's thin hands close on each other. He turned to her. "Perhaps, Lady Charles, you will be able to clear this point up for us," he said. "Can you tell us who took Lord and Lady Wutherwood down in the lift?"

"No. I'm sorry. I didn't notice. One of the twins came out to the landing as soon as I asked for someone to work the lift." She looked at the twins with a painful nakedness of devotion, made as if to speak to them, and was silent.

Alleyn waited. Fox returned and went silently to his chair. Nanny cleared her throat.

"Did anyone else," asked Alleyn, "notice which twin remained here and which went down in the lift?"

The twins looked at the fire. Frid made a sudden impatient movement. Henry lit a cigarette.

"No?" said Alleyn. "Then we'll go on."

There was a sort of stealthy shifting of positions. For the first time they all looked directly at him and he knew that they had expected him to pounce on this queer behaviour of the twins and were profoundly disconcerted by his refusal to do so. He went on steadily.

"When Lady Charles came and asked for someone to work the lift, Lady Frid and Lady Patricia were in their mother's bedroom, and their brothers were here in the drawing-room?"

"Yes," said Henry.

116

"Where had you been before that?"

"In the dining-room."

"All of you?"

"Yes. All of us. All the children and Roberta. Miss Grey."

"While your father and Lord Wutherwood were talking in here?"

"Yes."

"When did you leave the dining-room?"

"When the girls went out. The twins and I came in here."

"And you, Miss Grey?"

"I stayed in the dining-room with Mike—with Michael."

"And Michael," said Alleyn, "is of course now in bed?"

"He is," said Nanny.

"Were you all in the dining-room when Lord Wutherwood called out?"

"Yes," said Henry. "He shouted 'Violet!' twice. We were in the dining-room."

"At what stage did Michael appear in the dining-room?"

Henry leant forward and pulled an ash-tray towards him. "Not long before Uncle Gabriel called out. He'd been messing about with his trains in 26."

"Right. *That's* perfectly clear. We've got to the moment when Lady Wutherwood and her escort went into the lift. Did you go out on the landing, Lady Charles?"

"I stood in the hall door and called out good-bye."

"Yes? And then?"

"I turned back to come in here. I'd just gone to that table over there to get myself a cigarette when I heard—" she only stopped for a second—"when I heard my sister-in-law screaming. We all went out on the landing."

"I'll go on," said Henry. "We went out to the landing. The lift came up. Aunt Violet was still screaming. Then whichever twin it was opened the lift doors and she sort of half fell out. Then we saw him."

"Yes. Now, to go back a little way. This call Lord Wutherwood gave—Did it strike none of you as at all odd that he should sit in the lift and shout for Lady Wutherwood?"

"Not in the least," said Frid. "It was entirely in character. I can't tell you—"

"My brother," interrupted Lord Charles hurriedly, "was like that. I mean he did rather sit still and shout for people."

"I see. You wouldn't say, on thinking it over, that there was any particular urgency in his voice?"

"I see what you mean, sir," said Henry. "I'm sure there was nothing wrong when he shouted. I'll swear nothing happened until after that."

"But wait a moment." Lady Charles leant forward and the light from a table lamp caught her face at an exacting angle. Shadows appeared beneath her eyes, her cheekbones; shadows prolonged the small folds at the corners of her mouth and traced out the muscles of her neck. By that trick of lighting a prefiguration of age fell across her. Her voice sharpened. "Wait a moment, all of you. Is it certain that he wasn't calling out in alarm? How do we know? How do we know that he hadn't seen something—someone?"

Alleyn saw Lord Charles look sharply at her.

"We don't *know*, of course," he said slowly.

"Would any of you say there was an unusual quality in his voice?" asked Alleyn. For a moment nobody answered and then Henry said impatiently: "He only sounded irritable."

Frid said: "Aunt V. had kept him waiting."

Alleyn looked at Roberta. "Lord Wutherwood was a comparative stranger to you, Miss Grey?"

"Yes."

"Would you say that there was any particular ring of urgency or alarm in his voice?"

"I only thought that he sounded impatient." said Roberta.

Alleyn waited for a moment and then with a freshening of his voice he said: "Well now, to sum up. Each time Lord Wutherwood shouted, the younger members of the party were in the dining room, Lady Charles was in her bedroom and Lord Charles was in here. Lady Wutherwood and Lady Katherine Lobe were with Lady Charles at the time of the first call. At the time of the second call they had gone severally to the bathroom and the other room at the far end of Flat 26."

"Neat as a new pin," said Frid, and lit a cigarette.

"It doesn't take us very far, however," said Alleyn. "It merely leaves us with the presumption that at these times Lord Wutherwood was still uninjured." He turned sharply in his chair, recrossed his long legs and looked thoughtfully at the twins. The twins continued to stare at the fire while, under their clear skins, their faces rapidly turned a dull red. "Yes," said Alleyn. "We arrive at a difficulty. The next step, as you will understand, is to find out the condition of Lord Wutherwood when Lady Wutherwood and one or the other of these two gentlemen entered the lift. As both of these gentlemen agree that only one of them went down in the lift and as each of them protests that he was that one, it would appear that neither of their statements can be particularly valuable. At the moment I don't propose to argue this point. I propose, when she can see me, to ask for Lady Wutherwood's impressions of what happened when she entered the lift, and to find out from her exactly when the two uninjured occupants of the lift first realized what had happened. In the meantime, if I may, I should like to see Lord Wutherwood's chauffeur." Alleyn glanced at his notes. "Can his name be Giggle?"

"Yes, yes," said Lady Charles drearily. "The servants in both our families always have names like that. One of you boys go and find Giggle, will you?"

Alleyn watched the twin on the left-hand end of the sofa hitch himself up and walk away. "That's the one that stammers," thought Alleyn. "He's got a mole behind his left ear."

"Thank you, Stephen," murmured his mother. The other twin stared uneasily at her, met Alleyn's glance and looked quickly away.

Alleyn asked Lady Charles when Dr. Kantripp was expected to come back. She said that he had told her he had two visits to make and would call in to see Lady Wutherwood on his return. An image of Lady Wutherwood began to take hold of Alleyn's imagination and, while he waited for Stephen Lamprey to fetch the chauffeur, he made a picture of her. She would be lying on Lady Charles's bed in the second room on the left in Flat 26, the room next to that other where her husband waited for the police mortuary van. What was she like, this woman whose screams had risen with the returning lift, who had stumbled through the doors into Lady Charles's arms, who was (he remembered Lord Charles's profound uneasiness) not English? What lay at the back of her apparently severe prostration? Grief? Shock? Fear? Why did the Lampreys, incredibly garrulous on all other topics, close down on the subject of their aunt? It was not his habit to speculate on the characters of people whom he was about to interview, and he checked himself. Time enough for him to form an idea of Lady Wutherwood when he met her.

The far door opened. Stephen Lamprey came in, followed by a tall man in a dark grey chauffeur's uniform.

"This is G-Giggle," said Stephen.

iii

Evidently Giggle was nervous. He stood to attention and kept closing and unclosing his mechanic's hands. He sweated lightly and was inclined to show the whites of his eyes. He had a large palish face and bleached eyebrows that met in a thicket over his snub nose. He eyed Alleyn with an air half-mulish, half-apprehensive, but gave his answers crisply enough, thinking for a moment, and then speaking without hesitation. Alleyn began by asking him if he knew what had happened to Lord Wutherwood. With an uneasy look at Lord Charles, Giggle said Mr. Baskett had told him his lordship had met with a fatal accident.

"We are afraid," said Alleyn, "that it was not an accident."

"No, sir?"

"No. It looks very much as though there has been foul play. You will understand that the police want to know the whereabouts of everyone in the flat from the time Lord Wutherwood was last seen, uninjured and apparantly unthreatened, until the moment when the injury was discovered."

He stopped and Giggle said doubtfully: "Yes, sir."

"All right. Now, did you hear his lordship call out after he went out on the lift landing?"

"Yes, sir."

"Where were you?"

"In the passage, sir, in the flat, I'd been helping Master Michael with his train, sir."

"Was Master Michael with you?"

"No, sir."

"Do you know where he was?"

Giggle shifted his weight from one foot to the other. "Well,

120

sir, we was in the passage outside her ladyship's room and Master Michael saw a parcel in her ladyship's room and said something about giving it to his lordship. I mean his late lordship, sir."

"Did Master Michael get this parcel?"

"Yes, sir."

"And went away with it?"

"Yes, sir."

Lord Charles cleared his throat and uttered a small deprecating sound. Alleyn turned to him.

"I'm so sorry, Alleyn. I quite forgot to tell you. Not that I imagine it can have the smallest bearing on anything. Michael had planned to give my brother a little present and actually came in here with it just before my brother went out."

"I see, sir. There was no parcel in the lift."

"No." Lord Charles touched his moustache. "No. Actually he didn't—he must have forgotten to take it."

"Then it's still here?"

"I suppose so. I—"

"There it is," said Frid. She went to the far end of the room and returned with a square brown-paper parcel. "Do you want to see it, Mr. Alleyn? Routine and all that."

"Yes, please." Alleyn took the parcel in his long hands. "So he didn't open it?"

"Well—well, no," said Lord Charles. "Actually I was talking to my brother and told Michael to put the parcel down. I didn't want to be interrupted."

"I see, sir." Alleyn turned the parcel over in his hand.

"Please, Mr. Alleyn!" said Lady Charles suddenly. "It's rather precious and terribly breakable."

"I'm so sorry. I didn't realize. May I ask what it is?"

"A piece of Chinese pottery. As old as the hills and perfectly hideous I think."

"Good heavens!" Alleyn put the parcel delicately on the table. "Am I in a muddle," he asked, "or was Lord Wutherwood a collector? I seem to remember a loan exhibition—"

"That's right," said Frid. "There's a Ming or Ho or something gallery at Deepacres. All horses and smug goddesses, you know."

"Well, Giggle," said Alleyn, "Master Michael got this parcel

121

and went away with it. What did you do?"

"I waited for a while, sir, and then I heard his lordship call for her ladyship so I came along to this flat and got my coat and cap, sir, from the staff sitting-room and I looked in at the door to say I was going. Then I went downstairs, sir. Master Michael came as far as the landing."

"I see. In coming across to this flat you used the landing?"

"Yes, sir."

"Where was Lord Wutherwood?"

"His lordship was in the lift, sir."

"Were the doors shut?"

"Yes, sir. I think they were."

"Did he speak to you?"

"He told me to go down to the car, sir."

"So you fetched your coat and hat, spoke to Master Michael, and returned to the landing?"

"Yes, sir."

"Did you hear his lordship call a second time?"

"I can't say I remember, sir. I don't think so, sir."

"Were the lift doors still shut when you returned?"

"I can't say, sir. I hurried downstairs, sir, without looking at the lift."

"Yes, I see. What did you do then?"

"I went straight to the car, sir."

"Meet anybody?"

"Beg pardon, sir? Yes, I did pass the commissionaire, sir."

"Speak to him?"

Giggle turned a deep crimson. "I just mentioned his lordship seemed to be in a bit of a hurry, sir."

"How long were you in the car?"

"I couldn't rightly say, sir. Not long before Miss Tinkerton came down. She's her ladyship's maid, sir. She came downstairs and sat with me."

"And then?"

Giggle looked towards Roberta. "The young lady came and fetched us, sir."

"You did, Miss Grey?"

"Yes."

"We thought they might be wanted," said Henry.

"Oh, yes. Thank you, Giggle, that'll do for the moment. I may want to see you later."

"Thank you, sir."

Giggle went away. Alleyn looked round that circle of politely attentive faces. "That carries us to the time when Lord Wutherwood first called out and, rather patchily, a little way beyond it. There's one small point we may as well clear up. I should like to know who wiped away the marks on the lift wall?"

"What marks?" asked Lord Charles while Roberta's heart sank into a chasm. "I didn't notice any marks."

"I did," said Roberta, in a much louder voice than she intended. "I wiped them off."

"Why did you do this, Miss Grey?"

"I don't quite know." Why had she wiped away the marks? "I think it was because they looked so beastly. And I thought if other people used the lift—the lift was still working."

"I see." He was smiling at her. "Just tidying up?"

"Yes."

"You shouldn't, you know," said Alleyn, dismissing it. "Well," he said, "I don't think any purpose can be served by keeping you all together. I'm so sorry, Lady Charles, but I'm afraid I ought to see your small son." Alleyn looked deprecatingly at Nanny. "I know it's all against nursery law," he said.

"The boy's worn out already, sir," said Nanny.

"Oh, Nanny, he *isn't*," said Patch.

"That will do, Patricia."

"Well, anyway—"

"It'll be a very nasty shock for him, m'lady," said Nanny. "Waking him up in the middle of the night and telling him his uncle's been done away with."

"I'll explain, Nanny," said Lady Charles.

"You needn't bother, Mummy," said Patch. "When I came out Mike was looking in the playbox for that magnifying glass you gave him. We guessed it was a murder and he thought he'd like to do some private detection."

"*Honestly!*" said Frid, and burst out laughing.

"Look here, Nanny," said Alleyn. "Suppose you take me along to the nursery and stand by. If you think I'm exciting him you can order me out."

Nanny pulled down the corners of her mouth. "It's for his mother to say, sir," she said.

"I think I'll just explain and bring him here to see you, Mr. Alleyn."

Alleyn stood up. The movement had the effect of calling them all to attention. Lady Charles rose and the men with her. She faced Alleyn. There was a brief silence.

Alleyn said: "I think, if you don't mind, I'll go with Nanny. Of course if they think it would be advisable, his parents may be present while I speak to him." Some shade of inflection in his voice seemed to catch the attention of the parents. Lady Charles said: "Yes, I think I'd rather..." hesitated, and glanced at her husband.

"I'm sure Mr. Alleyn will be very considerate with Mike," he said and, behind the somewhat stylized courtesy which he was beginning to recognize as a characteristic of Lord Charles's, Alleyn thought he heard a note of warning. Perhaps Lady Charles heard it too for she said quickly: "Yes, of course. I expect Mike will be *too* thrilled. Nanny, will you wake him and explain?"

Alleyn went to the door and opened it. "I don't expect we shall be very long," he said.

Henry laughed unpleasantly: Frid said: "When you've met Mike, Mr. Alleyn, you'll realize that no one on earth could prime him with any story."

"Don't be an ass, Frid," said Colin.

"What you may not realize," said Henry suddenly, "is that Mike is a most accomplished little liar. He'll think he's telling the truth but if an agreeably dramatic invention occurs to him he'll use it."

"How old is Michael?" Alleyn asked Lady Charles.

"Eleven."

"Eleven? A splendid age. Do you know that in the police-courts we regard small boys between the ages of ten and fifteen as ideal witnesses? They almost top the list."

"Really?" said Henry. "And what type of witness do the experts put at the bottom of the list?"

"Oh," said Alleyn with his politely depracting air, "young people, you know. Young people of both sexes between the ages of sixteen and twenty-six."

"Why?" asked the twins and Henry and Frid simultaneously.

"The text-books say that they are generally rather unobservant," Alleyn murmured. "Too much absorbed in themselves and their own reactions. May we go, Nanny?"

Without a word Nanny led the way into the hall. Alleyn followed her and shut the door but not before he heard Frid say: "And that, my dears, takes us off with a screech of laughter and a couple of loud thumps."

CHAPTER X

Statement from a Small Boy

Mike was fast asleep and therefore looked his best. The treachery of sleep is seen in the circumstances of its adding years to the middle-aged and taking them away from children. Mike's cheeks were filmy with roses, his lips were parted freshly and his lashes made endearing smudges under his delicate eyelids. His mouse-coloured hair was tousled and still moist from his bath. Near to his face one hand, touchingly defenseless, lay relaxed across the handle of a Woolworth magnifying glass. He looked about seven years old and alarmingly innocent. Nanny, scowling hideously, smoothed the bed-clothes and laid a gnarled finger against Mike's cheek. Mike made a babyish sound and curled down closer in his bed.

"Damn' shame to wake him," Alleyn said under his breath.

"Needs must, I suppose," said Nanny, unexpectedly gracious. "Michael."

"Yes, Nanny?" said Mike and opened his eyes.

"Here's a gentleman to see you."

127

"Gosh! Not a doctor!"

"No," said Nanny grimly, "a detective."

Mike lay perfectly still and stared at Alleyn. Alleyn sat on the edge of the bed.

"I'm so sorry to rouse you up," he said civilly, "but you know what these cases are. One must follow the trail while it's fresh."

Mike swallowed and then, with admirable nonchalance, said: "I know."

"I wonder if you'd mind going over one or two points with me."

"O.K.," breathed Mike. He uttered a luxurious sigh. "Then it *is* murder," he said.

"Well, it looks a bit like it!"

"Golly!" said Mike. "What a whizzer!" He appeared to think deeply for a moment and then said: "I say, sir, have you got a clue?"

"At the moment," said Alleyn, "I am completely baffled."

"Jiminy cricket!"

"I know."

"Well, it wouldn't be any of us, of course."

"Of course not," said Nanny. "It was some good-for-nothing out in the street. One of these Nazzys. The police will soon have them locked up."

"An outside job," said Mike deeply.

"That's what we're working on at the moment," agreed Alleyn. "But there are one or two points." He looked at Mike's parted lips and brilliant eyes and thought: "I must keep this unreal and how the devil I'm to do it's a problem. No element of danger but plenty of fictitious excitement." He said, "As a matter of fact it's quite possible that the bird has flown to a hide-out miles and miles away from here. We just want to check one or two points and I think you can help us. You were in the flat this afternoon, weren't you?"

"Yes. I was having a bit of a go with my Hornby train. Giggle helped me. He's absolutely wizard with trains. Being a motor expert helps, of course."

"Yes, of course. Where do you do it? Not much room in here, is there?"

Mike shrugged his shoulders. "Hopeless," he said. "We used the passage. And then, just when he'd got the coupling mended and everything, Giggle had to go."

"So I suppose you simply carried on without him?"

"As a matter of fac', I didn't. Ackshully, Robin was going to play with me. You see I had to give Uncle G. the parcel." Mike looked out of the corners of his eyes at Nanny. "I say," he said, "it's pretty funny to think of, isn't it? I mean, where *is* dead?"

"Heaven," said Nanny firmly. "Your Uncle Gabriel's as happy as the day's long. Well content, he is, you may depend upon it."

"Well, Henry said this afternoon that Uncle G. could go to hell for all he cared."

"Nonsense. You didn't hear Henry properly."

"Where was the parcel?" asked Alleyn.

"In Mummy's room. Just by the screen inside the door. I couldn't find it when Robin said Mummy wanted me to give it to Uncle G."

"When was that?" asked Alleyn, taking out his cigarette case.

"Oh, before. After they'd done their charade. The others were horribly waxy because Uncle G. didn't look at the charade. Stephen said he was an old—"

"That'll do, Michael."

"Well, Nanny, he did. I heard him when I was looking for the parcel."

"Did you give the parcel up as a bad job?" asked Alleyn.

Mike shrugged again. It was a gesture that turned him momentarily into a miniature of his mother. "Sort of," he admitted. "I went back to Giggle and the Hornby and then I saw the parcel. We were by the door."

"Was anyone in the bedroom?"

"Mummy and Aunt V. and Aunt Kit had come in. They were gassing away behind the screen."

"So what did you do?"

"Oh, I just scooped it up and took it to Uncle G. in the drawing-room. Uncle G. looked as waxy as hell."

"Michael!"

"Well, sorry, Nanny, but he did. He didn't say anything. Not thank you or anything like that. He just goggled at me and Daddy told me to put it down and bunk. So I bunked. Patch said they had the manners of hogs and I think they had too. Not Daddy, of course."

"Don't speak like that, Michael," said Nanny "It's silly and rude. Mr. Alleyn doesn't want to hear—"

129

"I *say*." Mike sat up abruptly. "*You're not Handsome Alleyn, are you?*"

Alleyn's face turned a brilliant red. "You've been reading the lower type of newspapers, young Lamprey."

"I say, you are! Gosh! I read all about the Gospell murder in the *True Detective!* A person in my form at school knew a person whose father is a friend of—Gosh, of yours. He bucked about it for weeks. He won't buck much longer, ha-ha. I say, sir, I'm sorry I mentioned that name. You know—H.A."

"That's all right."

"I suppose you think it's a pretty feeble sort of nickname to have. At school," said Mike lowering his voice, "some people call me Potty. Potty Lamprey."

"One lives down these things."

"I know. Ackshully, I suppose you wouldn't remember a person called N. Bathgate. He's a reporter."

"Nigel Bathgate? I know him very well indeed."

Mike achieved an admirable expression of detachment. "So," he said off-handedly, "as a matter of fac' do we. He told me he called you Hand—you know—as a sort of joke. In the paper. To make you waxy."

"He did."

Mike giggled and gave Alleyn a sidelong glance.

"I suppose there's not much hope nowadays," he said, "for anybody to get into detection. I suppose you have to be rather super at everything."

"Are you thinking of it?"

"As a matter of fac' I am, rather. But I suppose I'm too much of a fool to be any use."

"It's largely a matter of training. What sort of memory have you got?"

"He's the most forgetful boy *I* ever had the training of," said Nanny. Mike gave Alleyn a man-to-mannish look.

"Let's see how you shape," Alleyn suggested. "Have a stab at telling me as closely as you can remember just exactly what happened, let's say from the time you picked up the parcel and onwards. Go along inch by inch and tell me exactly what you saw and heard and smelt for the next fifteen minutes. That's the sort of stuff you have to do at this game." He opened his notebook. "We'll say you're an expert witness and I'm taking your statement. Off you go. You picked up the parcel? With which hand?"

"With my left hand because I had a Hornby signal in my right."

"Good. Go on."

"Everything?"

"Everything."

"Well, I stepped over the rails. Giggle was fitting two curved bits together. I said I wouldn't be a jiffy and he said 'All Right, Master Mike.' And I walked down the passage past the curtain of Robin's room. Robin's room is generally a sort of hall in 26 but Mummy had the curtains put there to make a room and a passage. Is this the right way, sir?"

"Yes."

"The curtains were shut. They're a kind of blue woolly stuff. The door at the end of the passage was shut. I opened it and went onto the landing."

"Did you shut the door?"

"I don't think so," said Mike simply. "I hardly ever do. No, I didn't, because I heard Giggle winding up the engine of the Hornby and I looked back at him."

"Good. Then?"

"Well, I crossed the landing."

"Was the lift up?"

"Yes, it was. You can see the light through the glass in the tops of the doors. There wasn't anybody on the landing or outside the lift. Not standing up, anyway. So I went into the hall of No. 25 and I don't suppose I shut the door. I'm afraid I'll be a bit feeble if you say I've got to describe the hall because there were all the things the others had had for their charade. They'd just sort of bished them into the cupboard and they were bulging out and there were coats lying on the table and . . ." Mike stopped and screwed up his eyes.

"What is it?"

"Well, sir, I'm just sort of trying to *see*."

"That's right," said Alleyn quietly. "You know your brain is really rather like a camera. It takes a photograph of everything you see, only very often you never develop the photograph. Try to develop the photograph your brain took of the hall."

Nanny said: "The boy's getting flushed."

"I'm *not*," said Mike, without opening his eyes. "*Honestly*, Nanny. Well, in my photograph the light is sort of coming through the window in front of me. Into my eyes. So

131

everything has got its shadow coming my way. There's a thing of flowers on the round table and a bowler. I think it was Uncle G.'s bowler. And I saw Henry's gloves. And a scarf and some race glasses and one of those hats people wear in hot places. Wait a bit, sir. There's something else. It's sort of on the edge of the picture. Not quite developed, like you said."

"Yes?"

"I'll get it in a jiffy, all right. It's a shining kind of thing. Not 'zackly big but long and bright."

Nanny uttered a brusque exclamation and made an anxious gesture with her hands as though she fended something away from herself and from Mike.

"Wait a bit," Mike repeated impatiently. "Don't tell me. Long and thin and bright."

He opened his eyes and stared triumphantly at Alleyn. "I've got it," he said. "It was on the edge of the table. One of those long pointed things they keep in the sideboard drawer. A skewer. That's what it was, sir. A skewer."

ii

Mike paused and regarded Alleyn with some complacency. Nobody stirred. The nursery clock ticked loudly on the mantelpiece. A little gust of wind shook the window-panes. Down below in Pleassaunce Court a sequence of cars changed gears and accelerated. A paper-seller yelled something indistinguishable and somebody shouted "Taxi!" Nanny's roughened hands, working together stealthily against her apron, made a faint susurration.

"They used it in their charade," said Mike. "I heard Frid yelling out for it."

"The charade?" Alleyn echoed. "Well, never mind. Go on."

"About the skewer? Well, there's one thing..."

Mike stopped. His face lost its look of eagerness and, as small boys' faces can, became extremely blank.

"What's up?" asked Alleyn.

"I was only wondering. Is the skewer a clue?"

"Anything might be a clue," said Alleyn carefully.

"I know. Only—"

"Yes?"

Mike asked in a small voice: "What *happened* to Uncle G.?"

Alleyn took his time over this. "He was hurt," he said. "Somebody went for him. It's all over now. Nothing of the sort can possibly happen again."

Mike said: "What was wrong with his eye?"

"It was hurt. People's eyes bleed rather easily, you know. Are you a boxer?"

"A bit. I was only wondering—"

"Yes?"

"About the skewer. You see I sort of remembered. After I tried to give the parcel to Uncle G. I went to the dining-room and after I went to the dining-room I went back with Giggle to the landing because Giggle was going away and we went through the hall and I said good-bye to Giggle because he's rather a friend of mine, and I saw him go downstairs and I leant on the table and—well I was only just mentioning it because I happened to remember—well, anyway, the skewer wasn't on the table then."

"Michael," said Nanny loudly, "don't make things up."

"It *wasn't*. I put my hands where it would have been."

There was another silence. Mike sat up and clasped his arms around his knees. "Shall I go back?" he asked. "Back to where I took the parcel to Uncle G.?"

"Yes," said Alleyn, "go back."

"Well, that's everything I can remember about the first time in the hall. I went through the hall into the drawing-room. Daddy and him were by the fire. So I gave him the parcel. Well, I mean I didn't give it to him because of what Daddy told me. I mean it was a bit awkward."

"What was awkward?"

"Uncle G. being in such a stink about something. Gosh, he was in a stink."

"You mean he was upset?"

"Absolutely livid. Gosh, you should have seen his face! Jiminy cricket!"

"Don't exaggerate," said Nanny. "You're letting your fancy run away with you."

"I am *not*," cried Mike indignantly. "He wants me to tell him ezackly all I can remember and I am telling him. You are silly, Nanny."

"That will do, Michael."

"Well, anyway—"

"Never mind," Alleyn interrupted. "Have you any idea why your uncle was angry?"

Nanny said: "I don't think Michael ought to answer these questions without his parents say that he may."

"O *Nanny!*" cried Mike in accents of extreme provocation. "You are!"

"Then we shall ask them to come in," said Alleyn. "Bailey." A figure stepped out of the shadows on the other side of the scrap-covered screen by Mike's bed. "Will you give my compliments to his lordship and ask him if he would mind coming to the nursery?"

"Very good, sir."

"Is he another detective?" asked Mike when Bailey had gone.

"He's a finger-print expert."

Mike suddenly gave a galvanic leap, ending in a luxurious writhe among the blankets. "I suppose he's brought his insnufferlater," he said.

"All his kit," agreed Alleyn gravely. "What happened when you left the drawing-room?"

"Well, I went to the dining-room and talked to Robin. The others had gone out. And then Giggle came along and said he had to go because Uncle G. was yelling in the lift. So I went to the landing with Giggle and he went downstairs. When he'd gone Uncle G. yelled out for Aunt V. So I bunked into 26. Gosh, he did sound livid. Absolutely waxy. I bet I know why."

"Are you sure he called out after Giggle had gone?"

"Yes, of course I am. Certain-sure."

"Did you see anybody else?"

"What? Let's see. Oh, yes. I saw Tinkerton in the hall. I sort of just spotted her out of the tail of my eye. She was tidying up the wardrobe, I think."

"Nobody else?"

"No." Mike thrashed his legs about. "Well, anyway," he said, "I'll jolly well tell you why—"

"You wait for your father, Michael," said Nanny. Somewhat childishly, Mike thrust his fingers in his ears and, fixing a defiant gaze on his nurse, he shouted. "It was because Mr. Grumball and all the other—"

"Michael," said Nanny in a really terrible voice. "Do you hear what I tell you? Be quiet." She reached out and pulled

Mike's hands away from his ears. "Be quiet," she repeated.

Mike flew into a Lamprey rage of some violence. His cheeks flamed and his eyes blazed. He roared out a confused sequence of orders. Nanny was to leave him alone. Must he remind her that he was no longer under her complete authority? Did she realize his age? Why did she continue to treat him like a child? "Like a silly damned kid," roared poor Mike and, pausing to take breath, glared about him and encountered the cold gaze of his father. Lord Charles had come round the corner of the screen.

"Mike," he said, "may I ask why you are making an ass of yourself?"

"Overexcited, m'lord," said Nanny. "I knew how it would be."

Mike opened his mouth, found nothing to say, and beat on the counterpane with closed fists.

Alleyn, who had risen, said: "You're not shaping too well at the moment, you know. You won't make anything of a policeman if you can't keep your temper."

Mike stared at Alleyn. Tears welled into his large eyes. He hauled the bed-clothes over his head and turned his face to the wall.

"Oh, damn!" said Alleyn softly.

"What *is* all this?" asked Lord Charles rather peevishly. Alleyn looked significantly at the crest of mouse-coloured hair which was all that could be seen of Mike, and turned down his thumb.

"I've blundered," he said.

"Come outside," said Lord Charles.

In the nursery passage, Alleyn closed the door and said: "I'm afraid Michael is upset because your nurse quelled the remarkably steady flow of his narrative. He told me that in your interview with him Lord Wutherwood had been annoyed about something. Nanny very properly suggested that you should be present. Michael, who is an enthusiastic maker of statements, resented her taking a hand."

"Did he—"

"Yes, I'm afraid he did deliver himself of one rather curious phrase. I'm so sorry he's upset. If I may I should like to try and mend matters a little. If I could just say good night to him?" Alleyn looked at Lord Charles and added rather drily: "I hope you will come with me, sir."

"The horse having apparently bolted," said Lord Charles, "I shall be glad to assist at the ceremony of closing the stable door."

They returned to the nursery. Nanny had tidied up the bed. Mike lay with the sheet clutched to the lower part of his face. His eyes were tightly shut and his cheeks stained with tears.

"Sorry to wake you up again," said Alleyn. "I just wanted to ask if you would very kindly lend me that lens of yours. I could do with it."

Without opening his eyes, Mike scuffled under the pillow and produced his Woolworth magnifying glass. He thrust it up. Alleyn took it. Mike was shaken by a sob and retreated farther under the sheet.

"It's a jolly good glass," said a muffled voice.

"I can see that. Thank you so much. Good night, Lord Michael."

The sheet was thrown back and Mike's eyes opened accusingly upon his father.

"*Daddy!*" he said. "It's not going to be *that!*"

"Well," said Lord Charles, "well, yes. I'm afraid—well, yes, Mike, it is."

"Good lord, that puts the absolute lid on it! Good lord, that's absolutely frightful! Good lord," repeated Mike on a note of tragedy, "it's a damn' sight worse than Potty!"

iii

Mr. Fox had remained in the drawing-room with the Lampreys and Roberta Grey. Alleyn, on his return with Lord Charles, found Fox sitting in a tranquil attitude on a small chair, with the family grouped round him rather in the manner of an informal conversation piece. Fox had the air of a successful raconteur, the Lampreys that of an absorbed audience. Frid, in particular, was discovered sitting on the floor in an attitude of such rapt attention that Alleyn was immediately reminded of a piece of information gleaned earlier in the evening: Frid attended dramatic classes. On his superior's entrance, Fox rose to his feet. Frid turned upon Alleyn a gaze of embarrassing brilliance and said: "Oh, but you *can't* interrupt him. He's telling us all about *you.*" Alleyn looked in astonishment at Fox who coughed slightly and made no remark. Alleyn turned to Lady Charles.

"Has Dr. Kantripp come back?" he asked her.

"Yes. He's seeing my sister-in-law now. The nurse says she's a good deal better. So that's splendid, isn't it?"

"Splendid. We can't go very much further without Lady Wutherwood. I think, as you have kindly suggested, Lady Charles, the best plan will be for us to use the dining-room for a sort of office. I shall ask the police-constable on duty on the landing to come in here. Fox and I will go to the dining-room and as soon as we have sorted out our notes I shall ask you to come in separately."

Fox went out into the hall. "What's the time?" asked Henry suddenly.

Alleyn looked at his watch. "It's twenty past ten."

"Good God!" Lord Charles ejaculated. "I would have said it was long past midnight."

"I think we ought to ring up Aunt Kit again, Charlie," murmured Lady Charles.

"I think we ought to ring up Nigel Bathgate," said Frid.

"Bathgate!" cried Alleyn, jerked to attention by this recurrence of his friend's name. "Bathgate? But why?"

"He's a friend of yours, isn't he, Mr. Alleyn? So he is of ours. As he's a press-man I thought it would be nice," said Frid, "to let him in at the death."

"Frid, darling!" her mother expostulated.

"Well, Mummy darling, it *is* just that. Shall I ring Nigel up, Mr. Alleyn?"

Alleyn stared at her. "It's not a matter for us to decide, you know," he said at last. "He might serve to keep his fellow scavengers at bay. I may say that you will be creating a precedent if—if you actually invite a press-man to your house when . . ." His voice petered out. He drove his fingers through his hair.

"Yes, I know," said Lady Charles with an air of sympathy. "We no doubt seem a very unbalanced family, poor Mr. Alleyn, but you will find that there is generally a sort of method in our madness. After all, as Frid points out, it *would be* a help to Nigel Bathgate who works desperately hard at his odious job and, as *you* point out, it may save us from masses of avid, red-faced reporters asking us difficult questions about Gabriel and poor Violet. Ring him up, Frid."

Frid went to the telephone and a uniformed constable came in from the hall and stood inside the door. With the mental sensations usually associated with the gesture of throwing up one's hands and casting one's eyes towards heaven, Alleyn joined Fox in the hall. He drew Fox onto the landing and shut the door behind them.

"And what the hell," he asked, "have you been telling that collection of certifiable grotesques about me?"

"About you, Mr. Alleyn? Me?"

"Yes, you. Sitting there, with them clustered round your great fat knees as if it were a bed-time story. Who do you think you are? Oie-Luk-Oie the Dream God, or what?"

"Well, sir," said Fox placidly, "they asked me such awkward questions about this case that one way and the other I was quite glad to switch off onto some of the old ones. I said nothing but what was to your credit. They think you're wonderful."

"Like hell they do!" muttered Alleyn. "Where's that doctor?"

"In with the dowager. I strolled along the passage but I couldn't pick anything up. She seems to be shedding tears."

"I wish to high heaven he'd give her a corpse-reviver and let her loose on us. I'll go along and wait for him. I've told that P. C. to note down anything they said."

"I hope he'll keep his wits about him," said Fox. "He'll need 'em."

"He's rather a bright young man," said Alleyn. "I think he'll be all right. I'll tell you one thing about the Lampreys, Br'er Fox. They're only mad nor' nor'-west and then not so that you'd notice. They can tell a hawk from a handsaw, I promise you, or from a silver-plated meat skewer, if it comes to that. Get along to the dining-room. I'll catch the doctor as he comes out and I'll join you later."

But as Alleyn crossed the landing he heard a muffled thump somewhere beneath him. He moved to the stairhead and looked down. Somebody was mounting the stairs, slowly, laboriously. He heard this person cross the landing of the flat beneath. He caught sight of a pancakelike hat, a pair of drooping shoulders, an uneven skirt. This new arrival assisted herself upstairs with her umbrella. That was the origin of the thumping sound. He heard breathing and another faint, sibilant noise. She appeared to be whispering to herself. A sentence of Henry's came into Alleyn's memory. He coughed. The toiling figure, now quite close, paid no attention. Alleyn coughed stertorously but to no effect. He moved so that his shadow fell across the stairs. The pancake hat tilted backwards, revealing a few strands of grey hair and a flushed elderly face wearing an expression of exhausted inquiry.

"Oh," she whispered, "I didn't see—The lift doesn't seem to—Oh, I beg your pardon. I thought for a moment you were one of my nephews."

Alleyn, remembering her name and praying no Lampreys would hear him and come out, said loudly "I'm so sorry if I startled you, Lady Katherine."

"Not a bit. But I'm afraid I don't quite—I've got such a very bad memory."

"We haven't met before," shouted Alleyn. "I wondered if I might have a word with you." He saw that she hadn't heard him and in desperation groped for one of his official cards. Feeling ridiculous, he offered it to her. Lady Katherine peered at it, uttered a little cry of alarm and gazed at Alleyn with an expression of horror.

"Not the police!" she wailed. "It hasn't come to that? Not already!"

iv

Alleyn wondered distractedly if there was anywhere at all in the flat where he could yell in privacy into the ear of this lady. He decided that the best place would be in the disconnected lift with the doors shut. By a series of inviting gestures he managed to lure her in. She sank onto the narrow seat. He had time to reflect that Bailey and Thompson had finished their investigation of the lift. He leant against the doors and contemplated his witness. She was a little like a sheep, and a rapid association of ideas led him instantly to the White Queen. He bent towards her and she blinked apprehensively.

"I didn't realize," he said loudly, "that you knew this had happened."

"What?"

"You know all about the accident?"

"About what?"

"This tragedy," shouted Alleyn.

"Yes, indeed. Too distressing! My poor nephew."

"I'm afraid it had proved to be serious."

"He told me all about it this afternoon."

"What!" Alleyn ejaculated.

"All about it, poor fellow."

"Who did, Lady Katherine? Who told you?"

She shook her head at him. "Very sad," she said.

"Lady Katherine, *who told you what?*"

"Why, my nephew, Lord Charles Lamprey, to be sure. Who else? I do hope—" she peered again at the card—"I do hope, Mr. Alleyn, that the police will not be too severe. I'm sure he regrets it very deeply."

Alleyn swallowed noisily. "Lady Katherine, what did he tell you?"

"About Gabriel and himself. My nephew Wutherwood and my nephew Charles. I was so terrified that it would come to this."

"To what?"

"Even now," said Lady Katherine, "after this has happened, I still hope that Gabriel may soften."

Across Alleyn's thoughts ran a horrible phrase: "Gabriel shall grow hard and Gabriel shall grow soft." He pulled himself together, reassorted Lady Katherine's series of remarks and thought he began to see daylight.

"Of course," he said, "you left before—I mean when you left, Lord Wutherwood was still living."

"What did you say?"

"I'm afraid," roared Alleyn, changing his course again, "I have bad news for you."

"Very bad news," agreed Lady Katherine with one of those half-knowledgeable phrases by which the deaf bewilder us. "Very bad indeed."

Alleyn threw all delicacy overboard. He placed his face on a level with Lady Katherine's and shouted, "He's dead."

Lady Katherine turned very pale and clasped her hands together. "No, no!" she whispered. "You didn't say—dead? Did you? I don't hear very well and I thought—Please tell me. It wasn't that?"

"I'm afraid so."

"But—Oh, how terrible. And such a grave sin if—Did he

140

lay hands upon himself? Oh, poor Charlie! Poor Immy! And poor children!"

"Good God!" cried Alleyn. "Not Lord Charles! *Lord Wutherwood. Lord Wutherwood is dead.*"

He saw the colour return in patches to her large, soft cheeks.

"Gabriel?" she said quite loudly. "Gabriel is dead?"

Alleyn nodded violently. For perhaps thirty seconds she said nothing and then on a sort of sigh she whispered astoundingly: "Then I needn't have taken all this trouble."

CHAPTER XI

Conversation Piece

Roberta had thought that when the two Scotland Yard officials went to the dining-room they would all be able to relax a little, and talk to each other in a normal fashion. It seemed to Roberta that since the appearance of Alleyn and Fox neither herself nor the Lampreys had been real persons. She was conscious, perhaps for the first time in her life, of making a deliberate and strenuous refusal to examine her own thoughts. Near the surface of her mind there waited, with the ominous insistence of images in a nightmare, a sequence of ideas and conjectures; and as, even during the experience of a nightmare, the dreamer may sometimes fight down his own images, so Roberta fought down the rising terrors of her thoughts, thrust them into the background, covered them with other thoughts less menacing to the love that six years ago she had so queerly dedicated to each one of the Lampreys. It seemed to her that the Lampreys themselves had completely withdrawn from her and that, without having had an opportunity to consult in private, they had nevertheless come to some understanding among themselves. She had hoped that when at last she was alone with them they would draw her towards them and, by an exhibition of the devasting frankness that so many of their friends mistook for a sign of flattering confidence, would let her join the common front they were to present to the police.... But it appeared that they were not to be alone. Alleyn and Fox left a large policeman behind them and, more than anything else that had happened during that incredible evening, the sight of this stolid figure with scrubbed face and shining buttons, standing inside the drawing-room door, sent an icy thrill of panic through Roberta. Apparently the Lampreys were not so affected. Obeying a murmur from his mother, Colin offered the constable an arm-chair and asked him if he would like to move nearer to the fire at the opposite end of the room. With a glance at the man's note-book, Colin turned on a table lamp at his elbow. At this astonishing anticipation of his activities the constable turned a deep crimson, put away his note-book and hurriedly took it out again. Colin begged him to take the chair and in some confusion he finally sat down.

Colin rejoined his family at the other end of the room.

"Eh bein," said Frid, *"maintenant, nous parlerons comme si le monsieur n'etait pas la."*

"Frid!" cried her mother. *"Attention!"* Frid peered down the length of the room and, raising her voice, said to the constable: "I do hope you won't mind us trying to talk in French. You see, we have got one or two things to discuss and as they are sort of rather private it will be less embarrassing for all of us, won't it? I mean, you won't feel that we are too odiously rude, will you?"

The policeman rose, cleared his throat and said: "No, Miss," and, as though he ardently desired a ruling on the point, cast an anguished look at the door. After a moment's hesitation he again took the arm-chair offered by Colin, and now all the Lampreys could see of him was the top of his head, which was red.

"That's all right, then, Mummy," said Frid. *"Alors. A propos des jumeaux..."*

Roberta's heart sank. Charlot and Lord Charles, she knew, spoke French with some fluency. Frid had been to a finishing school in Paris. Henry and the twins had attended the university at Grenoble and had spent most of their holidays with friends on the Cote d'Azur. Even Patch and Mike, in the New Zealand days, had made life hideous for a sweating Frenchwoman who had followed the Lampreys to England and was still sporadically employed during the holidays. Roberta, on the contrary, had merely taken French at school and knew from bitter experience that when the Lampreys spoke in that language their conversation resembled a continuous rattle of fricatives and plosives, maddeningly leavened with occasional words that Roberta could understand. They were at it now. Lord Charles seemed to expostulate, Henry to argue. The twins were comparatively silent and looked mulish. Once, in answer to a prolonged harangue from Frid, Colin said: "*Laisse-tu donc tranquille,* Frid. In fact, shut up."

Henry said: "This is fun for Robin, I must say."

"Darling Robin," said Charlot, "you don't mind, do you?"

"Of course I don't. And I *have* followed a bit."

"*Taisez-vous, donc!*" commanded Frid dramatically. "*Ecoutez!*"

"What's the matter?" asked Henry testily.

"Listen, all of you."

As though from a distant part of the flat came the sound of a deep voice.

"It's Mr. Alleyn," said Frid. "What's he yelling like that for?"

"Perhaps he's flown into a black rage," suggested Patch.

"Perhaps he's arresting Nanny or someone," said Stephen.

"I must say I don't see why he should roar at her, even if he is. And anyway," added Frid, "he doesn't sound like that. He sounds as if he's yelling to some one downstairs."

"Or to some one deaf," Stephen amended.

"Good heavens," cried Charlot, "can it be Aunt Kit?"

"Really, Immy!" said Lord Charles. "Why on earth should Aunt Kit come back here at this hour?"

"Everything is so odd that I don't consider the return of Aunt Kit at midnight would be at all surprising."

"It isn't midnight," said Patch.

"Mr. Alleyn is growing fainter," observed Colin. "He must be going downstairs and roaring as he goes."

"Perhaps," suggested Patch, "he's sitting in the lift and shouting to find out *si nous avons parle vrai, au sujet de mon oncle.*"

145

"Patch, darling!" lamented Charlot, "your *accent*. Honestly!"

"Well, I suppose we can't go and find out," said Frid with a glance at the back of the constable's head.

"Good God," ejaculated Lord Charles. "It *is* Aunt Kit."

Through the door into the drawing-room came Lady Katherine Lobe.

"Immy *darling*," she whispered, as she embraced Charlot. "So *terrible* but in a way such a dispensation. His ways are indeed mysterious and no doubt He has chosen this instrument. Charlie, my dear!"

"Aunt Kit, where have you been?"

"To Hampstead. By tube and bus. I should have returned sooner but most unfortunately I caught the wrong bus and then again Mr. Nathan took such a long time. And all for nothing as it turns out. Though even now with the death duties—"

"Whom did you go to see at Hampstead?"

"A Mr. Isadore Z. Nathan, Charlie. I thought I should find him in his shop but of course when I left here it was after closing hours. But I found his private address in the telephone book and luckily he was at home. Such an amazing house, Immy. Enormous pictures and a great deal of velvet. But Mr. Nathan was charming."

"You *can't* mean Uncle Izzy from the pop-shop round the corner!" Frid ejaculated.

"What, darling?"

"Not the pawnbroker in Admiral Street, Aunt Kit?"

"Yes. You see, Charlie, I had often thought of doing it for my lame ducks, because. it *did* seem rather extravagant and useless to pay all those large premiums when I am not well off, but as they were family things and almost the only family things that I had, I always imagined that Mama would not have approved, so I didn't. But this was *quite* different because you *are* the family and it gave me the very greatest pleasure, darling. I *couldn't* be more pleased. Now, perhaps, you will feel you would like to redeem them, though, for the time being—"

"Aunt Kit," said Lord Charles hastily, "you're not talking about the Indian pearls?"

"What, dear?"

"Not Great Aunt Caroline's pearls?"

"It's such luck that I always wear them." Lady Katherine fumbled in her reticule and produced a slip of paper over which she closed Lord Charles's nerveless fingers. "There, Charlie, my dear. And I'm *so* glad. I'm sure Mr. Nathan is perfectly all right. He took a very long time examining them and you see I knew their value because of the insurance and I drove quite a shrewd bargain with him. I asked him to make the cheque out to you because—"

Charlot, rather belatedly, interrupted Lady Katherine with a loud patter of French. Lady Katherine peered towards the far end of the room uttered a whispered ejaculation, and sank into the nearest chair. Lord Charles stared through his glass at the cheque, seemed to try to speak to his aunt, made a small helpless gesture and turned to his wife.

"Darling Aunt Kit," began Charlot and stopped short. "*C'est trop . . .*" She stopped again. "I simply cannot go on *yelling* French," said Charlot. She glanced at the top of the policeman's head, went to the desk near Roberta, drew out a sheet of paper, and took up her pen.

"Surely," said Lady Katherine, "he can't dream of thinking of you . . ." She turned with an air of tragedy to her nephew. "It's too impossible," she whispered. "He seemed to be a gentleman."

"Give her this," said Charlot. Into Roberta's hand she thrust a sheet of paper on which she had written in block capitals: "DARLING, DID YOU TELL HIM WE ASKED GABRIEL FOR TWO THOUSAND?"

In obedience to signals from the rest of the family, Roberta displayed this communication to them before handing it to Lady Katherine, who instantly began to fumble for her glasses. These secured and slung across her nose, she read Charlot's message, her lips forming the words, her hands trembling. She laid the paper on her knees and, looking piteously from one to the other of the Lampreys, she whispered: "I didn't tell him how much."

Frid groaned. There was a short silence. Roberta watched Lady Katherine's hand, swollen a little with arthritis and still trembling very much, grope in her bag for a handkerchief. Suddenly Henry walked over to his aunt and stooped to kiss her.

"Dear Aunt Kit," said Henry gently. "You are so kind."

It was perhaps at this moment that Roberta first realized

that she was in love with Henry.

It is not easy to thank a deaf person for a large sum of money when every word of thanks may compromise the speaker in the ears of an attentive policeman. The Lampreys pulled themselves together and made a pretty good job of it. Lady Katherine seemed to have some difficulty in hearing French though she whispered away at it herself with great fluency. The conversation was therefore conducted along bilingual lines, the Lampreys' less dangerous remarks being made in English, though Roberta thought there seemed to be very little point in disguising the deplorable state of Lord Charles's finances if Lady Katherine had already told Alleyn about the object of the interview with her brother, and if Inspector Fox knew about Mr. Grumball.

After a few minutes there was a tap on the far door, which the constable opened. Fox's voice was heard in a brief mumble and in a moment he came in.

"Mr. Alleyn, my lord," said Fox, "would be obliged if Lady Patricia could come to the dining-room for a few minutes."

"Off you go, Patch," said her mother. Her voice had lost nothing of its crispness, but, as Patch passed her, she took her hand and gave her a smile that to Roberta seemed like a brief flash of desperate anxiety. Patch went out.

"It's rather like French Revolutionary films," said Frid. "You know, the ones where the little group of aristocrats gets thinner and thinner."

"For God's sake, Frid," said Henry, "hold your tongue."

"Manners, love," said Frid in Cockney.

The door opened again and Dr. Kantripp cme in. Roberta wondered if this endless night was to be punctuated by visits from Dr. Kantripp. Each time he came in it was with the same hurried air of concern. Each time, he shook hands with Charlot and with Lord Charles.

"Well," he said, "she'll do all right, Lady Charles. She's better. Had a sleep and less agitated. Still rather upset of course. Inclined to be..." He made an expressive gesture.

"Mad?" asked Frid. "Stark ravers, would you say?"

"My dear girl, not that of course, but rather unsettled and unlike her usual self, no doubt."

"My poor Dr. Kantripp," said Charlot, "you don't know her usual self."

"She's pretty grim even when at her jolliest, poor Violet," said Lord Charles gloomily.

"Has there ever been any trouble?" asked Dr. Kantripp delicately. "Up aloft, you know? Hysteria and so forth?"

"We've always considered her a little odd," said Lord Charles.

"A *little*, Daddy," said Frid. "My dears, let's face it, she's ga-ga. You know she is, Daddy. What about that nursing-home she used to whizz off to?"

"An occasional *crise-de-nerfs*," Lord Charles muttered.

"She's seen an alienist?"

"Yes, yes, I think so. Not for some time, though. She became a Christian Scientist about five years ago and I daresay my brother hoped that would help. But it didn't last very long and lately she's been tremendously taken up with some kind of occultism."

"Black magic," said Frid. "She's a witch."

"Dear me!" said Dr. Kantripp mildly. "Well," he added, "I've suggested that she should see her own doctor."

"What did she say to that?" asked Charlot.

"She didn't say anything." Dr. Kantripp glanced at the constable. "She doesn't say very much."

"I know," agreed Charlot. "She just stares. It's rather alarming."

"Do you know if she's in the habit of taking anything? Ah—aspirin? Anything to make her sleep?"

"I don't know," said Charlot sharply. "Why?"

"Oh, I merely thought that if there was anything already prescribed she might as well go on with the same dosage."

"Tinkerton would know."

"She doesn't know of anything."

"Dr. Kantripp," Charlot began, "what are you—" She was interrupted with some violence by Stephen.

"What's that!" he demanded loudly. *"Listen!"*

There was a distant rumbling. A doorbell rang.

Baskett's step sounded in the passage and in a moment he came in.

"If Mr. Fox might speak to you, my lord?"

"Yes, Baskett, of course." Lord Charles hurried out. The door shut, but not before Roberta heard a sort of muffled rattle from the direction of the landing.

"That was the l-lift," said Stephen. "I thought the police had d-disconnected it."

"They had," said Henry.

"I think I know what it is," said Dr. Kantripp. "Don't worry, Lady Charles. The police are attending to things, you know, and we have been expecting the—ah—the—"

"They're taking him away?"

"Yes."

"I see. Does my sister-in-law know?"

"I asked the nurse to explain. Lady Wutherwood is so very—I didn't suggest that she should be present. Only distress her. If you'll excuse me I think I'd better have a word with Alleyn."

He went out, meeting Patch in the doorway.

"I say," said Patch, "there are more men going into 26. They're using the lift."

"Shut the door," said Colin.

But even with the door shut they could hear unmistakable and heavy sounds of Uncle G.'s departure. Even the Lampreys had nothing to say and sat in an uncomfortable hush, listening and yet not appearing to listen. With a clank and a heavy mechanical sigh, Uncle G. went down again in the lift.

Henry moved to a window of the drawing-room, pulled aside the curtains and looked down into the street. The others watched him uneasily and in a moment the twins joined him. Unwillingly, Roberta read in their faces the stages of Uncle G.'s progress. Henry opened his window more widely. Down in Pleasaunce Court, doors were shut. An engine started, a motor horn sounded, Henry dropped the curtain and turned back into the room.

"I suppose," he said, "I shall not be promoted to first suspect if I merely observe, thank God for that."

"Patch," said Charlot, "has Mr. Alleyn finished with you?"

"Yes, Mummy."

"Then go to bed, darling. I'll come and say good night if I can. But don't stay awake for me. Run along."

Patch wandered to the door where she turned. "He hardly asked me anything," she said. "Only what we were all doing in the dining-room when—"

"Pas pour le jeune homme," said Frid warningly.

Patch made a rapid grimace at the constable's chair and opened the door.

"Here, wait a minute," cried Frid in alarm. But she was too late: Patch had gone.

"Look here," said Frid to the constable, "can I go after her? I want to ask her something."

"I'm afraid you can't, Miss. I can ask the young lady to come back, if it's any use," offered the constable, who had risen to his feet.

"I don't think it is," said Frid gloomily. "Her French isn't up to it." She wandered in a desultory manner round the room.

Lord Charles came in from the hall and went to the fireplace. He leant his arms on the mantelpiece and his head on his arms.

"Well, old man," said Charlot.

"Well, Immy," he said without changing his position, "they've taken him away. You didn't know him when he was a young man, did you?"

"No."

"No. When we were boys we were good friends. It seems a queer thing for him to go away like this."

"Yes," said Charlot, "I expect it does." He went and sat beside her.

"Well," said Henry, "what happens now?"

"Examination of witnesses continues, I trust," said Frid. "Who do you say he'll ask for next? I'm longing for my turn."

"Frid, my dear," said her father, "don't."

"Don't what, Daddy?"

"Don't be so quite so whatever it is you are being. We're all rather tired. Immy, ought I to ask if I may see Violet?"

"I don't think so, darling. Dr. Kantripp says she seems to be much quieter and more sensible. No doubt she'll—"

The drawing-room door opened slowly. The young constable scrambled to his feet, followed, one after another, by the Lampreys. Framed in the doorway, supported on one hand by a uniformed nurse and on the other by her maid, stood the Dowager Lady Wutherwood.

Roberta had been given a good many frights that evening and perhaps her resistance to shock had been weakened. There is no doubt that the appearance of Lady Wutherwood in the drawing-room doorway struck terror to her heart. It was as if some malicious stage-manager had planned this

151

entrance along the best traditions of Victorian melodrama. By some chance of lighting, the colour of the green-painted door-jamb was reflected in Lady Wutherwood's face. Her chin was lowered and her cavernously set eyes were in shadow while her mouth, which was wet but which still retained a trace of rouge, caught the light and glittered. The coils of dyed hair had become loosened and hung forward. Perhaps she had thrust Tinkerton aside, for her dress was ill-fastened and much in disarray. She seemed to have no bones. Even her hands showed no clear highlights on fingers and wrists, but hung puffily among the folds of her dress. Propped up by the nurse and maid, her posture was so odd that it suggested to Roberta a horrid notion. She thought Lady Wutherwood looked for all the world as though she dangled by the neck like some ill-managed puppet. Her lips moved and so still was the room that Roberta heard that clicking sound as Lady Wutherwood arranged her mouth for speaking; but when she did speak it was in an unremarkable voice, a voice that held no overtones of tragedy or horror.

"Charles," said Lady Wutherwood, "I've come to see the police."

"Yes, Violet. I'll tell them."

"I've come to see them because there is something they must understand. They have taken away Gabriel's body. It must come back to me, to my house. The funeral will be from my house and nowhere else. I want to tell them that. Gabriel must come back."

iii

Charlot hurried to her sister-in-law's side and Roberta heard her speak in the voice she had used in the old days, when one of the children was hurt or distressed. It was a tranquil voice but Lady Wutherwood seemed scarcely aware of it. The nurse, professionally soothing, said: "Now, come along. We'll just sit and wait while they bring the doctor."

"Not in there," said Lady Wutherwood. "I don't go into that room."

"Now, now, dear."

"Where is the detective? I must see the people in

authority." Lady Wutherwood's head turned with a rolling movement and from the shadowed caverns of her eyes she seemed to look at Charlot. "Go away," she said loudly.

Lord Charles turned to the constable. "Will you tell Mr. Alleyn?"

He said: "Yes, my lord, certainly," and looked at Lady Wutherwood who, with her escort, completely blocked the doorway.

"There's a chair in the passage, nurse," said Charlot.

Tinkerton said: "Come along now, m'lady," in a thin voice but with an air of authority. Her mistress leant towards her and with a clumsy lurch turned and went into the passage, still supported by the two women. Charlot shut the door and eyeing her family spread out her hands and shrugged her shoulders.

"What," she began, "do you suppose—"

But Frid interrupted her. Frid, standing in the centre of the room, urgent, and for once unconsciously dramatic, harangued her family in a sort of impassioned whisper.

"Look here," she said, "he's out of the way. What are we going to do? What has Patch said we did in the dining-room?"

"Obviously," said Henry, "she told the truth."

"She may have lied like a book."

"Shall I whizz out and ask her?" Stephen suggested.

"My dear," said Charlot, "the place is solid with policemen. You'd be arrested."

"Well," said Frid impatiently, "what shall we say? Quick. Before he comes back."

"You will tell Alleyn the truth, Frid," said Lord Charles.

"But, Daddy—"

"You will tell him the truth." He looked at Lady Katherine. "After all," he added, "nothing matters much now, after what has been already told."

"But—all right, Daddy," said Frid. "The truth it is. I don't know what everybody else thinks, but to me it's pretty obvious who did it."

The others stared at her. Frid gestured towards the door.

"Oh, no," said her father.

"Daddy, but of *course*. She's mad. She's stark ravers. You know how they hated each other. And Mummy, you said that you left her alone when you came here to ask one of the boys to work the lift. She must have done it then. Who else?"

"Charlie, do you think..."

Lord Charles stared at his wife. "Who else, Immy?" he said. "Who else?"

"I think Frid's right," said Stephen.

"Then," said Henry, "for God's sake come off your racket, you and Colin, and tell us who went down in the lift with them."

Colin said: "I went down in the lift."

"Don't be a bloody fool," said Stephen. "If Aunt V. did it, what do you want to muck in for? You're mad."

"You're both mad," said Henry. "If Aunt V. did it—"

"If Violet killed Gabriel," said Charlot suddenly, "it is not our business to do anything but clear ourselves."

"Immy, my dear—"

"If it's you, Charlie, or one of my children, against Violet, then I'm against Violet. I believe Frid's right. If Violet killed Gabriel she's mad. She's been shut up before; she'll be shut up again. Does that matter so much? Does it matter so much, even if she didn't do it?"

"Immy!"

"A mad woman, and, what's more, a horrible woman. You know you think she's horrible, Charlie. And if she wasn't demented before, she is now. She'll have to be shut up anyway. When I see Mr. Alleyn I shall make it perfectly clear that Violet had the opportunity. And if he asks what the relationship has been between them I shall tell him. Why not? Why, in God's name, shouldn't I? You yourself say we should speak the truth. What is it but the truth that Violet and Gabriel have hated each other for years? We all know they have. Let us say so. What about that woman you told me Gabriel installed—"

"Immy—"

"I know, you've never told the children. Tell them now. Tell them."

"It's all right, Mama," said Henry, "we know all about Uncle G.'s bits of nonsense."

"Mummy's right," said Frid. "For God's sake let's stick to it. Aunt V. won't be hanged. It's odds on she did it. Then let them know as much as we know. The twins have put themselves in a pretty bad light with their Sydney Carton stuff. Let's get them out of it. If it's a twin or Aunt V., personally I prefer the twin. If she jabbed Uncle G. in the eye with a meat skewer—"

"I know," said Henry, "but if she didn't?"

"If she didn't, she only gets shut up. Which is what she ought to be anyway."

"What," asked Henry, "does Robin think?"

But Robin, jerked abruptly into the picture, her thoughts racing down strange corridors, could only say with desperate emphasis that she knew none of them had done it, that she would do anything to save them from suspicion. And then, catching her breath over the implication of this avowal, she stopped short and looked with something like horror into Henry's eyes.

"It's no good, Robin," said Henry, "you've got your views. So have I. I've only just realized it. But I've got them."

"What do you mean, Henry?" demanded Charlot, clenching her hands. "We've only got a few seconds. That man will be back."

"We can still talk in French," said Frid.

"It's not the same. We don't understand each other in the same way."

"We don't understand each other now," said Henry.

"I don't know what you mean," cried Charlot.

"I mean that I don't think Aunt V. killed Uncle G."

"Why, why, why?"

"Because she's asked for his body."

"She's mad," said Frid.

"Mad or sane, and in my opinion she's not as mad as all that, I don't believe she'd want his company if she'd dug a skewer into his brain and murdered him."

Nobody answered Henry. The silence was broken by Lady Katherine Lobe. Lady Katherine had turned her deaf, inquisitive face to each of the Lampreys as they spoke. She now rose and going to her nephew laid her hand upon his arm.

"Charlie, my dear," she said, "what has happened to Violet? She looks like a lost soul. Charlie, what has Violet done?"

But before Lord Charles could answer his aunt the door opened, and the constable returned.

CHAPTER **XII**

According to the Widow

Alleyn sat at the head of the dining-room table with Fox at his right hand and Dr. Curtis at his left. Lady Wutherwood sat at the far end, with Tinkerton and the nurse standing behind her chair like a couple of eccentric parlour-maids. In the background, and just inside the door, stood a constable, looking queerly at home without his helmet. A little closer to the table and gravely attentive, Dr. Kantripp looked on at this odd interview. At their first meeting Dr. Kantripp had warned Alleyn that Lady Wutherwood was greatly shaken. "I suppose she is," Alleyn had said; "one expects that, but you mean something else, don't you?" And Kantripp, looking guarded, muttered about hysteria, possible momentary derangement, extreme and morbid depression. "In other words, a bit dotty," Alleyn grunted. "Curtis had better have a look at her, if you don't mind." He left the doctors together and afterwards accepted Dr. Curtis' view that Kantripp was walking like Agag but that it might be as well to wait a bit before they attempted an interview with Lady Wutherwood. "She's got a nasty eye," Curtis said. "I couldn't get her to utter. Can't say anything on a mere look at the woman but she don't seem too bright. Kantripp's their family doctor but he's never seen *her* before. He seems to have got wind of a dubious history. Private home. Periods of depression. I should go slow."

So Alleyn went slow, finished his examination of the flat and the servants, had his general interview with the family and his separate interviews with Mike and Patch. Patch, under pressure and with evidence of the livliest reluctance, had informed him that while father and uncle talked together in the drawing-room she and her brothers and sister, together with Roberta, had lain on the dining-room floor. It had been a kind of game, she said. "Game be damned," Alleyn had said after Patch left them. "Look at that corner of the room. It's out of the regular beat and the carpet retains its pristine pile. That's where they lay. There's a smudge of brown boot polish off the toes of one of those blasted twin's shoes. Come over here." He knelt by the sealed door. "Yes, and there's a bit of red close to the crack. I can hear a murmuring of voices. Have a listen, Br'er Fox."

Fox lay on the carpet and advanced his brick-coloured face towards the crack.

"By gum," he said, "They're talking French. It's the twin that doesn't stammer. Can you beat that? *Taisez-vous, donc.* That's French."

"So it is," said Alleyn. "Leave them to it, just now, Br'er Fox. Yes, there's no doubt about it they had their ears to that sealed-up door there. Listening. Have you seen the bum, Fox?"

"Yes, Mr. Alleyn. It's a matter of forty-one pounds. Lane & Eagle, house decorators of Beauchamp Place, put him in. Carpet, and a couple of arm-chairs. His name is Grimball, not Grumball. They wouldn't know. I wouldn't be surprised if this Giggle is really called Higgins or something. They're like that—funny."

"If they continue funny through this case," Alleyn rejoined, "it'll be a tour de force. Let them crack jokes at the coroner and see how he likes it."

"Grimball says they're a very nice family."

"So they may be. Damn' good company and as clever as a cage full of monkeys. They'll diddle us if we don't look out, Br'er Fox. The Lady Friede's as hard as they come. They've taken a line and they're going to stick to it. Look at those blasted twins. The noble lords Stephen and Colin, doing a Syracuse and Ephesus comedy turn. How the devil are we to find out which of them went down in the lift?"

"The widow?" Fox suggested.

"Don't you believe it. If they weren't very certain of themselves they wouldn't have taken the risk. I'll bet you their aunt will say she didn't know which twin it was. Equally I'll bet you their mother knows, and has taken her cue from her lily-white boys. Of course she knows. Can a mother's tender care muddle up the kids she bare, bad luck to them?"

"I never heard anything like it," said Fox warmly. "Trying to work off this twin stuff on the investigating officers. It's unheard of. You can't *have* that sort of nonsense."

"And what are you going to do about it?"

"It's disgraceful. Come to think of it, it's a kind of contempt."

"It's no good getting cross, Foxkin. Let us but once lose our tempers with the Lampreys and we're done. Yes? Come in. Open the door, Gibson."

The red-headed constable, who had tapped on the door, was admitted by his mate.

"Why have you left your post?" snapped Fox.

"What is it, Martin?" asked Alleyn.

"I beg your pardon, sir, but I thought I'd better come. The Dowager Lady Wutherwood's in the passage and wants to see you. So I thought I'd better come."

"And as soon as you turned your back," said Fox angrily, "they got together and agreed on the tale they'd tell."

"They've already done that, sir."

"What!"

"While you were there?" asked Alleyn.

"Yes, sir. They spoke in French, sir. I've got it down in shorthand. They speak quite good French, with the exception of Lady Patricia. I thought that before proceeding, you'd like to see what they said."

"Here!" said Fox. "Do you understand French?"

"Yes, Mr. Fox. I lived at Concarneau until I was fifteen. I didn't know, Mr. Alleyn, what the ruling was about listening-in under those circumstances. I don't remember anything in the regulations as to whether it could be put in as evidence. Seeing they didn't know."

"We'll look it up," said Alleyn drily.

"Yes, sir. Will you see the Dowager Lady Wutherwood, sir?"

"Give me your notes," said Alleyn, "and three minutes to look at them. Then bring her along. Wait a second. Did they say anything of importance?"

"They argued a good deal, sir. Principally about the two younger gentlemen. The twins. His lordship and Lady Friede wanted them to come clean. Her ladyship seemed to be frightened and rather in favour of nobody knowing which twin went down in the lift. Lord Henry was non-committal. They spoke principally about the motive against themselves, sir. I gather that Lord Charles—Lord Wutherwood—"

"Stick to Lord Charles," said Fox irritably. "The whole thing's lousy with lords and ladies. I beg your pardon, Mr. Alleyn."

"Not a bit, Br'er Fox. Well, Martin?"

"It seems he's in debt for about two thousand, sir. Pressing, I mean. He asked Lord Wutherwood to lend him two thousand and he refused."

"Yes, I see." Alleyn had been looking at the notes. "Well done, Martin. Now go and tell Lady Wutherwood that I shall be very pleased and grateful and all the rest of it, if she'll be good enough to come in here. Then return to your shorthand. What's your impression of Lady Wutherwood?"

"Well, sir, she looks very peculiar to me. Either she's out of her mind, sir, or else she'd like everybody to think she was. That's how she struck me, sir."

"Indeed? Well, off you go, Martin."

The red-headed constable went out and Fox stared at Alleyn. "We get some unexpected chaps in the force these days," he said. "In your time, sir, you were a bit of a rarity. Now they go round splitting foreign tongues all over the place. Did you know he spoke French?"

"I did, as it happened, Br'er Fox."

"I must get him to try some on me," said Fox with his air of simplicity. "I don't get on as fast as I'd like."

"You're getting on very nicely. Here she comes. Or rather, I fancy, here they come. I think I hear the voices of the medical gents."

The door opened and the curious procession came in.

And now Alleyn faced the woman whom he had previously begun to think of as his principal witness. It was his practice to discourage in himself any imaginative speculation, but on seeing her he could not escape the feeling that with the belated appearance of Lady Wutherwood the case had darkened. She was, he thought, such a particularly odd-looking woman. She sat very still at the foot of the table and stared at him with remarkable fixedness. The presence of Dr. Kantripp, and of the nurse and the maid, lent an air of preposterous consequence to the scene. Lady Wutherwood might almost have been holding some sort of audience. There was no doubt that she was antagonistic, but she had asked to see Alleyn and he decided that he would wait for her to open the conversation; and so it fell out that Lady Wutherwood and Alleyn, for perhaps half a minute, contemplated each other in silence across the long table.

At last she spoke. Her deep voice was unemphatic, her enunciation so level as to suggest that English was not her native tongue.

"When," asked Lady Wutherwood, "will my husband's body be given to me? They have taken him away. He must return."

"If you wish it," said Alleyn, "certainly."

"I do wish it. When?"

"To-morrow night, perhaps?" Alleyn looked at Curtis who nodded. "To-morrow night, Lady Wutherwood."

"What are they going to do with him?"

Curtis and Kantripp made deprecatory noises. The nurse put her hand on Lady Wutherwood's shoulder. Tinkerton the maid, clucked thinly.

"Under the circumstances," said Alleyn, "there will be an examination."

"What will they do to him?"

Dr. Kantripp went to her and took her hand. "Now, now," he said, "you must not distress yourself by thinking about these things." He might have been a hundred miles away for all the notice she paid him. She did not withdraw her hand but he moved away, quickly and awkwardly.

"Will they do dreadful things to him?" she asked.

"The surgeon will examine the injury," Alleyn said.

She was silent for a moment and then, on the same level note, "Before he returns," she said, "tell them to cover his face."

Curtis murmured something inaudible. Alleyn said: "That will be done."

"Tell them to cover it with something heavy and thick. Close down his eyes. The eyes of the dead can see where the eyes of the living are blind. That is established, else how could they find their way, as they sometimes do, into strange houses?"

Mr. Fox wrote in his note-book; the nurse looked significantly towards Dr. Kantripp. Tinkerton, over her mistress' shoulder, executed a little series of nods and grimaces and shakes of the head. Alleyn and Lady Wutherwood stared into each other's faces.

"That is all," said Lady Wutherwood, "but for one thing. It must be understood that I will not be touched or persecuted or followed. I warn you that there is a great peril in wait for anybody who intercepts me. I have a friend who guards me well. A very powerful friend. That is all."

"Not quite," said Alleyn. "Lady Wutherwood, if you had not asked for this interview I should have done so. You see, the circumstances of your husband's death have obliged me to make very close inquiries."

Without changing her posture or the fixed blankness of her gaze, she said: "You had better be careful. You are in danger."

"I," murmured Alleyn. "How should I be in danger?"

"My husband died because he offended against one greater than himself. I have not been told by whose agency he died. But I know the force that killed him."

"What force is that?"

The corners of the shifting mouth moved up. Small wrinkles appeared about her eyes. Her face became a mask of an unlovely Comedy. She did not answer Alleyn's question.

"I must tell you," he said, "that, if you know of anything that would explain even the smallest detail in the sequence of events that led to his death, you should let the police know what it is. On the other hand we cannot compel you to give information. You may think it advisable to send for your solicitor who, if he considers that you are likely to prejudice yourself by answering any question, will advise you not to do so."

"I know very well," said Lady Wutherwood, "by what means I may be brought to betray myself into a confession of things I have not done and words I have never uttered. But I remember Marguerite Luondman of Gebweiler and Anna Ruffa of Douzy. As for a solicitor, I have no need or desire for such protection. I am well protected. I am in no danger."

"In that case," said Alleyn equitably, "you will not object, perhaps, to answering one or two questions."

She did not reply. He waited for a moment and had time to notice the scandalized expression of Mr. Fox, and the alert and speculative glances of the two doctors.

"Lady Wutherwood," said Alleyn, "who took you down in the lift?"

She answered at once: "It seemed to be one of his nephews."

"Seemed?"

Lady Wutherwood laughed. "Yes," she said, "seemed."

"I don't understand that," said Alleyn. "Lady Charles Lamprey asked for one of her sons to take you down in the lift, didn't she?"

Lady Wutherwood nodded.

"And one of them came out of the flat and, in fact, entered the lift and took you down? You saw him come out? And you stood close beside him in the lift? It was one of the twins, wasn't it?"

"I thought so, then."

"You thought so, then," Alleyn repeated and was silent for a moment. Lady Wutherwood laughed again and her laughter, Alleyn thought, was for all the world like the cackle of one of the witches in a traditional rendering of "Macbeth." This idea startled him and he went back in his mind over the string of inconsequent statements to which she had treated them. He was visited by an extremely odd notion.

"Lady Wutherwood," he began, "do you think it is possible that somebody impersonated one of the twin brothers?"

She gave him an extraordinary look and, with a movement that startled them all by its abruptness and shocking irrelevancy, wrapped her arms across her breast and hugged herself. Then with a sidelong glance, horridly knowing, she nodded again very slightly.

"Was there any recognizable mark?" asked Alleyn.

Her right hand crept up to her neck and round to the back of it. She moved her head slightly and, catching sight of the nurse, hurriedly withdrew her hand and laid one of her fingers across her lips. And through Alleyn's thoughts ran the memory of three lines:

> You seem to understand me
> By each at once her choppy finger laying
> Upon her skinny lips.

"Only," thought Alleyn, "Lady Wutherwood's finger is not choppy nor are her lips skinny. Damnation, what the devil is all this?" And aloud he said: "He stood with his back towards you in the lift?"

"Yes."

"And you noticed the mark on the back of his neck?"

"I saw it."

"Just there?" asked Alleyn pointing to the startled Fox.

"Just there. It was a sign. Ssh! He does that sometimes."

"The Little Master?" asked Alleyn.

"Ssh! Yes. Yes."

"Do you think it happened before you were there? The attack on your husband, I mean."

"He sat huddled in the corner, not speaking. I knew he was angry. He called for me in an angry voice. He had no right to treat me as he did. He should have been more careful. I warned him of his peril."

"Did you speak to him when you entered the lift?"

"Why should I speak to him?" This was unanswerable. Alleyn pressed his questions, however, and gathered that Lady Wutherwood had scarcely glanced at her husband, who was sitting in the corner of the lift with his hat over his eyes. With an unexpected turn for mimicry she slumped down in her own chair and sunk her chin on her chest. "Like that," she said, looking slyly at them from under her brows. "He sat like that. I thought he was asleep." Alleyn asked her when she first noticed that something was amiss. She said that when the lift was half-way down she turned to rouse him. She spoke to him and finally, thinking he was asleep, put her hand on his shoulder. He fell forward. When she had reached this point in her narrative she began to speak with great rapidity. Her words clattered together and her voice became shrill. Dr. Kantripp gave the nurse a warning signal and they moved nearer to Lady Wutherwood.

"And there he was," she gabbled, "with a ring in his eye and a red ribbon on his face. He was yawning. His mouth was wide, *wide* open. To see him like that! Wasn't it wonderful, Tinkerton? Tinkerton, when I saw him, I knew it was all true and I opened my mouth like Gabriel and I screamed and screamed—"

"She's off," said Dr. Curtis gloomily, and rose to his feet. Lady Wutherwood's voice soared in the indecent crescendo of hysteria. Fox began methodically to shut the windows. Dr. Kantripp issued crisp orders to Tinkerton, who showed signs of following the example of her mistress and was thrust out of the room by the nurse. The nurse suddenly became a dominant figure, bending in an authoritative manner over her patient. Alleyn went to the sideboard, dipped a handkerchief in a jug of water, and looked on with distaste while Dr. Kantripp slapped it across and across the screaming face. The screams were broken by gasps and the disgusting sound of gnashing teeth. Kantripp who had his fingers on her wrist said loudly: "You'll have to bring me that jug of water, nurse, if you please."

Alleyn fetched the water. Curtis said: "Unfortunate for the carpet," and pulled a grimace. The nurse said in a firm, brightly genteel voice: "Now, Lady Wutherwood, I'm afraid we must pour this *all* over you. *Isn't* that a shame?" Lady Wutherwood scarcely seemed to be aware of this impending disaster, yet her paroxysms began to abate and in a few minutes she was led away by Dr. Kantripp and the nurse.

III

"Open the window again, Br'er Fox, if you please," said Alleyn. "Let's get some air into the room. That was a singularly distasteful scene."

"I suppose you know what you were both talking about," said Dr. Curtis, "but I'm damned if I did."

"What's your opinion of her, Curtis? No sign of epilepsy, was there?"

"None that I could see. Plain hysteria. That doesn't say there's nothing wrong mentally, of course."

"No. What about it? Think she's ga-ga?"

"Ah," said Dr. Curtis, "you're wondering if she's the answer to the detective's prayer for a nice homicidal lunatic."

"Well," said Alleyn, "what about it? Is she?"

Dr. Curtis pulled down his upper lip. "Well, my dear chap, you know how tricky it is. She seemed to speak very wildly, of course, although I must say you appeared to take an intelligent hand in the conversation."

"What was she getting at, Mr. Alleyn?" asked Fox. "All that stuff about having a powerful protector and it *seemed* to be one of the twins. You don't seriously suggest anybody impersonated one of those young fellows?"

"I don't, Fox, but she does."

"Then she *must* be dotty. What was the big idea, anyway?"

"It's so damned preposterous that I hardly dare to think I'm on the right track. However, I'll tell you what I imagine was the burden of her song."

Dr. Kantripp returned. "The nurse and the maid are getting her to bed," he said. "The maid will come along as soon as she can."

"Right. Sit down, Dr. Kantripp, and tell us what you know of this lady's history."

"Very little," said Dr. Kantripp instantly. "I never saw her until to-night. As far as I can gather from Lady Charles and the others, there's a history of eccentricity. You'd better ask them about that."

"Yes, of course," agreed Alleyn with his air of polite apology, "but I thought that first of all I would just ask you. I suppose they didn't happen to mention whether the lady was interested in black magic."

"Now, how the devil," asked Dr. Kantripp, "did you get hold of that?"

"I was just going to explain. You heard her saying something about Marguerite Luondman of Gebweiler and Anna Ruffa of Douzy?"

"I've got them down in these notes," said Fox, "though I didn't know how to spell them."

"Well, unless my extremely unreliable memory is letting me down, those two were a brace of medieval witches."

"Oh, lor'," said Fox disgustedly.

"Go on," said Curtis.

"Taking them in conjunction with her suggestions that she had a powerful protector, that her husband had been punished, that she had warned him of his peril, that she recognized her lift conductor by a mark on his neck, that this was a sign from her Little Master, together with all the rest of her mumbo jumbo, I came to the preposterous conclusion that Lady Wutherwood thinks her husband was destroyed by a demon."

"Oh no, really!" cried Dr. Curtis. "It's a little too much."

"Have you ever come across a book called *Compendium Maleficorum*?"

"I have not. Why?"

"I don't mind betting Lady Wutherwood's got a copy."

"You think she's been mucking about with some sort of occultism and gone so far that she actually has hallucinations or illusions."

"Is it so very unusual among women of her age, restless by temperament, to become hag-ridden by the bogus-occult?"

"You come across some funny things," said Fox, "in these fortune-telling cases. I suppose you might say this is only going a step further."

"That's it, Br'er Fox. If it's genuine."

"You surely don't believe—" began Dr. Kantripp.

"Of course not. I mean, if Lady Wutherwood's apparent condition is genuine, she's just another gullible woman with a taste for the occult. But is her condition genuine?" Alleyn looked at Dr. Kantripp. "What do you say?"

"I should like to see more of her and hear more of her history before venturing on an opinion," said Dr. Kantripp uneasily.

"And also," murmured Alleyn, "you would like, I fancy, to consult with the family."

"My dear Alleyn!"

"I'm not trying to be offensive. Please don't think that. But as well as being the Lampreys' family doctor you are, aren't you, personally rather attached to them?"

"I think everybody who gets involved with the Lampreys ends by falling for them," said Dr. Kantripp. "They've got something. Charm, I suppose. You'll fall for it yourself if you see much of them."

"Shall I?" asked Alleyn vaguely. "That conjures up a lamentable picture, doesn't it? The investigating officer who fell to doting on his suspects. Now, look here. You are two eminent medical gents. I should be extremely grateful for your opinion on the lady who has just made such a very dramatic exit. Without prejudice and all that which way would you bet? Was the lady shamming or was she not? Come now, it won't be used against you. Give me a snap judgment, do."

"Well," said Dr. Curtis, "on sight I—it's completely unorthodox to say so, of course,—but on sight and signs I incline to think she was not shamming. There was no change in her eye. The characteristic look persisted. And when you turned away there were no sharp glances to see how you were taking it. If she was shamming it was a well-sustained effort."

"I thought so," said Alleyn. "There was no 'See how mad I am' stuff. And there was, didn't you think, that uncanny thread of logic that one finds in the mentally unsound? But of course she may be as eccentric as a rabbit on skates and not come within the meaning of the act. 'It is quite impossible,' as Mr. Taylor says, 'to define the term "insanity" with any precision.'"

"In this case," said Kantripp, "you needn't try. It doesn't arise."

"If," said Fox in his stolid way, "she'd killed her husband?"

"Yes," agreed Alleyn, "if she had done that?"

Dr. Kantripp put his hands in his trousers pockets, took them out again, and walked restlessly round the room.

"If she had done that," Alleyn repeated, "the question of her sanity or degree of insanity would be of the very first importance."

"Yes, yes, that's obvious. As a matter of fact I understand that she has paid visits to some sort of nursing-home. You can find out where and what it is, no doubt. Frid seemed to suggest there had been a bit of mental trouble at some time but—see here, Alleyn, do you suspect her of murder? Have you any reason to suppose there's a motive?"

"No more reason, perhaps, than I have for suspecting motive with the Lampreys."

"But, damn it all," Dr. Kantripp burst out, "you can't possibly think any one of those delightful lunatics is capable— To my mind it's absolutely grotesque to imagine for one moment—I mean, look at them."

"Look at the field, if it comes to that," said Alleyn. "The Lampreys, Lady Katherine Lobe, Lady Wutherwood—"

"And the servants."

"And the servants. The nurse, the butler, the cook, and the housemaids belonging to this flat; and the chauffeur and lady's maid belonging to the Wutherwoods. Oh, *and* a bailiff's man at present in possession here."

"Good Lord!"

"Yes. I expect when Messrs. Lane & Eagle learn in the morning's paper that Lord Charles has come in for the peerage, they will slacken the pressure. But in the meantime there is Mr. Grimball, the bum-bailiff, to be added to the list of possibles. A fanciful speculation might suggest that Mr. Grimball fell for the Lamprey charm and, moved by remorse and distaste for his job, altruistically decided to murder Lord Wutherwood; or, if you like, that Mr. Grimball dispatched Lord Wutherwood as an indirect but certain method of collecting the debt."

"I'd believe that," said Dr. Kantripp rather defiantly, "before I'd believe one of the Lampreys did it."

"How would you describe the Lampreys?" asked Alleyn abruptly.

"You've met them."

"I know. But to some one who hadn't met them. Suppose you had to find a string of appropriate adjectives for the Lampreys, what would they be? Charming, of course. What else?"

"What the devil does it matter how I describe them?"

"I should like to hear, however."

"Good Lord! Well, amusing, and ah—well ah—"

"Upright?" suggested Alleyn. "Businesslike? Scrupulous? Reliable? Any of those jump to the mind?"

"They're kind," said Dr. Kantripp, turning rather red. "They're extremely good-natured. They wouldn't hurt a fly."

"Never do anybody any sort of injury?"

"Never wittingly, I am sure."

"Scrupulous over money matters?"

"Very generous. Look here, Alleyn, I know what you're driving at but it's no good. They may be in a hole. They may be a bit vague about accounts and expenses and what not. I don't say they're not. Since we're being so amazingly unprofessional, I don't mind confessing I wish they did tidy up their bills a bit more regularly. The whole thing is that while they've got money they blue it and when they haven't they can't haul in their sails. But it's only because they're vague. It never occurs to them that other people don't live in the same way. They don't really think that money is of any importance. They would never in this world do anything desperate to get money. They couldn't. It's the way they are bred, I suppose."

"Oh, no," said Alleyn. "I don't agree with that. Business consciences aren't entirely bounded by the little fences of class, are they? However, that is beside the point."

"Well, look here," said Dr. Kantripp hastily, "I really must run along. Curtis has got my address if you should want me. I asked Lady Wutherwood about her own doctor and she said she hadn't one. Hadn't had a consultation for three years. I've got *his* man, if it's relevant. Cairnstock, the brain man we called in, you know, has left a report. He couldn't wait to see you, but Mr. Fox was here."

"Yes, Fox got the report."

"Right. Well, good-bye, Alleyn." Dr. Kantripp offered his hand. "I—ah—I hope you'll find—ah—"

"Somebody," suggested Alleyn with a faint twinkle, "that nobody is at all fond of?"

"Oh well, dammit, it's a nasty business, isn't it?" said Dr. Kantripp, who presented the agreeable paradox of a man in a tearing hurry unable to take his departure when there was nothing to stop him. "She'll do all right. Lady W., I mean. I've given her a sedative and so on." He went to the door and executed a little shuffle. "Ah—Curtis will tell you we noticed—ah—a slight condition of the—ah—the eyes."

"Pin-point pupils?" asked Alleyn.

"Oh, you saw that, did you? Well—ah—Good-bye. Good-bye, Fox. Good-bye."

"Very awkward for him," said Alleyn, after the door had shut.

CHAPTER XIII

The Sanity of
Lady Wutherwood

"It'll take that Abigail some time to stow away her mistress for the night," said Alleyn. "Before she comes back, let's go over what we've got. Check me as I go, Br'er Fox. We've got, in a half-baked sort of way, the positions of the Lampreys & Co., according to themselves, from the time their charade came to an end until the time they carried him, dying and unconscious, out of the lift. We now know which of the twins took him down in the lift."

"Do we?" asked Dr. Curtis.

"Oh, yes, rather. I'll come to that in a bit. We know the Lampreys are in deep water and we gather they had hopes of extracting two thousand pounds from the victim. We know they used the skewer in their charade, that it was lying on the hall table just before Lord Wutherwood left the drawing-room, and that it had disappeared a few minutes later. Young Michael is our authority, here, and he's very positive about it. So it looks as though our homicide was somebody who was in the hall for a moment after Lord W. went to the lift and before

Michael returned to the hall from the dining-room. According to evidence, during this brief interlude the Ladies Friede and Patricia went from the dining-room to Lady Charles's bedroom in Flat 26, and therefore passed through the hall. The Ladies Wutherwood and Katherine Lobe went from the bedroom to their respective lavatories and did *not* pass through the hall. Lady Katherine afterwards stole out to visit a pawnbroker. She tells me she didn't enter this flat. Lord Charles remained in the drawing-room where he was later joined by his sons who did not pass through the hall; Giggle, the chauffeur, went from the passage in 26 to the servants' hall in this flat, thence to the dining-room where he collected Michael, who saw him go downstairs. The fact that Lord Wutherwood was heard to call out again in a normal manner, after this, is a good mark for Giggle but will have to be checked. As for the servants, you've found, haven't you, Fox, that the butler, Baskett, was in the servants' sitting-room with the exception of a trip to the hall where he put Lord W. into his coat and gave him his scarf and bowler. From this trip to the hall, he returned directly to the sitting-room. One maid was out, the other was in the kitchen with the cook and the sinister Mr. Grimball. Nanny, a redoubtable dragon, was in the room with Lady Wutherwood's maid, Miss Tinkerton. Presumably Tinkerton left to get her bonnet and tippet from the servants' hall and subsequently went downstairs. But Tinkerton's movements are vague, as she has been too much in waiting on her mistress for us to question her. That will be attended to in a moment. Now then, all this is hellishly involved, but one infuriating fact emerges. According to their several accounts of themselves it would have been possible for any one of them to have slipped into the hall, grabbed the skewer, and subsequently have visited the lift. If one of the Lampreys did this, the others will no doubt lie like flat-fish to save his or her mutton. The girls will swear they did not separate. So will the boys. But Lord Charles and Lady Charles *were* alone for some of the time. So, by the way, was that quiet little New Zealander, who I must say has visited her Motherland in time for a pretty holiday. All right. At the moment we can't wipe anybody off the slate with the exception of the cook, the maid, and the bum. As a lively coda to all this rigmarole, follows the suggestion that Lady W. did not love her lord, and although she screamed industriously all the way up in the lift, was not altogether astonished that he should die of a meat skewer in the eye. And, by that same token, Curtis, wouldn't you expect him to die a bit sooner? That thing must have made a filthy mess of his brain, surely?"

"Just now," said Dr. Curtis, "you quoted Taylor. Do you remember the American Crowbar Case?"

"Phineas P. Gage?"

"The same. Do you remember that an iron rod forty-three inches long and one and a quarter inches in diameter, with a tapering point and weighing thirteen and a quarter pounds, passed completely through Phineas' head?"

"'There was much haemorrhage,'" Alleyn chanted drearily, "'and escape of brain matter.'"

"He eventually recovered all his faculties of body and mind..."

"'...with the loss of the injured eye.' I knew you'd flatten me with Phineas P. And what of Mr. J. Collyer Adam (Public Prosecutor, Madras) and his case of the man with the knife in his forehead?"

"Well," said Dr. Curtis with a grin, "with those examples before you, what d'you mean by asking why he didn't die sooner? For all we know, until I've had a peep inside, he might have survived to tell you 'oo done it and saved us all a night's work."

"He got a swinging great crack on the temple," Alleyn observed.

"Yes. I was going to ask you how you account for it."

"The smudge, inefficiently removed off the chromium steel boss in the lift wall, accounts for it. So, I fancy, do the bruises on the right temple and round the eyes, and the cut on the left temple, as well as a dent in the side of Lord W.'s bowler and the bloodstains on a pair of driving gloves we found in the lift. Henry Lamprey's gloves, they are, as he very airily admitted. Michael saw them in the hall, so no doubt they were taken at the same time as the knife. I get a picture of a great buffet on the side of the head. Then I see a picture of a left hand laid thumb downwards across the eyes, with the heel of the hand against the wall. While the left hand is still in position and the subject unconscious, the point of the skewer, held in the right hand and guided through the fingers of the left, completes a singularly nasty piece of work."

"A bit conjectural, isn't it?"

"Before they took the body away, Fox and I made an experiment. We stopped the lift at the uninhabited flat below this one and reconstructed the scene. Luckily rigor was not far advanced. The body fitted the marks exactly. The dent in the bowler tallies with a bit of chromium steel fancy work above the stain. Thompson's taken some shots of it. The results should be illuminating and calculated to give a tender juryman convulsions. And here, I fancy, comes Miss Tinkerton."

ii

Tinkerton was a thin, ambling sort of woman of about fifty. The only expression observable in her face was one of faint disapproval. She was colourless, not only in complexion, or merely because she gave no impression of character, but all over and in detail. Her eyes, her lashes, her lips, her voice, and her movements, were all without colour. It was as if she existed in a state of having recently uttered the phrase "not quite nice," and forgotten its inspiration, while her mouth idiotically maintained the form given by the sentiment. She was dressed with great neatness in clothes that, a long time ago, might have belonged to some one else but had since absorbed nonentity. She wore pince nez and a hair net. When Alleyn asked her to sit down, she edged round a chair and, with an air of suspicion, cautiously lowered her rump. She fixed her eyes on the edge of the table.

"Well, Tinkerton," said Alleyn, "I hope her ladyship has settled down more comfortably."

"Yes, sir."

"Is she asleep, do you know?"

"Yes, sir."

"Then she won't need you again, we hope. I've asked you to come in here because we want you, if you will, to give us as detailed an account as you can of your movements from the time you came here this afternoon until the discovery of Lord Wutherwood's injury. We are asking everybody who was in the flat to account as far as possible for their movements. Can you remember yours, do you think?"

"Yes, sir."

"Right. You arrived with Lord and Lady Wutherwood in their car. We'll start there."

But it was a thin account they got from Tinkerton. She did

not seem actually to resent the interview, but she maintained a question-and-answer attitude, replying in the most meagre phrases, never responding to Alleyn's invitation for a running narrative. It seemed that she spent most of the visit with Nanny in her sitting-room, from which she emerged at some vague moment and went to the servants' hall in Flat 25. By dint of patient and dogged questions, Alleyn discovered that on leaving Nanny's room she found Giggle and Michael playing trains in the passage, and the rest of the Lamprey children in the hall of Flat 25, dressing themselves for their charade. Tinkerton waited modestly on the landing until they went into the drawing-room and then slipped across into the passage and the servants' hall where she met Baskett, with whom she enjoyed conversation and a glass of sherry. She also called on cook. She could give no idea of the time occupied by these visits. On being pressed for further information, she said that she washed her hands in Flat 25. From this ambiguous employment she went down the passage towards the hall, meaning to return to Nanny in Flat 26. However she saw Baskett in the hall, putting Lord Wutherwood into his coat. She immediately went into the servants' sitting-room, heard Lord Wutherwood yell for his wife, collected her handbag, and hurried to the landing in time to see Giggle go downstairs. Alleyn got her to repeat this. "I want to be very clear about it. You were in the passage. You looked into the hall where you caught a glimpse of Lord Wutherwood and Baskett. You went into the servants' sitting-room, which was close at hand, picked up your bag, went out again, walked along the passage, through the hall, and onto the landing. Did you meet any one?"

"No," she said. She answered nothing immediately but met each question with an air of obstinate disapproval.

"You simply saw Giggle's back as he made for the stairs. Any one else?"

"Master Michael was going into the other flat."

"Where was Lord Wutherwood when you reached the landing?"

"In the lift."

"Sitting down?"

"Yes, sir."

"Sure?"

"Yes, sir."

"All right. Will you go on please?"

Tinkerton primmed her lips.

"What did you do after that?" asked Alleyn patiently.

Tinkerton said huffily that she followed Giggle downstairs. She remembered hearing Lord Wutherwood yell a second time. When he did that she was already some way downstairs. She joined Giggle in the car and remained there with him until the young lady came to fetch them. This came out inch by reluctant inch.

Alleyn made very careful notes, taking her over the stages of her movements several times. She seemed to be perfectly sure of her own accuracy and repeated monotonously that she had seen nobody but Giggle and Michael, as she went along the passage, through the hall, across the landing and downstairs.

"Please think very carefully," Alleyn repeated. "You saw nobody else? You are absolutely positive?"

"Yes, sir."

"All right," said Alleyn, cheerfully. "And now, what did you talk about all the afternoon?" At this sudden change of tone and of tactics, Tinkerton's air of disapproval deepened. "I really couldn't say, sir," she said thinly.

"You mean you don't remember—"

"I don't recollect."

"But you must remember *something*, Tinkerton. You had a long chat with Lady Charles Lamprey's nurse, didn't you? It must have been a long chat, you know, because when you came out Giggle and Master Michael were playing trains and they didn't do that until some time after your arrival. What did you and Nanny (Mrs. Burnaby, isn't she?) discuss together?"

Tinkerton primmed her lips again and said several things were mentioned.

"Well, let us hear some of them."

Tinkerton said: "The young ladies and gentlemen came up."

"Of course," said Alleyn amiably, "you would discuss the family. Naturally."

"They came up," Tinkerton repeated guardedly.

"In what connection?"

"Mrs. Burnaby brought them up," said Tinkerton, as if Nanny had suffered from a surfeit of Lampreys and had taken an emetic for it. "Miss Friede's theatricals. I should," added Tinkerton, "have said 'Lady Friede.' Pardon."

"I suppose you are all very interested in her theatricals?"

A slightly acid tinge crept over Tinkerton's face as she agreed that they were.

"And in all the family's doings, I expect. Did Lord and Lady Wutherwood often pay visits to this flat?"

Not very often it seemed. Alleyn began to feel as if Tinkerton was a bad cork and himself an inefficient corkscrew, drawing out unimportant fragments, while large lumps of testimony fell into the wine and were lost.

"So this visit was quite an event," he suggested. "Have you been in the London house for long?"

"No."

"For how long?"

"We have not been there."

"You mean you arrived in London to-day." She didn't answer. "Is that what you mean? Where did you come from?"

"From Deepacres."

"From Deepacres? That's in Kent, isn't it? Did you come straight to this flat?"

"Yes, sir."

"Had his lordship ever done that before, do you know?"

"I don't recollect."

"When were you to return to Deepacres?"

"Her ladyship remarked to his lordship, on the way up, that she would like to stay in Town for a few days."

"What did he say to that?"

"His lordship did not wish to remain in Town. His lordship wished to return to-morrow."

"What decision did they come to?" asked Alleyn. Was it imagination, or had he got a slightly firm grip in the cork?

"His lordship," said Tinkerton, "remarked that he had been dragged up to London and wouldn't stay away longer than one night."

"Then," said Alleyn, "they had come to London solely on account of this visit to the flat?"

"I believe so, sir."

"Where were you to spend the night?"

"In his lordship's Town residence," said Tinkerton genteelly. "Twenty-four Brummel Street, Park Lane."

"At such short notice?"

"A skeleton staff is kept there," said Tinkerton. "Of course," she added.

"Do you know why this visit was undertaken?"

"His lordship received a telegram yesterday."

"From Lord Charles Lamprey?"

"I believe so."

"Have you any idea why Lord Charles wanted to see his brother?"

Tinkerton's expression of disapproval became still deeper. Alleyn thought he saw a glint of complacency behind it. Perhaps, after all, Miss Tinkerton was not altogether proof against the delights of gossip.

"Her ladyship," she said, "mentioned that it was a business visit. H'm."

"And do you know the nature of the business?"

"It came up," said Tinkerton, "on the drive during conversation between his lordship and her ladyship."

"Yes?"

"I sat with Mr. Giggle in front and did not catch the remarks, beyond a word here and there."

"Still, you gathered—"

"I did not listen," said Tinkerton, "of course."

"Of course not."

"But his lordship raised his voice once or twice and said he would not do something that his brother wished him to do."

"What was that, do you know?"

"It was money matters." Something very like a sneer appeared on Tinkerton's lips.

"What sort of money matters?"

"The usual thing. Wanting his lordship to pay out."

He could get no more from her than that. She showed no particular reluctance to answering his questions and no particular interest in them. He began to wonder if she had any warmth of feeling or any sense of partisanship in her make-up. As an experiment, he led the conversation towards Lady Wutherwood, and found that Tinkerton had been in her service for fifteen years. Her ladyship, she said mincingly, was always very kind. Alleyn remembered those lack-lustre eyes and that sagging mouth and wondered wherein the kindness lay. He asked Tinkerton if she had noticed any change in her mistress. Tinkerton said dully that her ladyship was always the same, very kind. "And generous?" Alleyn ventured. Yes, it seemed her ladyship was generous and considerate. Pressing a little more persistently Alleyn asked if she had noticed no mental instability in Lady Wutherwood. Tinkerton instantly became an oyster and to his next questions either answered no, or did not answer at all. She did not think

Lady Wutherwood's behaviour was so very peculiar. She could not say whether Lady Wutherwood was interested in the occult. Lady Wutherwood did not take any medicine or drug of any sort. Lady Wutherwood's relations with her husband were not in any way unusual. She couldn't say what sort of nursing-home it was that Lady Wutherwood went to. She did not notice anything very odd in Lady Wutherwood's manner a few minutes ago. Her ladyship was upset, said Tinkerton of her own accord, and people often spoke wildly when they were upset. It was only natural.

"Was that why you made signs to the nurse over her ladyship's shoulder?" asked Alleyn.

"Her ladyship is suffering from shock," said Tinkerton in a burst of comparative candour. "I understand her ladyship. I knew she ought not to be upset by questions. I knew she ought to be in bed."

It was the same thing when they came to the late Lord Wutherwood. He was, said Tinkerton, a very quiet gentleman. She wouldn't describe him as mean nor would she describe him as generous. She couldn't say whether he had understood his wife. By using the strictest economy of words Tinkerton managed to convey the impression that Alleyn was making an exhibition of himself and, if that was really her opinion, he was inclined to agree with her. He ran out of questions and sat looking at this infuriating woman. Suddenly he rose to his feet and, walking round the table, stood over her. Unlike most tall men Alleyn had the trick of swift movement. Tinkerton stiffened uneasily on the edge of her chair.

"You know, of course, that Lord Wutherwood was murdered?"

She actually turned rather pale.

"You know that?" Alleyn repeated.

"Everybody is saying so, sir."

"Who is everybody? You have been with Lady Wutherwood ever since it happened. Does she say her husband was murdered?"

"The nurse said so."

"Did the nurse tell you how he died?"

"Yes, sir."

"What did she tell you? Describe it, exactly, if you please."

Tinkerton moistened her lips. "The nurse said he was injured with a knife."

"What sort of knife?"

"I mean a skewer."

"How was it done?"

"The nurse said he had been stabbed through his eye."

"Who did it?"

Tincerton gaped at him.

"You heard me, I think," said Alleyn. "Who murdered Lord Wutherwood?"

"I don't know. I don't know anything about it."

"You know he must have been killed by some one in this flat."

"The nurse said so."

"It was so. Very well, then. You understand that if you can prove it was impossible for you to have stabbed Lord Wutherwood through his eye into his brain, you had better do so."

"But I said—I said I was downstairs when he was still calling her ladyship. I said so."

"How am I to know that is true?"

"Mr. Giggle will have heard. He knew I was behind him. Ask Mr. Giggle."

"I have asked him. He doesn't remember hearing Lord Wutherwood call a second time."

"But he did call a second time, sir. I tell you I heard him, sir. Mr. Giggle must have been too far down to have heard. I was behind Mr. Giggle."

"And you say you met nobody and saw nobody as you passed along the passage, through the hall, and across the landing?"

"Only Mr. Giggle, sir, and he didn't notice me. I just caught sight of his back as he went down and Master Michael's back as he went into the other flat. Before God, sir, it's true."

"You are voluble enough," said Alleyn, "when it comes to your own safety."

"It's true," Tinkerton repeated shrilly. "I've said nothing that wasn't true."

"You've been with Lady Wutherwood fifteen years yet you don't know the name of the nursing-home she went to or why she went. You don't know whether she is interested in the supernatural or whether she isn't. You say she never takes any medicine or drug. Do you still insist that all three statements are truthful?"

"I won't talk about my lady. My lady hasn't done anything wrong. She's frightened and ill and shocked. It's not my place to answer questions about her."

Her hands worked drily together against the fabric of her skirt. Alleyn watched her for a moment and then turned aside.

"All right," he said. "We'll leave it at that. Before you go I want you to mark on this plan your exact position when Master Michael went into the other flat and when you saw Lord Wutherwood sitting in the lift."

"I don't know that I remember exactly."

"Try."

He put his sketch plan on the table with a pencil.

Tinkerton took the pencil in her left hand and, after consideration, made two faint dots on the plan.

"Your statement will be written out in longhand," said Alleyn, "and you will be asked to sign it. That's all for the moment. Thank you. Good night."

iii

"You were remarkably crisp with the woman," said Curtis. "I've never heard you less amiable. What was wrong?"

"She's a liar," said Alleyn.

"Because she wouldn't talk about her mistress? Wasn't that rather commendable?"

"Not because of that. She told a string of lies. Have a look at the statement later on and you'll spot them."

"You flatter me, I'm afraid. Why was she lying, do you suppose?"

"Not because she murdered Master," grunted Alleyn. "It's a right-handed job if ever there was one."

"She may be ambidextrous."

"I don't think so. She opened and closed the door, marked the plan, and took out her handkerchief with the left hand. She used the left hand every time she ministered to Lady Wutherwood. She's not our pigeon, unless she's an accessory to the blasted fact. What do you think, Fox?"

"I should say she's got a snug job with her ladyship," said Fox, glancing up from his notes and over the top of his glasses.

"Well, I must be off," said Curtis. "See about this P.M. Fox rang up the coroner. I'll start first thing in the morning. Cairnstock has an operation to-morrow and said he'd come and have a look later on. Don't expect we'll find anything of interest to you. I'll ring you up about mid-day. Good night."

He went out. Fox closed his note-book and removed his spectacles. Somewhere in the flat a clock struck eleven.

"Well, Br'er Fox," said Alleyn. "So it goes on. We'd better see another Lamprey. What's your fancy? Suppose we follow Master Henry's suggestion and talk to his mother."

"Very good," said Fox.

"We'd better let Lady Katherine go home. We can't keep them all boxed up in here indefinitely, I suppose." He looked at the constable. "My compliments to Lady Charles Lamprey, Gibson, and I'd be grateful if she could spare me a few minutes. And say that we shall not trouble Lady Katherine Lobe any further tonight. You won't call them Lady Lamprey and Lady Lobe, will you? And warn the man on duty in the entrance that Lady Katherine is to be allowed out. She lives at Hammersmith, Fox. We'll have to keep an eye on her, I suppose."

"She's not exactly the cut of a murderess, is she?" Fox remarked.

"You wouldn't say so. You wouldn't say she was the cut of a fairy, either, but apparently she vanishes."

"How d'you make that out, Mr. Alleyn?"

"According to herself, she met Michael on the landing just as he was going into the other flat. Tinkerton saw Michael but didn't see Lady Katherine."

"Perhaps the young gentleman made two trips, Mr. Alleyn."

"The young gentleman is our prize witness up to date, Fox. He tells the truth. As far as one can judge the family talent for embroidery has given him a miss. He's a good boy, is young Michael. No. Either Tinkerton added another lie to her bag or else—"

Gibson, the constable, opened the door and stood aside. Lady Charles Lamprey came in.

"Here I am, Mr. Alleyn," she said, "but I hope you don't expect any intelligent answers because I promise you that you won't get them from me. If you told me that Aunt Kit was steeped in Gabriel's blood I should only say: 'Fancy. So it's Aunt Kit after all. How too naughty of her.'"

He pulled out the arm-chair at the foot of the table and she

182

sank down on it, taking the weight of her body on her wrists as elderly people do.

"Of course you must be deadly tired," Alleyn said. "Do you know, that is the one thing that seems to happen to all people alike when a case of this sort crops up? Every one feels mentally and physically exhausted. It's a sort of carryover from shock, I suppose."

"It's very unpleasant whatever it is. Would you be an angel and see if there are cigarettes on the sideboard?"

The box was empty. "Would you like to ring for some," Alleyn asked, "or would these be any use?" He opened his case and put it on the table in front of her with an ash-tray and matches. "They are your sort, I think."

"So they are. That *is* kind. But I must see that there are some here, because if we are going to be any time at all I shall smoke all these and then what will *you* do?"

"Please smoke them. I'm not allowed cigarettes on duty."

He watched her light the cigarette and inhale deeply. Her hands were not quite steady.

"Now I'm ready for anything," she said.

"It won't be a solemn affair. I just want to check over your own movements, which seem to be very plain-sailing, and then I'll ask you to tell me anything you can think of that may help us to sort things out a little."

"I expect I'm much more likely to muddle them up, but I'll try to keep my head."

"According to my notes," said Alleyn, looking dubiously at them, "you went to your room with Lady Wutherwood and Lady Katherine Lobe and remained there until you heard Lord Wutherwood call the second time. Then, followed by Lady Wutherwood, you went to the drawing-room."

"Yes. She didn't come into the drawing-room, you know. I hurried on ahead of her."

"To ask for some one to take them down in the lift?"

"Yes," she said steadily. "That's it."

"Did you see anybody else on your way to the drawing-room?"

"I think Mike was in the passage. Nobody else."

"And Lord Wutherwood was in the lift?"

"I suppose he was. I didn't look. He sounded cross so I rather skidded past, do you know?"

"I see. And then you asked for some one to work the lift and Mr. Stephen Lamprey went out and worked it."

Alleyn felt, rather than heard, her draw in her breath. She said lightly: "No, that's not quite right. You remember that we don't know which twin went out."

"I think I know," said Alleyn. "I'm not trying to trap you into an admission. We'll leave it that a twin went out and you followed, as far as the hall, to say good-bye. Lady Wutherwood got into the lift and you returned to the drawing-room. That's all right?"

"About me—yes."

"I'll ask you to sign it later, if you will. What I hope you will do now is give us some sort of side-light of Lord Wutherwood himself. I'm afraid many of my questions will sound impertinent. Perhaps the most offensive part of police investigation is the ferreting. We have to ferret, you know, like anything."

"Ferret away," said Lady Charles.

"Well, can you think of anybody who would want to kill Lord Wutherwood?"

"That's not ferreting; it's more like bombing. I can't think of anybody who, in their right minds, would actually and literally want to kill Gabriel. I expect lots of people have, as one says, *felt* like killing him. He was a frightfully irritating fellow, poor dear. Not a fragment of charm and so drearily *ungay*, do you know? I mean, it does help if people are *gay*, doesn't it? I set *enormous* store on gaiety. But of course one doesn't kill people simply because they are not exactly one's own cup of tea and I suppose he had his grey little pleasures. He was passionately interested in plumbing and drainage, I understand, and carried out all sorts of experiments at Deepacres where one pulls chains when one would expect to turn taps and the other way round. So, what with his drains and his Chinese pots, I daresay he had quite a giddy time. And with Violet wrapped up in her black magic, you may say they both had hobbies."

"I thought I smelt black magic in Lady Wutherwood's conversation."

"She *didn't* start off about it to you!"

"Well, there were some rather cryptic allusions to unseen forces."

"Oh, *no*. Really, Violet is *too* odd."

"Lady Charles," said Alleyn, "do you think she's at all—"

"Dotty?"

"Well—"

"You needn't be apologetic, Mr. Alleyn. Violet popped into the drawing-room on her way to see you and if she kept up the form she showed then I'm surprised that you didn't whisk a strait jacket out of your black bag. Was she very queer?"

"I thought her so, certainly. I wondered if it could all be put down to shock."

Lady Charles said nothing but solemnly shook her head.

"No?" murmured Alleyn. "You don't think so?"

"No. I'm afraid I can't honestly say I do."

"Has there ever been serious trouble?"

"Well, of course, we don't see very much of them. My husband rather lost touch with Gabriel when we were in New Zealand but we did hear, from Aunt Kit and people, that she had gone away to a private nursing-home in Devonshire. It had been recommended by old Lady Lorrimer whose husband, as everybody knows, has been under lock and key for a hundred years. We heard that Violet's trouble comes in sort of bursts, do you know? Cycles."

"Is there anything of that sort in the family history?"

"Of that one hasn't the faintest idea. Violet is a Hungarian, or a Yugo-Slav. One or the other. Her name isn't Violet at all. It's something beginning with 'Gla,' like Gladys, but ending too ridiculously. So Gabriel called her Violet. I think her maiden name was Zadody, but I'm not sure. She was nobody that anyone knew, even in Hungaria or Yugo-Slavia, which was quite another country, of course, in Gabriel's wild-oatish youth. Gabriel said he had found her at the Embassy. I'm afraid Charlie used to say it was at a cabaret of that name or something slightly worse. You must remember her when you were a young man at parties. Or perhaps you are too young. He had her presented, of course, and everything. She was rather spectacular in those days, and looked like a Gibson Girl who didn't wash very often. Of course you *were* too young, but I remember them both very well. I believe that even then there were *crises-de-nerfs.*"

"That must have been rather difficult for Lord Wutherwood."

"Yes, *miserable* for him. Luckily there were no children. Luckily for us too, I suppose, as things have turned out, although I must say I don't think it's the pleasantest way of becoming the head of the family."

Her cigarette had gone out and she lit another. Alleyn felt quite certain that there was more than a touch of bravura in this rapid flow of narrative. It was a little too bright; the inconsequence was overstressed; the rhythm somewhere at fault. He thought that he was being shown a perilous imitation of the normal Lady Charles Lamprey by a Lady Charles Lamprey who was by no means normal. Once or twice he heard the faintest suggestion of a stutter and that reminded him of Stephen who, he felt sure, was overwhelmingly present in his mother's thoughts. Extreme maternal devotion had never seemed to Alleyn to be a sentimental or a pretty attachment, but rather a passionate concentration which, when its object was threatened, developed a painful intensity. Maternal anxiety, he thought, was the emotion that human beings most consistently misrepresent, degrading its passion into tenderness, its agony with pathos. He was too familiar with the look that appears in frightened maternal eyes to miss recognizing it in Lady Charles's and, though he was perfectly prepared to make use of her terror, he did not enjoy the knowledge that he had stimulated it. He heard her voice go rattling on and knew that she was trying to force an impression on him. "She wants me," he thought, "to believe that her sister-in-law is insane."

"...and I'm so terrified," she was saying, "that this really will throw her completely off her balance although, to be quite honest, we all thought she was very alarming when she arrived this afternoon."

"In what way?"

"Well, quite often she didn't answer when you spoke to her and then when she did speak it was all about this wretched supernatural nonsense, unseen forces, and all the rest of it. The oddest part about it was—"

"Yes?" asked Alleyn, as she hesitated.

"Perhaps I shouldn't tell you this."

"We shall be grateful if you will tell us anything that occurs to you. I think," Alleyn added without emphasis, "that I can promise you we shall not lose our sense of proportion."

She glanced at Fox who was placidly contemplating his notes.

"I'm sure you won't," she said. "It's only that I'm afraid of losing mine. It's just that it seems so strange, now, to remember what Violet said to me."

"What was that?"

"It was when we were in my bedroom. Gabriel had been rather acid about Violet's black magic, or whatever it is, and apparently she rather hated him sort of sneering at her. She sat on my bed and stared at the opposite wall until really I could have shaken her, she looked so gloomy and odd, and then suddenly she said in a very bogus voice (only somehow it wasn't *quite* bogus, do you know): 'Gabriel is in jeopardy.' It was so melodramatic that it made one feel quite shy. She went on again, very fast, about somebody who foretold the future and had said that Gabriel's sands were running out at a great rate. I supposed she must go in for a little fortune-telling or something, as a kind of relaxation from witchcraft. It all sounds too silly and second-rate but she herself was so wildly incoherent that I honestly *did* think she had gone completely dotty."

Lady Charles paused and looked up at Alleyn. He had not returned to his chair but stood with his hands in the pockets of his jacket, listening. Perhaps she read in his face something that she had not expected to see there—a hint of compassion or of regret. Her whole attitude changed. She broke into a storm of words.

"Why do you look like that," Lady Charles cried out. "You ought to be an effigy of a man. Don't look as if you were sorry for somebody. I..." She stopped as abruptly as she had begun, beat twice with her closed hands on the wooden arms of her chair, and then leant towards him. "I'm so sorry," she said. "I'm afraid you are quite right about people's nerves. Mr. Alleyn, it's no use for me to beat about the bush, with you looking on at my antics. I'm not a clever or a deliberate woman. My tongue moves faster than my brain and already I am in a fair way to making a fool of myself. I think perhaps I shall do better if I'm terribly frank."

"I think so, too," Alleyn said.

"Yes. I'm sure you have guessed my view of this awful business. Everything that I have told you is quite true. I do exaggerate sometimes, I know, but not over important things, and I haven't exaggerated or over-stressed anything that I have told you about Violet Wutherwood. I think she is quite mad. And I believe she killed her husband."

The point of Fox's pencil broke with a sharp snap. He looked resignedly at it and took another from his pocket.

"You will think," said Lady Charles, "that I am working for my husband and my children. I know Aunt Kit told you we were practically sunk and had asked Gabriel for money. I know that will look like a pretty strong motive. I know the twins have behaved idiotically. I don't even expect you to believe me when I tell you that it's always been their way, when one of them is in trouble, for both to stand the racket. I realized that all these things must make you a bit wary of anything I say and I can't expect you to be very impressed when I tell you I know, as surely as I breathe, that none of my children could, under circumstances a thousand times worse than ours, hurt any living creature. But if they were not my children, if I'd only been a looker on, like Robin Grey, only less interested, less of a partisan than Robin, I would still be certain that Gabriel was killed by his wife."

"It's a perfectly tenable theory," said Alleyn, "at present. Can you give me anything more than her condition and her conversation in the bedroom? Motive?"

"They had been at daggers drawn for years. Once or twice they had separated. Not legally. Gabriel would never have considered a divorce, I'm sure. He wouldn't like the idea of displaying his failure; he would never admit that anything he did was a mistake. And I don't suppose Violet has ever been normal enough to think of getting rid of him. She seemed to have merely settled down to hating him. And even if she had ever thought of it I don't suppose she'd altogether fancy the idea. I mean there *are* certain amenities—Deepacres and the London house and all the rest of it. She *could* have divorced him, of course. He had a series of rather squalid little affairs that everybody knew about and nobody mentioned. They'd loathed each other for years, in a dreary sort of way, but this afternoon there was something quite different. I mean Violet seemed to be actively venomous. It was as if *she* had poured all her dislikes of other people or things into one enormous hatred of Gabriel. That's how it was, exactly."

"I see. When do you think she could have done it?"

"I've been thinking it out. You see, she left Aunt Kit and me in the bedroom round about the first time Gabriel yelled for her. She didn't come back until after the second time he yelled, and then we both went along to the landing and I went into the drawing-room. There was no one else on the landing or in the hall."

"Did she seem very odd at that time?"

"I can't *tell* you how strange and ominous. I put out my hand to bring her along the passage but she drew away as thought I'd hit her and followed behind me. I was almost alarmed. I scuttled away as quickly as I could to get out of her reach. But she muttered along after me. It was like having a doubtful dog at one's heels. At any moment I expected her to growl and snap."

There was a pause. Alleyn had turned aside and moved to one of the windows. Fox looked up in surprise.

"*Mr. Alleyn,*" said Lady Charles, "what are you doing? You—you're not *laughing?*"

Alleyn turned round. His face was scarlet. He stood before her, his hands stretched out. "Lady Charles," he said, "I fully deserve that you should report me and have me turned out of the force. I've done the unforgivable thing—there's no excuse for me but I do apologize with all my heart."

"I don't want you to be turned out of any force. But why did you laugh?"

"It—I'm afraid the explanation will only add to the offence. I—you see—"

"It was at me," said Lady Charles with conviction. The strain had gone from her voice. "People do laugh at me. But what did I say? Mr. Alleyn, I insist on knowing what it was."

"It was nothing. There are some people who can't hold back a nervous laugh when they hear of somebody's death. Heaven knows a detective officer isn't one of them, but I'm afraid that if I hear anything very sinister and dramatic related with great *empressement* it sometimes has that effect on me. It was the way you described Lady Wutherwood as she followed you, muttering. I—it's no use. I'm abject."

"I suppose you're not a relation of ours by any chance," said Lady Charles thoughtfully.

"I don't think so."

"You never know. All the Lampreys laugh at disastrous pieces of news so I thought you might be. We must go into it sometime. I'm a distant Lamprey myself, you know. Nothing hygienically sinister. What was your mother's maiden name?"

"Blandish," said Alleyn helplessly.

"I must ask Charlie. Blandish. But in the meantime hadn't we better go back to poor Violet?"

"By all means."

"Not that there's very much more to say. Except that she might have done it *instead* of going to the lavatory or *while* I was in the drawing-room, although she would have to be pretty nippy to manage it then."

"Yes."

"Is that all?"

"One other question. Can you give the name of the doctor Lady Wutherwood saw before she went to the nursing home?"

"Good heavens, no! It was years ago."

"Or the nursing-home?"

"It was in Devonshire. Could it have been on Dartmoor or am I thinking of something else?"

"How did you get on, *Maman?*" asked Frid in French.

"Not so badly," answered her mother in the same tongue. "I have made him laugh, at least."

"Laugh!" Lord Charles ejaculated. "*Mon Dieu,* what at?"

"I had to work for it," said Charlot wearily. "He thinks I'm a sort of elderly *enfant terrible*. He thinks he made the most formidable gaffe in laughing at me. He apologized quite charmingly."

"I hope you didn't overdo it, Immy."

"Not I, darling. He hasn't the faintest inkling of what I was up to. Don't worry. *Soyez tranquil.*"

"*Soyez tranquil,*" wrote P. C. Martin faithfully, on the last page of his note-book and with, a sigh, took a fresh one from the pocket of his tunic.

"Blast that woman!" said Alleyn in the dining-room. "She

was determined to break me up, and, damn her, so she did. I hope she thinks she got away with it."

"You apologized very nicely, Mr. Alleyn," said Fox. "I expect she does."

"We'll have the twins, Gibson," said Alleyn.

CHAPTER **XIV**

Perjury by Roberta

"You see," said Alleyn, looking carefully at the twins, "you are not absolutely identical. In almost everybody the distance between the outer corner of the left-hand eye and the left-hand corner of the mouth is not precisely the same as the distance between the outer corner of the right-hand eye and the right-hand corner of the mouth. A line drawn through both eyes and prolonged is hardly ever parallel with a line drawn along the lips and prolonged. You get an open-angled and close-angled side to every face. That's why reflection in a looking-glass of somebody you know very well always seems distorted and queer. In both of your faces, the close-angle is on the left. But in Lord Stephen the angle is the least fraction more emphatic."

"Is this the B-B-Bertillon system?" asked Stephen. "*P-portrait parle?*"

"A version of it," said Alleyn. "Bertillon paid great attention to ears. He divided the ear into twelve major sections and noticed a great many subdivisions. Yours are not quite identical with your brother's. And then, of course, there's that mole on the back of your neck. Lady Wutherwood noticed it in the lift." He turned to Colin. "So you see you really would be rather foolish if you persisted in saying you went down in the lift. It would be a false statement and the law is not very amiable about false statements.

"Bad luck, Col," said Stephen with a shaky laugh. "You're sunk."

"I think you're trying to bamboozle us, Mr. Alleyn," Colin said. "You've got a fifty-fifty chance, after all. I don't believe Aunt V. would have noticed a carbuncle, much less a mole, on anybody's neck. She's too dotty. I stick to my statement. I can tell you exactly what happened."

"I'm sure you can," said Alleyn politely. "But do you know, I don't think we want to hear it. You both had plenty of time to put your heads together before the police arrived. I'm sure the stories would tally to a hair's-breadth, but I don't think we'll trouble you for yours. I won't ask you for a statement. I don't think we need bother you any longer. Good night."

"It's a trap," said Colin slowly. "I'm not going. You'll damn well take my statement, whether you like it or not."

"We're not allowed to set traps, I promise you, I should be setting a trap if I pretended not to know which of you worked the lift and so encouraged you to carry on with your comedy of errors."

"Do p-pipe down, Colin," said Stephen rapidly. "It's no go. I didn't want you to do it. Mr. Alleyn, you're quite right. I didn't kill Uncle G. but, on my word of honour, I t-took him down in the lift and Colin stayed in the drawing-room. Don't commit any more p-perjury, Col, for God's sake, just go b-buzz off."

The twins, white to the lips, stared at each other. It so chanced that each of them reflected the other's pose to the very slant of their narrow heads. The impression made by identical twins is always startling to strangers. It is accompanied by a sensation of shifted focus. It seems to us that the physical resemblance must be an outward sign of mental unity. It is easy to believe that twins are aware of each other's thoughts, difficult to imagine them in dissonance; and Alleyn wondered if these twins were in agreement when Colin suddenly said: "Let me stay here while you talk to Stephen, please. I'm sorry I was objectionable. I'd like to stay."

Alleyn did not answer and Colin added: "I won't butt in. I'd just be here, that's all."

"He knows everything about it," Stephen said. "I t-told him."

"If he first tells us what he did while you were in the lift," said Alleyn, "he may stay."

"Please do, Col," said Stephen. "You'll only make me look every kind of bloody skunk if you d-don't."

"All right," said Colin, slowly. "I'll explain."

"That's excellent," said Alleyn. "Suppose you both sit down."

They sat on opposite sides of the table, facing each other.

"I'd rather explain first of all," Colin began, "that it's not a new sort of stunt, our joining with the same story. It's a kind of arrangement we've always had. When we were kids we fixed it up between us. I daresay it sounds pretty feeble-minded and sort of ' "I did it, sir!" said little Eric,' but it doesn't strike us like that. It's just an arrangement. Not over everything but when there's a really major row brewing. It doesn't mean that I think Stephen bumped off Uncle G. I know he didn't. He told me he didn't. So I know."

Colin said this with an air of stolid assurance. Stephen looked at him dully. "Well, I didn't," he said.

"I know. I was only explaining."

"Later on," said Alleyn, "we'll look for something that sounds a little more like police-court evidence. In the meantime, what did you do?"

"Me?" asked Colin. "Oh, I just stayed in the drawing-room with Henry and my father."

"What did you talk about?"

"I didn't. I looked at a *Punch*."

"Henry said: 'Have they gone?' and my father said 'Yes,' and Henry said 'Three rousing cheers.' I don't think anybody said anything else until Aunt V. started yelling, and then Henry said; 'Is that a fire engine or do they ring bells?' and my father said 'It's a woman,' and Henry said: 'How revolting!' and my father said: 'It's coming from the lift,' and Henry said: 'Then it must be Aunt V. and she's coming back.' It had got a good deal nearer by then. I think Henry said 'How revolting!' again and then my father said; 'Something has happened,' and went out of the room. Henry said: 'She's gone completely crackers, it seems. Come on.' So he went out. My mother and

Frid and, I think, Patch, were on the landing and the lift was up. Stephen opened the doors and came out. He held the doors back. Aunt V. came screeching out. The rest of it's rather a muddle and I daresay you've heard it already."

"I should like to know when your brother decided to take up the option on your agreement."

"I didn't want—" Stephen began.

"Shut up," said Colin. "While they were all fussing round and ringing up doctors and policemen Stephen said: 'I'm going to be sick,' so I went with him and he was. And then we went to my room and he told me all about it. And I said that if anything cropped up like you, and so on, the arrangement would be good. Stephen said he didn't want me to crash in on the party but I did, of course, as you know. That's all."

"Thank you," said Alleyn. Colin lit a cigarette.

"I suppose I say what happened in the lift," said Stephen.

"If you will," Alleyn agreed. "From the time Lady Charles came to the drawing-room."

Stephen played a little tattoo with his fingers on the table. His movements as well as his speech, Alleyn noticed were much more staccato than his twin's. Colin had spoken with a deliberation so marked as to seem studied. He had looked placidly at Alleyn through his light eyelashes. Stephen spoke in spurts; his stutter became increasingly marked; he kept glancing at Alleyn and away again. Fox's notes seemed to disturb him.

"My mother," Stephen said, "asked for someone t-to work the lift. So I went out."

"To the lift?"

"Yes."

"Who was in the lift?"

"He was. Sitting there."

"With the doors shut?"

"Yes."

"Who opened them?"

"I did. Aunt V. was sort of hovering about on the landing. When I opened the d-doors she tacked over and floated in."

"And then? Did you follow at once?"

"Well, I stopped long enough to wink at my mother and then I got in and s-simply t-took the lift down—"

"Just a moment. What were Lord and Lady Wutherwood's positions in the lift?"

"He was sitting in the corner. His hat was on and his scarf pulled up and his c-coat collar turned up. I—th-thought he was asleep."

"Asleep? But a minute or so before, he had shouted at the top of his voice."

"Well, asleep or sulking. As a matter of fact, I rather thought he was s-sulking."

"Why should he do that?"

"He was a sulky sort of man. Aunt V. had kept him waiting."

"Did you notice his hat?"

"It was a poisonous hat."

"Anything in particular about it?"

"Only that it looked as if it belonged to a bum. As a matter of fact I couldn't see him very well. Aunt V.—Violet stood b-between us and the light wasn't on."

"Was she facing him?"

"N-no. Facing the doors."

"Right. And then?"

"Well, I p-pushed the button and we went down."

"What happened next?"

"When we'd got about half-way d-down, she started screaming. I hadn't looked at either of those two. I just heard the scream and jumped like hell and sort of automatically shoved down the stop button. So we stopped. We were nearly down. Just below the first floor."

"Yes?"

"Well, of course, I turned round. I didn't see Uncle G. She was between us, with her b-back to me, yelling in a disgusting sort of way. It was b-beastly. As sudden as a train whistle. I've always hated t-train whistles. She moved away a bit and I l-looked and s-saw him."

"What did you see?"

"You know what it was."

"Not exactly. I should like an exact description."

Stephen moistened his lips and passed his fingers across his face. "Well," he said, "he was sitting there. I remember now that there was a dent in his hat. She had hold of him and she sort of sh-shook him and he s-sort of t-tipped forward. His head was between his knees and his hat fell off. Then she pulled him up. And then I s-saw."

"What did you see? I'm sorry," said Alleyn, "but it really is important and Lady Wutherwood's description was not very clear. I want a clear picture."

"I wish," said Stephen violently, "that I hadn't got one. I c-can't—Col, tell him I c-can't—it was t-too beastly."

"Do you know," said Alleyn, "I think there's something in the theory that it's a mistake to bury a very bad experience. The Ancient Mariner's idea was a sound one. In describing something unpleasant you get rid of part of its unpleasant-ness."

"*Unp-pleasant!* My God, the skewer was jutting out of his eye and blood running down his face into his mouth. He made noises like an animal."

"Was there any other injury to his face?" Alleyn asked.

Stephen put his face in his hands. His voice was muffled. "Yes. The side of his head. Something. I saw that when—I saw it!" His fingers moved to his own temple. "There."

"Yes. What did you do?"

"I had my hand near the thing—the switchboard—you kn-know. I must have p-pushed the top b-button. I don't think I did it on purpose. I d-don't know. We went up. She was screaming. When I opened the d-doors she sort of fell out. That's all." Stephen gripped the edge of the table and for the first time looked steadily at Alleyn. "I'm sorry I'm not clearer," he said. "I don't know why I'm like this. I've been all right t-till now. I even sort of wondered why I *was* so all right."

"Shock," said Alleyn, "seems to have a period of incubation with some people. Now, as you went down in the lift you faced the switchboard?"

"Yes."

"All the time?"

"Yes."

"Did you hear any sort of movement behind you?"

"I d-don't remember hearing anything at all. It's not long, is it?"

"It's precisely thirty seconds to the bottom," said Alleyn. "You don't go all the way. Did you hear any sort of thud?"

"If I did, I don't remember it."

"All right. To go back a little. While your father interviewed Lord Wutherwood, you were all in here, lying on the carpet in that corner."

Stephen and Colin exchanged glances. Colin silently framed the word "Patch" with his lips.

"No," said Alleyn. "Lady Patricia only told us you lay on the floor. She said it was a kind of game. We noticed it took place in that corner where a door has been boarded up. There's a trace of lip-stick on the carpet close to the crack under the door and a bit of boot polish farther out. It's difficult to avoid the presumption that your game involved listening to the conversation next door."

"I say," said Stephen suddenly, "do you speak French? Yes, I suppose you do. Yes, of course you do."

"Shut up," said Colin.

"I haven't been lying on the carpet," said Alleyn. "And Mr. Fox only stayed there long enough to catch a phrase, spoken. I think, by you. *'Taisez-vous, donc!'*"

"He's always saying it," Stephen muttered gloomily. "In English or in French."

"And a fat lot of notice you take," Colin pointed out. "If you'd only—"

"We won't go into that," said Alleyn. "Now, when this unusual game was ended, and after your brother Michael had come in, you two, with your elder brother, went into the drawing-room, while your sisters went into Flat 26. Did you go together and directly into the drawing-room?"

There was a moment's silence before Colin answered: "Yes. We all went out together. The girls went first."

"Henry just had a little snoop d-down the passage."

"In which direction?"

"Towards the hall. He was only a second or two. He came into the d-drawing-room just after we did."

"And did you all stay in the drawing-room until Lady Charles came?"

"Yes," said the twins together.

"I see. That pretty well covers the ground. One more question, and I think I may put it to both of you. You'll understand that we wouldn't ask it unless we felt that it was entirely relevant. What impression did you get of Lady Wutherwood during the afternoon?"

"Mad," said the twins together.

"In the strict sense of the word?"

"Yes," said Colin. "We all thought so. Mad."

"I see," said Alleyn again. "That's all, I think. Thank you."

ii

When the twins reappeared in the drawing-room Roberta thought they had a slightly attenuated and shivery air, rather as if they had been efficiently purged by Nanny. They looked coldly at the rest of their family, walked to the sofa and collapsed on it.

"Well," said Colin after a long silence, "I see no reason why we should announce in anything but plain English the fact that the gaff is blown, the cat out of the bag, and the balloon burst."

"What do you mean!" cried Charlot. "You didn't—"

"No, Mama, we didn't tell him because he already knew," said Stephen. "I was the l-liftman. I did it with my little button."

"I told you so," Frid observed. "I told you that you'd never get away with it."

Stephen looked icily at her. "Is it possible," he said, "that any sister of mine can utter that detestable, that imbecilic phrase? Yes, Frid, dear, you told us so."

"But, Stephen," said Charlot in a voice so unlike her own that Roberta wondered for a second who had spoken, "Stephen, he doesn't think—you—*Stephen?*"

"It's all right, Mum," said Colin. "I don't see how he could."

"Of course not," said Lord Charles loudly. "My dear girl, you're so upset and tired you don't know what you're saying. The police are not fools, Immy. You've nothing to upset yourself about. Go to bed, my dear." And he added, without great conviction, an ancient phrase of comfort. "Things will seem better in the morning," said Lord Charles.

"How can they?" asked Charlot.

"My darling heart, of course they will. We're in for a very disagreeable time no doubt. Somebody has killed Gabriel and, although it's all perfectly beastly, we naturally hope that the police will find his murderer. It's a horrible business, God knows, but there's no need for us to go adding to its horror by imagining all sorts of fantastic developments." He touched his moustache. "My dear," he said, "to suppose that the boys are in any sort of danger is quite monstrous; it is to insult them, Immy. Innocent people are in no kind of danger in these cases."

Frid looked towards the far end of the room, where the constable's red head showed over the back of his chair. "Do you agree to all that?" she said loudly. The constable, slightly startled, got to his feet.

"I beg your pardon, Miss?"

"It would be grand," Frid said, "if we knew your name."

"Martin, Miss."

"Oh. Well, Mr. Martin, I asked if you would say innocent people are as safe as houses, no matter how fishy things may look?"

"Yes, Miss," said the constable.

"My good ass," said Henry, glaring at Frid, "who looks fishy?"

"Henry, don't speak like that to Frid."

"I'm sorry, Mama, but *honestly!* Frid is."

"I'm *not*," said Frid. "We all look fishy. Don't we?" she demanded of the constable. "Don't we look as fishy as Billingsgate?"

"I couldn't say, Miss," said the constable uneasily, and Roberta suddenly felt extremely sorry for him.

"That will do, Frid," said Lord Charles. Roberta had not imagined his voice could carry so sharp an edge. Frid crossed the room stagily and sat on the arm of her mother's chair.

There was a tap at the door and the constable, with an air of profound relief, answered it. The usual muttered colloquy followed, but it was punctuated by a loud interruption outside. "It's perfectly all right," said a cheerful voice in the hall. "Mr. Alleyn knows all about it and Lady Lamprey expects me. If you don't believe me, toddle along and ask."

"It's Nigel!" cried the Lampreys and Frid shouted: "Nigel! Come in, my angel! We're all locked up but Mr. Alleyn said you could come."

"Hul*lo*, my dear!" answered the voice. "I know. I'll be there in a jiffy. They're just asking—oh, thanks. Tell him I'll come and see him later on, will you? Where are we? Thanks."

The constable admitted a robust young man who, to Roberta's colonial eyes, instantly recalled the fashionable illustrated papers, so compactly did his clothes fit him, and so efficiently barbered and finished did he seem, with his hair drilled back from his reddish face, his brushed-up moustaches, and his air of social efficiency. He came in with a lunging movement, smoothing the back of his head and grinning engagingly, and rather anxiously, at the Lampreys.

"Nigel, my dear," cried Charlot, "we're so *delighted* to see you. Did you think it *too* queer of Frid to ring up? Everyone else did."

"I thought it marvellous of Frid," said Nigel Bathgate. "Hullo, Charles, I'm terribly sorry about whatever it all is."

"Damnable, isn't it," said Lord Charles gently. "Sit down. Have a drink."

"Robin," said Henry, "You haven't met Nigel, have you? Mr. Bathgate, Miss Grey."

Roberta, while she shook hands, had time to be pleased because Henry did not seem to forget she was there. As soon as Henry remembered Roberta, so did all the other Lampreys.

"Poor Robin," said Charlot, "she's just this *second* arrived from the remotest antipodes to be hurled into a family homicide. Do get your drink quickly, Nigel, and listen to our frightful story. We're so dreadfully worried, but we thought that if we were having a *cause celebre* you might as well get in first."

"And perhaps stave off the press-men," added Frid. "You will, won't you, Nigel? It really is a scoop for you."

"But *what* is?" asked Nigel Bathgate. "I only got your message ten minutes ago and of course I came round at once. Why are Alleyn and his merry-men all over the place? What's occurred?"

The Lampreys embarked on a simultaneous narrative. Roberta was greatly impressed by the adroit manner in which Nigel Bathgate managed to disentangle cold facts from a welter of Lampreysian embroideries. His round red face grew more and more solemn as the story unfolded. He looked in dismay from one to another of the Lampreys and finally, with a significant grimace, jerked his head in the direction of the constable.

"Oh, we've given up bothering about him," said Frid. "At first we talked French but really there's nothing left to conceal. Aunt Kit told Mr. Alleyn about the financial crisis and Daddy had to come clean about the bum."

"*What?*"

"My dear Nigel," said Lord Charles, "there's a man in possession. Could anything look worse?"

"And as for the twins," said Frid, "your boy friend turned them inside out and hung them up to dry."

"And I m-may t-tell you, Frid," said Stephen, "that he knows just what we did in the dining-room. You would wipe your painted mouth on the carpet, wouldn't you?"

"Good Lord!" Henry ejaculated, and he threw two cushions down in front of the sealed door. "Why the devil didn't we think of that before?"

"Oh," said Stephen, "he says he didn't bother to listen. I suppose we all give ourselves away t-too freely for it to be necessary."

"But what *is* all this?" demanded Lord Charles. "What did you do in the dining-room?"

Rather self-consciously, his children told him.

"Not very pretty," said Lord Charles. "What can he think of you?"

There was a short silence. "Not much, I daresay," said Henry at last.

"You had better..." Lord Charles made a small despairing gesture and turned away. Frid spoke rapidly in French. Roberta thought she said that they had not been asked to give an account of the interview.

"But no doubt," said Colin, "anything that we haven't told him has been madly divulged by Aunt V. So why be guarded?"

"But," Nigel interrupted firmly, "where is your Aunt Violet? Where is Lady Wutherwood?"

"Asleep in my bed," said Charlot, "with a nurse on one side of it and her maid, who is determined not to leave her, on the other. So where Charlie and I are to spend the night is a secret. We don't know. We've also got to bed down somewhere a chauffeur called Giggle, in addition to Mr. Grumball."

"Yes, but look here, this is really serious," Nigel began.

"Well, of course it is, Nigel. We know it's serious. We're all shaken to our foundations," said Frid. "That's partly why we asked you to come."

"Yes, but you don't *sound*..." Nigel began and then caught sight of Charlot's face. "Oh, my dear," he said, "I'm so terribly sorry. But you needn't worry. Alleyn—"

"Nigel," said Charlot, "what's he like? You've so often talked about your friend and we've always thought it would be such fun to meet him. Little did we know how it would come about. Here I've been, sitting in my own dining-room, trying to sort of *see* into him, do you know? I thought I'd got the interview going just my way. And now, when I think it over, I'm not so sure."

"My dear Imogen," said Nigel, "I know you're a genius for diplomacy but honestly, with Alleyn, if I were you, I wouldn't."

"He laughed at me," said Charlot defensively.

"Are you certain, Mummy," said Frid, "that it wasn't sinister laughter? 'Heh-heh-heh'?"

"It wasn't in the least sinister. He giggled."

"I wish he'd send for me," Frid muttered.

"I suppose you think," Henry began, "that you're going to have a fat dramatic scene, ending in Alleyn throwing up the case because you're *trop troublante*. My dear girl, your histrionic antics—"

"I shan't go in for any histrionic antics, darling. I shall just be very still and dignified and rather pale and very lovely."

"Well, if Alleyn isn't sick, he's got a stronger stomach than I have."

Frid laughed musically. The constable answered a tap on the door.

"This is my entrance cue," said Frid. "What do you bet?"

"It may be your father or Henry," said Charlot.

"Inspector Alleyn," said the constable, "would be glad if Miss Grey would speak to him."

iii

Roberta followed a second constable down the passage to the dining-room door. Her heart thudded disturbingly. She felt that she wanted to yawn. Her mouth was dry and she wondered if, when she spoke, her voice would be cracked. The constable opened the dining-room door, went in, and said: "Miss Grey, sir."

Roberta, feeling her lack of inches, walked into the dining-room.

Alleyn and Fox had risen. The constable pulled out a chair at the end of the table. Through a thick mental haze, Roberta became aware of Alleyn's deep and pleasant voice. "I'm so sorry to worry you, Miss Grey. It's such bad luck that you should find yourself landed in such a disagreeable affair. Do sit down."

"Thank you," said Roberta in a small voice.

"You only arrived yesterday, didn't you?"

"Yes."

"From New Zealand. That's a long journey. What part of New Zealand do you come from?"

"The South Island. South Canterbury."

"Then you know the McKenzie Country?"

The scent of sun-baked tussock, of wind from the tops of snow mountains, and the memory of an intense blue, visited Roberta's transplanted heart. "Have you been there?" she asked.

"I was there four years ago."

"In the McKenzie Country? Tekapo? Pukaki?"

"The sound of the names makes the places vivid again." He spoke for a little while of his visit and like all colonials Roberta rose to the bait. Her nervousness faded and soon she found herself describing the New Zealand Deepacres, how it stood at the foot of Little Mount Silver, how English trees grew into the fringes of native bush, and how English birdsong, there, was pierced by the colder and deeper notes of bell-birds and mok-e-moks.

"That was Lord Charles's station?"

"Oh yes. Not ours. We only lived in a small house in a small town. But you see I was so much at Deepacres."

"It must have been rather a wrench for them, leaving such a place."

"Not really," said Roberta. "It was only a New Zealand adventure for them. A kind of interlude. They belong here."

"Did Lord Charles like farming?"

Roberta had never even thought of Lord Charles as being a farmer. He had merely been at Deepacres. She found it difficult to answer the question. Had he enjoyed himself in New Zealand? It was impossible to say, and she replied confusedly that they had all seemed quite happy, but of course they were glad to be home again.

"They are a very united family?"

Roberta could see no harm in speaking of the Lampreys' attachment to each other, and she quite lost her apprehensions in the development of this favourite theme. It was easy to relate how kind the Lampreys had been to her; how, although they argued incessantly, they were happiest when they were together, how she believed they would always come to each other's aid.

"We had an example of that," Alleyn agreed, "in the present stand made by the twins."

Roberta caught her breath and looked at him. His eyes, with their turned-down corners, seemed to express only sympathetic amusement, as though he invited her to laugh a little with him at the twins.

"But they have always been like that," cried Roberta. "Even at Deepacres when Colin took the big car . . ." and she was off again, all her anecdotes of the Lampreys tending to show their devotion to each other. Alleyn listened as though everything Roberta said amused and interested him, and she had ridden her hobby-horse down a long road before she stopped suddenly, feeling herself blush with embarrassment.

"I'm sorry," she stammered, "I'm talking too much."

"Indeed you're not. You're giving me a delightful picture. But I suppose we must get down to hard facts. I just want to check your own movements. You were in here from the time Lord Charles had his interview with his brother right up to the discovery of the accident. That right?"

"Yes." Roberta had sorted this out carefully and gave him a clear account of her talk with Michael and her final move to the landing.

"That's grand," said Alleyn. "Crisp and plain. There are two points I want to check very carefully. . . . The times when Lord Wutherwood shouted. You tell me that when he first called you were all in here."

"Yes. Including Mike. He had just come in. But the others went out a second or two after he called out."

"And the second time?"

"Mike went away with Giggle. A very short time after that Lord Wutherwood called out the second time."

"You're quite certain?"

"Yes, quite. Because it was so quiet in the room when they had gone. I remember that, after he had called again, I heard the sound of the lift. Then I heard some one call out in the street below and the voices next door in the drawing-room. It's all very clear. I heard the lift again just as I took a cigarette out of that box. After that, I remember I walked about hunting for matches. I'd just lit my cigarette and was leaning out over the window still looking at London when I heard her—Lady

Wutherwood. It was awful, that screaming."

"I want you to go through that again if you will."

Roberta went through it again and, greatly to her astonishment, again. Alleyn read over his notes to her and she agreed that they were correct and signed them. He was silent for a moment and then returned to the subject of the family.

"Do you find them much changed now you have seen them again?" he asked.

"Not really. At first they seemed rather fashionable and grown-up but that was only for a little while. They are just the same."

"They haven't grown up as far as their pockets are concerned," Alleyn said lightly. But Roberta was ready for this and said that the Lampreys didn't worry about money, that it meant nothing to them. With a sensation of peril she carried her theme a little further. They would never, she said, do anything desperate to get money.

"But if they are faced with bankruptcy?"

"Something always happens to save them. They know they will fall on their feet. They *seem* desperately worried and inside themselves they continually forget to be worried." And seeing that he listened attentively to her, she went on quickly: "Even now this has happened they are not remembering all the time to be alarmed. They know they are all right."

"All of them?"

Roberta said truthfully: "Perhaps not . . . Charlot—Lady Charles. She is frightened because Colin pretended he was in the lift and she wonders if that may make you think Stephen is hiding something. But I am sure, inside herself, she knows it will be all right." Roberta was silent and perhaps she smiled a little to herself for Alleyn said: "Of what were you thinking, Miss Grey?"

"I was thinking that they are like children. You can see them remembering to be solemn about all that has happened and then for a time they are quite frightened. But in a minute or two one of them will think of something amusing to say and will say it."

"Does Lord Charles do this?"

A cold sensation of panic visited Roberta. Was it, after all, Lord Charles whom they suspected? Again it seemed to her that it was impossible to guess at Lord Charles's thoughts. He was always politely remote, a background to his family. She discovered that she had no understanding of his reaction to his brother's murder. She said that of course it was more of a tragedy for him. Lord Wutherwood had been his only brother. She regretted this immediately, anticipating Alleyn's next question.

"Were they much attached to each other?"

"They didn't meet often," Roberta said and knew that she had blundered. Alleyn did not press this point but asked her what she had thought of Lord Wutherwood. She said quickly that she had seen him for the first time that afternoon.

"May we have your first impression?" Alleyn asked. But Roberta was nervous now and racked her brains for generalities. Lord Wutherwood, she said, was not very noticeable. He was rather quiet and colourless. There had been so many people she hadn't paid any particular attention . . . She broke off, disturbed by Alleyn's gently incredulous glance.

"But it seems to me," he said, "that you are a good observer."

"Only of people who interest me."

"And Lord Wutherwood did not interest you?" Roberta did not speak, remembering that she had watched both the Wutherwoods with an interest inspired by the object of their visit. A vivid picture of that complaisant yet huffy face rose before her imagination. She saw again the buck teeth, the eyes set too close to the thin nose, the look of speculative disapproval. She couldn't quite force herself to deny this picture. Alleyn waited for a moment and then as she remained stubbornly silent he said: "and what about Lady Wutherwood?"

"You couldn't *not* notice her," Roberta said quickly. "She was so very odd."

"In what way?"

"But you've seen her."

"Since her husband was murdered, remember."

"There's not all that difference," said Roberta bluntly.

Alleyn looked steadily at her. Under cover of the table Roberta clasped her hands together. What next?

Alleyn said: "Did you join the reconnaissance party, Miss Grey?"

"The—I don't understand."

"Perhaps reconnaissance is not quite the word. Did you listen with the others to the conversation next door?"

208

It hadn't seemed such an awful thing to do at the time, Roberta told herself wildly. The Lampreys had assured her that Lord Charles wouldn't mind. In a way it had been rather fun. Why, oh why, should it show so shabbily, now that this man asked her about it? Lying on the floor with her ears to the door! Spying! Her cheeks were burning coals. She would not unclasp her hands. She would sit there, burning before him, not lowering her gaze.

"Yes," said Roberta clearly, "I did."

"Will you tell me what you heard?"

"No. I'd rather not do that."

"We'll have to see if any of the servants were about," said Alleyn thoughtfully. A hot blast of fury and shame prevented Roberta from understanding that he was not deliberately insulting her, deliberately suggesting that she had behaved like an untrustworthy housemaid. And she could say nothing to justify herself. She heard her own voice stammering out words that meant nothing. In a nightmare of shame she looked at her own indignity. "It wasn't like that—we were together— we weren't doing it like that—it was because we were anxious to know . . ." The unfamiliar voice whined shamefully on until out of the fog of her own discomfiture she saw Alleyn looking at her with astonishment, and she was able to be silent.

"Here, I say, hi!" said Alleyn. "What's all this about?" Roberta, on the verge of tears, stared at the opposite wall. She felt rather than saw him get up and come round the table towards her. Now he stood above her. In her misery she noticed that he smelt pleasantly. Something like a new book in a good binding, said her brain, which seemed to be thinking frantically in several directions. She would not, *she would not* cry in front of these men.

"I'm so sorry," the deep voice was saying. "I see. Look here, Miss Grey, I wasn't hurling insults at you. Really. I mean it would have been perfectly outrageous if I had suggest-ed . . ." He broke off. His air of helplessness steadied Roberta. She looked up at him. His face was twisted into a singular grimace. His left eyebrow had climbed half-way up his forehead. His mouth was screwed to one side as if a twinge of toothache bothered him. "Oh damn!" he said.

"It's all right," said Roberta, "but you made it sound so *low*. I suppose it was really."

"We're all low at times," said Alleyn comfortably. "I can

see why you wanted to hear the interview. A good deal depended on it. Lord Charles asked his brother to get him out of this financial box, didn't he?"

Desperate speculations as to the amount of information he had already collected joggled about in Roberta's brain. If he knew positively the gist of the interview she would do harm in denying Lord Charles's appeal. If he didn't know he might yet find out. And what had Lady Katherine told him?

She said: "I may have listened at door cracks but at least I can hold my tongue about what I heard." And even that sounded bad. If Alleyn had been mistaken, of course she would have said so. "He knows," she thought desperately. "He knows."

"You will understand," Alleyn said, "that from our point of view this discussion between the brothers is important. You see we know why Lord Wutherwood came here. We know what it was hoped would be the result of the interview. I think you would all have been only too ready to tell us if Lord Wutherwood had agreed to help his brother."

What would Henry and Lord Charles tell him? They had spoken about it in French. She had caught enough of the conversation to realize what they were talking about. What had the twins told him? Had they agreed to lie about it? Why not? Why not, since Uncle G. was dead and could not give them away? But Alleyn could not have asked the twins about the interview or they would have said so on their return. So it was up to her. The word perjury was caught up in her thoughts with a dim notion of punishment. But she could do them no harm. Only herself, because she lied to the police in the execution of their duty. That wasn't right. Lying statement. False statement. She must speak now. *Now*. With conviction. She seemed to hover for eternity on the edge of utterance and when her voice did come it was without any conscious order from her brain.

"But," said Roberta's voice, "didn't they tell you? Lord Wutherwood promised to help his brother."

"Do you speak French, Miss Grey?" asked Alleyn.

"No," said Roberta.

Back in the drawing-room Roberta returned to her fireside seat. The Lampreys watched her with guarded inquisitiveness.

"Well, Robin," said Henry, "I trust your little spot of inquisition passed off quietly."

"Oh yes," said Roberta. "Mr. Alleyn just wanted to know where I was and all that." And nerving herself, she said: "You know, my dears, I've been thinking you must be very glad he was so generous after all. It'll be nice to remember that, won't it?"

There was a dead silence. Roberta looked into Lord Charles's eyes and then into Henry's. "Won't it?" she repeated.

"Yes," said Henry after a long pause. "It'll be nice to remember that."

CHAPTER XV

Entrance of Mr. Bathgate

"Courageous little liar," said Alleyn, "isn't she?"

"I suppose so," said Fox.

"Of course she is, Br'er Fox. Do you imagine if it were true they wouldn't have been out with the whole story as soon as we mentioned the interview? They've shied away like hell whenever we got near it. She's a good, plucked 'un is the little New Zealander. She can't understand French and unless they managed to slip her a message she's decided to lie like hell and take the consequences. If Martin isn't careful she'll manage to warn Master Henry and his father. Let's see what the bilingual Martin has to say in his notes. Yes. Here we are. Have a look."

Fox eyed the notes. "I'd have to get it out in longhand," he said. "May I trouble you to translate, Mr. Alleyn?"

"You may, Foxkin. They seem to have discussed the twins' proposition and got no further. Here Lady Charles cut in and said: 'It's very necessary that we should come to some decision about Gabriel and the money.' That devilish girl seems to have chipped in with a remark to the effect that what we didn't know wouldn't hurt us."

"Lady Friede, sir?"

"The same. Master Henry said that only their father knew what had happened at the interview. I catch the warning note here, Foxkin. He was instructing his brothers and sisters to forget they had overheard the interview. It's evident that Lord Charles didn't know they had listened."

"What did his lordship say?"

"His lordship is cryptic. He doesn't say much. Here's a stray observation. *'Par rapport a Tante Kit.'* Oh! He says: Considering what Aunt Kit has probably told us, we're not likely to suppose they were out of the financial wood. Very true. Lady Charles asks what Gabriel said at the interview and Lord Charles replies that he thinks it will be better if his family can truthfully say it doesn't know. I imagine an awkward silence among members of the carpet party. By this time, no doubt, the twins will have told their parents all they seem to have said about the interview between the brothers. You'd better have another go at the servants, Br'er Fox."

"I don't think the butler would give anything away, sir. He's a quiet old chap and seems to like the family. If that parlour-maid overheard anything, she might be persuaded to speak up."

"Go and have a word with her. Use your charm. And in the meantime, Fox, I'll deal with Master Henry."

So Fox went off to the kitchen and the constable fetched Henry. Alleyn came straight to the point with Henry, asking him whether his uncle had promised to lend his father a sum of money. Henry instantly said that he had.

"So the financial crisis was over?"

"Yes."

"Why did none of you tell me of this before?"

"Why should we?" asked Henry coolly. "It didn't arise."

"The question of the guilt or innocence of every single one of you arises," said Alleyn. "As you no doubt realize, Lady Katherine has told us of your financial difficulties. Lord Charles has told us that there is a bailiff in the flat. People do not murder a man who is on the point of rescuing them from bankruptcy."

"Well," said Henry, "we didn't murder Uncle G."

"Who, in your opinion, did murder him?"

"I've no opinion about it."

"You don't share your mother's conviction of Lady Wutherwood's homicidal insanity?"

"Does my mother feel convinced about that?"

"She told me so." Henry said nothing. "In plain words," said Alleyn, "do you think Lady Wutherwood is insane and killed her husband?"

"I don't see how one can possibly know," said Henry slowly. "I think she's mad."

"That's an honest speech," said Alleyn unexpectedly. Henry looked up, quickly. "I think she's mad, too," Alleyn said, "but like you I don't know if she killed her husband. I wonder if we hesitate for the same reason. It seems strange to me that a woman who murdered her husband should demand his body."

"I know," said Henry quickly, "but if she's mad—"

"There's always that, of course. But to me it doesn't quite fit. Nor to you, I think?"

"To me," said Henry impatiently, "nothing fits. The whole thing's a nightmare. I know none of us did it and that's all I do know. I can't think either of their servants are murderers. Giggle's been with them since he was a kid. He's a mild, stupid man and plays trains with Mike. Tinkerton is objectionable on the general grounds that she's got a face like a dead flounder and smells of hair combings. Perhaps *she* killed him."

"We'd get on a good deal faster, of course," Alleyn murmured, "if everybody spoke the flat truth."

"Really? Don't you think we're telling the truth?"

"Hardly any of you except your brother Michael. Of course we have to be polite and make sympathetic, gullible noises but when all's said and done it's little but a hollow mockery. You'll give yourselves away in time, and that's the best we can hope for."

"Do you often talk like this to your suspects? It seems very un-Yardlike to me," said Henry lightly.

"We vary our tune a bit. Why didn't you go straight to the drawing-room with your brothers?"

Henry jumped, seemed to pull himself together, and said: "I didn't at first see what you meant. Hustling tactics, I perceive. I went to the hall door to see if they'd gone."

"Anybody in the hall?" Henry shook his head. "Or the landing?"

"No."

"Or the passage?"

"No."

"How long were you about it?"

"Not long enough to find a meat skewer and kill my uncle."

"Where was the meat skewer?"

"*I* don't know," said Henry. "We had it in our charade. I suppose it was either in—"

"Yes?"

"It must have been in the hall with all the other stuff."

"You were going to say in the drawing-room or in the hall?"

"Was I?" said Henry.

"Well," said Alleyn amiably, "I'm only asking. Were you?"

"Yes, but I stopped because I realized it couldn't have been in the drawing-room. If any one had taken it from there we should have seen them."

"I see by my notes," said Alleyn, "that Lord Charles was alone in the drawing-room for some time."

"Then," said Henry stolidly, "he would have seen anybody who came in and took the skewer."

"Did you happen to look at the hall table on this visit?"

"Yes, I did. I looked to see if his hat and coat were gone. Of course they were. He was in the lift, I suppose, by then."

Alleyn clasped his hands together on the table and seemed to contemplate them. Then he raised his head and looked at Henry. "Can you remember seeing anything on the table?"

"I remember very well that there was nothing on it but a vase of flowers."

"Nothing? You are positive?"

"Quite. I remember the look of the table very clearly. It reflected the light from the window. Some one must have given the vase a knock because there was some water lying on the table. It's rather a favourite of my father's and I remember thinking that the water ought to be mopped up. I gave it a wipe with my handkerchief, but it wasn't very successful. I didn't do anything more about it. I was afraid that Aunt V. might come out of cover and I'd had a bellyful of Aunt V. I went into the drawing-room. But there was nothing on the table."

"Would you swear to that? I mean, take a legal oath?"

"Yes," said Henry, "I would."

"What did you talk about when you went into the drawing-room?"

For the first time during the interview Henry seemed to be disconcerted. His eyes went blank. He repeated: "Talk about?" on a note that held an overtone of helplessness.

"Yes. What did you say to your father and your brothers or they to you?"

"I don't remember. I—oh, yes, I asked if the Gabriels had gone."

"Anything else?"

"No. I don't think anybody said anything."

"And yet," said Alleyn, "you must have all been feeling most elated."

"We—yes. Yes, of course, we were."

"Everything all right again. Lord Wutherwood had promised to see you out of the wood. Crisis averted."

"Yes. Oh, rather. It was wonderful," said Henry.

"And yet you all sat there saying nothing except to ask if the benefactor was out of the way. Your younger sister tells me that she and Lady Friede, who went into Flat 26 at this stage of the proceedings, also had nothing to say. A curious reaction."

"Perhaps our hearts," said Henry, recovering his poise, "were too full for words."

"Perhaps they were," said Alleyn. "I think that's all. Thank you so much."

Looking rather startled, Henry got up and moved to the door. Here he paused and after a moment's hesitation returned to Alleyn.

"We didn't do it, sir," he said. "Honestly. None of us. We are not at all a homicidal family."

"I'm glad of that," said Alleyn tranquilly.

Henry stared at him and then shrugged his shoulders. "Not an impressive effort on my part, I see," he said.

"Have you been honest with us?"

Henry didn't answer. His face was quite colourless. "Well, good night," he said and, on some obscure impulse, held out his hand.

ii

Fox had not returned. Alleyn looked at his watch. Almost midnight. They'd done not so badly in four hours. He added another column to a tabulated record of everybody's movements from the time of Lord Wutherwood's first yell up to the return of the lift. P. C. Gibson, at the door, coughed.

"All right," said Alleyn without looking up. "We'll get going again in a moment. Been following the statements?"

"Yes, sir."

"And what do you think about it?" asked Alleyn, scowling at his notes.

"Well, sir, I seem to think there's a good deal in the old lady myself."

"Yes, Gibson, and so will everybody else. But why, why, why does she want the body? Can you tell me that, Gibson?"

"Because she's mad, sir?" Gibson ventured.

"It won't cover everything. She screamed the roof off when the injury was discovered. She wouldn't go and see him when he was dying. If she killed him why, mad or sane, should she want to take him home? The funeral could have been arranged to leave from the house with all the trappings and the suits of woe, if that's what she's after. It may be, and yet—and yet—it doesn't seem to me like the inconsistency of a *homicidal* lunatic, but lord knows I'm no alienist. I don't think I've got the dowager right, somehow, and that's a fact. All right, Gibson. My compliments to his lordship and I'd be glad if he'd see me. The others may go to bed, of course."

"Yes, sir. Martin asked me to mention, sir, that Mr. Bathgate has arrived and is with the family. He's been asking if he could see you."

"So they did ring him up," Alleyn muttered. "Incredible! I'd better see him now, Gibson, before you give the message to Lord Charles."

"Very good, sir."

Nigel lost no time in making his appearance. Alleyn heard him hurrying along the passage and in a moment he burst into the dining-room.

"Look here, Alleyn," Nigel cried, "I've got to talk to you."

"Talk away," said Alleyn, "but not at the top of your voice and not, if you've any mercy, at great length. I'm on duty."

"I can't help it if . . ." Nigel broke off and looked at Gibson. "It's—I'd like to see you alone."

Alleyn nodded good-humouredly at Gibson, who went out.

"Now what is it?" Alleyn asked. "Have you come to tell me I mustn't speak to your friends as if there's been a murder in their flat?"

"I've come to tell you it's utterly out of the question that any

218

of them should be implicated. I've come to save them, if possible, from opening their mouths and putting their feet in them. See here, Alleyn, I've known the Lampreys all my life. Known them well. They're as mad as May flies but there's not a vicious impulse in the make-up of a single one of them. Oh hell, I'm not going about this in the right way! I got such a damned jolt when they told me what was up that I'm all anyhow. Let me explain the Lampreys."

"Two of their friends have already explained them, this evening," said Alleyn. "Their descriptions tallied fairly well. Boiled down to a few unsympathetic adjectives they came to this: 'Charming. Irresponsible. Unscrupulous about money. Good-natured. Lazy. Amusing. Enormously popular.' Do you agree?"

"Nobody knows better than you," said Nigel, "that people can *not* be boiled down into a few adjectives."

"I entirely agree. So what do you suggest we do about it?"

"If I could make you understand the Lampreys! God knows what they've been saying to you! I can see that in spite of the shock it's given them they're beginning to look at this business as a sort of macabre parlour game with themselves on one side and you on the other. They're hopeless. They'll try to diddle you merely to see if they can get away with it. Can you understand that?"

"No," Alleyn said. "If they're making false statements for the sheer fun of the thing, I've completely misjudged them."

"But, Alleyn—"

"See here, Bathgate, you'd much better stay out of this. We had the same difficulty when we first met. The Frantock case is almost seven years old now, isn't it? Do you remember how hot you were about our work over that case? Because the people involved were friends of yours? It's the same thing over again. My dear old Bathgate, it's only fun being friends with a policeman when you're not also friends with his suspects."

"Then," said Nigel turning very pale, "do you suspect one of them?"

"They were in the flat, together with some eight other persons of whom there are also possible murderers. We've only been four hours on the damned case and haven't had much of a chance to thin out names. I tell you quite honestly, we've only got the faintest glimmering so far."

"I'd risk everything I've got in the world on the Lampreys being out of it."

"Would you? Then you've nothing to worry about."

"I know. But I'm so deadly afraid of what they may take it into their heads to say. They're such lunatics."

"So far, beyond a few superficial flourishes they haven't behaved like lunatics. They've behaved with an air of irresponsibility, but considering that they're working under police supervision they've managed to keep their misrepresentations pretty consistent. They've displayed a surprising virtuosity. They're nobody's fools."

"Alleyn," said Nigel, "will you let me stand by? I'm not pretending I'm any good at this sort of thing. 'Oh God, you're only Watson' is my cry. But I—I would like to—to sort of look out for the Lampreys."

"I don't think I'd advise you to do it. I tell you we don't know—"

"And I tell you I'm prepared to risk it. I'm only asking to do what I've so often done before. I'll cover the case for my paper. They've actually given me carte blanche for that. Did you ever hear of such a thing? Frid said it was a nice scoop for me. And so, of course, it is," added Nigel honestly. "Better me than one of the others, after all."

"You may stay if you think it advisable, of course. But suppose that as things fall out we find ourselves being drawn to—"

"I know what you're going to say and I'm convinced it's entirely out of the question."

"Then you're in?"

"I'm in."

"All right," said Alleyn. "Gibson!" The door opened. "I'm ready for Lord Charles, if he can come."

iii

Alleyn had grown accustomed to Lord Charles's walk. It recalled vividly a year out of his own past. From 1919 to 1920 Alleyn's youthful and speculative gaze had followed tail-coated figures hurrying with discretion through the labyrinths of diplomatic corridors. These figures had moved with the very gait of Lord Charles Lamprey and Alleyn wondered if at any time he had been among them. He came into the dining-room with this well-remembered air, taking out his eye-glass as he moved to the table. There was a kind of amateurish gravity about him, linked to an expression of guarded courtesy. He was one of those blond men at whose age it is difficult to guess. Somewhere, Alleyn thought, between forty-five and fifty.

"You will be glad to hear, sir," said Alleyn, "that we have nearly finished for to-night."

"Oh yes," said Lord Charles. "Splendid. Hullo, Nigel. Still with us? That's good."

"He's asked for an unofficial watching-brief," Alleyn explained. "Subject, of course, to your approval."

"Do you mind, Charles?" asked Nigel. "As you know, I'm Alleyn's Watson. Of course, you'll tell me if you'd rather I made myself scarce."

"No, no," said Lord Charles, "do stay. It was our suggestion. I'm afraid, Alleyn, that by this time you must have decided that we are a fantastically unconventional family."

The old story, thought Alleyn. It seemed to him that the Lampreys showed great industry in underlining their eccentricity.

He said: "I think it was a very sensible suggestion, sir. Bathgate is remarkably well equipped as a liaison officer between the press, yourselves, and the police." This remark met with a silence. Nigel fidgeted and Lord Charles looked blank. Alleyn said: "As far as your own movements are concerned we've got a complete statement. You didn't leave the drawing-room from the time Lord Wutherwood arrived until the lift returned after the injury was inflicted?"

"No. I was there all the time."

"Yes. Well, now, I think I must ask you for some account of your conversation with Lord Wutherwood after the others left you alone together."

Lord Charles rested his right arm on the table, letting his hand hang from the wrist. His left hand was thrust into his trousers pocket. He looked a little as though he sat for a modish portrait. "Well, Alleyn," he began, "from what my Aunt Kit tells me and from what I have already told you and Mr. Fox, I expect you will have guessed why my brother called to-day. I was in a desperate financial case and I appealed to my brother for help. This was the subject of our conversation. My appalling children tell me they overheard us. No doubt they have given you a highly coloured account."

"I should like to have your own account, sir."

"Would you? Well, I told Gabriel how things were and he—ah—he read me a pretty stiff lecture. I fully deserved it. I don't know how it is but I have never been able to manage very well. I think I may plead that I've had extraordinarily bad luck. A little while ago things seemed to be most promising. I ventured into business with a very able partner but unfortunately, poor fellow, he became mentally deranged and—ah—was foolish enough to shoot himself."

"Sir David Stein?"

"Yes, it was," said Lord Charles, opening his eyes very wide. "Did you know him?"

"I remember the case, sir."

"Oh. Ah yes, I suppose you would. Very sad and, for me, quite disastrous."

"You explained all this to Lord Wutherwood?"

"Oh, yes. And of course he scolded away about it. Indeed, we quite blazed at each other. It's always been like that. Gabriel would give me hell and we would both get rather angry with each other and then, poor old boy, he would come to the rescue."

"Did he come to the rescue this time?"

"He didn't write a cheque there and then," said Lord Charles. "That was not his way, you know. I expect he wanted me to have a night to think over my wigging and feel properly ashamed of myself."

"Did he promise to do so?" There was a fraction of a pause.

"Yes," said Lord Charles.

Alleyn's pencil whispered across his note-book. He turned a page, flattened it, and looked up. Neither Lord Charles nor Nigel had stirred but now Nigel cleared his throat and took out a cigarette case.

"He promised," said Alleyn, "quite definitely, in so many words, to pay up your debts?"

"Not exactly in so many words. He muttered that he supposed he would have to see me through as usual, that—ah—that I would hear from him."

"Yes. Lord Charles, your children, as you evidently have heard, lay in the corner there and listened to the conversation. Suppose I told you they had not heard this promise of your brother's, what would you say?"

"I shouldn't be in the least surprised. They could not possibly have heard it. Gabriel had walked to the far end of the room and I had followed him. I only just heard it myself. He—ah—he mumbled it out as if he was half ashamed."

"Then suppose, alternatively, that I tell you they state they did hear him promise to help you, would you say that they were not speaking the truth?"

"Somebody once told me," said Lord Charles, "that detective officers were not allowed to set traps for their witnesses."

"They are not allowed to hold out veiled promises and expose them to implied threats," said Alleyn. "It is not quite the same thing, sir. I'm sure you know that you may leave any question unanswered if you think it advisable to do so."

"I can only repeat," said Lord Charles breathlessly, "that he promised to help me and that I think it unlikely that they could have heard him."

"Yes," said Alleyn, writing.

Nigel leant across the table, offering his cigarettes to Lord Charles. Lord Charles had not changed his modish attitude. He looked perfectly at his ease, perfectly aware of his surroundings, and yet he did not notice Nigel's gesture. There was something odd in this unexpected revelation of his detachment. Nigel touched his sleeve with the cigarette case. He started, moved his arm sharply and, with a murmured apology, took a cigarette.

"I really don't think there's very much else," said Alleyn. "There's a small point about the arrival of your three elder sons after Lord Wutherwood left. In what order did they come into the drawing-room?"

"The twins came in first. Henry appeared a moment or two later."

"How long, should you say, sir? A minute? Two minutes?"

"I shouldn't think longer than two minutes. I don't think any one had spoken before he came in."

"You didn't at once tell them that Lord Wutherwood had promised to see you out of the wood?"

"I didn't, no. I was still rather chastened, you see, by my scolding."

"Oh, yes," said Alleyn politely. "Of course. That really is all, I think, sir. I'm so sorry but I'm afraid I shall have to litter a few men about the flat for a little while still."

"Surely we may go out to-morrow?"

"Of course. You won't, any of you, want to leave London?"

"No."

"The inquest will probably be on Monday. I wonder, sir, if you can give me the name of Lord Wutherwood's solicitors."

"Rattisbon. They've been our family lawyers for generations. I must ring up old Rattisbon, I suppose."

"Then that really is everything." Alleyn stood up. "We shall ask you to sign a transcript of your statement tomorrow, if you will. I must thank you very much indeed, sir, for so patiently enduring all this police procedure."

Lord Charles did not rise. He looked up with an air of hesitancy. "As a matter of fact," he said, "there's one other thing that rather bothers us, Alleyn. Tinkerton, my sister-in-law's maid, you know, came into the dining-room just now in a great state. It seems that my sister-in-law, whom I may say we all thought was safely asleep in my wife's bed, has now waked up and is in a really appalling frame of mind. She says she must have something or another from their house in Brummell Street and that Tinkerton and only Tinkerton can find it. Some patent medicine or another, it seems to be. Well now, your men are allowing no one to leave the flat. I explained all that to Tinkerton and she went off only to return saying that Violet was out of bed trying to dress herself and proving too big a handful for the nurse. The nurse, for her part, says she won't tackle the job singlehanded. We've rung up for a second nurse but now Tinkerton, although she's perfectly willing to carry on with the nurses, has obviously taken fright. It's all a frightful bore, and Imogen and I are both at our wits' end. I won't pretend we wouldn't be most relieved to see the last of poor Violet, but we also feel that if you allowed her to go she ought to have somebody who is not a servant or a strange nurse to be with her in that mausoleum of a house. Imogen says she will go but that I will not have. She's completely fagged out and where she is to sleep if Violet stays here for the rest of the night I simply don't know. I—really the whole thing is getting a little more than we can reasonably be expected to endure. I wonder if you could possibly help us?"

"I think so," Alleyn said. "We can arrange for Lady Wutherwood to go to her own house. We shall have to send some one along to be on duty there, but that can easily be done. I can spare a man from here."

"I'm extraordinarily relieved."

"About somebody else going—who do you suggest?"

"Well..." Lord Charles passed his hand over the back of his head. "Well, Robin Grey—Roberta Grey, you know—has very nicely offered to go."

"Rather a youthful guardian," said Alleyn with a lift of his eyebrow.

"Ah—yes. Yes, but she's a most resourceful and composed little person and says she doesn't mind. My wife suggests that Nanny might go to keep her company. I mean she will be perfectly all right. Two trained nurses and Tinkerton, who for all her fright insists that she can carry on as usual and says Violet will be quite quiet when she has had this medicine of hers. You see Frid, my eldest girl, may be a bit shaken, and of course Patch—Patricia—is too young. And we feel it ought to be a woman—I mean just for the look of things. You see, the nurse says that without some one besides Tinkerton she feels she can't take the responsibility until the second nurse comes. So we thought that if Robin—I mean, of course, with your approval."

Alleyn remembered a steadfast face, heart-shaped and colourless, with wide-set eyes of grey. His own phrase "a courageous little liar" recurred to him. But it was no business of his who the Lampreys sent to keep up the look of things in Brummell Street. Better perhaps that it should be the small New Zealander who surely did not come into this tragi-comedy except in the dim role of confidante and whole-hearted admirer of the family. With a remote feeling of uneasiness Alleyn agreed that Miss Grey and Nanny Burnaby should go in a taxi to Brummell Street; that Lady Wutherwood, Tinkerton, and the nurses, should be driven there by Giggle with Gibson as police escort. Lord Charles hurried away to organize these manoeuvres. Nigel, with a dubious look at Alleyn, murmured something about returning in a minute or two and slipped out after Lord Charles. Alleyn, left alone, walked restlessly about the dining-room. When Fox returned Alleyn instantly thrust the notes of Lord Charles's statement at him.

"Look at that," he said, "or rather don't. I'll tell you. He said that when they got to the far end of the drawing-room his brother promised in a mumble to help him. He said that none of his precious brood could have heard it. He was in a fix. He didn't know what they'd told me. I tripped him, Br'er Fox."

"Nicely," said Fox, thumbing over the notes.

"Yes, but, damn him, it still might be true. *They* may have lied but he may have spoken the truth. I'll swear he didn't, though."

"I know he didn't," said Fox.

"Do you, by George?"

"Yes, sir. I've been talking to the parlour-maid."

"With parlour-maids," said Alleyn, "you stand supreme. What did she say?"

"She was in the pantry at the time," said Fox, hauling out his spectacles and note-book. "The pantry door was open and she heard most of what was said between the brothers. I got her to own up that she slid out into the passage after a bit and had a good earful. I asked her why none of the other servants heard what she says she heard and her answer was that they all hung together with the family. She's under notice and doesn't mind what she says. Rather a vindictive type of girl with very shapely limbs."

"That's nice," said Alleyn. "Go on. What's her name?"

"Blackmore's the name. Cora. She says that the two gentlemen got very hot with each other and there was a lot of talk about the deceased cutting his brother out of everything he could. Blackmore says he went on something terrible. Called his present lordship everything from a sponger to a blackguard, and fetched up by saying he'd see him in the gutter before he'd give him another penny-piece. Then she says his present lordship lost his temper and things got very noisy until the boy—Master Michael—went into the drawing-room with a parcel. When Blackmore saw Master Michael she made out that she was doing something to the soda-water machine in the passage. He went in and they pulled up and said no more to each other. The deceased came away almost at once. As he got to the door he said, speaking very quiet and venomous according to Blackmore: 'That's final. If there's any more whining for help I'll take legal measures to rid myself of the lot of you.' Now, sir," said Fox, looking over the top of his spectacles, "Blackmore was playing round behind the soda-water machine which is close to the wall. She *says* she heard his present lordship say, very distinctly: 'I wish that there was some measure, legal or illegal, by which I could get rid of *you!*"

"Crikey!" said Alleyn.

"That's what I thought," said Fox.

CHAPTER XVI

Night Thickens

It was in a sort of trance that Roberta offered to spend the rest of an endless night in an unknown house with the apparently insane widow of a murdered peer. Lord Charles had displayed an incisiveness that surprised Roberta. When Charlot said she would go to Brummell Street he had said: "I absolutely forbid it, Immy," and rather to Roberta's surprise Charlot had at once given in. Frid offered to go, but not with any great show of enthusiasm, and Charlot looked dubious. So Roberta, wondering whether she spoke out of turn or whether at last hers was something she could do for the Lampreys, made her offer. With the exception of Henry they all seemed to be gently relieved. Roberta knew that the Lampreys, persuaded perhaps by dim ideas of pioneering hardihood, were inclined to think of all colonials as less sheltered and more inured to nervous strain than their English contemporaries. They were charmingly grateful and asked if she was sure she wouldn't mind.

"You won't see a sign of Aunt V.," said Frid, and Charlot

added: "And you really ought to see the house, Robin. I can't *tell* you what it is like. All Victorian gloom and glaring stuffed animals. *Too* perfect."

"I don't see why Robin should go," said Henry.

"Robin says she doesn't mind," Frid pointed out. "And if Nanny goes she'll feel as safe as a Crown jewel. Isn't Robin sweet, Mummy?"

"She's very kind indeed," said Charlot. "Honestly, Robin darling, are you *sure?*"

"I'm quite sure if you think I'll do."

"It's just for *somebody* to be there with the nurses. If Violet should by any chance make some sort of scene you can ring us up. But I'm sure she won't. She needn't even know you are there."

And so it was arranged. P. C. Martin, no longer in his armchair, stared fixedly at a portrait of a Victorian Lamprey. Lord Charles went off for his interview with Alleyn. Frid did her face; the twins looked gloomily at old *Punches;* Charlot, having refused to go to bed until the interviews were over, put her feet up and closed her eyes.

"Every moment," said Henry, "this room grows more like a dental waiting parlour. Here is a particularly old *Tatler*, Robin. Will you look at it and complete the picture?"

"Thank you, Henry. What are you reading?"

"The Bard. I am reading 'Macbeth.' He has a number of very meaty things to say about murder."

"Do you like the Bard?"

"I suppose I must, as quite often I find myself reading him."

"On this occasion," Stephen said. "I call it bad form t-to read 'Macbeth.'"

"'Night thickens,'" said Frid in a professionally deep voice.

> "And the crow makes wing to the rooky wood:
> Good things of day begin to droop and drowse,
> While night's black agents to their preys do rouse."

"You *would*," said Colin bitterly.

Roberta turned over the pages of the *Tatler*, unsolaced by studio portraits of ladies looking faintly nauseated and by snapshots of the same or closely similar ladies, looking either partially concussed or madly hilarious. She would have liked to put down the *Tatler* but was prevented from doing so by the circumstance of finding, whenever she looked up, that Henry's eye was upon her. Strange thoughts visited Roberta. She supposed that many of the ladies in the *Tatler* were personally known to Henry. Perhaps the mysterious Mary was one of them. Perhaps she was long-limbed, with that smooth, expensive look so far beyond the reach of a small, whey-faced colonial. So why, thought Roberta, with murder in the house and nobody being anything but vaguely kind, and with smooth ladies everywhere for Henry, should she be feeling happy? And before she could stop herself she had pictured the smooth ladies gliding away from Henry because he was mixed up in murder while she, Roberta Grey, dawned upon him in her full worth. With these and similar fancies her mind was so busily occupied that she did not notice the passing of the minutes, and when Lord Charles and Nigel Bathgate returned she thought that Alleyn must have kept them a very short time in the dining-room. She roused herself to notice that Lord Charles looked remarkably blank and Mr. Bathgate remarkably uneasy.

"Immy, darling," said Lord Charles, "why haven't you gone to bed?"

"If any one else tells me to go to bed," said Charlot, "knowing full well that my bed is occupied by a mad woman, I shall instantly ask Mr. Martin to arrest them."

"Well, it won't be occupied much longer. Alleyn says she may go home and that Robin and Nanny may go with her. He's sending a policeman too, so you'll be quite safe, Robin, my dear. The rest of us are—" Lord Charles fumbled for his glass—"are free to go to bed."

"Except me," said Frid. "Mr. Alleyn will want to see me. He's evidently saved me for the last."

"He didn't say anything about you."

"Wait and see," said Frid, touching her hair.

Fox came in.

"Excuse me, my lady," Fox said. "Mr. Alleyn has asked me to thank you and his lordship and the other ladies and gentlemen for their patience and courtesy and to say he will not trouble you any further tonight."

"Make a good exit out of that, if you can," said Henry unkindly to Frid.

Could it possibly, Robin pondered confusedly, be no longer than forty hours ago that she packed this little suitcase in her cabin? Time, she thought, meant nothing at all when strange things were happening. It was incredible that she had slept only one night in England. The bottom of the suitcase was littered with small objects for which she had not been able to find a place: the final menu card of the ship, with signatures that had already become quite meaningless, snapshots of deck sports, a piece of ship's notepaper. They belonged to a remote experience but for a fraction of a second Roberta longed for the secure isolation of her cabin and thought of how in the night, sometimes, she would listen contentedly to the sound of the ship's progress through the lonely ocean. She packed the suitcase, trying to keep her head about the things she would need and wondering how long she would have to stay with the Lampreys' mad aunt in Brummell Street. There were sounds of activity next door in Charlot's room and presently Roberta heard the door open. A dragging, clumsy footstep sounded in the passage and the nurse's voice, professionally soothing: "Now, we shall *soon* be home and tucked up in our own bed. Come along, dear. That's the way." Then that deep grating voice: "Leave me alone. Where's Tinkerton?" And Tinkerton: "Here, m'lady. Come along, m'lady. We're going home." Roberta heard them pass and go out to the landing. She had fastened down the lid of her suitcase but was still sitting on the floor when the curtains of her improvised room rattled and, turning quickly, she saw Henry.

He wore a great-coat and scarf and in his hands he held a small heap of clothes.

"Oh, Robin," Henry said, "I'm coming to Brummell Street instead of Nanny. Do you mind?"

"Henry! I don't mind at all. I'm terribly glad."

"Then that's all right. I asked Alleyn. He seems to think it's in order. I'll just pack these things and then we'll get a taxi and go. Mama has rung up Brummell Street and told the servants. Tinkerton has told Aunt V."

"What did she say?"

"I don't think she was particularly ravished at the thought. Patch is having nightmares and Nanny isn't coming."

"I see."

Henry looked gravely at Roberta and then smiled. There was a quality in Henry's smile that had always touched Roberta and endeared him to her. He made a comic family grimace, winked, and laid his finger against his nose. Roberta made the same grimace and Henry withdrew. With an illogical singing in her heart she put on her own overcoat and hat and took her suitcase out into the passage to wait for Henry. This time last night they had been dancing together.

It was not very pleasant crossing the landing where a policeman stood on guard by the dark lift but Henry lightened the situation by saying; "We're not fleeing from justice, officer."

"That's quite all right, sir," answered the policeman. "The Chief Inspector told us all about you."

"Good night," said Henry, piloting Roberta down the stairs.

"Good night, sir," said the policeman and his voice rang hollow in the lift well.

Roberta remembered her last trip down the stairs when she went to fetch Giggle and Tinkerton and how like a nightmare it had seemed. Now the stairs seemed a way of escape. It was glorious to reach the ground floor and see the lights of traffic through the glass doors. It was splendid when the doors were opened to breathe the night air of London. Henry took her elbow and they moved forward into a blinding whiteness that flashed and was gone. A young man came up to Henry and with a queer air of hardened deference said: "Lord Rune? I wonder if you would mind?"

"I'm afraid I would, do you know," said Henry. "Taxi!"

A cruising taxi drew up at once but before they could get in there was another flash and this time Roberta saw the camera.

Henry bundled her in and slammed the doors, keeping his face turned from the window. "Damn!" he said. "I'd forgotten about Nigel's low friends." And he yelled the address through to the driver.

"Lord Rune," said Roberta's thoughts. "Henry is Lord Rune. The Earl of Rune. Press-men lie in wait for him with cameras. Everything is very odd."

She was awakened by Henry giving her a little pat on the back. "Aren't you the clever one?" he said.

"Am I?" asked Roberta. "How?"

"Tipping us the wink about what you'd told Alleyn."

"Do you think that policeman noticed?"

"Not he. You know I didn't exactly enjoy lying to Alleyn."

"I hated it. And, Henry, I don't think he believes it—about your Uncle G. promising the money."

"'More do I. Oh well, we could but try." He put his arm round Roberta. "Brave old Robin Grey," said Henry. "Going into the witch's den. What have we done to deserve you?"

"Nothing," said Robin with spirit. "Without the word of a lie you're a hopeless crew."

"Do you remember a conversation we had years ago on the slope of Little Mount Silver?"

"Yes."

"So do I. And here I am still without a job. I daresay it would have been a good thing if Uncle G. had lived to chortle at our bankruptcy. It would take a major disaster to cure us. Perhaps when the war comes it will do the trick. Kill, as they say, or cure."

"I expect you'll manage to slope through a war in the same old way. But don't you call this a major disaster?"

"I suppose so. But you know, Robin, somehow or another, although I feel very bothered and frightened, I don't, inside myself, think that any of us are bound for the dock."

"Oh *don't*. How *can* you gossip away about it!"

"It's not affectation. I ought to be in a panic but I'm not. Not really."

The taxi carried them into Hyde Park Corner. Roberta looked up through the window and saw the four heroic horses snorting soundlessly against a night sky, grandiloquently unaware of the less florid postures of some bronze artillerymen down below.

"We shan't be long now," said Henry. "I can't tell you how frightful this house is. Uncle G.'s idea of the amenities was a mixture of elephantine ornament and incredible hardship. The servants are not allowed to use electricity once the gentry are in bed so they creep about by candlelight. It's true, I promise you. The house was done up by my grandfather on the occasion of his marriage and since then has merely amassed a continuous stream of hideous *objets d'art*."

"I read somewhere that Victorian things are fashionable again."

"So they are, but with a difference. And anyway I think it's a stupid fashion. Sometimes," said Henry, "I wonder if there is such a thing as beauty."

"Isn't it supposed to exist only in the eye of the beholder?"

"I won't take that. There are eyes and eyes. Fashion addles any true conception of beauty. There's something inherently vulgar in fashion."

"And yet," said Roberta, "if Frid dressed herself up like a belle of 1929 you wouldn't much care to be seen with her."

"She'd only be putting her fashion back eleven years."

"Well, what do you want? Nudism? Or bags tied round the middle?"

"You are unanswerable," said Henry. "All the same . . ." and he expounded his ideas of fashion, giving Roberta cause to marvel at his detachment.

The taxi bucketed along Park Lane and presently turned into a decorous side-street where the noise of London was muffled and the rows of great, uniform houses seemed fast asleep.

"Here we are," Henry said. "I *think* I've enough to pay the taxi. How much is it? Ah yes, I can just do it *with* the tip. So that's all hotsy-totsy. Come on."

As Henry rang the front doorbell, Roberta heard a clock chime and strike a single great note.

"One o'clock," she said. "Where is it striking?"

"I expect it was Big Ben. You hear him all over the place at night-time."

"I've only heard him on the air before."

"You're in London now."

"I know. I keep saying so to myself."

"It's a damn shame you should be landed in our particular soup. Here comes somebody."

The great door swung inwards. With the feeling that an ominous fairy tale was unfolding, Roberta saw a very old woman dressed in black satin and carrying a lighted candle in a silver candlestick. She stood against a dim background of stuffed bears, marble groups, gigantic pictures and a wide staircase that ascended into blackness. Henry said: "Good morning, Moffatt," to this woman and added, "I expect Tinkerton has explained that Miss Grey and I have come to

235

stay with her ladyship." The woman answered: "Yes, Mr. Henry. Yes, my lord." And like all the portresses of elfland she added: "You are expected."

They followed her, crossing a deep carpet and ascending the stairs. They climbed two flights up to a muffled landing. The air was both cold and stuffy. Moffatt whispered an apology for her candle. A detective had arrived and insisted that the light should not be turned off at the switchboard but at least they could keep his poor lordship's rule and not go using the lights before, as Moffatt said with relish, he was scarcely cold. Great shadows marched and stooped across unseen walls as Moffatt walked ahead with her candle. There was no sound but the stealthy whisper of her satin hem. Sometimes, as she held the candle before her, she was a black figure with a golden rim, but sometimes she turned to light them, and then her shadow sprang up beyond her. They came at last to a doorway which Moffatt opened. With a murmured apology she went in before them. Roberta, pausing on the threshold, saw a dim reflection of Moffatt in a dark looking-glass. Branched candlesticks stood on an immense dressing-table. Moffatt lit the candles and looked at Roberta, who on this hint entered her new bedroom. Henry followed.

"If there is anything you require, Miss?" suggested Moffatt. "Perhaps I may unpack for you? We only keep two maids when the family is not in residence and they are both in bed."

Roberta said that she would unpack for herself and Moffatt and the candle and Henry went away.

The bedroom had a very high ceiling with a central plaster ornament. The walls were covered with a heavily patterned paper and hung at intervals with thick curtains. Enormous pieces of furniture stood about the room, perpetuating some Victorian cabinetmaker's illegitimate passion for mahogany and low relief. But the bed was a distinguished four-poster with fine carvings, a faded French canopy, and brocaded curtains where gold threads shone among rose-coloured flowers. The carpet was deep and covered with vegetable conceits. Upon the walls Roberta found four steel engravings and one colour print of a child with a kitten. There was a great charm in this print, so artlessly did the beribboned child simper over the blue bow of the tiny animal. Beside her bed Roberta found a Bible, a novel by Marie Corelli, and a tin of thick, dry biscuits. She unpacked her suitcase and, too timid to hunt down back passages for a bathroom, washed in cold water provided by a garlanded ewer. There was a tap at the door. Henry came in wearing his dressing-gown.

"Are you all right?" he asked.

"Yes."

"Isn't it frightful? I'm over the way so if you want anything you've only to cross the passage. There's nobody else on this side. Aunt V. is across the landing in a terrible suite. Good night, Robin."

"Good night, Henry."

"You interrupted me," said Henry. "I was going to add, 'my darling.'"

He winked solemnly and went out.

iii

A wind got up during the small hours. It hunted desolately about London, its course deflected by sleeping buildings. It moaned about Peasaunce Court Mansions, shaking the skylight of the lift well. The policeman on duty there stared upwards and wished the black, rattling panes would turn grey for the dawn. It blew the curtains of Patch's windows across her face, giving her another nightmare and causing her to make horrid noises in her throat. The rest of the family, hearing Patch, turned fretfully in their beds and listened for the thud of Nanny's feet as she stumped down the passage. Gathering strength in the open places of Hyde Park, the wind howled across Park Lane and whistled up Brummell Street so that the old chimney-cowls in No. 24 swung round with a groan and Roberta heard a voice in the chimney moaning "Rune—Rune—Rune." Out at Hammersmith the wind ruffled the black waters of the Thames and the blameless dreams of Lady Katherine Lobe. Indeed the only actor in the Pleasaunce Court case who was not disturbed by that night wind was the late Lord Wutherwood who lay in a morgue awaiting his tryst with Dr. Curtis.

"Wind getting up," said Fox in the Chief Inspector's room at Scotland Yard. "Shouldn't be surprised if we had rain before dawn." He pulled a completed sheet and two carbons from his typewriter, added them tidily to the stacked papers on his desk, and took out his pipe.

"What's the time?" asked Alleyn.

"Five-and-thirty past two, sir."

"We've about finished, haven't we, Fox?"

"I think so, sir. I've just got out the typescript of your report."

Alleyn crumpled a sheet of paper and threw it at Nigel Bathgate, who was asleep in an office chair. "Wake up, Bathgate. The end's in view."

"What? Hullo, are we going home? Is that the report? May I see it?" asked Nigel.

"If you like. Give him a carbon, Fox. We'll all have a brood over the beastly thing." And for twenty minutes they read and smoked in a silence broken by the rustle of papers and occasional gusts that shook the window frames.

"That covers it, I think," said Alleyn at last. He looked at Nigel, who with the nervous, half-irritated concentration of a press-man was still reading the report.

"Yes," said Fox heavily, "as far as the family goes it's all pretty plain sailing. Their truthful statements seem to hang together and so, if you can put it that way, do their untruthful statements."

Nigel looked up. "Are you so positive," he said, "that some of their statements are not true?"

"Certainly," Alleyn said. "The story of Wutherwood promising to pay up is without doubt a tarradiddle. Roberta Grey tipped the wink to Lord Charles and Master Henry. Martin, the constable on duty, heard her do it. She said: 'You must feel glad he was so generous, after all. It'll be nice to remember that.' You'll find it in the report. I said she was a courageous little liar, didn't I?"

"Is it the only lie she handed in?" asked Fox deeply.

"I'm sure it is. She made a brave shot at it but she had her ears laid back for the effort. I should say she was by habit an unusually truthful little party. I'll stake my pension she hadn't the remotest notion of the significance of her one really startling bit of information. She was absolutely sure of herself, too. Repeated it twice, and signed a statement to the same effect."

"Here, wait a bit," Nigel ejaculated and hastily turned back the pages of his report.

"If she's right," said Fox, "it plays bobs-a-dying with the whole blooming case."

"It may make it a good deal simpler. Is that commissionarie fellow all right, Fox? Dependable?"

"I should say so. He noticed the eccentric old lady—Lady Katherine Lobe—all right. She *walked* down but he didn't miss her. And he didn't miss that chap Giggle or Miss Tinkerton either. Passed the time of day with them as they went out. And, by the way, you'll notice he confirms Tinkerton's story that she got downstairs just after Giggle."

"Miserable female," Alleyn muttered. "There's a liar if you like! Still, the commissionarie seems sound enough."

"Rather an observant sort of chap I should say," Fox agreed. "They get a knack of noticing people at that job."

"And he says the lift was not used between the time the Wutherwoods went up and what I feel sure Bathgate's paper will call the fatal trip?"

"That's right. He says he can't be mistaken. He always has a look to see who comes down or goes up because it's his job to keep that IN-and-OUT affair up to date. After the Wutherwoods went up to the flat the lift didn't return. He says the people on the first floor never use it. The second floor's away on a holiday and the third is unlet. The lift is really only used by the Lampreys just now."

"Ah, well," said Alleyn. "It's a line of country. We'll have to follow it up."

"What is?" Nigel demanded. "What are you talking about?" He pored over the report for a minute and then said: "Here! Are you thinking of those two servants? Giggle and Tinkerton?"

"Have you read that report carefully?"

"Yes, I have. I know what you mean. Young Michael says Wutherwood yelled out for his wife after Giggle went downstairs. Suppose that was a blind? Suppose Giggle came back and did the job?"

"Passing Tinkerton on his way up and probably running into Lady Charles as she came through the landing? Remember Lady Charles came out of 26 and went to the drawing-room in the other flat."

"Then whoever the murderer was, he took the risk of meeting her."

"The murderer," said Alleyn, "took great risks but I'm

inclined to think that was not one of them."

"For God's sake, Alleyn, what do you mean by that?"

"I told you it would be better if you kept out of it. I can't discuss the case fully with you. It wouldn't be fair to any of us. If we find ourselves drawn away from the Lampreys you'd burst to tell them so. If we find ourselves drawn towards one of them—what then? Your position would be intolerable. Better keep out."

"No," said Nigel. "I'll stick. What about this Tinkerton who's a liar?"

"She's almost the only member of the crowd of whom I am certain. She didn't kill Wutherwood. It's actually a physical impossibility."

"Then," said Nigel, "in my mind there's only one answer. It must be the dowager. Homicidal lunacy. She must have taken the skewer when Imogen went into the dining-room to ask for a twin to work the lift."

"The skewer had gone by then. *Vide* Michael."

"Well, if he's right, she took it before that and did the trick while she was supposed to be in the lavatory."

"Yes," said Alleyn, "that's arguable. But see what Roberta Grey says."

"Oh, damn Roberta Grey. What do you mean, Roberta Grey?"

"If you want to see thing as a whole," said Alleyn, "get it down as a sort of table. Take Lord Wutherwood's movements from the time he left the drawing-room until the lift returned, not forgetting the two yells he gave for his wife. Then look at the statement and correlate all the other people's moves with his. You'll find that after Wutherwood called the second time the landing was deserted until Lady Charles went from 26 to the drawing-room. During that period, according to statements, Lord Charles and his three eldest sons were in the drawing-room, Lady Charles and her daughters in her bedroom, Lady Wutherwood and Lady Katherine in the two lavatories, Giggle on his way downstairs, Tinkerton following him, Baskett in the servants' hall, Roberta Grey in the dining-room, Michael in Flat 26, and Nanny in her bedroom. The other servants and the bum were in the kitchen, and during that same period Lady Katherine Lobe went downstairs and into the street."

"And that's the crucial time?"

"It's unlikely that he yelled for his wife in what they all agree was his normal voice after he'd got a skewer in his brain."

"Can you cut that period down a bit further?"

"Lady Katherine told me that she slipped away after Lady Charles crossed the landing. That means that she herself was on the landing and making for the stairs. She looked at the lift but could see nobody inside. With those doors you can't see anybody who is sitting down. Wutherwood must have been in the lift then but his murderer, unless he sat beside the victim, was not there. Nor, of course, was he on the landing. A moment later Stephen Lamprey came out to work the lift."

Nigel dabbed his finger on the carbon copy.

"And when Stephen went out on the landing his aunt was there—alone."

"That is what he gave in his statement," said Alleyn without emphasis.

"Have you any reason to doubt this statement?"

"At the moment, none."

"Very well, then. She had been alone on the landing."

"I thought your argument was that she did it before that, in which case why did she stay on the landing?"

"I'm only showing that she had opportunities."

"All right."

"Alleyn," said Nigel, "please tell me. Do you think she did it?"

"There you go, you see," said Alleyn wearily. "Stick to your press-manship, my boy. Go away and write a front-page story and let me see it before you hand it over to your evening screecher. Come on. We'll go home to our unfortunate wives and Fox to his blameless pallet."

They parted on the Embankment. Nigel hailed a taxi; Fox, his head bent sideways, his hand to his bowler and his overcoat flapping about his formidable legs, tacked off into the wind, making for his lodgings in Victoria. Alleyn crossed the Embankment and leaning on the parapet looked down into the black shadows of Westminster Pier. The river slapped against wet stones and Alleyn felt a thin touch of spray on his face. He stood for so long that a constable on night duty paused and finally marched down upon his superior, flashing his torch into Alleyn's face.

"It's all right," said Alleyn. "I'm not yet tired of life."

241

"I beg your pardon, sir, I'm sure. Mr. Alleyn isn't it? Didn't recognize you for a minute. It's a thick night."

"It's a beastly night," agreed Alleyn, "and we're at the worst part of it."

"Yes, sir. That's right, sir."

"Dull job, night duty, isn't it?"

"Chronic, sir. Nothing much to do as a general rule except walk and think."

"I know."

Gratified by this encouragement, the constable said: "Yes, sir. I always reckon that if there's any chap or female on this beat, hanging off and on, wondering whether they'll make a hole in the river or not, it's between two and four of the morning they'll go overboard if they're ever going. The river patrols say the same thing."

"Yes," said Alleyn. "So do doctors and nurses. It's the hour of low vitality." He did not move away and the constable, still further encouraged, continued the conversation.

"Have you ever read a play called 'Macbeth,' sir?" he asked.

"Yes," said Alleyn, turning his head to look at the man.

"I wonder if it'd be the same thing, sir. The one I have in mind is by this Shakespeare."

"I think it'll be the same."

"Well, sir, I saw that piece once at the old Vic. On duty there, sir, I was. It's a funny kind of show. Not the type of entertainment that appeals to me as a general rule. Morbid. But it kind of caught my fancy and afterwards I got hold of a copy of the words and read them. There's one or two bits I seem to be reminded of when I am on night duty. I don't know why, I'm sure, because the play is a countrified affair. Blasted heaths and woods and so on."

"And witches," said Alleyn.

"That's so, sir. Very peculiar. Fanciful. All the same there's one or two bits that stick in my mind. Something about 'night thickens' and it goes on about birds flying into trees, and 'good things of day begin to droop and drowse'—and—er—"

"'While night's black agents to their prey do rouse.'"

"Ah. It's the same, then. Gives you a sort of sensation, doesn't it, sir?"

"Yes."

"And there's another remark that took my fancy. This chap

Macbeth asks his wife, 'What is the night?' meaning what's the time and she says 'Almost at odds with morning, which is which.' It's the kind of way it's put. They were a very nasty couple. Bad type. Superstitious, like most crooks. She was the worst of the two, in my opinion. Tried to fix the job so's it'd look as if the servants had done it. Do you recollect that, sir?"

"Yes," said Alleyn slowly, "yes."

"Mind," said the constable, warming a little, "I reckon if he hadn't lost his nerve they'd have got away with it. No finger-printing in those days, you see. And you know how it'd be, sir. You don't *expect* people of their class to commit murder."

"No."

"No, you don't. And with the weapons lying there beside these grooms or whatever they were, and so on, well the first thing anybody would have said was: 'Here's your birds.' Not that there seemed to be anything like what you'd call an inquiry."

"Not precisely," said Alleyn.

"No, sir. No," continued the constable, turning his back to the wind, "if Macbeth hadn't got jumpy and mucked things up I reckon they'd have got away with it. They seemed to be well-liked people in the district. Some kind of royalty. Aristocratic, like. Well, nobody suspects people of that class. That's my point."

Alleyn pulled his hat on more firmly and turned up the collar of his coat.

"Well," he said, "I'll go off duty."

"Yes, sir. I beg pardon, sir. Don't know what came over me speaking so freely, sir."

"That's all right," said Alleyn. "You've put a number of ideas in my head. Good night to you."

CHAPTER **XVII**

Mr. Fox Finds an Effigy

The north wind that had come up during the night brought clouds. Before dawn these broke into teeming rain. At nine o'clock Roberta and Henry breakfasted in a room heavy with Victorian appointments. The windows were blind with rain and the room so dark that Henry turned on the lights.

"I don't suppose that's ever been done before except in a pea-soup fog," he said cheerfully. "How did you sleep, Robin?"

"Not so badly," said Roberta, "but for the wind in the chimney. It would drone out your name."

"My name?" said Henry quickly. "I've never heard the north wind make a noise like 'Henry.'"

"Your new name."

"Oh," said Henry, "that. Yes, it is rather flatulent, isn't it?"

"Have you heard how Lady Wutherwood is this morning?"

"I met Tinkerton on the landing. She says Aunt V. slept like a log. 'Very peaceful,' Tinkerton said, as if Aunt V. was a corpse."

"Don't."

"I suppose it's real," said Henry, returning with eggs and bacon from the side table. "I suppose somebody did kill Uncle G. last night. This morning it scarcely seems credible. What shall we do all day, Robin? Do you imagine if we go out our footsteps will be dogged by a plain-clothes detective? It might be fun to see if we could shake him off. I've always thought how easy it must be to lose a follower. Shall we try, or is it too wet?"

"There's a policeman down in the hall."

"How inexpressibly deadly for him," said Henry. "I think the hall is possibly the worst part of this house. When we were small the direst threat Nanny had for us was that we should be sent to live in Brummell Street. Even now I slink past that stuffed bear, half expecting him to reach out and paw me to his bosom."

"It's such a large house," said Roberta, "even the bear looks smallish. Has it been your family's house for long?"

"It dates from a Lamprey who did some very fishy bit of hanky-panky for Good Queen Anne or one of her ministers. A pretty hot bit of work, one would think, to be rewarded with such a monstrous tip. She made him a Marquis into the bargain. The house must have been rather a fine affair in those days. It took my grandfather to ruin it. Uncle G. and Aunt V. merely added a few layers of gloom to the general chaos."

"I suppose it's your father's house now."

Henry paused in the act of raising his cup. "Golly," he said, "I wonder if it is. One could make rather a lovely house of it, you know." And to Henry's face came a speculative expression which Roberta, with a sinking heart, recognized as the look of a Lamprey about to spend a lot of money.

"There'll be terrific death duties," she cried in panic.

"Oh, yes," said Henry, grandly dismissing them.

They finished their breakfast in silence. An extremely old manservant, who Roberta thought must be Mrs. Moffatt's husband, came in to say Henry was wanted on the telephone.

"I'll answer it in the library," said Henry, and to Roberta: "It'll be the family. Come on."

In a dimly forbidding library Roberta listened to Henry on the telephone: "Good morning, good morning," said Henry brightly. "Anybody arrested yet or are you all at liberty?"

…Oh, good.…Yes, thank you, Mama…No, but Tinkerton says she's all right.…" He ambled on in a discursive manner and Roberta's attention strayed but was presently caught again by Henry ejaculating: *"Baskett!* Why on earth?…Good lord, how preposterous." He said rapidly to Roberta: "That vast person Fox has been closeted with Baskett and Nanny for an hour and they're wondering if he thinks Baskett…All right, Mama.…No, I thought of showing Robin the house and then we might pay you a visit.…Tonight?…Oh. Oh I see…Yes, if you think we ought to.…Yes, I know it's monstrous but it might be made rather pleasant don't you think?" Henry lowered his voice. "I say, Mum," he said guardedly, "will it be Aunt V.'s or ours?…Oh. Oh, well good-bye darling."

He hung up the receiver. "I'm afraid we'll have to stay tonight, Robin," he said. "They're bringing him here, you see."

"I see."

"And Mama rather thinks we get this house. Let's have a look at it."

ii

At eleven o'clock Alleyn got the surgeon's report on the post-mortem. It was accompanied by a note from Dr. Curtis. The skewer, he said, had been introduced into the left orbit and had penetrated the fissure at the back of the eye and had entered the blood vessels at the base of the brain.

That's all the coroner or his jury need to know [wrote Dr. Curtis] but I suppose I shall have to give them a solemn mumbo jumbo as usual. They don't think they've got their money's worth without it. For your information, this expert must have groped a bit before finding the gap and played his weapon about as much as he could after it got through into the brain. Nasty mess. No doubt about it being a right-handed job. I shall say that the wound on the left temple was caused by its coming into sharp contact with the chromium steel boss on the lift wall and that he was probably unconscious when the stuff with the skewer was done, and that death was caused by injury to the brain. Hope you get him (or her).

Yours,

S. C.

Alleyn brooded over the report, put it aside, and rang up Mr. Rattisbon, the Lamprey's family solicitor. Mr. Rattisbon was an old acquaintance of Alleyn's. He said that he was just leaving to wait upon the new Lord Wutherwood but would call on Alleyn in an hour's time. He sounded extremely bothered and fussily remote. Alleyn was heartily thankful that the Lampreys had not sent for Mr. Rattisbon last night. If any one could keep their tongues from uttering indiscretions it was surely he. "I shall get very little out of him," Alleyn thought. "He'll be as acid as a lime and as dry as a biscuit. He will look after the Lampreys." And with a sigh he turned back to his report. Presently Fox came in, beaming mildly, with his white scarf folded neatly under his wet mackintosh and his umbrella and hat in his hand.

"Hullo, Br'er Fox. Enjoy your game of Happy Families this morning?"

"I got on nicely, thank you, Mr. Alleyn. I looked in at the house in Brummell Street. I didn't see Mr. Henry Lamprey—Lord Rune, rather—or Miss Grey, but I understand they passed a quiet night. Her ladyship's quieted down a lot too, so the nurse told me. She thinks one nurse will be enough to-night. I saw that chap Giggle, the chauffeur, and passed the time of day with him. He didn't seem to like it."

"Your method of 'passing the time of day' is sometimes a bit ominous, Foxkin. What did you say to Giggle?"

"I thought I'd have a shot at shaking his story about when he went downstairs. He got very nervous, of course, when I hammered away at it, but he stuck to it that he went down just after Lord Wutherwood called out the first time."

"It's the truth," said Alleyn. "Young Michael saw him go. You won't shake that story, Br'er Fox."

"So I found, sir. I left the chap in a great taking on, however, and went along to Pleasaunce Court. They all seem to be much the same. Quite enjoyed signing their statements. I don't fancy they slept a great deal, but they were as bright as ever and uncommonly friendly."

"A fig for their friendliness," muttered Alleyn.

"Lady Friede seemed very put out that you didn't interview her last night," Fox continued as he opened the door and shook his dripping umbrella into the corridor.

Alleyn grunted.

"You appear to have made quite an impression, sir."

"Shut that door, and put your gamp away and come here, damn you."

Fox obeyed these instructions with an air of innocence. He sat down and took out his official notebook. Alleyn reflected that his affection for Fox must be impregnable since it survived the ordeal of watching him moisten his forefinger on his lower lip whenever he turned a page, a habit that in any other associate would have filled Alleyn with a desire to be rid of him.

"Yes," said Fox, finding his place. "Yes. Baskett. Well now, Mr. Alleyn, I've been able to get very little out of him beyond what we already knew. He helped his late lordship into his coat and went back to the servants' hall. He states positively that he didn't meet Miss Tinkerton on the way. Says he didn't see her at all. But if her story's correct that she saw Baskett and his lordship from the passage and fetched her things from the servants' hall, then they must have met in one place or another. He seems a straightforward old chap, too."

"And she doesn't seem a straightforward middle-aged girl. No, by gum, Fox, she doesn't. But she's not our pigeon, you know."

"I reckon she was up to something, however, and I fancy I've found what it is."

"Have you, now! This is what we keep you for, Foxkin."

"Is that so?" said Fox with his slow smile. "Well, Mr. Alleyn, I thought I'd better finish in the flat and let them get it straight again. Following your suggestion I had a look round the hall. Now, as you know, the hall was in a mess. The young people had had these charades and hadn't done much to clear up beyond slinging things into the cupboard. Now the cupboard was open. The cupboard door is flush with the hall door. All right. *On* the floor, half in and half out, was one of those thin, transparent mackintoshes that ladies go in for nowadays. All right. *Inside* the cupboard and *on* the mackintosh I found a couple of prints. Female shoes, with what they call Cuban heels, pointing inwards and to the left. Now one heel has gone through the stuff and the other has made a deep dent. Very nice prints, the surface being a bit tacky and taking a good impression. Now, sir, which of those ladies wore Cuban-heeled shoes?"

"Tinkerton, for one," said Alleyn. "What about the parlour-maid?"

"No. I checked up on Cora. She wears round heels. I've brought away that mackintosh, Mr. Alleyn, and with your approval I'll take a chance and try to lay my hands on Miss Tinkerton's shoes."

"Better ask Master Henry or Miss Grey to do it for you," said Alleyn drily. "They'll be only too pleased if they think we're sniffing round after the servants."

"Should you say they were dependable?"

"She is. But I don't give it as a serious suggestion. Br'er Fox. What do you think Tinkerton may have been up to?"

"I was going to ask you for an opinion."

"Having one of your own up your sleeve, you old dog. Well Fox, the cupboard is in the hall between the hall and the drawing-room. Isn't it at least possible that the lady in the cupboard was listening to the conversation in the drawing-room?"

"Ah," said Fox. "When?"

"There's only one possible time if it was yesterday afternoon."

"*Which* it was," said Fox. "Baskett says the cupboard was all spick and span before the charade. We're lucky it wasn't tidied up later on. He was going to put things straight when the accident happened and after that our chaps told him not to. So it must have been during the conversation between the brothers. I got the old nurse talking. She won't say anything against the family but she's got her knife into Miss Tinkerton. You know what these old girls are like, sir. Mrs. Burnaby kept sort of hinting at things, suggesting Miss Tinkerton's a very inquisitive sort of woman and very much in with her ladyship and against his late lordship. I reckon Miss T. and Mrs. B. had a row at some time or other and Mrs. Burnaby doesn't forget it. I reckon they're kind of bosom enemies if you know what I mean."

"I do. Not very reliable evidence."

"No, but there may be something in it all the same. She

couldn't say a good word for Miss Tinkerton but there was nothing you could get your teeth into. At one time it was Miss Tinkerton carrying on with the menservants—that Giggle, as Mrs. B. called him, in particular."

"Good lord!"

"Yes. At another time it was Miss Tinkerton repeating gossip about Miss Friede, as Mrs. Burnaby calls her."

"What sort of gossip?"

"Oh, saying the stage was a funny life for a young lady. Nothing definite. She kept saying 'those two.'"

"Who did she mean?"

"That's what I asked her, and she gave a bit of a laugh and said: 'Never mind, but they were hand in glove against his late lordship and there was more in it than met the eye.' Seemed as if she meant Tinkerton and her ladyship. Later on she said her ladyship would be properly in the soup if it wasn't for Miss T. *I* don't know," said Fox. "Search me what she was driving at half the time, but I've got it all down and you can see it, sir, for what it's worth. Based on imagination from start to finish, as like as not, but it did seem to suggest that Miss Tinkerton's a bit of a sly one. And taking the prints in the cupboard into consideration, if they *are* hers, I wondered if she was sort of keeping watch—well, for somebody else. Naming no names, as Mrs. B. would say."

"On the other hand," Alleyn said, "she may have been merely snooping for the love of the sport, like your friend Cora."

"That's so. You know, sir, I sometimes wonder how people would react if they heard everything their servants said about them."

"I should think the Lampreys would laugh till they were sick," said Alleyn. "I remember one afternoon, when my brother George and I were conceited youths, we took a couple of deck chairs and our books to a spot which happened to be under the window of the servants' hall. The window was open and we heard a series of very spirited imitations of ourselves and our parents. The boot-boy was particularly gifted. George was conducting a not very reputable affair of the heart of which I knew nothing. But the boot-boy had it all pat." Alleyn broke into one of his rare laughs. "It was damn good for us," he said.

"Would you say they were usually correct, though? If this

old nurse lets on that Miss Tinkerton and the chap Giggle are carrying on a bit, or that Miss T. is in some sort of cahoots with her mistress, or that Miss T.'s got her knife into the Lampreys, is she more likely to be lying or talking turkey?"

"If she's got her knife into Miss T.," said Alleyn, "it's a fifty-fifty chance. I should say Nanny Burnaby was a bit of a tartar. Inclined to be illogically jealous and touchy but a very faithful old dragon with the family. I bet you didn't get her to say anything about them."

"Lor' no. They were a bunch of cherubs."

"Yes, I daresay. I wonder if it'd be a good idea to see Giggle again. If he's Tinkerton's boy friend (and it's a grim thought) he may possibly throw a new ray of light on that unlovely figure. We'll see him, Fox. Ring up the Brummell Street house and get him to come here. And I tell you what, Foxkin," said Alleyn gloomily, "it looks very much as if we'll have to go into that Kent visit. It'll be one of those little jaunts that sound such fun in the detective books and are such a crashing bore in reality. Do you read detective novels, Br'er Fox?"

"No," said Fox. And perhaps with some idea of softening this shortest of all rejoinders he added: "It's not for the want of trying. Seeing the average person's knowledge of the department is based on these tales I thought I'd have a go at them. I don't say they're not very smart. Something happening on every page to make you think different from what you thought the one before, and the routine got over in the gaps between the chapters. In two of the ones I tried, the investigating officers let the case run for a couple more murders and listened in to the fourth attempt in order to hear the murderer tell the victim how the first three were done. Then they walked in and copped him just before the cosh. Well, you don't do that sort of thing in the department. There'd be questions asked. I don't say it's not clever but it's fanciful."

"A little, perhaps."

"The truth is," said Fox gravely, "homicidal cases are not what people would like them to be. How often do we get a murder with a row of suspects, each with motive and opportunity?"

"Not often, thank the lord, but it has happened."

"Well, yes. But motives aren't all of equal weight. You don't have much trouble in getting at the prime motive."

"No."

"No. Mostly there's one suspect and our problem is to nail the job on him."

"What about this case?"

"Well, sir. I'll give you there's two motives. First, money. In which case either one of the family or one of the servants did the job. Second: insane hatred. In which case it's her ladyship we're after. That's on the face of it; never mind what we've found out since we came in on the job. Something else may crop up but if so I'll be surprised if it doesn't fit in with one or the other motive. Do you know if he's left anything to the servants, sir?"

"I'll try and get it out of Mr. Rattisbon. I don't suppose he'll object to telling me. None of them gives a tuppenny damn about the servants. Except Lady Wutherwood. She'd find Tinkerton hard to replace."

"Maybe," said Fox, "she won't be wanting a maid."

iii

Mr. Rattisbon came mumbling in with his chin poked forward and his leather case under his arm. He was a family solicitor who reeked of his trade. A story was told of him that on emerging from his chambers one summer evening he was accosted by a famous film producer who walked halfway along the Strand with him, imploring him to play the part of a family solicitor in his new picture. Mr. Rattisbon's refusals were so gloriously in character that each titupping, pernickety refusal stung the producer into making a fresh financial assault until, so the story said, Mr. Rattisbon threatened him shrilly with the Municipal Corporation Act of 1822 and looked about him for a constable.

When he saw Alleyn he hurried across the room, shook hands, snatched his claw away, looked sharply from Alleyn to Fox, and finally took a chair. He then formed his mouth into a tight circle and vibrated the tip of his tongue rather as if he had taken a sip of scalding liquid.

"We are very grateful to you for coming, sir," said Alleyn.

"Not at all, not at all," grabbled Mr. Rattisbon. "Shocking affair. Dreadful."

"Appalling."

Mr. Rattisbon repeated the word with great emphasis: "A-PALL-ing" and waited for Alleyn to make the first move. Alleyn decided that his only hope lay in direct attack. He said: "I expect you know why we have asked to see you, sir."

"Frankly," said Rattisbon, "no."

"For the usual reason, I'm afraid. We hope you will tell us something about the late Lord Wutherwood's estate." Mr. Rattisbon's tongue vibrated rapidly in preparation for utterance and Alleyn hurried on. "We realize, of course, that you are in a—how shall I put it—a confidential position: a position that might become delicate if we began to press in certain definite directions. But in what we still trustfully call the interests of justice—"

"In those interests, Chief Inspector," Mr. Rattisbon cut in neatly, "I have a duty to my client."

"Of course, sir."

"I have, as you know, this morning had an interview with the present Lord Wutherwood. I may tell you that at the inquest I shall watch proceedings on his behalf. I think I may, with propriety, add that my client is naturally most anxious to give the police every assistance that lies in his power. He desires above all things that his brother's assailant shall be brought to justice. You will appreciate, however, that as regards any information prejudicial to my client (should such information exist which I by no means suggest), my own attitude is—most clearly defined."

Alleyn had expected nothing better and he said: "And as Lady Wutherwood's solicitor—"

"The present Lady Wutherwood?"

"The Dowager Lady Wutherwood, sir."

"Mm—a—a—ah," said Rattisbon with a formidable and sheeplike cry. "I am not the Dowager Lady Wutherwood's solicitor, Chief Inspector."

"No, sir?"

"No. I understand that she has in the past consulted solicitors. I have this information from a reliable source. I think I may tell you that I understand her solicitors to be Messrs. Hungerford, Hungerford and Butterworth."

"Thank you," said Alleyn, making a note of it. "Then, sir, our position is not so delicate as I supposed." He paused, wishing heartily that Mr. Rattisbon's conversational style was less infectious. "Perhaps," he said, "you won't mind telling me how Lord Wutherwood's widow is affected by the will."

"I anticipated this question. I may say I have considered it closely and—in short, Chief Inspector, I have decided that there are certain details of the will with which I may acquaint you." With his entire person Mr. Rattisbon effected a kind of burrowing movement which, in a less emaciated person, would have suggested he was settling down to a square meal. "The Dowager Lady Wutherwood," he said rapidly, "by her marriage settlement becomes possessed of a very considerable fortune. Apart from this actual fortune she inherits a life interest in the Dower House of Deepacres St. Jude, Deepacres, Kent, and a Manor House near Bognor Regis."

"She will be a very wealthy woman, then?"

"Very wealthy?" repeated Mr. Rattisbon as if the expression was altogether too loose and unprofessional. "Ah—you may say she will be possessed of a very considerable, I may say a very handsome, inheritance. Yes."

"Yes." Alleyn knew very well that it was no good trying any approach to the Lamprey side of the picture. Better, he thought, to make what he could of Mr. Rattisbon's "unprejudiced" information. He said: "I believe I may be quite frank about Lady Wutherwood. Her behaviour since the catastrophe has been, to put it mildly, eccentric. From what I've been able to learn from the others, one cannot put her eccentricity to shock. It's an old story. You'll understand, sir, that in the course of routine we are concerned with the relationship between Lord Wutherwood and his wife. Now, do you feel inclined to tell me anything about it?"

Mr. Rattisbon executed several small snatching gestures which resulted in the appearance of a pair of pince-nez. These he waved at Alleyn. "Under less extraordinary circumstances..." he began, and Alleyn listened to an exposition of Mr. Rattisbon's professional reticence under less extraordinary circumstances. Gradually, however, small flakes of information were wafted through the dry wind of his discourse. It appeared that Mr. Rattisbon knew a good deal about Lady Wutherwood. Alleyn learnt that she was the daughter of a Hungarian minor official and a Russian cabaret artiste, that her maiden name was Glapeera Zadody. He learnt that, from the beginning, the marriage had been disastrous and that at one time Lord Wutherwood had seriously considered the advantages of divorce. Mr. Rattisbon had been consulted. The question of insanity had been discussed. All this, though it was something, was not much, and Alleyn perceived that Mr. Rattisbon hovered on the brink of more daring disclosures. At last, after a series of sheeplike cries and strange grimaces, Mr. Rattisbon told his secret.

"It occurs to me," he said, for all the world as if he were some stray Dickensian character embarking on a tale within a tale, "It occurs to me that a certain incident, which, though I dismissed it as childish when I was made aware of it, should be brought to your attention. No longer ago than February last, the late Lord Wutherwood called upon me at my rooms. He appeared to be in an unusual state of agitation. I may say that I was quite startled by his manner which I can only describe as furtive and uneasy. It was some time before I got from him the object of his visit, but at last it appeared that he wished to know if he could take legal measures to protect himself from menaces to his person threatened by his wife. I pressed him for closer information and he gave it me. I may say that his story seemed to me ridiculous and, if it pointed to anything, merely furnished us with additional proof of his wife's mental condition."

Mr. Rattisbon cleared his throat, darted an uncomfortable glance at Alleyn, waved his pince-nez and gabbled rapidly. "He informed me of a discovery. He had found in a drawer of Lady Wutherwood's dressing-table—maa—a—ah— evidence, or so he assured me, of an attempt upon her part to—ah—to ah perform upon him by some supernatural agency."

Alleyn uttered a stifled ejaculation.

"You may well say so," said Mr. Rattisbon. "Fantastic! I questioned him rather closely, but he would give me no sort of evidence to support his story though he hinted at definite and concerete proof. He became quite hysterical and was utterly unlike himself. I—really I found myself at a loss how to deal with him. I pointed out that anything in the nature of legal protection was out of the question. He actually replied that the laws against witchcraft should not have been repealed. I suggested an alienist. He raised the extraordinary objection that if Lady Wutherwood were placed in confinement she would still find some means of harming him. I should add that while he was obviously in a state little removed from terror, he also professed to ridicule the idea of danger. His manner was extraordinary and illogical. He contradicted himself repeatedly and became more and more agitated. I could do little to reassure him. He displayed irritation and hostility. When he finally left me he turned in the doorway and—and—ah—"

Mr. Rattisbon vibrated his tongue and sucked in his breath. "Lord Wutherwood," he said, "made this final statement. He said: 'You mark my words. If somebody doesn't do something to stop her she'll get me yet!'"

"Oh, hell!" said Alleyn.

"Well, now," said Mr. Rattisbon after a long silence, "you may dismiss this incident, Chief Inspector, as absurd and irrelevant. I assure you that I deliberated at some length whether I should acquaint you with it."

"I'm very glad you decided to tell me about it. What did he do with this concrete proof of her activities, whatever it may have been?"

"He locked it away in some hiding place of his own. It appeared that for some superstitious reason, which I don't pretend to understand, he was unwilling to destroy it, though he refused to tell me what it was."

"Had he ever discussed the affair with his wife, do you know? Taxed her with it?"

"Never. I asked the same question. Never."

"No. No, I suppose he wouldn't. Well, it's a strange story."

"Is it a significant story?"

"It fits into the pattern, I think."

"Ah," said Mr. Rattisbon who knew Alleyn. "The pattern. Your pet theory, Chief Inspector."

"Yes, sir, my pet theory. I hope you may provide me with another lozenge in the pattern. Did he leave any large sums to his servants?"

"He made the customary bequests of a man in his position. One hundred pounds to each servant who had been in his employment for five years or more. In the cases of old family servants the legacies were in some cases considerable."

"What about the two servants who were with them yesterday? William Giggle and Grace Tinkerton."

"William Stanley Giggle," said Mr. Rattisbon, "is the son of Lord Wutherwood's late coachman and the grandson of his father's coachman. He receives a more substantial inheritance in the form of an invested sum that should produce three hundred pounds per annum together with a small freehold property—a cottage and some three acres of land on the outskirts of the village of Deepacres."

"Is this a recent bequest?"

"No, no. Lord Wutherwood has made several wills and many alterations but this bequest appears in the earliest of them. I understand that it was done at the request of Lord Wutherwood's father."

"And Tinkerton?"

"Is that Lady Wutherwood's personal maid?"

"Yes."

"Nothing."

Alleyn grimaced and dropped his pencil on the desk before him.

"Isn't it strange under the circumstances that Lady Wutherwood receives so much?"

"She would have received a great deal less," said Mr. Rattisbon, "if the late Lord Wutherwood had lived until noon today." And with some appearance of relishing the effect of this statement he added: "I was to wait upon the late Lord Wutherwood this morning with the purpose of obtaining his signature to a will. By that will Lady Wutherwood received the minimum which the law insists and not one penny-piece more."

iv

Giggle's arrival coincided with Mr. Rattisbon's departure. He was brought in by Mr. Fox. The stolid indifference of the previous night had deserted him. He was very pale and seemed to make no attempt to conceal his obvious alarm. Evidently, thought Alleyn, his morning's interview with Fox had shaken him. He stood to attention turning his chauffeur's cap around in his hands, and staring with signs of the liveliest distrust at Mr. Fox.

"Now then, Giggle," Alleyn said, "there's no need to worry, you know, if you've given us a straight-forward account of yourself."

"I have so, sir. I've told the truth, sir, so help me. I wasn't there, sir, honest I wasn't. Master Michael will bear me out, sir.

He saw me go downstairs, and they say they heard his lordship sing out after I'd gone, sir."

"All right. We only want the facts, you know. If you've given us the facts you've nothing to worry about."

"If I might ask, sir, has Master Michael spoken for me?"

"Yes, he has. He says he saw you go down."

Giggle wiped his hand across his mouth. "Thank God! I beg your pardon, sir, but young gentlemen of his age don't always notice much, and I've been that worried."

"We've asked you to come here this morning," Alleyn said, "to see if you can give us any further information."

"I will if I can, sir, but I don't know a thing. I've got nothing to do with it. I never wished his lordship dead. His lordship always treated me fair enough."

"Even to the extent of leaving you a nice little property, I understand."

Giggle burst into a clumsy tirade of self-defence. It was not his doing, he cried, that his lordship had favoured him. "It was along of what my dad did for his lordship's father. I never asked for anything nor never expected it. You can't pin anything on me. It's always the same. If it's gentry and workingmen in trouble the police go for the workingmen every time. My Gawd, can't you understand..." Alleyn let him talk himself to a standstill. At last he was silent and stood there sweating freely and showing the whites of his eyes like a startled horse.

"Now you've got that off your chest," said Alleyn, "perhaps you'll listen to one or two questions. Sit down."

"I'd as soon stand."

"All right. You tell us you went downstairs to the car, and that the first thing you knew about the tragedy was when Miss Grey came for you. Very well. Now, as you went downstairs did the lift overtake you and go to the bottom?"

"No, sir."

"It didn't come down at all while you were on the stairs?"

Giggle seemed to shy all over. "What's this about the lift? It was up top. I never seen it after I went down."

"That's all I wanted you to tell me," said Alleyn.

"Oh cripes!" said Giggle under his breath.

"Another point. How did his lordship get on with his servants?"

"Good enough," said Giggle cautiously.

"Really?"

"I'm not going to get myself trapped—"

"Don't talk silly," said Inspector Fox austerely. "What's the matter with you? The Chief Inspector asked you a plain question. Why can't you answer it? You're making yourself look awkward, that's what you're doing."

"Come along, now, Giggle," said Alleyn. "Pipe up, there's a good fellow."

"Well, sir, I'm sorry, but I'm all anyhow. His lordship got on good enough with his staff in a manner of speaking. There was some thought he was a bit on the near side and there was some didn't like his sarcastic ways but I never minded. He treated me fair."

"Did some of the staff prefer her ladyship to his lordship?"

"They might of."

"The maid for instance?"

"She might of."

"Are you friendly with her maid?"

"We get on all right," said Giggle, eyeing Alleyn suspiciously.

"Any attachment between you?"

"What the hell's that got to do with this business?" roared Giggle. "Who says there's anything?"

"Away you go again," observed Alleyn wearily. "Will you answer the question or won't you?"

"There's nothing between us, then. We might have been a bit friendly, like. What's there in that? I don't say we're not friendly."

"Would you say that Tinkerton took Lady Wutherwood's part against her husband? Sympathized with her?"

"She's very fond of her ladyship. She's been with her a long time."

"Quite so. *Did* she sympathize with Lady Wutherwood when it came to any differences between them?"

"I suppose so."

"Then there were differences between Lord and Lady Wutherwood?"

"Yes, sir," said Giggle, obviously relieved at this turn of the conversation.

"What did they quarrel about, do you know?"

"Her ladyship's got funny ideas. She takes up with funny people."

"Do you think she's normal mentally?"

Giggle shuffled his feet and looked at his cap. His lips were trembling.

"Come on," said Alleyn.

"It's pretty well known she's a bit funny. Grace Tinkerton doesn't like it said, but it's a fact. She was shut up for a time and she's never what you'd call the same as other people. I think most of us on the staff have that opinion."

"Except Miss Tinkerton?"

"She knows," said Giggle, "but she won't let on. Loyal-like."

"All right," said Alleyn. "That's everything, I think."

Giggle wiped his face with a shaking hand. He seemed to hover on the edge of speech.

"What is it?" Alleyn asked.

"Gawd, sir, I'm that upset! It's got me down. Thinking about it." He stopped again and then with a curious air of taking control of himself said rapidly, "I beg pardon, sir, for forgetting myself. I got that rattled thinking about it when Mr. Fox came at me again this morning—"

"That's all right," said Alleyn, "good-bye."

Giggle gave him a terrified glance and went out.

V

A mid-day train took Alleyn, Fox and Nigel Bathgate into Kent. Nigel rang up Alleyn two minutes before he left for Victoria and climbed into the restaurant carriage two seconds after it had started moving. "Ever faithful, ever sure," he said and ordered drinks for the three of them.

"You won't get much out of this," said Alleyn.

"You never know, do you? We sent a cameraman down there this morning. I hope to fix up some trimmings for the pictures."

"Have you seen your friends this morning?"

"Yes." Nigel looked doubtfully at Alleyn, seemed about to speak, but evidently changed his mind.

"Let's have lunch," said Alleyn.

During the journey he was amiable but uncommunicative. After lunch Fox and Nigel went to sleep and did not wake until they reached Canterbury. Here they found the sun shining between ponderous clouds moving slowly to the south. They changed to a branch line, arriving at Deepacres Halt at three o'clock.

"Out we get," said Alleyn. "The local superintendent is supposed to have sent a car. It's three miles, I understand, to the chateau Wutherwood. There's our man."

The superintendent himself waited for them on the platform and led the way out to a village road and the police car. He was evidently much stimulated by this visit from the Yard and showed great readiness to discuss Deepacres Park and the Lamprey family. As they drove away from the village he pointed to a pleasant cottage standing back from a side lane.

"That'll be Bill Giggle's property now," he said.

"Nice for Bill Giggle," said Alleyn.

"Very nice. Funny, the way he's come by it. Ancient history, it is. Bill Giggle's old man was coachman to his late lordship's father and saved his life. Runaway horse affair, it was. His old lordship promised Bill Giggle's dad the cottage for his work which was very courageous and smart but, in the end, it was horses did for his old lordship, just the same, for he was killed in the hunting field. Only lived a few minutes but in the hearing of them that were there he said he was sorry he'd never made that addition to his will, and asked his son—that's his late lordship—to make it good. Well, his new lordship's, as he was then, didn't actually hand over the cottage, being a bit on the near side, but he sent for his lawyers and made his will and let it be known young Bill Giggle would get the place when he himself was dead and gone."

"I see."

"Yes, and they're going to take the railroad that way now, so it looks as if Bill Giggle's in for a nice thing, doesn't it?"

"Yes," said Alleyn, "it does."

He was rather silent after that. They drove through country lanes past a mild sequence of open fields, small holdings, spinneys, and a private golf course, to the gates of Deepacres Park. The house was hidden by trees and as they climbed a long winding avenue Fox began to look solemnly impressed.

"A show-place, seemingly," said Fox.

"Wait till you see the house," said the superintendent. "It's as fine a seat as you'll find in Kent after Leeds Castle. Not so big, but impressive, if you know what I mean."

He was right. The great house stood on a terrace above a deer park. It was built at the time of John Evelyn and that industrious connoisseur of fine houses could have found no fault in it. Indeed he might have described it as perfectly uniform structure, observable for its noble site, and showing without like a diadem. The simile would have been well chosen, thought Alleyn, for in the late afternoon sunshine the house glowed like a jewel against the velvet setting of its trees.

"Lummy!" said Nigel. "I never knew it was as grand as all this. Good Lord, it's funny to think of the Lampreys coming home to this sort of roost."

"I suppose Lord Charles was born here?" observed Alleyn.

"Oh, yes. Yes, I suppose so. Yes, of course he was. Rather terrific, isn't it?" And Nigel's fingers went to his tie.

"I've told the servants to expect you," said the superintendent. "They'll be in a fine taking on over this, I'll be bound."

But the butler and housekeeper, when Alleyn saw them, seemed to be less agitated than bewildered. They were more concerned, it seemed, with the problem of their own responsibilities and, for the moment, were made uneasy by the lack of them. They had heard of his lordship's death through the stop-press column of the newspaper. They had received no orders. Should they and a detachment of servants go up to London? Where was his lordship to be buried? Alleyn suggested they should ring up Brummell Street or the Pleasaunce Court flat. He produced a search warrant and got to work. It would take weeks to go over the whole of Deepacres but he hoped to bring off a lucky dip. Lord Wutherwood's secretary, it appeared, was away on his holiday. Alleyn did not regret his absence. He asked to see the rooms Lord Wutherwood used most often and was shown a library and a sort of office. Fox went off to a dressing-room in a remote wing. Nigel sought out the housekeeper to get, so he said, the faithful retainer's angle on the story. Alleyn had brought a bunch of keys taken from Lord Wutherwood's body. One of them fitted the lock of a magnificent Jacobean cupboard in the library. It was full of bundles of letters and papers. With a sigh he settled down to them, pausing every now and then to glance through the tall windows at the formal and charming prospect outside.

He found little to help him in the Jacobean cupboard.

There were gay begging letters from Lord Charles, acidly blue-pencilled by his brother: "*Answered 10/5/38, Refused. Answered 11/12/38. Final refusal.*" But Lord Charles's letters still came in and there were further final refusals. The late Lord Wutherwood, Alleyn saw, had been a methodical man. But he had not always refused to help his brother. A letter from New Zealand was blue-pencilled "*Replied 3/4/33. £500*" and a still earlier appeal: "*£500 forwarded B. N. Z.*" These appeared to be the only occasions on which Lord Charles had not drawn a blank. There were letters from Lady Katherine Lobe in which the writer reminded her nephew of his obligations to the poor and placed her pet charities before him. These were emphatically pencilled "*No.*" Among a bundle of ancient letters Alleyn came upon one from the Nedbrun Nursing Home, Otterton, Devon. It reported Lady Wutherwood's condition as being somewhat improved. He made a note of the address.

It was Fox who made the strange discovery. The sun had crept low on the library windows and the room had begun to be filled with a translucent dusk when a door at the far end opened and Fox, bulkily dark, materialized from the shadows of the hall beyond. Alleyn was down on the floor, groping in the bottom shelf of the cupboard. He sat back on his heels and watched Fox advance slowly from dark into thick golden light. Fox looked a huge and portentous figure. He seemed to carry some small object on the palms of his hands. Without speaking Alleyn watched him. The carpet was deep and he advanced as silently as a robust ghost. It was not until he drew quite near that Alleyn could distinguish the object he held in his hands.

It was a small and very ugly doll.

Without a word Fox put it on the carpet. It was a pale, misshapen figure, ill-modelled from some dirtily glossy substance of a livid colour. It was dressed, after a fashion, in a black coat and grey trousers. On the tip of its deformity of a head were stuck a few grey hairs. Black-headed pins formed the eyes; a couple of holes the nostrils. A row of match ends projected horridly from beneath a monstrous upper lip. Alleyn advanced a long finger and pointed to the end of the figure where the feet should have been. They had dwindled away like the feet of the suffering Jews in Cruikshank's drawing for *The Ingoldsby Legends*.

"Melted," said Fox loudly.

Alleyn's finger travelled up to the breast of the doll. A long pin stuck out from its travesty of a waistcoat.

"Where was it?"

"In the back of his dressing-table drawer."

"This is the thing he wouldn't show old Rattisbon. I wonder why."

"Perhaps he was afraid he'd laugh."

"Perhaps," said Alleyn.

CHAPTER **XVIII**

Scene by Candlelight

There was no break that day in the clouds over London. From morning to night it rained inexorably. Whenever they went to the library window in Brummell Street, Roberta and Henry looked down on a pattern of bobbing umbrellas, on the glistening mackintosh of the Brummell Street policemen, on the roofs of wet cars and on the jets of water that spurted from under their wheels. When, after lunch, they went out into Brummell Street under a borrowed umbrella, the wind drove them sideways, and Henry tucked Roberta's hand under the crook of his elbow. In spite of everything that had happened, Roberta felt her heart warm to this adventure, to the Londoners hurrying intently through the rain, to the lamplit shop-windows, to the scarlet buses that sailed above the traffic, to the sea of noise, and to Henry who piloted her through the rain. She was glad that Henry had no more than one and elevenpiece in his pockets and that, instead of borrowing her proffered ten shillings and taking a taxi, he suggested they should go roundabout by bus and tube to

Pleasaunce Court. Splendid, sang Roberta's heart, to mount the swaying bus and go cruising down Park Lane, splendid to plunge into the entrance of the tube station, to smell the unexpected sweetness of air that was driven through the world of underground, to sink far below the streets and catch a roaring subterranean train. Splendid, she thought, to sit opposite Henry in the tube and to see his face, murkily lit but smiling at her.

"Like London?" he asked, guessing at her thoughts, and she nodded back at him, feeling independent and adventurous. Best of all, it seemed to Roberta, was this sense of independence. Nobody in the crowded tubes knew she was Roberta Grey from New Zealand. She didn't matter to them or they to her and she warmed to them for their very indifference. It didn't even matter that she and Henry must be back at Brummell Street before Uncle G. came home in his coffin. It was ridiculous to suppose that the Lampreys were in any sort of danger. For Roberta was twenty and abroad in London.

The behaviour of the Lampreys did nothing to subdue her mood. Charlot was resting and Lord Charles had gone to see his bank manager but the others, though rather black under the eyes, displayed flashes of their usual form. They all had tea in the dining-room including Mike, who wore an air of triumph. Frid absent-mindedly poured tea in all the cups before her and then strolled about the room smoking. Patch consumed oranges from a side table and the twins ate quantities of toast.

"I suppose you've heard," said Colin, "that Mr. Grumball's gone."

"And his name is Grimball," said Stephen.

"He went," explained Patch, "because Daddy's all hotsy-totsy now as regards money."

"You don't suppose, do you," said Henry, "that Uncle G.'s hoarded gold becomes ours in the flash of an eye? There are death duties, my child."

"What are death duties?"

None of the Lampreys seemed to know the answer to Patch's question. Even Henry, though vaguely depressing, was uninformed.

"Oh, well," said Patch, "there's always Aunt Kit's money from the pearls she popped. Perhaps that'll square the death duties."

"Or pay for learned counsel to defend one of us," said Frid.

"You *would* think of that, Frid," said Henry.

"Well, let's face it, one of us may—"

"*Pas pour le jeune homme*," said Colin.

"I know what that means," said Mike. "But you needn't worry. Chief Detective-Inspector Alleyn'll solve the mystery sometime to-day, I should think. Robin, did you know Chief Detective-Inspector Alleyn happened to have rather an important talk with me last night?"

"Did he, Mikey? That was fun, wasn't it?"

"Not bad. He happened to want to know one or two things and I happened to remember them. I must say he's an absolute whizzer. Well," added Mike, "I mean he's the kind of person another person knows bang off for a whizzer. You can kind of recognize it. I say, Robin, do you know he hadn't got his magernifying-glass with him and I happened to be able to lend him mine? I bet he finds some pretty hot clues with my magernifying-glass. Hoo!" said Mike, kicking the leg of his chair, "I bet old B-K's chops fall when I tell him about the magernifying-glass."

"Who's old B-K?"

"A person," said Mike. "As a matter of fac' it's Benham-Kaye in my form at school. He's pretty high-hat. I bet he won't be so high-hat when I tell him—"

"Your conversation," said Frid, "is like a round of catch sung by one person only."

"What did you tell Mr. Alleyn, Mike?" asked Henry.

"Oh, about when the skewer was in the hall and when it wasn't and who I saw and when. He said I was a pretty good witness."

"Robin," said Henry, "it's half-past five. I think we should return to duty."

II

The return trip to Brummell Street was not quite so satisfactory. Henry, having borrowed a little money from Nanny, took a taxi. He was very silent and Roberta had time to think of the night that awaited them in the Brummell Street house. She had time to wonder where they would put Uncle G. and whether Aunt V., hitherto invisible, would appear for dinner. It seemed that Roberta and Henry were expected by

Charlot to remain at Brummell Street and she began to wonder nervously if Henry would be bored by a long evening with her in that cadaverous library. Perhaps the aunt would be there too, and Roberta began to imagine how Aunt V. would sit and stare at Henry and herself and how, when bedtime came, they would climb the stairs and walk silently through the long passages. Perhaps they would have to pass the door of the room where Uncle G. lay in his coffin. Perhaps Aunt V. would madly insist on their looking at Uncle G. Roberta wished the rain would stop and that the clouds would roll away and let a little evening sun into Brummell Street. For the first time since she came to England she felt lonely. She decided that after dinner she would write to her own unknown middle-class aunt who, thought Roberta with an inward smile, must have been rather shaken by her evening paper. The evening papers were evidently full of Uncle G. At street corners Roberta saw placards with: "DEATH OF A PEER" and "SHOCKING TRAGEDY. LORD WUTHER-WOOD KILLED." She couldn't help wondering if inside these papers there were photographs of herself and Henry coming out of Pleasaunce Court Mansions. Perhaps underneath the photograph would be written: "Lord Rune and a friend leaving the fatal flat last night." Henry stopped the taxi at a street corner and bought a paper. "This is Nigel's affair," he said. "Let's see what sort of gup he's handed out, shall we?" They read the paper in the taxi and, sure enough, there was the flashlight photograph with their faces, appropriately haggard, like white puddings with startled black-current eyes. Roberta thought the letter-press quite indecently frightful but Henry said it might have been worse and that Nigel had spared them a lot. The taxi drew up at 24 Brummell Street. They left the paper behind and once more entered the heavy house. They were immediately aware of a sort of subdued activity. They smelt flowers and there, climbing the stairs, was a maid with a great wreath of lilies in her arms. Moffatt, the old manservant who had let them in, told them that part of the Deepacres staff were coming up to London by the morning train. "But we've managed very well, my lord," said Moffatt. "Everything is prepared. The flowers are beautiful."

"Which room?" Henry asked.

"The green drawing-room, my lord. On the second landing."

"Upstairs?" said Henry dubiously.

"Her ladyship wished the green drawing-room, my lord."

"Is her ladyship dining, Moffatt?"

"Not downstairs, my lord. In her room."

"How is she, do you know?"

"I—I understand not very well, my lord. Miss Tinkerton tells me not very well. If it is convenient, my lord, perhaps the nurse on duty may dine with you."

"Oh, lord, yes." said Henry.

Tinkerton appeared in the shadows at the far end of the hall. Henry hailed her and asked after her mistress. She came nearer and with a glance at the stairs replied in a whisper that Lady Wutherwood was not well. Very restless and strange, she added and, as Henry said no more, glided away into the shadows.

"Very restless and strange," Henry repeated gloomily. "That's jolly."

A clock in the rear of the hall struck six. At the moment, in Lady Wutherwood's bedroom at Deepacres, Alleyn looked up from a copy of the *Compendium Maleficorum*.

"Fox," he said, "how many men did we leave at Brummell Street?"

"One, sir. Campbell. The house is being watched." And staring at his superior's face, Fox asked: "What's wrong?"

Alleyn's long finger went out in that familiar gesture. "Read that."

Fox put on his glasses and bent over the *Compendium*. "THE SECOND BOOK," he read, "DEALING WITH THE VARIOUS KINDS OF WITCHCRAFT AND CERTAIN OTHER MATTERS WHICH SHOULD BE KNOWN."

"Go on."

"CHAPTER I. OF SOPORIFIC SPELLS. ARGUMENT." Fox read on in his best police-court manner until Alleyn stopped him. "Well," said Fox, "It seems to be very silly sort of stuff. It's marked in the margin so she evidently made something of it. I suppose it's given her ideas."

"There are several more works on witchcraft down in the library. Some of them are very rare. Yes, I think it's given her ideas, Fox. I'm wondering if we've bumped our heads on the keystone of her behaviour. How soon can we get back?"

"To London? Not before eleven thirty, sir."

"Damn. Fox, I've got a very rum notion, so rum that I'm

half ashamed of it. I believe I know why she wanted his body brought home."

"Lor'!" said Fox. "You don't think she would get up to any of these capers?"

"I wouldn't put it past her. I'm uneasy. Fox. Pricking of the thumbs or something. When are they delivering the goods? About ten, isn't it?"

"Yes, sir. The mortuary van—"

"Yes, I know. Let's get back to London."

iii

It was a few minutes after ten when they brought Uncle G. to Brummell Street. Henry and Roberta were in the library. The rain made a great drumming noise on the windows and the wind soughed in the chimney but they were at once aware of new sounds inside the house and Henry said: "You stay here, Robin. I'll come back soon."

He went out, shutting the door but not shutting away the heavy sounds of Uncle G.'s progress across the great hall and up the long stairway. Roberta sat on the hearthrug and held her hands to the fire. Her heartbeat was faster than the bump of feet on the stairs. In their morning's exploration she and Henry had visited the green drawing-room. It was over the library and soon the ceiling gave back to her the sound of Uncle G.'s progress. The footsteps stopped for a little while and then lost their heaviness. Now the men were coming downstairs again, crossing the hall, leaving 24 Brummell Street for the kindlier storm-swept streets. She heard the great front door close. In a little while Henry came back. He carried a tray with a decanter and two glasses.

"I got them out of the dining-room," he explained. "We'll have a little drink, Robin. Yes, I know you don't, but to-night I prescribe it."

The unaccustomed glow did drive away Roberta's cold, sunken feeling. Henry threw more logs on the fire and for half an hour they sat before it talking of the old days in New Zealand.

"I am quite determined," Henry said, "that after this is all over I shall get a job. Yes, I know I've talked about it for six years."

"And now," said Robin tartly, "when, for the first time, it isn't a crying necessity—"

"I make up my mind to do it. Yes. I shall continue in the territorials in my humble but exacting capacity. I shall sit for strange examinations and thus prepare myself for the obscure and unattractive performance known as 'doing one's bit.' And when war comes," said Henry in a melancholy manner, "Henry Lamprey, Earl of Rune, will take his place among the flower of England's manhood guarding an entrance to some vulnerable public convenience."

Roberta knew that Henry was trying to brighten this ominous night and although his jokes were not quite up to Lamprey standard she contrived to laugh at them. The clock struck eleven. They couldn't stay all night by the library fire. Sometime those stairs must be climbed, those passages traversed. In an exhausted, uncertain fashion Roberta longed for her bed. She ached for sleep yet was not sleepy. Her throat and mouth kept forming half yawns and her head throbbed.

"How about it, Robin?" asked Henry presently. "Bed?"

"I think so."

Past the stuffed bear with his open mouth and extended paws.... Past the cold marble persons at the foot of the stairs.... Past the second landing where Aunt V. and her nurses and perhaps Tinkerton slept or watched behind closed doors.... Then the long passage, lit now by electric lights....

"I asked them to put a fire in your room, Robin." Heavenly of Henry to think of that.... Better by far to undress by this cheerful fire.... And when she crept out in her dressing-gown, there was Henry in his dressing-gown, and they went into the bathroom together and Henry sat on the edge of the tub in a friendly manner while Roberta brushed her teeth. They returned together to their bedroom doors.

"Good night, Robin darling. Sleep well."

"Good night."

The Kentish slow train was late. The police car had punctured a tyre half a mile from Deepacres Halt and they had missed their connection with the express. At every station the slow train halted, breathing long steamy sighs which were echoed by Alleyn.

"What's biting you, Inspector?" asked Nigel cheerfully.

"I don't know."

"I've never seen you so jumpy."

"That fellow Campbell was told to keep his wits about him, Fox?"

"Yes, Mr. Alleyn."

"Good God, we're stopping again!"

iv

Roberta's heart beat so thickly that she wondered if it alone had awakened her. She lay with her eyes opened upon blackness. She could not see so much as the form of the curtains that hung beside her head or the shape of her hand held close to her eyes. For a moment she was confused. The memory of this room was gone from her. She had no sense of her position or of her invisible surroundings but felt as though she had opened her eyes on nothingness. She dared not put out her hand lest the wall should not be there. Now she was wide awake. She remembered her room and knew that round the curtains on her left side she should be able to see the fire. She touched the curtain, so close yet invisible, and it moved. Somewhere beyond her bed glowed a point of redness. The fire was almost dead; she had slept a long time. Outside it was still raining and the wind still moaned in the chimney but neither the wind nor the rain had awakened Roberta. She knew that some one had walked past her door. She began to reason with herself, telling her thumping heart that there was no cause for fear. Perhaps it was the man on guard in the house, making some cold round of inspection. Yet even while she sought in panic for comfort she knew, so densely woven are the strands of thought, that the footstep in the passage was the secondary cause of her alarm and that it was another sound that had horrified her dreams and rushed her upwards into wakefulness. She lay still and waited, tingling, for full realization. Presently it came. Beneath her, beyond the mattress of her bed, the carpet on the floor, the floor itself, the ceiling below the floor—beyond all these, there was a sound that fretted the outer borders of her hearing. It had a kind of rhythm. It suggested some sort of harsh movement with which Roberta was familiar. At the moment when she recognized it, it ceased, and she was left with a picture of a hand and a saw. Then she remembered that underneath her bedroom was the green drawing-room.

Perhaps if the sound had not begun again Roberta would have lain still in her bed. But there are degrees of terror and with the stealthy resumption of the sound she knew that she could not endure it alone. She snapped down the switch by her door but no light came and she supposed that it had been turned off at the main. She groped on her bedside table, found a box of matches and lit her candle. Now her room was there with her clothes lying across a chair. Her shadow reared up the wall and stretched halfway across the ceiling. She put on her dressing-gown and, taking her candle, went to her door and opened it. As she did this the sound stopped again.

Henry's door was wide open. Roberta crossed the passage and went into his room but before she looked at the bed she knew he would not be there. The clothes were turned back and there was no candle on his table. She found some comfort in being in Henry's room. It smelt faintly of the stuff he put on his hair. Roberta wrapped his eiderdown quilt round herself and sat on the bed. Henry had heard the noise and had gone to see about it. But at once she grew afraid for Henry and as the seconds went by this fear increased until it became intolerable. She went to the door and listened. The sound had stopped for some minutes and she heard only the rain, muffled here where there were no windows. She faced the passage and perceived a thinning of darkness at the far end, where the landing was and where the well of the house gaped up to the roof. As she peered down the passage this dimness changed stealthily to a faint shadow, moving slow. It must be Henry returning with his candle. Now she could see the landing with its gallery rail and stairhead. She caught a glint of light on a far wall and remembered that a looking-glass hung there. A glowing circle appeared on the landing floor. It widened and grew more clearly defined. Henry was coming upstairs. In a moment she would see him.

Framed by the black walls of the passage, a figure carrying a lighted candle moved from the stairs across the landing. It paused, and slowly turned. The light from the candle shone upwards into its face. It was Lady Wutherwood. Her head was slanted as if she listened intently; her eyes were turned upwards towards the next landing. She moved away, became a receding shape rimmed by a golden nimbus, and disappeared.

Roberta, in the dark passage, stood still. Henry's door, caught in a draught from his open window, banged shut, and her whole body leapt to the sound and was still again. At last the landing began to grow light once more. The manner of its lighting was so exactly as it had been before that her nerves expected Lady Wutherwood to come upstairs again like a ghost that punctually repeated its gestures. But of course it was Henry. He shielded his candle with his hand and seemed to look directly into Roberta's eyes. Forgetting she was invisible she wondered at his look, which held nothing of the comfort she had expected. Then, realizing that he had not seen her, she went down the passage to meet him.

"Robin! Why have you come out! Go back." He scarcely breathed the words.

"I can't. What's happening?"

"What have you seen?"

"I saw her. I think she went up to the next landing."

"Go back to your room," Henry said.

"Let me stay. Give me something to do."

He seemed to hesitate. She touched his arm. "Please Henry."

"What wakened you?"

"A noise in that room. Like sawing. Have you been there?"

Again Henry hesitated. "It's locked," he said.

"Where's the detective? Shouldn't you find him?"

"Come with me."

So he was going to let her stay with him. She followed him across the landing. He paused at a door, bent down to listen. Then, very gingerly, he turned the handle and with his head motioned Roberta to come closer. She obeyed. Through the crack of the door came the sound of snoring, very deep and stertorous.

"Night nurse," breathed Henry and closed the door.

"What are you going to do? Find the detective?"

"I'd like to find out for myself what she's up to."

"No, Henry. If anything's wrong it would look so strange. Ssh!"

"What?"

"Look."

A circle of light bobbed up the stairs and across the landing. "Damn!" whispered Henry. "He's coming."

He walked swiftly to the stairhead. "Hullo," he said softly, "who's that?"

"Just a minute, sir."

The man came up quickly, flashing his torch on Henry. As he moved into the candlelight Roberta saw he wore a heavy overcoat and muffler and remembered that she herself was cold.

"What's wrong here, sir?" asked the man. "Who's been interfering with these lights? I said they were to be left on."

Henry told him quickly that he had been awakened by a sound from the green drawing-room, and that he had seen Lady Wutherwood walk across the landing with a candle in her hand. "Miss Grey saw her too. Miss Grey came out soon after I did."

"Where did she go, sir?"

"Upstairs."

"You stay here, if you please, sir. Both of you. Don't move."

He threw his torch light on the upper stairs. They were half the width of the lower flight and steeper. The man ran lightly up and then disappeared. Roberta and Henry heard a door open and close, then another, and another. Then silence.

"Hell!" said Henry loudly, "I'm going..." Roberta snatched at his arm and he stopped short. Somewhere in the top floor of the house Lady Wutherwood screamed. Roberta knew at once it was she who screamed. It was the same note that had drilled through the silence of the lift well. It persisted for some seconds, intolerable and imbecilic, and then a door slammed it away into the background. Other voices sounded on the top floor. Somebody had joined them on the landing. It was the night nurse with her veil askew.

"Where's she gone?" cried the night nurse. "I don't accept the responsibility for this. Where's she gone?"

On the top floor the man in the overcoat was saying: "Get back to your rooms, the lot of you. Move along now. Do what you're told." And a voice, Tinkerton's: "I'm going to my lady." "You're doing what you're told. Into your rooms, now, all of you. I'll see you later."

"You can't lock me out."

"I have locked you out.Stand aside, if *you* please."

The man in the overcoat came downstairs.

"Where's my patient?" said the nurse. "I must get to my patient."

"You're too late," said the man, and to Henry: "You two come along with me, sir. I'm going to the telephone."

They followed him to a small study on the second landing. He sat down to a desk and dialled Whitehall 1212. His fingers shook and his mouth looked stiff.

"... Campbell here on duty at 24 Brummell Street. Mr. Alleyn, please. What's that? On his way? Right. There's been a fatality here. We'll want the divisional surgeon quick. Get him, will you, I'm single-handed."

He replaced the receiver.

"Look here," said Henry violently. "What was she doing? You can't drag us around like a brace of dummies and tell us nothing. What's happened? What's this fatality?"

The man Campbell bit his fingers and stared at Henry.

"Who locked the door of the room where the body is?" he demanded.

"I didn't," said Henry.

"But you knew it was locked, sir?"

"Of course I did. I heard a damned ghastly noise in the room and went down to investigate. What's happened upstairs?"

The man seemed to weigh something in his mind and come to a decision. "Come and see," he said.

They seemed to have forgotten Roberta but she followed them up the long stairs. On the next landing they picked up the nurse and went on to the top floor, a strange procession. The nurse and Campbell had a torch and Henry his candle. The top landing gave on to a narrow passage. The detective opened the first door. The Moffatts, two girls, and Tinkerton, fantastic in their night-clothes, were huddled round a candle.

"Here, you," said Campbell, "Mr. Moffatt. Go down and fix up the lights. Some one's pulled out the main fuse. Find it and get it back. Or have you got a spare?"

"Yes, sir."

"Well, fix it. Have you got a police whistle?"

"Yes, sir."

"Go to the front door and blow it. When the constable

comes, take him up to the door of the room where the body is and tell him I said he was to stay there. Detective-Sergeant Campbell. Then wait by the front door. Let in a doctor who will be here in a few minutes and send him upstairs to the top floor. Then wait for Chief Inspector Alleyn who's on his way from Victoria Station. Send him up too."

He passed the next door and paused by a third. "Your patient's in there, nurse. We'll take a look at her first. We'll have to see if there's a key on her. You come in with me, sir, and look out for yourself. She may give trouble." He turned to Roberta. "You slip in after us if you please, Miss, take my torch and shut the door. If we've got to hold her I may trouble you to help. And you, Nurse. Now then."

He unlocked the door, glanced at Henry, and then opened it quickly. He went in, with Henry on his heels. The nurse followed; Roberta slipped in behind her and shut the door.

It was an unused servant's bedroom. For a moment Roberta thought Lady Wutherwood was not there but the light from the torches found her. She sat on the floor at the head of the stretcher bed. She turned her head and looked blindly into the light and though her retracted lips at first suggested a snarl it was evident by the noise she made that she was laughing. Her hair hung about her eyes; the white discs at the corners of the mouth glistened; she turned her head gently from side to side. Her throat was bare and in its pale thickness a pulse beat rapidly. She wore a dark gown over her nightdress and her hands moved among its folds.

"Now, my lady," said Campbell, "nobody's going to hurt you. Here's Nurse come to take you back to bed."

The nurse in a most unnatural voice said: "Come along, dear. We can't stay in a nasty cold room can we? Come along." Lady Wutherwood shrank back against the wall. The nurse said; "We'll just help you up, shall we?" and moved forward.

Lady Wutherwood was on her feet with a swiftness that suggested some violent wrench of pain. She pressed herself against the wall. Her hands were in the pockets of her gown, holding them together, crushed tight against herself.

"That's better," said the nurse. Campbell moved closer to Lady Wutherwood and in answer to this signal Henry followed him.

"Now you come along with Nurse, my lady," said Campbell. "We'll just take your arms. *Look out!*"

Henry's candle rolled on the floor and went out. The nurse and Roberta pointed their torches at the three struggling figures. Lady Wutherwood struck twice at Campbell with her right hand before he caught her arm. Henry had her left arm. The left hand was still rammed down in the pocket of her dressing-gown but she fought with the violence of an animal. Suddenly the room was flooded by a hard white light. Roberta threw her torch on the bed. "Collar her low, Robin." said Henry's voice. Roberta was on the floor. Her arms embraced a pair of soft legs, struggling inside the folds of robe and nightgown. "Disgusting, *disgusting*," said her thoughts but she held on. "That's better," Campbell said, and abruptly they were all quiet, blinking in the glare. The nurse still pointed the torch at them. She was talking. "It's a case for a mental attendant. I should never have been asked to take the case," gabbled the nurse, carefully pointing her torch. "It's not a case for ordinary duty." Lady Wutherwood's left hand doubled inside her pocket, touched the top of Roberta's head. The hand and arm were rigid, yet they moved with their owner's violent breathing. A new voice, harsh and broken, sounded and was silent.

"What's she say?" Campbell demanded. "She said something. What was it?"

"German, I think," said Henry.

"What's she got in her pocket? Here, Nurse! Get rid of that torch." The nurse looked at her hand. "Oh. Silly of me," she said, and put the torch down.

"Now," said Campbell, "put your hand in her pocket and see what she's got hold of. Carefully. It may be a knife."

"Why a knife?" asked Henry.

Campbell didn't answer him. The nurse approached her patient and over Roberta's head gingerly slid her hand down Lady Wutherwood's arm into the pocket. Roberta, looking up, saw the nurse's face bleach out abruptly to the colour of parchment.

"What's the matter!" Campbell demanded.

"She's—she's—got—both her hands—in her pocket."

Henry said violently; "Don't be an ass, Nurse. What d'you mean?"

The nurse backed away from Lady Wutherwood, pointing at the pocket and nodding her head.

"I've got her right hand," said Campbell impatiently. "What are you talking about?"

"There are two hands in her pocket," said the nurse, and fainted.

CHAPTER **XIX**

Severed Hand

The taxi pulled up at 24 Brummell Street, discharged its fares and skidded off into the rain.

"Quiet enough," said Nigel. "You've got a jitterbug, Inspector."

"There's a light on in the hall," said Alleyn. "What about the entrance here, Fox? Wasn't there a man outside?"

"The P.C. on this beat," said Fox. "He was told to stay outside and another chap was put on the beat."

"Well, where is the P.C.?"

"Taking shelter, most likely," said Fox. "He'll hear about this," Alleyn rang the bell at 24. Immediately they heard inside the click of a lock.

"Hullo," said Alleyn. "That's sudden."

The door opened. Moffatt, very pale, with a rug clutched about him, stared at them.

"Are you from Scotland Yard, sir?"

"Yes. Anything wrong?"

"Yes, sir. Something terrible's happened. I don't know

what it is, but . . ." Moffatt followed them up, leaving the door open behind him.

"Where is it?" Alleyn asked. "We're all here. You'd better shut the door. Where's the man on duty?"

"Mr. Campbell, sir? He's upstairs, sir, and there's a doctor there too, sir."

"A doctor!" said Alleyn sharply.

"And there's a policeman outside the room where his lordship's lying. Something terrible—"

"We'll go up," said Alleyn. "How many floors?"

"Three, sir. And his lordship's lying on the next floor. Her ladyship, sir, has been screaming something frightful to hear and . . ."

Alleyn was half-way up the first flight. The others followed him, Moffatt bleating in the rear. The fourth-floor landing was brightly lit. On the top stair Alleyn found a group of three. A uniformed nurse, white to the lips, was on the floor, propped against the stairhead. Above her stood Henry Lamprey and Roberta Grey. They, too, were deadly pale. As soon as she saw Alleyn the nurse said: "I'm quite all right and ready for duty. I don't know what happened to me. It wasn't natural. I've never slept on duty before, never. If the doctor wants me—"

"Where is the doctor?"

"In the fourth room along that passage," said Henry. "Don't mistake it for the third room. My aunt is locked in there. Stark mad, with her husband's hand in her pocket."

"They took it away," said the nurse in a high voice.

Alleyn strode down the passage, followed by Fox.

"Henry," said Nigel, "what in heaven's name are you talking about?"

"Hullo, Nigel," said Henry. "Follow your boy friends and find out."

"But—"

"For God's sake," said Henry, "leave us alone."

Nigel followed Alleyn and Fox.

ii

In the fourth room along the passage Alleyn examined the body of William Giggle. He lay in his bed, on his right side, with the clothes drawn up to his mouth. There was a blood-stained dent on his left temple, a horseshoe-shaped mark pointing downwards towards the cheek with the arched end near the brow. When Alleyn drew down the bed-clothes he saw Giggle's throat. A razor lay on the sheet close to Giggle's head. Alleyn bent lower.

"Cooling," he said.

"He's been dead at least two hours," said Dr. Curtis.

"Has he, by gum?" said Fox.

The bed was against the left-hand wall of the room. There was a space between the head of the bed and the back wall. Alleyn moved into it and made a gesture over the throat.

"Yes," Curtis said, "like that. You notice it begins low down on the right near the clavicle, and runs upward almost to the left ear."

"There's no blood on any of them, sir," said Campbell. "Not on her or any of them."

Alleyn pointed to a slash in the collar of the pyjama jacket and Curtis nodded. "I know. It was done under the bed-clothes. Look at them. Yes," as Alleyn stooped to peer at an object at his feet. "She knocked him out with that boot. There's blood on the heel."

"Put it away carefully, Campbell. Chalk the positions. We'll want Bailey and Thompson."

"They're coming," said Curtis.

"Good." Alleyn took a counterpane from the end of the bed and covered the body with it. "The same idea, you see," he said, "with a difference. She's learnt that an injury to the brain doesn't always mean instant death but she's stuck to the preliminary knock-out. It works well. Two hours, you say?"

"Or more."

"We wouldn't have saved him, Fox, if we had caught the express."

"No, sir."

"If only I'd seen that book a little earlier. What have you got in there, Campbell?"

Campbell had taken a rolled-up towel from the top of the dressing-table.

"It just doesn't make sense," sakd Campbell. "My Gawd, sir, we found it in her pocket with the key of the room downstairs. It's like one of these damn-fool stories."

"The Case of the Severed Hand?"

"How did you know, sir?"

"Her nephew told me. I'll see the thing later."

"Mr. Alleyn expected it," said Fox quickly.

"I'm afraid it makes very good sense, Campbell," said Alleyn. "Where is Lady Wutherwood?"

"Next door," said Curtis. "I gave her an injection. Had to. She'd have hurt herself otherwise. She's quieter now. I've telephoned Kantripp."

"And the others?"

"The servants are all in the room at the end of the passage," said Campbell. "Her personal maid, Tinkerton the name is, keeps asking to see her."

"Let her stay where she is." Alleyn moved to the door, turned, and looked at the bed.

"Well," he said, "I suppose if he'd been asked he'd have preferred this."

"To what?" asked Nigel.

"To the quick drop, Mr. Bathgate," said Fox.

"Good God, was he the murderer?"

"Yes, yes," said Alleyn impatiently. "Come on."

iii

Alleyn sent Curtis to look at Lady Wutherwood, and Campbell to the servants' room where one of the maids could be heard enjoying fits of hysterics. Henry, Roberta, and the nurse were still on the landing. The nurse again expressed her devotion to duty and was told she could report to the doctor. Henry and Roberta were sent upstairs.

"If you can find a room with a heater," said Alleyn, "I should use it. I'll see you in a few minutes."

"I want to know—" Henry began.

"Of course you do. Give me a little longer, will you?"

"Yes, sir."

Alleyn and Fox went down to the green drawing-room, followed by a completely silent Nigel. Alleyn sent the policeman on guard there up to Campbell. He unlocked the door with the key that had been found in Lady Wutherwood's dressing-gown pocket. The room was heavy with flowers.

The sound of wind and rain was loudest here. Gilded chairs and china cupboards stood at intervals round the walls, which were hung with green silk. Behind those sad folds the wainscoting uttered furtive little noises. A monstrous chandelier chimed dolefully as some one walked along the passage overhead. On three trestles in the middle of the room lay Lord Wutherwood's body in an open coffin. The face was covered and a sheaf of lilies quite hid the breast. Alleyn moved them away. For a moment they were all silent. Then Nigel took out his handkerchief.

"God," said Nigel shakily, "this is—it's a bit too much."

"Hacked off at the wrist," said Fox. "Sawn off, isn't it?"

"Yes," said Alleyn. "If you're going to be sick, Bathgate, I implore you to go outside."

"I'm all right."

Alleyn slid his hand out of sight round the sharp outline of the body. After a moment he drew something out of the coffin. Nigel had turned away. He heard Fox's exclamation and then Alleyn's level voice: "So the tool, you see, was to be buried with the crime."

"It's from the kitchen," said Fox. "They saw up stock bones with them."

"Put it away, Fox. Bailey will have to see it. Thompson had better take a shot of the dismembered arm. In the meantime—"

Alleyn replaced the sheaf of lilies and stood for a moment looking at the shrouded figure.

"What sort of epitaph," he said, "can be written for the late Lord Wutherwood, killed by cupidity and mutilated in the interests of black magic? We'd better finish our job, Fox. We haven't got a warrant. She'll have to be taken away and charged later. You attend to that, will you? I'd better see that young man."

iv

"Robin may stay and listen too, mayn't she?" asked Henry.

"Certainly. In a sense," said Alleyn, "Miss Grey is the heroine in this case."

"I am?" asked Roberta. "How can that be?"

"Your statement last night gave us the first inkling as to Giggle's activities. You remember that you told us how, when you were alone in the dining-room, you heard the lift. Do you mind repeating that story once more?"

"Of course not. I heard Lord Wutherwood call out the second time. Then I heard the lift go down. Then I took a cigarette. Then I heard the lift again. Coming up. Then I hunted for matches and leant out of the window, smoking and listening to London. Then I heard Lady Wutherwood scream. The screams got louder and louder as . . ." Roberta stopped and stared at Alleyn. "Now I see," she said slowly. "That's why you made me repeat it twice over. The lift noises didn't fit with the screams."

"That's it," said Alleyn. "You see, according to all the other evidence, Lady Wutherwood began screaming while the lift was still going down and all the time it was coming up. But you heard the lift go down and come up with no disturbance. Then you leant out of the window and listened to London so you didn't hear the lift go down on the second trip. You only heard her scream as it returned."

"So there was a trip down and up unaccounted for," said Henry.

"Yes. But the commissionaire said positively that the lift only made one trip and that the fatal one, when your brother stopped it before it actually reached the ground floor but when it was within view of the hall. What of this other trip? The only explanation was that it didn't go all the way down. Now, when Miss Grey heard the lift, Michael and Giggle had just left her. They both say that Giggle went straight downstairs. Yet Giggle stated that the lift made no movement while he was going downstairs. He swore that it was at the top landing with Lord Wutherwood inside. It is at least true that Lord Wutherwood was inside. But we know it went down and we know Giggle must have seen it. The lift can be summoned from any floor at any time. The flat on that landing below yours is unoccupied. Our theory is that Giggle, on leaving Michael, went down to that landing. Michael saw him go and went into Flat 26. That gave Giggle his dubious alibi. He summoned the lift with Lord Wutherwood inside it. He entered the lift and inflicted the injuries. He was wearing your motoring gloves. He threw them under the seat, got out of the lift and went on down to the ground level where the commissionaire spoke to him. He then walked through the front entrance and got into the car."

"But why!" Henry said. "Why did he kill him?"

"Because he knew he would come into £300 a year and a small property."

"For so little!"

"Not so little to him. And I learnt that the property has increased considerably in value. He would have been comfortably set up for life. But there was another driving factor which we shall come to in a minute or two."

"One moment," said Henry. "Did Aunt V. know Giggle was the murderer?"

"We'll take her next. As your family pointed out with tireless emphasis, Lady Wutherwood is mentally unhinged. May I say in passing that the emphasis was just a little too pointed? They would have been wiser to have left us to form our own opinion. However, she is undoubtedly insane and—a point that you may have missed—she is almost certainly taking some form of drug; morphia, I should think. She has also become deeply interested in witchcraft and black magic. The interest, I think, is pathological. In the police service we see a good deal of the effect of superstition on credulous and highly-strung people. We learn of middle-aged men and women losing their money and their sanity in the squalid little parlours of fortune-tellers, spirit-mongers, and self-styled psychiatrists. Lady Wutherwood, I think, is an extreme example of this sort of thing. She has wooed the supernatural in the grand macabre manner and has paid for her enthusiasm with her wits."

"She's always been a bit dotty," said Henry.

"When Dr. Curtis and Fox and I interviewed her, we were puzzled by her reference to a couple of obscure mediaeval witches. A little later she certainly suggested that her husband had been killed by some supernatural agent who had taken the form of your brother Stephen."

"Well!" said Henry. "I must say I call that a bit thick. Why pick on poor old Step?"

"Simply because she saw him in the lift. Her behaviour at this interview was in every way extraordinary. She had, we were assured, screamed violently and persistently when she discovered the injury to her husband, yet one couldn't miss a kind of terrified exulting in her manner when she spoke of it.

Lastly, and most importantly, she insisted that his body was to be sent to their London house. I'm no psychiatrist but it seemed to me that, however insane she was, if she had murdered her husband she wouldn't desire, ardently, to spend a couple of nights in a half-deserted house with the dead body. *Unless*, and here's an important point, she had some motive connected with the body. Very stupidly, I could think of no motive and was therefore still doubtful if she was guilty of her husband's death, since Giggle's guilt was not certainly known. This afternoon at Deepacres Park I believed I had discovered the motive. In a copy of a mediaeval work on witchcraft we found a chapter dealing with the various kinds of soporific spells."

"My God!" Henry whispered, "'The Hand of Glory.'"

"Yes. The hand cut from the wrist of a corpse, preferably a felon or a murdered man. It renders the possessor safe from discovery since—but you know your *Ingoldsby Legends*, I see.

> Sleep all who sleep
> Wake all who wake
> But be as the dead for the dead man's sake.

"That's it. Lady Wutherwood determined to make the experiment. As soon as her copy of the *Compendium Maleficorum* opened itself at that chapter, as soon as I saw her pencilled marks in the margin, I guessed what was up. I ought to have guessed before."

"I don't see how you could," said Roberta.

"Lord, no," said Henry. "I call it quite remarkable to have got it when you did."

"Do you?" said Alleyn. "I'm afraid you're easily impressed. Well, there you are. She waited till the house was still and her night nurse was snoring. By the way, the night nurse's virtuous denials may have some foundation. I fancy she'd been treated to a morphia tablet in her cocoa. You will have noticed that her pupils were contracted."

"We didn't," said Henry. "But how cunning of Aunt V."

"Oh, Lady Wutherwood didn't do that," said Alleyn, "any more than she murdered Giggle."

Neither Henry nor Roberta spoke. Alleyn looked from one to the other and then at Nigel, who sat self-effacingly in a corner of the room. "Haven't you told them?" asked Alleyn.

"I—I thought I had," murmured Nigel.

"What *have* you told them?"

"I—that—well that Lady Wutherwood—"

"I left you with Fox. If you still held this remarkable theory surely you made certain, before you communicated it, that it was his idea too?"

"No," stammered Nigel. "No. You said 'she.' How the devil—"

"You've seen the files. Who hid in the hall cupboard and listened to the quarrel between Lord Charles and his brother? Who lied about it and gave us a string of impossible moves? Who brought the lift back to the top landing after Giggle had done the job downstairs? You've seen Giggle's body. What sort of murderer could inflict that sort of injury from behind the head of a victim lying on his right side in a bed by the left-hand wall of a room?"

"I—well. I—"

"A left-handed murderer to be sure. Tinkerton, you great gump, Tinkerton, Tinkerton, Tinkerton."

CHAPTER **XX**

Preparation for Poverty

Roberta was so deadly tired that she was not able to feel anything but a sort of dull astonishment and a sense of release. This was followed by the ironical reflection that once more the Lampreys, through no effort of their own, had got out of a scrape. They would not even have to face the distasteful ordeal of giving evidence against their uncle's widow. She looked at Henry and wondered if she only imagined there was an unfamiliar glint of purpose in his eye, or if in sober truth the horrors of the last thirty hours had developed some latent possibilities in his character. He seemed to be listening intently to Alleyn. Roberta forced herself to listen too.

"... all we had to work on," the pleasant voice was saying. "If she had done what she said she did, she would have met Baskett on his way from the hall or in the servants' sitting-room. She told us she met nobody. She didn't know, or had forgotten, that Baskett went down the passage while she was hiding in the hall cupboard. She heard Michael say good-bye to Giggle and remembered to fit that in with her story. But she told us that as she crossed the landing and followed Giggle downstairs she saw Lord Wutherwood sitting in the lift. You can't see any one who sits in that lift. The doors were shut and the window in the outer door is too high. If Tinkerton was innocent, why did she tell those purposeless lies? Our theory is that Tinkerton, knowing that Lord Wutherwood meant to refuse his brother, left Nanny Burnaby in Flat 26, got as far as the hall door, found the hall full of the charade party and, as she told us, hung back until they went into the drawing-room, then joined Baskett for a glass of sherry, saw Cook in the kitchen and, leaving the kitchen ostensibly to wash her hands, went back to the hall and slipped into the open cupboard where she left impressions of her heels. She overheard the quarrel between your father and his brother. We have a detailed account of that quarrel from Miss Cora Blackburn."

"Miserable little snooper," said Henry. "You can't open a door in that flat without finding Blackburn tiptoeing away on the other side."

"A good many people overheard the interview," Alleyn remarked.

"One up to you, sir," said Henry.

"But Blackburn's account happened to be the only one we felt inclined to believe."

"Robin," said Henry, "we have not distinguished ourselves, my darling. But why, Mr. Alleyn, did you reject our united story (unhappily somewhat fanciful) in favour of a curious parlour-maid's (probably correct)?"

"Well," Alleyn said, "it's a long story but the constable on duty in the drawing-room speaks French. That's one reason."

"Dear me! I must say we *have* made fools of ourselves."

"To go on with Tinkerton. Tinkerton heard the quarrel and thought it a wonderful opportunity to secure Giggle, together with a nice fat legacy, and throw suspicion of guilt on somebody else. She and Giggle would no doubt keep their respective jobs with Lady Wutherwood. Your old nanny told Fox there was something between them. Old nannies are not always reliable witnesses but—"

"She's right about that," said Henry. "I remember now. There was some row about it between Uncle G. and Aunt V. He said Tinkerton was debauching Giggle. How Giggle could! Imagine it!"

"We won't," said Alleyn. "To continue. Michael left Giggle

and took the parcel into the dining-room. The coast was clear for Tinkerton. We think she may have crossed the landing and got Giggle to come out there. She probably told him then of the quarrel. I fancy Tinkerton, like Lady Macbeth, was the brains of the party, and I may add that a casual conversation with a Shakespearian P.C. first gave me this idea. Sometime between Michael's departure to the dining-room and Lady Charles's return from Flat 26 the thing was concocted. Either a tentative plot was interrupted by Lord Wutherwood coming out and getting into the lift, or the whole thing took shape in Tinkerton's fertile brain after he was there. Here was their opportunity. He was alone and he had quarrelled violently with his brother who had audibly wished him dead. They made themselves scarce while Baskett put Lord Wutherwood into his coat. As soon as Basket had gone, out they came. Giggle got his instructions. He was to go to the deserted landing below, summon the lift with Lord Wutherwood inside it, kill him, and go on downstairs. Tinkerton would recall the lift and as soon as she had touched the button hurry down after Giggle leaving all of you upstairs with a very healthy motive. All went according to plan, except that neither of them knew that injuries to the brain are not always instantly fatal. As soon as Lord Wutherwood entered the lift she gave Giggle the skewer and gloves, sent him along to get Michael as his witness, took to her old hidy-hole until Giggle had gone, and then returned to the landing. She would see the lift go down and stop at the lower landing. She would hear the doors open. Possibly she would hear another more ominous sound. She would hear the doors close again. That was her cue. She pressed the button and followed Giggle downstairs. The lift returned to the top floor and Tinkerton, having summoned it, passed it on her way down. The commissionaire saw them go out to the car, one after another, just as they said. If it seemed impossible for Giggle to have killed him then it must seem equally impossible for Tinkerton to do so since she was on Giggle's heels. Michael provided the upstairs alibi. The pause on the second floor was sandwiched neatly between their two appearances."

"They took frightful risks, sir."

"They took one big risk. I think Giggle left the doors open while he attacked Lord Wutherwood. Tinkerton, in that case, would be quite safe, if she kept her thumb on the call button up above. That would prevent anybody summoning the lift to the ground floor and it would return to the top floor the moment Giggle left it and closed the doors behind him. The great risk was that somebody would come out on the landing and notice that the lift was not there, or catch it on its return, or even see it returning. In that case the job would have been up to Tinkerton. If somebody appeared as the lift was going down, she would have had to keep her thumb on the button and no sooner did it stop than it would return, with Lord Wutherwood angrily alive inside it. If somebody appeared during the few seconds after the attack but before the lift returned, and before Tinkerton got away, she would have had to distract the newcomer's attention. Ask if she might fetch Lady Wutherwood. Faint, like Lady Macbeth. Slam the hall door on her own finger. Anything to draw attention away from the lift. That was their difficult moment, but it only lasted a few seconds, and remember that Tinkerton knew pretty well what you were all doing. She wouldn't have been implicated but Giggle would. Giggle was the mug."

"Why did she kill him?"

"Because he'd lost his nerve. This morning we questioned him about the lift and about his legacy. He went to pieces. He was a stupid fellow, ready enough to act quickly when the brains of the party shoved the weapon in his hand and egged him on, but wildly incapable of keeping his head afterwards, when the mental rot set in. No doubt he returned to Brummell Street in a state of terror and Tinkerton decided he was dangerous. She's a clever, a desperate and a courageous woman. Moreover she is in her mistress' confidence. I'll bet you anything you like that Tinkerton is the buyer of whatever drug Lady Wutherwood takes and that she gets a little commission on the side. As Lady Wutherwood's confidante, she undoubtedly knows a great deal about the witchcraft business. We shall only find Lady Wutherwood's prints on the—" Alleyn checked himself—"on the objects connected with this last crime, but I'll stake my life that Tinkerton visited the kitchen sometime during the night and brought away an instrument which she laid ready to hand in the green drawing-room. You may be sure Tinkerton knew very well what her mistress meant to do during the small hours. You may be sure it was Tinkerton who suggested that Lady Wutherwood should test the power of the Hand of Glory and Tinkerton who slipped down the backstairs and pulled out the fuse plug.

One can imagine the instructions that were poured into that demented ear. First she was to secure the hand, then take it up to the top landing and down the deserted passage to the end room. There she would find a sleeping man. Let her make any noise she could think of, drop his heavy boots on the floor, scream, shake the bed. No one would stir, said Tinkerton, for all would be under the soporific spell of the severed hand."

"So poor Aunt V. was the cat's-paw."

"Yes. Tinkerton may even have persuaded her that her Little Master required the death of the chauffeur. She may have told her where to find the razor. Her prints on the razor would be useful and her reaction when she found Giggle already murdered wouldn't matter. Let her make whatever noise she liked. Let her be found there, with the razor in her hand. I'm sorry, Miss Grey, it's a beastly story but I think you'll feel better if you know exactly what happened, however unpleasant the recital."

"Yes," said Roberta. "But I still don't quite see."

"It may be Aunt V., after all," said Henry. "Egged on by Tinkerton."

"No. Only a left-handed person could have done it. I shan't describe the nature of the injury."

"I'd rather you did," said Henry. "Robin, dear, perhaps if you—"

"I'd rather know, too, Henry. It's beastly to wonder."

"Well," said Alleyn, "the murderer stood behind the head of the bed and the angle and position of the injury precludes any possibility of it being a right-handed attack. That's all you need to know, isn't it?"

"But why didn't she arrange it to look like suicide?" asked Henry and Alleyn saw with astonishment that the passionate interest of the amateur had already replaced in Henry's mind the horror of the scene with Lady Wutherwood. Henry had not seen Giggle and so, though he lay upstairs with his throat slit, his injury had an academic interest and Henry was prepared to discuss it.

"Tinkerton was very careful that it should not look like suicide," Alleyn said. "A theory of suicide might have led to the possibility of Giggle's complicity and that would have come altogether too close to Tinkerton. No. Tinkerton was desperate. With Giggle in a state of terror, blundering in his statements to the police, threatening perhaps to confess and be hanged, she had to revise her plans drastically and disastrously. We must now be led to plump for Lady Wutherwood as a homicidal maniac. The whole object of the first crime went west but Tinkerton was in terror of her life. She made up her mind to cut her losses and Giggle's throat."

"Won't it be very hard to prove all this, sir?"

"If Miss Grey hadn't heard the lift and if you both had slept through the night, we should have had little against her beyond the left-handed evidence and her earlier lies. As it is you heard Lady Wutherwood downstairs and saw her come upstairs and go to the top landing on the errand that was to be thought murderous. But when Campbell followed her to the chauffeur's bedroom and found her there with the body Giggle had been dead for over two hours. We've medical evidence for that. It was half past two then. The nurse will swear that at one o'clock Lady Wutherwood was in bed and had not stirred. The nurse had her cocoa in a thermos flask. Tinkerton brought it to her at eleven o'clock. The previous night she drank it immediately. To-night she was about to drink it, she had actually set out her cup and saucer before Tinkerton went away, when the storm reminded her that she had left the window open in the next room. She shut the window, decided to write a letter and forgot her cocoa. She did not drink it until two hours later. In the meantime Tinkerton had killed Giggle. The nurse drank her cocoa at two o'clock and immediately fell into a deep sleep."

"How much did Aunt V. know?"

"She knew, at least, that she must keep still and pretend to be asleep for as long as the nurse was waking. She had been well instructed, it seems. She has made one statement. I'm afraid it will not be much use as evidence but it is illuminating. Dr. Curtis tells me she has said over and over again: 'Why were they not asleep? She said they would all sleep like the dead.' And when he asks her: 'Who said this?' she answers 'Tinkerton'!"

ii

"Well, that's over," said Charlot, raising her black hat until it perched on her grey curls and tipped over her nose. "I must say that we do look a collection of old black crows."

"We always turn rather peculiar at funerals," said Frid. "I suppose it's because we all wear each other's clothes. Where did you get that hat, Mummy?"

"It's Nanny's. I haven't got a black. And these are Nanny's gloves. Aren't they frightful?"

"Really, it's rather as if we were dressed up for another charade," said Stephen. "Robin's the only girl among you who doesn't look p-peculiar." And perhaps remembering that Roberta's black clothes were rather tragically her own, Stephen hurried on. "Why didn't you all b-buy yourselves funeral garments, darling?"

"Much too expensive," said Charlot. "And that reminds me. You've all got to pay the greatest attention. I'm going to speak seriously to you."

"Immy," said Lord Charles suddenly, "where is Aunt Kit?"

"For pity's sake, Charlie, don't tell me Aunt Kit is lost again."

"No, Mummy," said Patch. "She's just 'disappeared' into 26."

"Well, you know what happened the last time she did that."

"Talking about hats," said Frid, "did you ever see anything to equal hers?"

"We are not talking about hats," said Charlot seriously. "We are talking about money."

"Oh gosh!" groaned Mike. He was lying on the hearth-rug with sheets of expensive note-paper scattered about him. He was writing.

"About money," Charlot repeated firmly. "I do think, Charlie darling, don't you, that we should make our plans at the very outset. Let's face it; we're poor people." And catching sight of Roberta's astonished eyes, Charlot repeated: "We're going to be very hard up for a long time."

"Well," said Colin, "Step and I are going to get jobs."

"And I shall be playing small but showy parts in no time," added Frid.

"My poor babies," Charlot exclaimed dramatically, "you *are* so sweet. But in the *meantime* . . ." She broke off. "What *are* you doing, Mike?"

"Writing a letter," said Mike, blushing.

"To whom, darling?"

"Chief Detective-Inspector Alleyn."

"What about?" asked Colin.

"Oh, something. As a matter of fac' I just wanted to remind him about something. We were talking about jobs and I said I might rather like to be a detective." He returned to his letter. Charlot shook her head fondly at him, lit a cigarette, and with an air of the greatest solemnity took up her theme. "In the meantime," she said, "there will be the most ghastly death duties and then we shall have Deepacres and Brummell Street, and all the rest of it, hung round our necks like milestones."

"Millstones, darling," said Henry.

"You're wrong," said Charlot. "Hung round our necks like the upper and nether milestones is the full expression. You're thinking of the mills of God. Charlie, how much do you suppose we'll have when everything has been paid up?"

"Really, darling, I don't quite know. Old Rattisbon will tell us, of course."

"Well, at a guess."

"I really—well, I suppose it should be about thirty thousand."

"Per annum," asked Patch casually, "or just the bare thirty thousand to last for ever?"

"My dear child; a year of course."

"And, of course," said Charlot, "at least half of that will go in taxes and then there will be people like Mr. Grumball to pacify and those enormous places to run. What shall we have left?"

"Nothing," said Colin deeply.

"So there you are, you see," cried Charlot triumphantly. "Nothing! I was thinking about it during the funeral and I clearly foresee that we must use our cunning and cut our capers according to our cloth. Now this is my plan. We'll never manage to let Brummell Street, shall we?"

"Well—" began Lord Charles.

"My dear, *look* at it! It's *monstrous*, Charlie. Still it's a house and it's quite large. My plan is that we get rid of this flat and live in it. Rent free. Until we decide whether we are to use Deepacres."

"Mummy, we *can't*," said Frid. "It's too ghastly."

"What?"

"The Brummell Street house."

"Do you mean Giggle or the furniture, Frid?"

"Well, both. The furniture, really. I don't believe in ghosts though of course it would be rather awful if Giggle's blood—"

"That will do, Frid," said Lord Charles.

"Drip, drip, drip."

"Frid!"

"What does Frid mean?" asked Michael.

"Nothing," said Frid. "But Mummy, 24 Brummell Street! *Honestly!*"

"My poor baby, I *know*. But attend to me. Let me finish. My cunning tells me that we can *improve* Brummell Street. Sell the most valuable of Aunt V.'s monsters—"

"Good heavens, Immy," Lord Charles interrupted, "what about V.? I mean, haven't we got V. on our hands? I mean she's mad."

"We must keep our heads about that," said Charlot capably. "Dr. Kantripp will help. As soon as she has given her evidence—"

"But will she give evidence?" Henry asked. "She'd cut a pretty queer figure in the witness-box talking about soporific spells."

"Do let's keep to the point," said his mother. "We were in Brummell Street. Now with what we save on rent we shall be able to make a few meagre alterations to the Brummell Street house. Paint the walls and change the curtains and get at least enough bathrooms for ordinary cleanliness. We could cover the worst of the chairs that we don't sell with something dirt cheap but amusing."

"French chintz?" suggested Frid, taking fire.

"Yes, I mean something that will simply tide us over our bad times. We'll consult a clever decorator. What I *do* want to *hammer* into your heads," said Charlot, "is that we are poor. Poor, poor, *poor*."

Henry, who had been watching Roberta, burst out laughing. Charlot gazed at him with an air of injury.

"What are you laughing at, Henry?"

"I was wondering if Robin could be persuaded to tell us her thoughts."

Roberta became very pink. She had been reflecting on that agreeable attitude of mind which enabled the Lampreys, after a lifetime of pecuniary hazards, to feel the pinch of poverty upon the acquisition of an income of thirty thousand pounds. There they were, as solemn as owls, putting a brave face on penury and at the same time warming to the redecoration of 24 Brummell Street.

"Robin," said Henry, "I shall guess at your thoughts."

"No, Henry, don't. But you can make another kind of guess. What family in fiction would you most resemble if you belonged to a different class?"

"The Macbeths?" asked Frid. "No. Because, after all, Daddy and Mummy didn't murder Uncle G. and the sleeping groom."

"I think I'm rather a Spartan mother," said Charlot. "Isn't there a Spartan family in a play? That's what we *shall* resemble in the future, I promise you."

"I think Mummy's Congrevian," said Stephen.

"Millament?" murmured Lord Charles.

"Robin means 'The Comedy of Errors,'" said Patch, "because of the twins."

"Jemima Puddleduck," said Mike and burst into one of his small-boy fits of charming laughter. "You're Jemima Puddleduck, Mummy, and you go pit-pat-paddle-pat, pit-pat-waddle-pat."

"Mikey!" cried Charlot. Michael screwed up a piece of the expensive note-paper and threw it at her. "Pit-pat-waddle-pat," he shouted.

"I'm afraid I know which family Robin means," said Henry. He took Roberta by the shoulders. "The Micawbers."

The others stared innocently at Robin and shook their heads.

"Poor old Robin," said Frid. "It's all been a bit too much for her."

"It's been a bit too much for all of us," said Charlot. "Which brings me to the rest of my story. I've got a little plan, Charlie darling. I think it would be such a good idea if we all crept away somewhere for a little holiday before the trial comes off or war breaks out and nobody can go anywhere. I don't mean anywhere smart like Antibes or the Lido but some *unsmart* place, do you know? Somewhere where we could bathe and blow away the horrors and have a tiny bit of mild gambling at night. I think the Cote d'Azur somewhere would be best because it's not the season and so we shouldn't need many clothes."

"Monte Carlo?" Frid suggested. "It's very unsmart nowadays."

"Yes, somewhere quite dull and cheap. After all," said

Charlot, looking affectionately at her family, "when you think of what we've been through you're bound to agree that we must have *some* fun."

"Well, there's Uncle G. under the turf at last," said Nigel. "What do you suppose the Lampreys will do now?"

"They're your friends," Alleyn grunted. "God forbid that I should prophesy about them."

"They'll be damned rich, won't they?"

"Pretty well."

"I wonder if they'll turn comparatively careful about money. People do sometimes when they get a lot."

"Sometimes."

"Henry's been talking about a job."

"Good lord! Not the little New Zealander?"

"I think so." Alleyn grimaced. "I told you she was a courageous little party," he said.

December 27, 1939
  Cashmere Hills,
  New Zealand

AGATHA CHRISTIE

"One of the most imaginative and fertile plot creators of all time!" —Ellery Queen

Miss Marple

____	THE MURDER AT THE VICARAGE	0-425-09453-7/$3.50
____	THE TUESDAY CLUB MURDERS	0-425-08903-7/$3.50
____	DOUBLE SIN AND OTHER STORIES	0-425-06781-5/$3.50
____	THE MOVING FINGER	0-425-10569-5/$3.50
____	THE REGATTA MYSTERY AND OTHER STORIES	0-425-10041-3/$3.50
____	THREE BLIND MICE AND OTHER STORIES	0-425-06806-4/$3.50